Secrets of the Unborn

UNBORN RISING

TRACEY BARSKI

Barski-Lyn Adventures

First edition ISBN: 978-1-961707-17-7

Contents

For my uncle, who read the first iteration of this story over a decade ago and loved it. Thanks for believing in this story, Uncle Nu Nu. Kick cancer's ass.

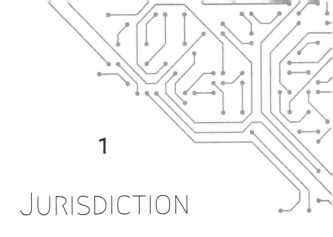

1

JURISDICTION

THE TATTERED BAG OF cucumbers went tumbling to the ground, and the thud drew Vic's attention from a few feet away. The vegetables rolled out, vulnerable and exposed, and were ground into the dirt by a ratty, worn boot.

Heat spread through her middle as her eyes bounced from the man who'd intentionally knocked the bag to the ground to the cluster of Organics who stood on the corner, watching intently. No hint of surprise marked their expressions.

Grim understanding settled within her, and Vic shifted her focus back to the man who'd knocked the bag over.

"Stupid bottle-bred hybrids," he muttered, shooting a sneer at Halle, who was trying to sell her surplus produce—now another casualty of the harassment that had become more and more commonplace.

To add insult to injury, the man flung the smashed cucumbers with his toe, narrowly missing Halle's aghast face. She ducked just in time, then clenched her hands at her sides, expression twisting with rage.

Vic cased the area again. The group on the corner rippled with energy, shifting endlessly, prepared to move when the time came. Like they were hoping for a fight. Two policemen approached from the opposite corner, their conversation halting as they observed the scene unfolding before them. One crossed his arms and leaned against a light pole, eyes going to slits.

That internal wiring, like a switch had been tripped, fired off inside of Vic, and she lurched forward, wrapping her fingers around Halle's wrist before the other woman could do something she—and possibly the rest of them—would regret.

Halle's head jerked around, blonde hair whipping and barely missing Vic's face. Her nostrils flared as she took in Vic's tight expression that said *not here, not now.*

Even though her chin shifted forward a fraction, defiance warring with submission in Halle's copper eyes, Vic's authority still held, even all these years later. Halle yanked her wrist from Vic's grasp, tensing as she caught sight of what Vic had already been aware of: the sheer number of Organics surrounding the square, including the officers who had no intention of doing a thing about what was happening until it got bad.

The Organic man wouldn't have been that brazen if he didn't have backup. He wasn't a complete idiot, even if he *was* a complete asshole. Having this many of the Unborn in one location was a serious risk if he'd been alone.

Halle crossed her arms, glaring at the bully who'd harassed her as he moved on. There were fewer Unborn at the market that day than usual, but a current of frustrated awareness rolled through those who were present.

Vic straightened, working to catch the eyes of the others. The number of Organics surrounding them might've been an even match for the rest of the Unborn who were there, but the police officers were her concern. Experience had taught her exactly whose side they'd be on. Considering every last one of them was an Organic, it was no surprise. Unborn were barred from even applying.

Which was typical. And such a waste.

Some of the other Unborn watched Vic, tuned for a signal she wouldn't give. The war might have been over, but they were fighters by design. Even in her own body, her genetic coding calculated odds, looked for weaknesses, and organized her squad for maximum damage.

Instead of entertaining those thoughts, she held incredibly still, her gaze following the man who joined his comrades, his hands curling and uncurling into fists, over and over. The group's desire for a fight was palpable, the malice plucking at their restless bodies. Something else had likely pissed them off—lack of food, depressed economy, crumbling infrastructure—and the Unborn were their scapegoat, as usual. It was easy to blame Vic and her people.

The police officers might land on the Organics' side during a scuffle, but starting something needlessly was still frowned upon, and they were cautious of those eyes on them, too.

Small mercies, she thought.

Halle's lip curled as she watched the group of Organics, and the sun caught the metallic glint in her irises as she sent Vic a scalding stare.

Vic gave her head a slight shake. The others caught it, too. Some of them shifted, frustration snapping their movements tight. The rest continued to watch her, wary of what might come next, not sure they wanted to start something, either.

And all of it was a weight that pressed around Vic, one that was stifling and uncomfortable against her skin. But as far as she knew, there weren't any other Silvers among their number, no one who could give her backup as the former leaders of their kind. So the decision remained hers, though the war was over and any official authority a Silver had once had was revoked. At least on paper.

A ripple of uncertainty crested first through the Organics spread out along Old Market, ending with the gang of instigators that lingered on the corner, their attention going to the west. The flame of unease caught as the Unborn became aware of what had spooked the rest of the bustling population.

Uniforms, gray and starched, flashed between bodies, and a stab of apprehension spiked Vic's blood. Even the two officers who'd been casually watching the crowd straightened and adjusted their own uniforms, shifting with discomfort.

Vic's eyes snagged on a small child who was jostled in the crowd and fell to the ground, his shrill wail getting lost in the anxious murmuring of the crowd. Vic's whole body twitched, and she took a step in that direction. Then an Organic woman snatched the boy up and clutched him close in her arms, darting out of sight.

Vic didn't want to find out what was next on the list of bad luck and turned to help the others pack up.

"I've got it," she told Halle, who'd bent to retrieve the bag at Vic's feet.

Halle said nothing, but her gaze lasered behind them toward the dispersing gang of Organics. Halle was more of a hothead than most, reminding Vic of Jamie. She pushed down the cold finger of guilt in her gut when she thought of her old friend, and put her hand on Halle's arm, urging her back toward their little village away from the city.

The Organics began to spread, breaking off from the larger gathering to slink back down alleys and into stores that had withstood the war, watching warily as the gray-uniformed contingent filtered through the mass of people.

Once Vic was sure her people were well on their own way out of sight, she split off and took a roundabout way back to what used to be a main thoroughfare for auto traffic. She hopped over a long-ago downed stoplight and scrabbled over a pile of brick rubble to get to a closed-off alley most people would avoid, sliding in the dirt as she reached the bottom of the crumbled concrete.

She started to brush herself off then heard the robotic-sounding footfalls and froze, pressing her back against the brick wall, stilling her breath.

Flashes of memory assaulted her, kicking her heartbeat into an erratic rhythm as the veritable army marched past the opening between the two bombed-out buildings.

Images of when she'd been behind enemy lines danced across her mind. A time when she'd lost half her squad to a sniper hiding in the rubble of a supposedly annihilated town, and she'd been determined to get the rest back alive.

Her pulse throbbed in her ears, and she fought to keep the oxygen flowing in and out. The pads of her fingers dug into the rough texture of the wall behind her, ripping the top layer of skin.

Pay attention, she ordered, clenching her jaw.

Air huffed through her teeth in bursts as she took in the sheer number of bodies that marched past, movements mechanical and precise. The sound of their footfalls reverberated in her chest, triggering a rattling unease that vibrated her bones.

So many. That wasn't good.

As soon as the last row of gray uniforms passed from view, she moved to the opening of the alleyway, climbing carefully over the heap of broken concrete that had kept her so well hidden.

An urgency sang in her veins to get back to the village. If the others had gotten back already, they might have informed the rest of the Unborn, but she wasn't sure they had the same sense of foreboding she did. She'd feel better once she was sure nothing was amiss among her people.

But this was not normal, and she wasn't the only one who was nervous. The way people reacted at the market earlier meant something was happening that didn't sit right with anyone. Uniforms were not a common sight.

She slid down to the street, wincing as small chunks of debris tumbled down behind her like concrete crumbs, making a ruckus she wasn't anticipating.

Sticking to the shadows and hidden pockets on the path home seemed like the wisest course of action as the marching bodies disappeared around a corner, heading—she assumed—to the more intact part of the city. Some of those buildings had been miraculously spared the obliterating bombs that had peppered almost every city in America. And those that weren't had wealthy patrons to finance the restoration process. It was a false veneer on a deteriorating city that mirrored the country at large.

As she walked into the less recognizable outer edges of the city, she wondered if the Uniforms were being put up in one of the hotels in the midtown district, which led her to thoughts of who might've been pulling the strings there. Political power had once been drawn from the will of society—or at least had pretended to be. These days, no one attempted to hide that it was all about money.

On the outskirts of the city was a suburban graveyard, its tombstones formed by the jagged pieces of what used to be houses that had once lined these cracked streets for miles. It was all that was left of the families that used to thrive here.

Now it was a haven for thieves and thugs, and Vic kept her eyes open for whoever could be lurking. Most would've trekked to the Old Market, probably to harass her people and steal from their own, and wouldn't be back until closer to nightfall. But that was assuming the Uniforms hadn't scared them home early.

The first few shacks at the edge of her shanty village came into view, a mockery of a suburban "development" that had been named Edge Wood because of its nearness to a thick forest. Squat little wood buildings barely large enough to hold more than a bed and a tiny kitchen—if you could call it that—was the government's gift to their bedraggled, lab-created army. Thanks for ending our war; here's a storage shed to live in.

The outer band of buildings were only a small step above what the Unborn had and housed the poorer of the Organics who didn't seem to mind living close to Vic's kind. Maybe it didn't bother them because their proximity to Unborn gave them a measure of protection from the crime that plagued the rest of the city. The whole area had been dubbed the Edge as if to separate it from what was the legit part of town, and even the whispers from the city-dwellers mentioned it with disdain.

Vic saw more families in the Organic part of the Edge than she generally did in the city, proving that life persisted even when the world was a crumbling mess.

A cluster of children sat on the sagging steps of one Organic house, watching her silently as she worked her way toward her village. Their faces were dirty and suspicious, but the littlest waved at her when she offered a small smile. Casting a final look behind her, Vic cut between two of the shacks in the outer row of her village to make her way to the center of the Edge where many of the Unborn congregated.

Fire pits made little craters in the dirt path at regular intervals, offering a space to gather and connect. The gardens that were meticulously cultivated to keep the community fed rested in rectangular boxes between the shacks that lined the main walk, giving everyone access. It was a community-wide rule that everyone helped maintain the produce and could take what they needed.

"Hey, Vic!"

She turned, the familiar voice drawing a smile to her face, though a low-level anxiety continued to bubble in her chest. It made her recheck her surroundings, just in case.

The only people milling around were those between jobs or whose work kept them in the village. She brought her attention back to the man who'd called out to her.

He stood under the eave of a nearby shack, leaning on the carved walking stick that acted as his left leg, which was missing from the hip down. His dark hair fell to his shoulders, unchecked now that he wasn't required to keep it at regulation length.

"Hey, Coop," she said, slowing to lean against the crooked beam that held the eave up.

His one good silver eye glinted as he grinned. "You look a little spooked."

She lifted a shoulder, unwilling to burden him with her worry about the Uniforms until she got a better read on the situation. Her gaze shifted to the activity down the row of shacks, though Coop's attention stayed on her. Halle was coming out of her own place right then and caught sight of Vic, her expression tightening before she turned away.

"You been causing trouble?" Cooper asked.

Vic glanced up at him, though his knowing look was trained on the other woman now. Cooper had fought in the war years before Vic had. He'd lost his leg and vision in one eye in a blast that had knocked out half his platoon. Though Unborn didn't age the same way Organics did, he was at least a decade older than Vic was. And yet he didn't seem to wear the mantle of his rank in civilian life the way she did.

"I was literally uncausing trouble." The humor didn't infuse her tone the way she'd intended, and her attempt at a smile was brittle at best.

Coop noticed and squinted at her.

She sighed. "We had some push-back from the Organics for being at the market."

"Let me guess," he said. "Someone was picking a fight. And instead of letting them have a what-for, you tugged on those reins, and our little bucking bronco didn't appreciate it."

She gave a mirthless laugh and stuffed her hands into her jacket pockets.

"Listen to me, Victoria."

Her glare snapped to his face at the use of her full name.

"The war's over. Those bars on your sleeve mean nothing here. And if Halle makes a decision—"

"That would affect everyone around her?" Vic interrupted, the heat spreading through her chest and tingling down her arms. Her hands clenched in her pockets.

Coop raised a brow, his expression mild. "You don't have to protect everyone all the time, Vic."

She turned her face away, fighting the urge to argue, to deny the truth of his words. And she fought herself, the inner voice that told her that's what she was made for.

"Good talk, Coop," she said instead, pushing away from the post.

"Hey, don't go getting offended on me." The sound of him shuffling forward—a soft footstep, then the thunk of the wooden cane—pulled her attention back to him.

"No offense taken, Cooper. I just have some other things to do," she lied. "You alright? Need anything?"

He narrowed his good eye on her. "I've got all I need, Cap."

She waved him off, choosing not to push back on that last little jab.

But it sat in her gut, heavy and churning, for the rest of the afternoon.

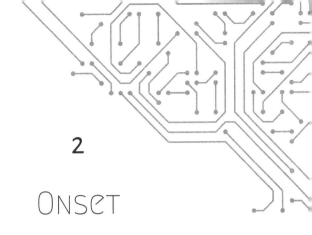

2

Onset

E VENING BROUGHT SILENCE WITH it. The solitude Vic had sought after her encounter with Coop, and the discomfort his words had given her, began to chafe once the sun dipped below the horizon. Electricity was a luxury few people could afford, and the little light provided by her solar lantern did nothing to dispel the nagging sense of loneliness that filled her.

The feeling drove her out into the crisp night air, the chill nipping at her through the layers of clothes she pulled on over her thin frame.

The fires had been lit, the flames making the shadows dance with the orange light that flickered along the sides of the buildings, drawing her in despite her reluctance to sit too close.

The phantom sensation of flames licking up her sleeve, voraciously consuming the fabric and then her flesh under her uniform always stung along the scar that marred her right shoulder and across her upper back. She wouldn't go so far as to say she was afraid of fire, but she gave it a wider berth than she would have otherwise. It still haunted her dreams.

And yet she was drawn forward, lured by sounds of connection and community, voices that rose and fell in a steady rhythm. Less laughter than usual, but there was hope in camaraderie. Interspersed with the serious conversation was a jocular tone that coaxed a nostalgia to the surface that Vic couldn't shake.

Memories of nights with those she'd grown up with, scraping out the vestiges of the childhood they'd been denied because of what they were and how they came to be, filled her mind. Alice had been their marshmallow—the soft, sweet one. Jamie had been the prankster, deriving so much joy from the booby traps she'd set for those who'd created and raised them. The scientists had wired them to be the perfect specimens—ultimate war machines. And that had been where Vic thrived. A rule follower and natural-born leader.

She'd been a favorite among the scientists who'd been teachers as well as parents for those short years during which they'd all grown at that abnormally quick rate—because what was the point of designing the perfect soldier to end your decades-long war if it took them eighteen full years to be able to fight it?

How that war changed them all. Jamie had turned from the fun-loving prankster to the hard, cynical woman who used incisive humor to call out those around her. That sharp wit cut to the bone sometimes.

Halle reminded Vic of Jamie, even down to the blonde hair, though Jamie's was lighter, bordering on platinum. It sent a pang of longing through her. And that familiar sting of guilt. She'd all but given up on trying to contact her childhood friends, the ones she called sisters. The resources available were meager and the process arduous. She'd run into more than one wall, and she had to wonder if that had been intentional.

Vic tried to convince herself the reason she sought out Halle now had little to do with her simmering guilt over Jamie and Alice. It was only because of what happened earlier that day.

"Uniforms?"

The word caught Vic's ear, and she skidded to a halt in the shadows. It was Andrew speaking. He lived a few houses down from her—a nice enough guy, though he kept to himself. Even now, he was hunched in on himself, sitting farther from the man he spoke with than the others who were gathered around that fire, participating in the conversation.

"Even the Adams got skittish about 'em." The response came from Garrett. He'd been with them in the market earlier. He seemed sweet on Halle, though Vic suspected the woman wasn't aware of the fact.

"Those mechs give me the creeps, man," someone else piped in. From this distance, Vic couldn't tell who it was. Probably Paul or one of the other guys Garrett hung around with.

"That's because they're robots."

"They're made of flesh and blood, too." Andrew's voice was quiet.

"As far as we know. Have you seen the way they move?" Garrett again. "The government built us, but we're still human. I think for myself. But those things. . . they're not human enough to need a life after war."

"Are we?" Andrew asked.

It was spoken so quietly, Vic almost missed it. But when it landed, it hit with the force of a bomb, and she recoiled.

It was not a conversation she wanted to listen to any longer, and she forced herself onward. It was at the last fire pit, the one that seemed the least lively, that she found Halle.

"Hey," Vic said as she approached.

Halle didn't turn, but her coppery eyes caught the firelight, casting little shining reflections across Vic's chest. "Hey, Cap."

Vic grimaced at the barb that was intended in the greeting. "I wanted to check in with you—"

"It's fine, Vic." Halle leaned forward, resting her forearms on her knees, and a shudder ran through Vic to see her so close to the flames. But it also revealed in her expression that it was anything but fine.

Vic stuffed her hands into her pockets, watching the fire. She wasn't sure what she wanted to say, what she'd hoped to get from this conversation. Because she wasn't sorry, not when she could see the exact sequence of events if she hadn't stepped in. Unnecessary bloodshed. And hadn't they had enough of that in the war?

Some people were wired for a fight more than others.

Vic liked to think she wasn't, but then why was she standing there, trying to convince someone that her decision had been the right one? It took effort, but she started to turn, arguing with herself to leave well enough alone. Halle said it was fine.

"The thing that kills me is that we could've taken that Adam and his buddies down so fast. There were enough of us." Halle's voice was dark and even.

Vic's fists clenched inside her pockets, and she turned back. So much for *fine*.

"But we always gotta do what the captain says, even if it's not the right thing."

Halle's bitterness blistered, and Vic fought to keep from stepping forward, heat surging through her. "Keeping everyone safe is usually the right thing."

"So we're just supposed to let them beat us down?" Halle stood now.

"Leave it be, Halle."

Vic's head jerked toward the woman who'd spoken, the smoky alto unmistakable. Geneva, who had been among the group that walked into the city, sat across the fire and turned her metallic eyes on them.

"What *you* didn't see, and Vic did, were the two police officers keeping an eye on the group when that Adam knocked the produce on the ground. We could've taken him and his buddies out, sure. But we also might have ended up in a worse position."

Halle sniffed and turned away as if the older woman hadn't spoken. "I saw them," she muttered.

"Did you?" Geneva asked, raising a brow.

Halle shifted at the challenge in Geneva's voice, but Vic redirected.

"It doesn't matter because Uniforms showed up." She watched the other two for a reaction, hoping that landed. "And who knows what kind of trouble that spells for us?"

Vic thought of the conversation she'd overheard. They still didn't know the Uniforms' purpose or where their loyalties lay—if they were even capable of such a thing. That was Vic's first encounter with them, though she'd heard plenty of speculation, even from the Organics.

When Halle refused to respond, Vic leaned forward, her defense of the *rightness* of her choice on the tip of her tongue, poised to leap. But she caught sight of Geneva jerking her head for Vic to head out. Geneva considered it a battle not worth pursuing, apparently. Or maybe she knew she had more influence with Halle as a peer. Always set apart, set above, Vic was not the woman for the job this time. She'd always be seen as the captain, someone who wanted to throw her weight around. Some people responded to that. Others took it like a challenge and needed to push back. Like Jamie.

It took everything in Vic to leave it be, to let someone misunderstand her intentions without defending them. But the frustration buffeted her in waves as she made her way back through the rows of shacks to her own. She clenched her body against the onslaught.

As if she would protect the Organics over her own.

Even though the Organics—or *Adams*, as some of the others liked to call them—were who'd they'd gone to war for, they certainly weren't the ones she'd fight for now. But she wanted no part of a conflict that could be avoided.

Even with her resentment stirring under the surface, she refused to use the derogatory *Adams*. Being referred to as *bottle-bred* or *hybrid* with vicious intent had made some of her fellow Unborn ready to respond in kind. It gave the hurt and anger something to latch onto, but it was a power move that was all bluster. None of it had real weight behind it, and fighting fire with fire wasn't always the answer. She'd learned that fairly quickly in the war.

Strategy, calculation, preparation—it all played a role in advancing the army.

Coop had said the war was over.

Sometimes she felt like it was just beginning.

Chaos reigned. Shouts, movement, flashing lights. Even the ground shook beneath her feet, and she crouched, the whomp whomp *of choppers flying overhead.*

It was a rare sight, but that sound reverberated in her chest as her heart punched at her ribs. She threw her hands over her head as a deluge of dirt washed over her, her eyes catching on a smashed flower—pink and delicate, lying pitifully between her dirty, ragged boots.

She hadn't even heard the bomb go off. How could she when her ears were ringing so loudly?

The tinnitus had plagued her for months now. But they'd been pinned down by the enemy for that long, unable to get communication back to command.

The last she'd heard, they were losing ground, and the desperation from the top brass had come down like a strangling fist, wringing last-ditch efforts out of them.

Another explosion rocked the ground under her, and a wave of dirt fell over her, a split-second blackness that made her forget for a moment where she was.

The ringing in her ears crested, rising as another blast caught them on the left. A wall of earth, a scream, and a sharp intake of breath greeted her in the darkness.

Darkness. An echo, like a voice from down a long hallway.

Warm skin beneath her palms, the flesh supple as her hands tightened. A breath brushed across her face.

And then the ringing and a haze around the edge of her vision broke through the dream-like state that held her captive.

Someone screamed, and she blinked, her vision clearing enough to see the face before her, recognize the ruptured blood vessels in the whites of the man's eyes.

Then she saw the hands around his throat, the way his mouth opened and shut like a fish out of water, trying to suck in air.

Someone help him! she wanted to shout, a tingling shooting down her arms into her hands. The hands around his throat flexed, and she registered that they were attached to her arms.

Those were *her* hands cutting off his airway.

It was sluggish, the command that slammed through her mind. Her hands eventually obeyed, releasing the man from her strangling grip, and she staggered backward, heavy with horror.

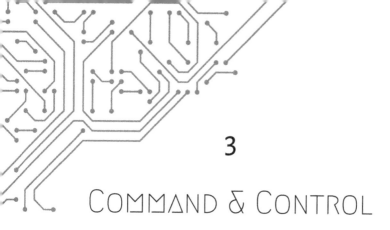

3

COMMAND & CONTROL

E VERYTHING IN HER BODY rebelled. It took seconds longer than it should have to command what each part of her did, like she was fighting someone else for control.

Vic's eyes wheeled around, unable to truly focus initially, but it was pandemonium. People fighting all around her.

Screams bit through the fog over her brain in snatches. But they weren't fear-filled. They were war cries that sent a chill down her spine, a zing straight through her.

A body knocked into her, and she registered none of what she saw until it was clear blue sky that steadied above her. Then pain sliced through her side, and her vision sharpened, the full force of sound rushing her ears.

The screams, the slamming doors, thuds, and—the one that scared her most—the rumble of a fire burning unchecked, humming with satisfaction as it devoured the dry wood planks of the shacks that made up this little village.

Locating the fire would have to come second. The current predicament came first—the person who was swinging a knife toward her face, which she blocked, the impact sending a jolt up her forearm.

It was Garrett's face that loomed over her, tight with effort but not rage. There was something cold and empty about his stare. She whipped her arm around his, locking her elbow and twisting, forcing him to drop the weapon with a grunt.

She held his wrist, pulling his arm into hyperextension, and wrapped her legs around his shoulder, pushing him away from her body. When he didn't give in, his free hand scrabbling to grab his blade again, she yanked back on his arm. Even though she'd expected it, the feel of his elbow snapping flipped her stomach, and he made a weird sound that wasn't quite a scream. It was muffled, like someone had covered his mouth.

Vic rolled and scrambled to her feet, kicking up dust as she staggered, running headlong between two shacks that hadn't caught the flames that raced down the row only a few buildings from her.

The searing ache of her scar sent a thrill of fear through her, urging her to put as much distance between her and that fire as possible before she realized she wasn't sure exactly where she was.

What she saw made no sense as she sprinted across one of the lanes that bisected two rows of homes, none of which were her own. The shadowy space between a pair of shacks called to her, even as she heard the footfalls behind her. A shock of adrenaline pulsed in her blood at being pursued.

But over the adrenaline, a coating of fear cut like ice when she took in the chaos around her. Bodies colliding and ripping each other apart, grunts and screams and blood.

Even in the war, the fighting hadn't been this barbaric. They were trained for hand-to-hand combat, the moves to take down an opponent drilled so deeply into them that it was almost second nature. But it had rarely been necessary. With modern weaponry and technology, they hid behind hardware and firepower.

How could they use those deadly skills on each other? What was wrong with everyone?

She skidded to a stop and narrowly missed getting hit by the bulk of a body that thudded to the ground in front of her. The man didn't get up, gaze wide and dark as he stared unseeingly right at her face.

She jerked when recognition lit through her, a torpedo of grief slicing at her from the inside.

The glinting silver of Cooper's good eye was almost swallowed by the black of his pupil, so unnaturally huge that it sent a shock of horror through her. That's what Garrett's eyes had looked like, too—wide and empty.

She stared at the trickle of blood that dribbled from the corner of Coop's mouth for a second too long, and a fist crashed against her face so hard she staggered sideways, her teeth rattling together and her vision blanking for a split-second. Numbness hit first, then the ache radiating through her cheekbone, spider-webbing across her entire face.

She jerked to her right, eyes wide. "Geneva?"

The woman had a head wound that wept rivulets of blood, her fingers stained red and curved like claws at her sides as she moved unsteadily toward Vic. Her chest heaved with effort, but there was no indication she recognized Vic or had registered her name.

Behind Geneva several others grappled.

What was happening?

Another person slammed into Geneva from the side, taking them both to the ground, and Vic stumbled backward, tripping over another body. She went down but quickly scrambled back, twisting around to climb to her feet again and run for the shadows.

She cast a glance behind her, confirming that no one pursued. But the flames that climbed higher caught her gaze, tongues of glowing orange licking at the dawn sky.

She faced forward, relief knocking when she saw the break at the edge of the village, the golden knee-high grass glowing under the touch of the rising sun. The edge of the woods beyond that remained dark, but the usual unease it inspired was replaced by a beckoning she felt deep in her bones. She would be safe in the depths of the trees. If only she could get there.

A hand shot out, snatching the lapel of her jacket, yanking her sideways until she collided with a solid body.

The first thing she registered was the starched wool clothing, clean and smooth and gray. Her eyes snapped up to the face of the man who held her captive. His expression was devoid of emotion, like everyone back in the village, but this was different.

She'd never been face-to-face with a Uniform before, and the eyes were the most unsettling part. They weren't the flat, almost empty black like Garrett's had been—like the pupils had swallowed the irises. But they were dark and visibly moved like a camera lens focusing. Robotic, mechanical—like a computer that was calculating exact measurements.

She saw the gun in her periphery as he raised it, that movement too smooth and fast. Another shot of adrenaline slammed through her, a bolt of electric sensation firing down her arm.

Before she realized what she was doing, her hand slammed forward to rip through his eye like a torpedo, the flesh on the surface warm until she felt the metal beneath and pushed harder. She gritted her teeth, clamping down on the agonized scream that clawed its way up her throat as the mechanics inside broke under the force of her hand, slicing at her skin with jagged edges and shocks of electricity.

His grip shuddered and loosened around her jacket, and he stumbled backward with jerking movements.

She didn't take a single second to think before she took off at a sprint for the open field and the forest that waited beyond. It wasn't until she'd gotten to the tree line that she started to feel the pain screaming in her hand, realizing she was dripping blood like breadcrumbs behind her.

When the shadows of the wood swallowed her, she tucked her torn hand into the flapping fabric of her jacket to stanch the flow and catch her breath.

She checked behind her as she moved farther into the trees, grateful they grew closer together the deeper she got. Still, she could see the light that permeated the edge of the wood and scanned back and forth to make sure she was alone.

Even as her wounds became more and more apparent, she kept trekking into the forest until she no longer saw the sunrise peeking between tree trunks, the air heavy with clinging nighttime moisture and stillness.

Still, she didn't stop. Not until she'd begun to trip over roots, the energy the adrenaline had given her leaching out like the blood seeping from the slice in her side and the gashes all over her hand.

She finally allowed herself to take a breather, putting her uninjured hand against a tree to determine her next move. But stopping her flight made the pain scream louder, and she huffed wild breaths through her teeth, sending radiating aches through her face. She'd almost forgotten about Geneva's fist hammering into her like it was made out of lead—no hesitation because of who she was hitting, nor was there consideration for her own well-being. Because a blow like that surely had broken at least a couple bones in Geneva's hand.

A reinforced skeleton only did so much when the bones were that fragile and thin. And if they hadn't been stronger than the average person's, Vic probably would have a fracture in her face. She wasn't entirely sure she didn't.

She pulled her hand from the cocoon of her jacket, wincing as the fabric stuck to the congealing blood oozing from her torn flesh. It was a mess, so it was hard to discern how much of her hand was damaged and how much was smeared blood. But she knew it was bad enough that it was not usable at the moment.

Lifting her shirt, she inspected the wound in her side next. It was clear from the beginning that the slice wasn't that deep, though it still leaked blood from the four-inch-long slash. It would stop eventually. The pain was negligible if she didn't focus on it.

But it was hard not to as she leaned back against the tree, casting her eyes skyward, snatches of blue visible between the interwoven branches above her, telling her the sun was fully blazing now.

It was absurd that it could be, that it would shine down on a day that had started this way, with her people ripping each other apart like wild animals, their eyes empty black pits.

Not one person had seemed to be in their right mind. Except for Vic.

But why?

Her brows pulled low over her eyes, a determination setting her jaw.

She grabbed the lining of her jacket and pulled until the seams popped, the thinner fabric tearing from the heavier canvas-like material of the outer shell. Once the lining had come away completely, she used her teeth to rip it into strips.

After they'd been sectioned off, she sucked in a breath as she wrapped her torn-up hand, hissing her exhale as her eyes traced the path she had taken through the trees.

Because she was going back.

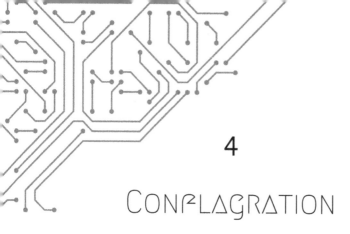

4

CONFLAGRATION

THE ENTIRE VILLAGE WAS consumed by the time Vic got to the edge of the woods, the sky filled with the black smoke that danced its glee at being fed so gluttonously.

From this distance, she couldn't see anyone. Were they all dead, then? Fodder for the flames?

She swallowed against the rising bile that threatened when she thought of the stench of burning flesh, still a vibrant memory in her mind. But even worse, the loss of life cut like a knife.

Cooper's eyes as he'd lain in the dirt flashed to the forefront, and she wanted to march back and demand why. Why them? And why not her?

Several gunshots rang out, and she flinched with each as if being struck by the bullets herself. Firearms were outlawed for the everyday citizen. No one in the Edge owned one.

Had that Uniform she'd run into been part of a larger group? He'd had a weapon, lifting the gun as if to shoot her. And she had no doubt he would have had she not reacted.

She should've stayed, should've investigated. It wouldn't have been the first time she'd been alone, surrounded by the enemy. She could've done recon, found out if there were more Uniforms. Maybe she would've found another person who wasn't controlled by the weird homicidal spell the rest had been under.

The *could have* and *should have* plagued her, threatened to force her from the shade of the trees to go back.

Make sure, that voice inside her urged, and her body lurched forward a fraction.

But bulky figures moved among the flames, dark silhouettes against the bright orange that made her slide behind a tree trunk as if they would see her. She could just make out the weapons they held as one gestured to another, the long, black shape of the rifles clear even from this distance. Her hands still knew the weight of those guns, the precise placement and balance necessary for accuracy from hundreds of yards away. Even now, her mind went through calculations of wind speed, approximate distance, lighting, the slope of the land.

Her fingers itched as the sense that these mechanized-men were her enemy rose inside her. Because all of those people. . . dead.

They must have done something to the Unborn. Had tried to do it to her, but she'd. . . what? Snapped out of it? But how? And why her?

Why, why, why?

What was so special about Vic that she'd been able to wrest control back?

Another gunshot echoed, and she jerked out of her spinning thoughts quickly enough to catch the silhouette of a body that tumbled to the ground, so starkly visible against the backdrop of the sinuous flames.

A cold, empty pit opened inside of her. Some sense that there was nothing left, that only flames and the Uniforms remained, twisted in her chest. Seeing that person fall made the last ounce of hope she'd clung to dissipate like a fine mist. Because it was clear the mechs would take care of anyone who managed to survive the absolute massacre that had taken place.

One heartbeat thundered in her ears before the realization sank in that she had to go; she had to find safety. From whatever was happening to the village but also what might happen to her. There was no telling if her ability to snap out of the mind control—or whatever it was—would be temporary.

She set out westward, though she wasn't sure why. It seemed right, like her subconscious knew something she didn't. Even as a numbness settled over her mind and body, a background loop started in her mind, lists of names of those she knew in the war who might have landed somewhere close enough that she could seek shelter, safety, and protection—for and from herself.

Jamie and Alice were too far. Somewhere on the East Coast, though they'd tried to push back on the decision. They'd been built together, both in those glass jars, and in their preparation for war. It had never crossed Vic's mind they wouldn't get sent home together. And yet. . .

There was some underlying assumption that they'd been separated for a reason. It hadn't been explicitly stated, but Vic had a gut feeling. It was one more thing to add to the tipped scale. Fight the Organics' war then start a life, but on the government's terms, not their own. Assigned towns, designated living areas. Take what you're given and shut up. Be a good little soldier and do what you're told.

But what kind of life was it to scrape by on the fringes of society because the people you'd fought for didn't want you? Not when the economy had crumbled and they were barely getting through life as it was.

Vic had a hard time truly blaming the Organics for their cold, unwelcoming attitudes. Why would they accept the Unborn as their own? They were scientifically created beings who were better in every way except one: connection. They were not tied to any human being, were no product of love. Just necessity.

A means to an end.

The tight skin of Vic's burn scar itched, and she glanced back at the fire that was still visible. Something kept her from moving away from the edge of the wood. It was like she needed to keep an eye on the blaze in the distance to remind herself that what had happened that morning wasn't simply a nightmare she couldn't shake, as much as she wished it had been.

Keep going, the machine of her mind told her as she stumbled with the weight of a grief so vast, it felt like she'd never reach the end of it. It soared through her, threatening to swallow her whole.

But she couldn't succumb, wouldn't let herself drown. And so she calculated.

In a few miles, there'd be a road. An old highway that was rarely used for much more than supply transport. Vehicles were an endangered species, protected and almost exclusively used by the government and the wealthy. But the road stretched like a river that weaved through fields and forest to the next largest town.

The next largest town.

She stopped in her tracks, thinking back to a conversation from years back, well before the war had ended.

She remembered Max, a man who'd smiled easily and often, his silver eyes always glowing with mirth. He'd brought a levity to the burden they all carried as leaders of their squads that she'd needed. She was usually too serious.

"You ever think about where you'd like to go if we end this thing?" he'd asked once. His dirt-smeared face had held a rare and fleeting solemnity.

The word "if" had been weighty then. Silvers were supposed to make it "when," but the letters had morphed and changed, dropped off like their numbers. She remembered the constant rumble of tanks and planes, the distant murmur of bombs like soft thunder, a storm on its way. It was a bleak moment, and it had made them all wistful or reckless—a result of the constant barrage, not showering in days, not eating a hot meal for weeks, not making progress. A weariness had made its home in their bones.

"No," she'd answered, her eyes on the horizon where flashes of light blinked against the overcast sky.

By then, the whole middle of America had been obliterated by nukes, a veritable empty wasteland where she had once resided, the lab she'd been created and raised in not even a dent in the landscape. There was nowhere for her to go.

Max's mouth had tipped up a little. He hadn't cared about her tone or lack of encouragement. "There's this place where sunrise and sunset make you feel like you'll drown in golden light. It's quiet and secluded."

She'd gone very still as his eyes grew distant, seeing something she didn't. Max had thrived in chaos and noise, hanging on the adoration of the soldiers under their command. He'd worked for it, though it seemed to come easy. But maybe it wasn't what he'd wanted for himself. Not in the end. Not when he was staring his own mortality in the face.

The name of the city flashed into her mind then, and she remembered looking at the map on the holoscreen when they'd been given their orders for relocation after the war. At the time, the name hadn't registered because she'd been too busy studying the location of her assignment in the west in relation to the only information she'd gotten about where Jamie and Alice were headed—the east coast. Might as well have been China with the Wasteland between the two halves of the country.

But the city Max talked about had stuck in her head, enough for her to take comfort in knowing someone she knew would be close enough to contact. Back when they thought they could get messages out, take trips, see more of the country as citizens instead of only going from one training location to another.

"You should come visit the ranch sometime. Check out the simple life when city living gets to be too much." Max had smiled genuinely then, and Vic knew he had meant it.

She started walking again, a renewed sense of purpose infusing her tired muscles. A vague idea of the direction she needed to travel kept her moving west to the highway.

Maybe there'd be a transport moving north from there, and she could hitch a ride—without the driver's knowledge. There was no telling who'd set the Uniforms on her village, and no one was to be trusted. Least of all her.

The walk churned out miles she had no way to keep track of, but hunger and the sun's position in the sky gave her some idea of the distance she trekked.

She made it through a suburban wasteland that filled her with a bubbling unease. Not one building had survived what had clearly been an early attack during the war. In the intervening years, nature had tried her best to reclaim the land that had been leveled. Buried under the rubble that was half-swallowed by moss and grass, exposed roots of trees clutching at the pieces like a child hoarding toys, Vic spotted the rusted wheel of a bicycle sticking out of the slumbering chaos—evidence that life had once flourished here.

She had no idea how far the highway was from where she'd started, but it was early afternoon by the time the forest curved and then thinned out to reveal the road that sliced through the trees. It was maintained well enough to allow the big, heavy trucks passage, but the asphalt was still riddled with cracks and potholes.

The problem was that there was nothing out here that would make a vehicle stop and allow her to sneak easily into the canvas-covered back, so she'd have to get creative.

The sound of a truck's engine kicking into a lower gear echoed against the trees, startling her. It was loud, groaning as it worked to climb the slope of the highway that steadily gained in elevation. She'd felt it as she'd walked—the uphill slant making her legs protest.

As the big truck came into view, its lethargic progress gave her hope. The driver took a weaving pattern to get around major potholes and craters in the asphalt. Some were left by bombs, others had formed due to neglect, but the rate at which he crawled through the pass was slow enough that she could sprint alongside. That would allow her to catch the handhold on the back and swing herself up and in if she timed it right.

She chalked this one up as recon because she didn't have the time or wherewithal to make a successful go. It was also wiser to aim for a night transport, when she would be less visible.

Figuring how infrequently these trucks cut through, it wasn't likely she'd come across another one for a few hours anyway. That suited her fine because her body ached, her hand throbbed, and the slice in her side burned. She settled against a tree closest to the edge of the road but still hidden from view, cradling her hand against her stomach.

She'd been shot twice before, but she'd rarely had to leave her wounds untreated this long. In the war, she'd always had the supplies on hand to address whatever injury she'd sustained, even if it was a temporary fix. Her pack would have been useful right about then. But it was gone now. Swallowed by flames.

Was the fire still raging or had it run out of fuel? Had anyone done anything about it? Maybe the Organics who lived on the outskirts of the Edge would get concerned about what had happened and do something. Or maybe they'd watched it burn.

If they weren't killed in the massacre.

Vic swallowed the bleak thought and leaned her head back, shutting her eyes. Behind her lids, flames flashed and fingers of heat licked along her skin. But she was too heavy with exhaustion to flinch away.

She didn't wake until the distant sound of another protesting engine reached her, jolting her from her restless doze. Disorientation reigned heavily as she took in the twilit forest around her, but her senses sharpened with the adrenaline that surged through her.

Even before she remembered what she was supposed to be doing, her body knew it was go-time and pulled her to her feet as if controlled by someone else. Ingrained training was its own master.

Headlights cast glowing beams along the trees, and Vic slid down the slight slope to the ditch along the road, pressing into the dirt as soon as she was at the edge of the asphalt, feeling the vibration of the truck's movement under her hands. It wasn't as dark as she would've liked, but given how long she'd had to wait between transports, she didn't want to squander the opportunity.

She was counting on the driver throwing all concentration into the effort of driving around the pock-marked road safely so that she could sneak in. The vibration intensified, and her muscles hummed in anticipation, tingles running marathons through her body as the truck came into view. She would launch herself once the front tires passed directly in front of her, and she pressed herself up into a low crouch to get ready.

The beams of headlights cut right above her head, and she froze, a jolt of nerves running through her. Hopefully the light hadn't given her away.

A wheel rolled past her face without stopping, alleviating her fears, and she shoved up, losing footing in the loose dirt for a second. She cursed as she stumbled up onto the asphalt a split second after the back of the truck passed her.

Heat and energy poured into her legs, and the wound in her side split open as she sprinted, pumping her arms.

It was only a few seconds until she was able to reach out, keeping her blistering pace steady enough to grip the handle on the corner of the truck set into the frame above the right brake light. Sucking in a breath, she pushed off the ground, her booted feet landing with a thunk on the bumper. Without pausing, she flipped open the canvas and slipped inside in time for the truck to hit a crater that sent her teeth clattering, and her feet stumbling.

She clamped her mouth shut to keep from crying out and landed sideways, allowing the momentum to take her down the aisle that had been made in the middle of whatever the truck was transporting.

Skidding along until she slammed against the cab, she froze, waiting for sounds of the truck stopping, of the driver questioning what was happening in the bed of the vehicle, any sign that he was aware she'd stowed away. But nothing changed.

It became clear why as the wheels bounced along another road imperfection and a crate crashed to the floor of the truck bed, something cylindrical rolling toward her. Apparently the other benefit of catching a nighttime transport was that they hit more of the damaged parts of the highway and were less likely to notice she was there.

Still, she didn't move for a long time. Not until she'd whacked her head against the floor two more times as they trundled over more divots in the road. The ache in her skull induced her to push to a sitting position, wincing as the newly opened slice in her side reminded her it was there.

It would have to be ignored for now. It wasn't like she had a way to treat it anyway.

She picked up the canister that had rolled toward her, barely allowing herself to hope it might be some kind of food. In the dark of the covered bed, she couldn't make out a label, but it certainly felt like some kind of canned good. She didn't have a knife or anything else to puncture the top, so it didn't matter, and she set the can on the nearest crate, working to keep her frustration in check.

She leaned her head back, staring into the dark, trying to ignore the renewed aches and pains from her sprint to the truck, wishing she could drop into sleep and get another reprieve for however long she could. Her mind wasn't tired enough to allow her the sleep she craved, so she rested her eyes, grateful she wasn't hoofing it the fifty-some miles to where she vaguely remembered Max's location to be.

A distorted squawk from the cab of the truck made her jerk upright, realizing how little insulation there was between where she sat and the driver.

It was hard to make out what garbled message was coming over the speaker until she heard a string of words that made her stomach drop out.

5

Rumors of Refuge

"**A**DVISED...LOOKOUT...Silver female Unborn."

"What?" The muttered question came from a young-sounding man, which sent a renewed ripple of uncertainty through Vic.

The broadcast came louder, so he'd clearly turned the volume up. "Authorities are looking for a Silver Unborn woman after an entire Unborn settlement was decimated early this morning. The Silver woman is wanted for questioning. Tall, dark hair, wearing a green jacket and black cargo pants. Authorities are asking for anyone to report this woman if seen."

A pause filled the cab with a tightness that cinched around Vic's chest like a vise.

"Reports are coming in that there were no other survivors in the settlement and that some of the nearby Organic population was affected by the attack. The Silver woman was last seen heading north and is presumed dangerous."

The Organics were affected in the attack? Every breath she took sent a spasm through her heart, and *no survivors* dropped like stones into her stomach. None of her people made it.

It was what she'd suspected, but to have it confirmed set a roiling in her gut. It was more jarring than the fact that people were being warned to look for her, though that was problematic, too.

Why would they be looking for her? Why would they care?

Unless they thought she had something to do with it, which was absurd. She'd been affected, too. Until she wasn't.

Her throat constricted.

But no, it had to be that someone had orchestrated the whole thing, and she was a loose end they needed to wrap up.

But, again, why? She was far from important. She had no special information, had no unique access to anything any other Silvers didn't. Unborn only got as far as captain in the military. The upper ranks were reserved for Organics, so even her knowledge of specifics in the war were relegated to assigned locations and keeping her squad organized and alive.

It had to be because she was the only one who'd snapped out of whatever mind control had trapped everyone else. But what was different about her that she'd been able to? She'd been created with the same meticulous and intentional precision, trained and groomed from birth, programmed with the skills and knowledge the rest of the Silvers were. Made, not born. Curated, not raised.

Dr. Angela Forman built her, and she'd spliced the DNA and picked every facet of each of Vic's podmates. If there was anything weird about Vic, wouldn't there be something about Jamie and Alice that was. . . off? And more than just something inside of Vic being different, what was it that might've been hard-wired into the Unborn that made them all go crazy? They might have been created to be weapons, but they wouldn't tear each other apart for no reason.

Something made them do it.

There was no doubt something sinister was at work. It was bad enough that her kind had been created for the sole purpose of ending a devastating war without thought of what would happen to them when they succeeded. But someone had built in a—what? Kill switch?

A chill danced down her spine, and the urge to take action, to *do* something electrified her muscles, dispelling the pain that had moments before threatened to take her entire focus. That innate need to find and eradicate the threat reared its ugly head, as much programming as it was an emotional pull to avenge all the people who'd needlessly lost their lives that day.

But she couldn't fight an enemy she hadn't identified, and she beat back the absolute need crawling through her, reminding the latent soldier inside her that she needed a plan first. And before she could plan, ideally, she should have rest, treat her wounds, and maybe get some food.

Unborn were designed to withstand harsh environments with only shreds of sustenance, to heal despite odds being stacked against them, to fight when they had no reserves left. There would be no point in building the ultimate soldier who had the same limitations as ordinary people. But she still couldn't go out swinging blindly.

She needed to regroup. She needed back up.

So she settled against the cab of the truck, hating the sense of helplessness that stole through her, her muscles still humming with the desire to be used.

Survival, she reminded herself. She had to survive this situation in order to get to that next step. She'd bide her time, knowing that at least the rest she got hiding in the back of that transport was the next best thing to food and proper wound treatment.

They rolled along for somewhere close to two hours, her mind lulled into a semiconscious twilight because she simply could not think anymore. Not when it was a merry-go-round of the same questions always boiling down to the most salient point: *why?*

But she snapped to full attention as the truck began to slow. Scrambling to the rear of the bed, she lifted the corner of the canvas flap to glance out. Bright lights cut through the late-night darkness, sending her heart into frantic flutters. But it looked like a ghost town aside from the fueling station the truck rumbled into.

It was the only building that looked updated and well-kept, its windows illuminated by blazing lights. The other buildings were dark, sallow, and sagging—not merely asleep, but dead. Killed by the abandonment of citizens who'd flocked to the major cities where more was available to them as the small towns floundered and drowned under the crumbling economy.

"Hey-o!"

The shouted greeting sent Vic jerking back into the recesses of the truck, bumping into a stack of crates and knocking one into the next stack. She tensed up, waiting for the crash, but it held, sitting precariously on the edge, its top leaning against the tower beside it.

"You hear that?" It was the young man who'd been driving, the sound of his voice coming from outside the truck now. The driver's side door slammed shut, rocking the vehicle.

"Probably knocked something loose," the other person responded, unconcerned as he moved toward the end of the truck. He was almost next to where she crouched, the sound of his footsteps on loose gravel giving him away.

"Did you get that broadcast over the radio a while ago?" the driver asked, his voice tight with apprehension. He'd moved down to stand near the other man.

The sound of the fuel pump being stuffed into the receptacle was loud in the cargo area.

"About the bottle-bred who escaped after torching her entire village? Some pretty messed up shit."

What?

"They think she did it?" the younger man asked.

"Read between the lines, Raleigh." The other man was amused, a dark humor infusing his mocking tone.

"They said she was last seen heading north."

"You think she's tucked away in your truck?" The second man laughed, and Raleigh, noticeably, didn't. "Come on, man. You haven't stopped in hours. When would she have the opportunity?"

Again, his mirth was not shared by the other man, who remained tensely quiet. She could feel his unease even on the other side of the canvas—probably because it was amplified by her own.

"If you're so worried about it, why don't you check?"

Vic shut her eyes briefly. Of course. Because she had all the luck in the world.

She lowered to a crouch and crept into a corner, hoping it would keep her hidden. It was dark enough with the flaps closed, but the blazing lights that surrounded the fueling station wouldn't do her any favors.

So much for night giving her good cover.

The driver hesitated, and the silence between the two men stretched.

"Want me to do it?" the second man asked, the edge in his voice giving away the malice under the humor.

"It's my truck," Raleigh said uncertainly.

No response.

But she heard the footsteps, felt the anticipation build in her blood, the hum of life coming to her muscles, possible angles and modes of attack forming in her mind.

The flap flipped back, light cutting along the edge of the opposite side of the truck bed from where she hid, pressing herself farther into the shadow.

And that's when she saw it: a little strip of fabric from her makeshift wrap around her hand had caught on something on the tailgate and pulled loose. She hadn't even noticed.

But the driver did, his young, smooth face wrinkling with confusion as he looked down where his hand rested next to the billowing piece of cloth. Blood stained the soft material, now dried and splotchy brown. Maybe he wouldn't realize it was—

"Blood," he breathed.

Damn it.

His head jerked up as if she'd spoken aloud, eyes scanning the truck for her, and she shifted to get her legs under her so she could launch herself at him.

And, again, as if she'd called out to him, his head swiveled in her direction, his mouth opening to call for his buddy, but she threw her body at him before he could speak.

He hadn't had a good grip on the tailgate and sailed backward, taking her with him. His body broke her fall on the concrete, and he went still. He was breathing when she checked, though she hoped the concussion wouldn't be too serious.

When she turned her attention to the other man, he was frozen, standing with his hands splayed outward for a second before he fumbled for a handgun that was strapped at his hip. Apparently, he'd been assigned out here and given a special dispensation for carrying. No doubt raiders came through, and he'd need some kind of protection.

But she spun off of the younger one, staying low to the ground as she swung her leg to take out the other man's ankles. She knocked his feet out from under him before he could unholster the weapon, and he grunted when he hit the concrete. She rose and strode toward him as he scuttled backward, scraping his knuckles along the concrete as he continued to fumble for the gun.

As soon as he had it, shakily pointing it up at her, she kicked it from his hands, the sound of it clattering away making his eyes go wide.

Typical to have someone so ill-trained to handle even the smallest weapon.

He flipped over, scrambling on his hands and knees for a moment before he lurched to his feet and sprinted back toward the guard building.

It was a waste of time to chase him down when she had access to a weapon and the truck, so she spun and ran to where the gun had landed, sliding on her belly to fit under the vehicle, stretching to reach it. Then she pushed to her feet, checking the safety before stuffing the gun into the back of her pants. Her eyes went to the building the man had disappeared into as she hurried to the driver's side door to swing herself in, twisting the key that had been left in the ignition.

She tested the heft of the vehicle as she punched the accelerator. It lurched forward, growling as it lumbered out of the station. A loud thunk sounded, rocking the truck for a moment.

In the side mirror, she saw that the fuel pump had still been attached, and she'd just broken it off of the pump station.

Collateral damage she could live with. Her eyes landed on the still form of the young man she'd tackled to the ground, hoping again that it was a minor concussion and nothing more. She wasn't sure how thick his head might have been.

As the truck lumbered along, she came to realize why it moved so slowly. Not only for the sake of the ruined road but because it wasn't built to move quickly, which made the nerves dance wildly in her stomach.

How swiftly could authorities get to her in their much faster vehicles? She wasn't sure how close the next town with a full police force was. And if everyone was on the lookout for her, there might have been a whole group designated to find her. Maybe they'd already been dispatched.

Pressing the pedal to the floor did little to increase her speed, but she drove for an hour with no signs of pursuit, stewing in her anxiety, checking the mirrors repeatedly. Which was a good thing since the engine was too loud for her to hear the sound of anyone approaching.

She crested the top of a hill and a swath of city lights greeted her, giving her both a sense of hope and a slug of fear.

The sign ahead alerted her that she was approaching her destination, and that hope took flight in her gut, even as the urgency radiated in her bones to abandon the truck and get as far away from it as she could.

There was no clear opening between the trees that she could see, and her heart sank at the realization. If she couldn't hide it well, she would be much easier to track.

She tapped a finger against the steering wheel as she debated. Should she keep going? Or barrel into the trees and make a hiding spot that would probably be just as easy to find as if she'd parked it in the middle of the road?

There were still no other vehicles in sight, so she pressed on, using the slope of the hill to push the truck faster down into the city Max had told her about.

"*A few miles east of town,*" he'd said once. "*Surrounded by trees, this old farmhouse-looking deal. It's something out of a story book.*"

"Did someone read you stories when you were young?" she'd asked with a dry smirk, though a twinge of sadness had overwhelmed her in the moment.

Someone *had* read stories to her. Angela had insisted they needed the fantastical tales as well as the tactical manuals they'd been forced to study at such a young age. It had painted Vic's dreams with adventure, even as she held herself to the strictest guidelines during training, forcing herself to live in the concrete, black-and-white world they'd been brought up in.

Max had grinned. *"There's this old path. Overgrown and hard to find. But the trail markers are still there. They point you in the right direction."*

She'd wondered back then why he had shared so many of the details with her, the specific turns and landmarks that would lead her there. He'd told her all of it so wistfully, she'd hardly paid attention.

It was a desperate day—one that had been hard and sleepless as bombs dropped around them almost constantly like incendiary raindrops and bullets zoomed by inches above their heads.

It was those times, when they thought things would end for them at any moment, when they were pinned down so long they could see but not get to their fallen comrades only a few feet in front of them, they talked of the things that brought them comfort or the things that kept them going.

Sometimes it was nonsense.

But the minute details Max had given her weren't nonsense. She simply needed to remember them.

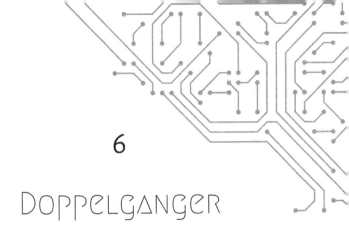

6

Doppelganger

"Eᴀsᴛ ᴏғ ᴅᴏᴡɴᴛᴏᴡɴ," sʜᴇ murmured, her own voice an overlay of Max's as it floated through her memory.

At least this far into the city, the truck could blend in with the other supply vehicles that trundled through the mostly-deserted streets. Depots were typically heavily guarded and many of the deliveries were made in the middle of the night to avoid raids by gangs.

This truck was probably expected at the warehouse, and she couldn't decide if it would be smarter to dump it or to try to take it into the depot. Taking it to its destination would keep anyone searching off her trail, but there were no guarantees she'd get past the guards. She had no identification and the driver she'd knocked out several miles back had worn a uniform she clearly didn't have.

Not to mention she had no clue where exactly the depot was.

So dumping it would have to do. Maybe leaving it on one of the crumbling side streets would give some innocent citizens access to much-needed supplies.

"Win-win," she murmured.

Urgency galloped through her as she parked the truck, her nerves sparking endlessly as she scanned the area for anyone witnessing what she'd done.

She hopped from the cab of the truck, tucked down an alleyway littered with dust and debris, then she took off east, first at a sprint, then at a jog until she came to the city limits.

The edge of town felt like a precipice, the crumbling buildings falling away so suddenly, it was as if two worlds had collided along an invisible line. The forest had stood at a distance from her little village, but here, it encroached at the boundary of the city like it was waiting for its chance to reclaim its territory.

It was lush and heavy with moisture amid the trees, the thick branches keeping it locked in, cultivating a veritable greenhouse where vegetation flourished. Every inch was green. Even the trunks of the trees were covered in vines and leaves and moss, leaving no surface unclaimed by plant life.

Which, she supposed, was a good thing. If the forest was harder to navigate, it would discourage those who might try to find the house Max had spoken of so fondly.

It was a problem for her, though, in the dead of night because it choked out the light of the moon and made it doubly hard for her to find her way through.

She trudged forth carefully until she felt safe enough in the dense brush to turn on the flashlight she'd pilfered from the truck. A sense of urgency and purpose drove her forward even as she stumbled with exhaustion over roots and barely missed whacking her head against low-hanging limbs.

The urgency bubbled up from the fear of being pursued, and the purpose was driven by the need to find answers. And so she continued doggedly into the darkness, instinct taking over more than calculation because she had little capacity left.

She was running on fumes by the time dawn touched the navy sky with bands of soft gray and orange, visible through the thinning canopy. Some kind of clearing lay before her, revealing the waning shine of stars above.

Uncertainty was a whisper along her skin. There was nothing that would suggest anyone was out there, but stepping into the open meadow made her feel exposed, especially with the sun rising. Its faint rays gave the clearing an ethereal, otherworldly feel as mist began to rise from the thick underbrush.

Vic clicked her flashlight off, allowing one breath of hesitation before she stepped out of the tree line. She didn't venture farther, though, opting instead to circle along the edge so she could duck back into the dense woods surrounding it if the need arose.

On the most eastern end, she paused, a little tickle brushing down her neck. Looking up, she spotted the cluster of leaves and vines that bulged from the trunk of the tree she stood next to where one of its largest branches sprouted.

A camera if she had to guess, though it was pretty cleverly disguised. Most people would think it was a bird's nest.

It sent a thrill of anxiety and anticipation through her. If someone had put up a camera in this clearing, that meant something was close, and they wanted to monitor who came and went.

Was this the haven Max had talked about? Or was it something else—an enemy she had no idea how to prepare for?

She cast one last glance around the clearing before shifting into the forest on this side, noting the faintest clearing of vegetation like this was a path used frequently enough to wear down to the dirt.

When she reached an old, half-grown-over wooden sign, she knew she must be close. It was confirmed in her mind when she became aware of a presence. It could have been an animal tracking her—mountain lions liked to stalk their prey—but she doubted it.

Somewhere off to her right, she made out the faintest sound of movement. Then, a few minutes later, to her left. Far enough away that one could chalk it up to an overactive imagination, but she was too on edge, too attuned to possible danger to dismiss it.

But if they didn't attack or alert her to their presence, she wouldn't let them know she was aware of them either.

It was like an exercise she'd had to do for training before the war had become the nightmare they'd never realized they'd had. Back then, she and her fellow soldiers-to-be were eager to prove themselves, eager to be used for the purpose for which they'd been created.

Being bred from the beginning as a leader meant that Vic had to endure training that went beyond the usual scope. And being dropped in the middle of an unfamiliar landscape, alone and with few supplies, was one of those tests she'd passed with flying colors.

They'd sent Jamie in after her to track and get the drop on her. A test of her friend's skills in tracking and taking out a single enemy to parallel Vic's objective of surviving and escaping from behind enemy lines. Neither had known it was the other who was their faux enemy.

Jamie had been so angry when Vic had taken her down. She'd always been a sore loser.

Under normal circumstances, Vic would have smiled at the memory. Instead, she tuned in to the movement on either side of her, keeping her own tread light as she neared the edge of the grouping of trees.

Beyond the forest, she could see what initially seemed like another clearing, but as her eyes swept the open field of tall grass before her, she spotted the gray house that stood several yards away. It looked ready to fall apart, its roof line sagging, the windows dark with dirt, vines growing unchecked up its side, edging their way under eaves and between the slats in the siding.

Was that really the house Max had longingly talked of?

She waited at the edge of the trees, knowing her trackers had stopped as well, monitoring her. It seemed pointless to sneak now. If this was the end of her journey, either positive or negative, there was no need to keep her presence secret.

But pride told her to make sure her trackers knew she was aware of them. She looked left and then right, pinpointing where she suspected they were with a long, narrowed stare before she stepped out of the shelter of the trees. Wisdom told her to keep her hands at her sides and slightly away from her body as she walked slowly forward.

As she'd expected, figures materialized from hiding spots around the old farmhouse, clad in dark, form-fitted clothing. Two women and two men, one walking forward in the front like he was the leader. His figure, the broad shoulders and slim waist, and the way he moved seemed familiar, but a hat obscured his face from view.

She cocked her head to the side, noting that two of the people with him held semi-automatic weapons. A pistol was resting in a holster at the leader's hip, his hand hovering over it like a Wild West outlaw ready to duel.

Slowly, Vic tipped her hands palm-out to show they were empty and came to a stop. The man halted as well, standing a few yards from her, his companions stopping just behind him.

Vic took in the three behind him that formed a V, one of the women—midnight-dark skin shimmering in the growing light—stood directly behind him, her long limbs spread like she was ready to attack. Her coppery eyes reflected the light, which also bounced off of the bronze in the second man's eyes. The shorter Copper woman on the other side of him squinted at Vic, her hands tightening ever so slightly on her weapon.

"State your name and business," the man in front said, his tone gruff. His fingers fluttered lightly, setting the corded muscle of his forearms feathering under sun-tanned skin.

But it wasn't his nervous little movement that struck her. It was his voice that sent a jarring thrill through her.

"Max?" she ventured.

He stiffened, and his companions shifted uncomfortably. The two in the back with the guns looked at each other.

Despite the odd reception—why hadn't he recognized her?—she pushed on.

"I followed your instructions to get here. I came to ask for safety, and for. . . help." God, those words grated as they scraped up her throat. Asking for help. . . How was it possible that all these years of having a community that relied so heavily on each other, she still couldn't come right out and ask for assistance when she most needed it?

"Safety from what?" he asked, his voice still edged with distrust. "From the reports, it would seem you're the one we'd need to protect ourselves from."

Her fingers curled into fists at her sides, and the two with the guns inched forward.

Her eyes flashed to the two in turn before landing back on Max. "Tell me you don't believe that kind of story. You know the Organics—"

"I know nothing," he interrupted, his voice still low, but it was tight with apprehension.

"Max, it's me, Vic." How could he not remember her?

She stepped forward, though the guns came fully up this time, aimed squarely at her chest and head. The shorter Copper woman's mahogany braid slid across her shoulders, swinging like a pendulum as she stabilized her stance and tipped her head to line up her sights. Vic went very still. Jumpy buggers.

Max reached up to pull off his cap, revealing the familiar square jaw that was shaded by a reddish-blond beard, the aquiline nose, and the eyes—she gasped.

The same shape, always a little squinted, like suspicion was his natural state of being. But it was a glacial blue that pierced her, sending a jolt down to her toes.

It was Max. It had to be Max. He looked and sounded exactly like him. But those eyes. . .

"How?" she breathed.

"Tell me your name," he said instead of answering her question.

"Victoria," she answered through a tight jaw. "But I go by Vic."

He never took those icy blue eyes from her face, but he dipped his chin in acknowledgment. He gave a hand signal and the guns lowered.

"She has a weapon."

She stiffened but didn't turn at the man's voice that came from behind her.

"*Brody,*" not-Max said. There was irritation and censure in his tone.

"She made us before she stepped out of the tree line. No point in hiding." There was a hint of amusement in Brody's voice.

"Toss your gun over," not-Max said to Vic, jerking his chin up.

Because she was surrounded and most of the people were Unborn, she swallowed her pride and the instinct to fight her way out and slowly reached to retrieve the gun that still rested against her lower back. She tossed it at not-Max's feet, turning her head enough to the side to get a quick glimpse of the two men who'd walked from the woods behind her. One was an Organic—the one called Brody who'd snitched about her gun.

"Do I get to know your name?" she asked not-Max, drawing his gaze to her face as he bent to pick up her gun.

He straightened and met her gaze before he responded, "Hunt."

The group pulled in close to her, stationing themselves at intervals, ready to defend an attack or escort her in. Hunt hadn't moved, but he folded his arms across his chest. She should have known it couldn't be Max. This man was tighter, gruffer, and clearly didn't smile often—not like Max, whose smile hardly ever disappeared. At least back then.

"Is this really necessary?" Vic lifted a brow.

"It might be," Hunt replied, his tone even.

She sighed, moving forward with her entourage as Hunt turned around and led the way back toward the house.

Based on the greeting, she wasn't sure this had been the right place to come. And if this Hunt person was in charge, something must have happened to Max. An Organic teamed up with Unborn was rare.

And it might just prove dangerous.

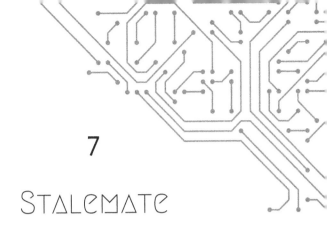

7

STALEMATE

T HE HOUSE WAS DARK inside, cluttered with worn furniture and evidence of an extinct way of life still being lived. There were paintings on the walls, shelves with well-loved books, and even homey candles half-burned down sitting on the coffee table. It felt like walking into one of those old movies Angela had let her watch when she was young. Homes like this were meant to be warm and inviting.

Another shiver of uncertainty tingled down Vic's spine as they walked through, single file, the gun-toting Unborn in front and behind her. This was anything but a welcome party.

Hunt led them through a cased opening that brought them into a kitchen with well-used but state-of-the-art appliances and a peeling linoleum floor that contrasted with the clean and tidy appearance. When he stopped, the rest of them filed in, spreading through the room around Vic, stationing themselves like guards.

Vic stood right inside the doorway, taking in the space and the blank expressions on everyone's faces. Light filtered in through a foggy window over the chipped sink, letting in diffused light behind Hunt's head.

"Have a seat." He gestured to the chair in front of her that was tucked into a small, round table between them.

She looked at the people around the room again.

"I won't bite," Hunt said, pulling his own chair out and sitting across from her. He placed his empty hands on the table as if to assure her it wasn't a trick.

She took a few steps forward, taking the chair he'd indicated. She set her own hands on the surface, mirroring his pose. Neither trusted the other, but she would do her damnedest to prove she was worthy of it.

His eyes landed on her wrapped and mangled hand.

"I had a tussle with a Uniform."

His eyes shot back to her face, the muscles contracting, enhancing the faint lines that fanned out from the corners. Not laugh lines, though. If she was calculating correctly, he was probably somewhere in his mid-thirties, the lightest peppering of silver in his blondish hair. It wasn't noticeable until they were this close.

"What happened back at your settlement?" he asked.

Something in the room palpably shifted, though no one had moved. It was everyone's uncertainty and tension coiling tighter, pressurizing the air.

She swallowed, recognizing in herself the same feelings, made worse by the fact that she still didn't understand what exactly *had* happened.

"I don't truly know." Her voice was a murmur, but she might have yelled for all the uncomfortable shuffling that went on around her. She shook her head, looking down at her hand for the first time in hours. The abrasions no longer stung the way they had. "I woke up yesterday morning, my hands around the throat of. . . a friend. My neighbor. I don't know why or how, but that was my first cognizant moment."

Hunt leaned forward a little, but she wasn't looking at him, barely registering the exchanged glances around the room. Her mind was replaying the nightmare.

"It was like I'd snapped out of some trance. And everyone else was still under its control. They were ripping each other apart." Phantom screams filled her ears, the rage-tinged sounds making her wince. "Killing each other. I didn't know what was happening or what to do. . ." She shuddered. "So I took off. Then I ran into that mech. Jammed my hand into his eye, slicing it up on the metal parts of his skull until he let me go. Ran again. Straight to the woods."

Shame whispered toxic accusations at her as she admitted to running from a fight. *From the unknown*, she reminded herself. *You can't fight an enemy you can't see.*

"You were the only one?" Hunt asked, drawing her attention back.

"As far as I know." The words scraped up her throat, Cooper's lifeless eyes flashed in her memory.

"You didn't go back?" someone—the dark-skinned woman—asked from behind her.

Vic fought to keep from making a fist. "Of course I did. The whole village was on fire by then, and the Uniforms were shooting anyone who hadn't already been killed." *By their friends.* She swallowed the added words. And the emotions.

Hunt leaned back and made eye contact with the rest of the people in the room. "And what about the Organics who were killed?"

The air she pulled into her lungs scorched at the question. Of course he would ask that; he was an Organic.

"They lived close by," she replied quietly. "I didn't know any had been hurt, though I'd wondered." The kind of madness that had overtaken everyone but her would've been hard to contain.

Hunt's gaze swept from her face to her hands and back, calculating. "So why did you snap out of this trance and the others didn't?"

She shut her eyes and sighed. "I don't know."

"You don't know?" His question sliced, a knife against an already gaping wound.

Her uninjured hand slammed against the table without her permission. "I don't know!"

The guards around the room moved closer, but Hunt hadn't even flinched, nothing in his expression changing as he stared at her.

She paid no heed to the warnings going off in her mind about how any movement she made would be perceived. She had to swipe the tear away before it fell from her eye, the hot liquid brimming against her bottom lid.

Thankfully, Hunt held his hand up to lock his companions in place. She caught the slightest softening of his features as he took in her show of emotion.

"I've been trying to figure it out since I took off," Vic said. "But I had to get somewhere safe before I could do anything else. Max was the first person I thought of. He told me about this place years ago, and if anyone would help me, I knew it would be him."

Her voice constricted around that last word, the fear of what might have happened to him threatening to overwhelm her. Admittedly, it was more because of the grief she hadn't processed. It added a level of emotion she would normally be able to control at the thought that Max hadn't made it. But it would be one too many lives lost right now.

Seconds crawled by, scraping along her mind like razor blades. All those people.

"We can't help you," Hunt finally said, standing abruptly.

She blinked. "Wait, what?" It was an effort to keep herself from jumping up to grab him and shake him.

The others seemed as shocked as Vic was.

"Hunt," the Copper man with the gun said, striding forward.

Hunt turned and fixed him with a hard stare, but the man was undeterred.

"We can't just—"

"We can, and we will, Ryan," Hunt interrupted.

"You're not the only one in charge here," the woman with the braid said.

"We cannot trust that whatever happened in her village wouldn't happen here, too," Hunt said between his teeth, his eyes going from the man to the woman.

"And maybe she has information we can use to protect ourselves if it does happen," she said, flinging an arm in Vic's direction.

"And what if it's her we need to protect ourselves from?" Hunt's gaze shot to Vic and danced back to the Unborn around him.

The silence grew heavy as that question sank in. She'd had the very same thought the day before, though that was part of why she'd come. She may have wrested her mind from the trance before, but if it happened again, would she be able to get control back a second time? If she was a danger to everyone around her, she needed help to stop it, even if that meant putting her down. With no idea what was causing it, who it would affect, and when it would happen, they needed answers as much as Vic did.

"You can keep me locked up," she blurted.

Everyone in the room tensed up, turning to look at her.

"You're right to be wary. So keep me in a separate room, if you have it. Give me a guard. Cuff my wrists. Whatever you have to do." Desperation leaked into her voice, and she despised herself for it. But she needed the help, needed her answers, and she needed to do the right thing. Protect others—from herself, if it came to it.

Hunt stared at her, the cogs in his mind working. She saw it in his eyes.

"If there's something wrong with me, you need to know what it is. We need to figure this out together." She stood slowly then. It was a step that no one pointed their weapons at her. "Because I could be the key to figuring out what that was and if it's coming for everyone."

The thought was frightening. It made her hands clammy simply thinking about it.

The other Organic man—Brody—tilted his head, and he and Hunt seemed to have a silent conversation. The others in the room still held the tension that pressed against Vic's skin as they waited for Hunt's final decision.

Whatever this place was, Hunt held a crazy amount of sway. Maybe she'd be able to figure him out and how that came to be if she was given the chance. Because she'd never seen an Organic aligned with Unborn. And there were two here.

Were there others?

Maybe her jaded view was the result of a lack of data. She really only had her own experience to base it on.

"Fine." Hunt's answer was blunt and begrudging, but it deflated the worst of the pressure that had built in the room.

He jerked his head, and they re-formed their little single-file line, the guns surrounding Vic again. This time, she expected it, welcomed it.

But still, a lump grew in her throat. Was there something about *her* that had triggered the homicidal rage in everyone else? Was she the ticking time bomb that would eradicate her kind because the integration of the Unborn wasn't going the way it was supposed to?

Regret over this decision grew into a stone in her gut, making her steps more and more cumbersome as she was led through a dark hall like a prisoner on the way to execution.

Hunt stopped at a door in the hallway, pulling out what looked like a square of fabric from the little closet. It only became clear to Vic what it was when he came toward her with it.

"We can't have you knowing where the entrance is," he said.

Was it her imagination that his eyes were asking permission?

That was fair. In his position, she would take every precaution to protect her people, too. She nodded.

The bag—a pillowcase, she realized—went over her head. She was not engulfed in darkness, but she might as well have been. Someone took her hand and placed it on their shoulder—a man's if she had to guess—so that she would know where she was going.

They shuffled along for a while, and since she wasn't familiar with the layout of the sprawling house, she wasn't sure where exactly they were or where they led her. Which was good from their standpoint.

She heard a door being opened, and she could tell when they passed through it. The floor abruptly changed under her feet, becoming more smooth and solid, and the scent on the air was different almost immediately. Less dank and more processed—like it was recycled through vents instead of the stagnant, humid smell she'd picked up inside the house.

The floor sloped downward unexpectedly, and she stumbled forward, falling into the man who was leading her.

"Sorry. Should've warned you." It was Hunt's voice, and she stiffened at the realization.

"It's fine," she muttered, pushing herself away from him. She wanted to take her hand from his shoulder, but she knew that wasn't wise.

"We're coming to a ladder," he warned. "So we're going to stop while some of the others go down first."

"Okay."

So it was underground, which explained the odd tang in the air. Was it an old bomb shelter? Some kind of bunker?

Hunt took her hand from his shoulder and kept it trapped in his own, his palm rough with callouses. He guided her forward.

"I'm going to lead you to the ladder."

The way he said it made uncertainty slink through her. "Okay," she said again.

"That means I'll have to touch you," he added.

"You are touching me."

Laughter sounded behind her, but she wasn't sure if his joined in.

"I mean on your body." Definitely sounded annoyed. Or maybe it was embarrassment.

She flinched when his hands landed on her hips, and it all made sense. He gently pushed so that she knew to turn around, then he backed her up, one hand leaving her waist.

"The edge is right behind you. Be careful." His voice was just a breath by her ear, stirring her hair. His other hand disappeared.

She lowered her foot until it connected with the top rung, then felt for a railing, clamping her hands around it, and began climbing down.

"Easy. I'm right below you," Hunt called up to her, and she slowed, listening intently for his steps, trying to match his speed.

She sucked in a breath when his hands abruptly landed on her hips again.

"We're at the bottom."

She took the last step, her foot landing on solid ground. He placed her hand on his shoulder again, though she could faintly make out the bright light that surrounded them through the fabric over her head.

"Why keep me blindfolded? We're already down here."

He was quiet for a moment, and she felt the tension in his body under her hand. "I'm not sure I want you to know where the exit is or where your room will be in relation to... everything else."

"Seems a little extreme, Hunt," Brody said, the smooth baritone of his voice coming from the front of their group.

"It's all right," she said. "Better overly cautious than not."

It was true, though it did sting. She'd never been on the receiving end of such distrust. Was there something more than this question mark about her being dangerous? Or did Hunt—an Organic—have a bias that ran deeper? It would be no different than every other prejudiced Organic she'd ever encountered.

Even in the war, the Organic commanders that were above her treated her more like some cog in their machine than a human being. Never mind that she was smarter, faster, and stronger than anyone of their rank.

Hunt might have been working with Unborn, holding some sort of leadership role among them, but that didn't mean much if she based it off her experience under the command of Organics. But surely these Unborn wouldn't be here against their will. Still, she couldn't help wondering about the dynamic.

They slowed, and she heard the sound of a door opening, a snick that made her think it was a pocket door sliding into a wall.

Hunt led her forward. "There's a lip here. Step high."

Despite the warning, she still stumbled over it, not having any sense of its location or height, but holding onto Hunt kept her from falling.

He led her further in, then the pillowcase flew off the top of her head, and she was blinking in the bright light.

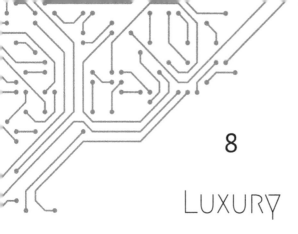

8

LUXURY

THE WALLS WERE A brilliant white and looked like fiberglass connected in square panels that spanned every surface—floor, ceiling, walls.

There was a bed in the corner, wide enough for a person to lay straight on it, and she wondered how comfortable it would be. There was a toilet and sink in the opposite corner. Otherwise, it was entirely empty.

Her heart beat a little bit faster as she noted the lack of windows and how it felt very much like an overly sterilized prison cell.

The door slid shut behind them, and she whipped around. All six of the others had crammed into the room with her, leaving little space to maneuver.

"You are not a prisoner," Hunt began.

Someone gave a mirthless snort from the doorway—the willowy dark-skinned woman—and Hunt's eyes shot to her, a warning in their icy depths.

"But until we get a handle on some things, we're going to take as many precautions as we can."

Vic nodded, trying to force her inner panic into submission. This was right. Keep everyone safe until they were sure. Until she was sure.

"Claire," Hunt said to the tall woman. "I need you to stay here. Help Victoria—"

"Vic," Claire corrected.

His eyes narrowed slightly. "Right. Vic. Help her get settled, keep her company. I'm going to get Doc to come check her out."

Claire gave one slicing nod, and the rest made to file out. Brody was the last to leave, and he turned a grin on Vic.

"Make yourself at home," he said, winking. He shot his smirk at Claire then and ducked out the door.

Claire rolled her eyes, holding the gun loosely in her hands, and rested her back against the wall, bronze eyes following Vic as she walked the small space, a sense of desolation stealing through her.

She had to remind herself that she was at least safe here, if not trusted. She could sleep. Maybe get food. How long had it been since she'd had either of those things?

Or a shower.

"How bad does it hurt?"

Vic jerked to look at Claire. The other woman's expression was fairly unreadable, though her attention was on Vic's hand. She lifted it in question.

A solemn nod.

"Not bad now." Vic turned it, examining the wraps crusted with dried blood. "It looks worse than it is. Just needs a good clean up."

"It's not the only thing. Seems you need a good clean-up," Claire observed, doing a head-to-toe sweep.

It was true. Vic was filthy with dried sweat, dirt, and blood. She could hardly tell what stain was what on her clothes. All of it was so smeared in.

"Yeah, well, I don't see a shower in here." Vic gave the other woman a lopsided grin.

Claire's brows quirked. "Not in here, no. But I'll see about taking you to the showers. Maybe after the doc looks at you. Though I'd argue that having you clean for your check-up would be better for her."

Vic shrugged. "Probably. But I don't think Hunt would agree."

She opted to sit on the floor instead of the bed. If a shower was in her future, she'd rather keep the bed pristine for that moment she'd finally get the chance to rest. The bed might've been small, but it was as good as sacred at the moment.

Claire didn't give much away. No flash of resentment danced across her delicate features, so Vic didn't think Hunt's authority was begrudged.

"Hunt can be overly cautious, but he's kept us all safe."

A hint of admiration shone in Claire's tone, and Vic pursed her lips in thought. So he was a leader that they all appreciated, even if they questioned him at times—openly, even in front of dubious interlopers.

She wanted to ask more questions, to understand this place and the people who lived here, but now that she was no longer moving, no longer in fight or flight, the exhaustion settled a weight into her bones she was losing a battle against.

"It's alright, Vic. You rest while you can."

Rest. Yes. Why not? She was safe. There was no worry that someone would attack her at any moment. Her eyes drooped. Even if this place was unfamiliar, she sensed no danger from these people.

Only herself.

The thought sent a shot of panic through her, but it wasn't strong enough to bring her back from the brink, and her mind went dark.

Voices brought her back. She wasn't sure how long it had been. The lighting in the room had not changed, but it was long enough that she woke up stiff.

She lifted her head, blinking the sleep from her eyes, but her mind was sluggish, unable to understand what was before her.

"There's a bed for a reason," Hunt said with a frown, hands on his hips.

Vic winced, shifting against the wall as her injuries came alive with complaints, aches and pains reminding her how much she'd been through in the last twenty-four hours.

Every time, she thought bitterly. Stop moving, and the body gave her a what-for about what it had suffered.

"She didn't want to get the bed dirty," Claire said dryly. "The polite thing would be to let her have a shower, a good meal, then let her rest."

Hunt crouched in front of Vic but tossed an exasperated look in Claire's direction. "I was getting that arranged." He turned back to Vic. "The doc will be by. Are you in pain?" His eyes shot to her hand, then traced over her as if to silently ask her if there were other injuries.

"You crowding our guest, Hunt?"

The voice was jarring. Since she couldn't see him, it was like Hunt had thrown his voice to the other side of the room, infusing it with uncharacteristic levity.

Hunt's mouth twitched up in one corner before he stood, stepping aside to reveal Max.

Vic scrambled to her feet, wincing. She'd given up hope about Max, thinking something must have happened to him. Something had, apparently, but he was alive and well, his smile as loose as ever.

He'd wheeled himself to the edge of the doorway, and her breath caught, though she tried to keep her reaction to his missing legs from showing on her face.

"I know. Shocking, isn't it? I used to be taller than you."

She choked on her surprise, but Hunt gave a soft chuckle behind her while Claire rolled her eyes with a smirk.

"God, you're morbid," Vic said with a laugh, letting her discomfort melt.

"Nothing ever changes," Hunt muttered.

Vic looked back at the other man, trying to wrap her head around it. It was uncanny how much the two looked alike. If she didn't know better, she'd have said they were twins. Though she apparently didn't know better, had no idea how they were possible. Max never mentioned Hunt in the time they'd fought together. It was a short assignment, but still.

"I see you've met my more friendly and welcoming brother," Max said with a wink.

Hunt rolled his eyes and shifted his weight while Claire snickered.

"Brother," Vic repeated dryly.

She didn't see the humor in the situation as she looked between the identical men. Their existence, their likeness, seemed impossible and was likely the result of illegal genetic manipulation. Maybe that was why Max had never mentioned it to her.

Hunt strode forward, mild irritation tightening the muscles around his mouth. "Genetically speaking, we are twins."

As if that were an explanation. That was already obvious.

"Claire and I will escort you to the showers," Hunt said, walking toward the door. "Doc is finishing something up. She'd prefer you all washed up, anyway." He ignored Max entirely, though an amused smile still lit Max's face.

Claire waited while Vic debated. Answers were what Vic really wanted in that moment, though she couldn't deny the call of a shower, the promise of clean clothes, the rest that would come after.

Hunt stopped right outside the door and turned to look at her. She supposed Max and the answers weren't going anywhere. And one step in getting a solid few hours of sleep on an actual bed would be to get clean and checked by the doctor.

So Vic marched forward, casting a look to Max that was full of promise of the future interrogation she was planning. He dipped his head in acknowledgment of the unspoken fact, rolling his wheelchair back to give them room.

Vic stepped over the lip in the doorway, raising a brow. "No blindfold this time?"

Hunt's mouth tightened again. "Put it to a vote. No one thinks it's necessary."

She wondered if "no one" actually meant "Max." Was he upset about the results or was he just a cranky bastard?

Vic glanced at Claire as the slender woman stepped over the lip in the door, and Vic wondered exactly how Max would have made it through in his wheelchair on his own. It was probably why he hadn't come all the way inside. If he'd been living there long enough, he'd likely figured out how to make the whole thing work or they'd made accommodations where necessary.

But there was still the problem of the ladder they'd used to get down there. No way he could make it up that thing with his legs gone from the knee down.

Which told her there was probably another way out.

They walked along the curving corridor, which was lined with doors at regular intervals. More rooms like hers?

It seemed unusually bright for being so far underground, and she looked up at the ceiling and walls for the source of light—strips that were tucked almost invisibly at the seams. It felt like what she imagined the inside of a spaceship would look like.

But what was their power source? Electricity was hard to come by, and if someone could afford it, the rolling blackouts were a pain to contend with and hard to predict.

The corridor opened into a large, round room bustling with people, and Vic's footsteps faltered a little as talk died down. Who knew so many Unborn could fit in this bunker, which seemed more like an underground colony? Several other curved corridors branched off the large room, and Hunt led her down the next one to their left.

It was more of the same—endless white panels and glowing strips of light. As they continued, she could see how easily she'd get turned around in the identical tunnels.

Hunt stopped at another door and moved to the side, gesturing for Claire to open it before he turned his back entirely on the room she revealed behind it.

Vic stepped inside, taking in the curtain that stretched from wall to wall only a few feet inside the room.

Claire came in behind her and slid the door shut.

When Vic took no further action, Claire jerked the curtain aside to reveal a row of stalls, five shower heads poking up just above, and a long bench. A pile of folded clothing rested on the bench next to a bar of soap.

"The left one is the hot water," Claire said as Vic slowly walked forward.

She spun to look at the other woman with wide eyes. "Wait, you have hot water?"

Claire's mouth curved upward then dropped as she made the realization. "How long has it been since you had a hot shower?"

Vic walked forward, touching the knobs with her fingertips. "Years," she murmured.

"Jeez," Claire breathed. "Take all the time you need. It's off hours, so if you use all the hot water, it should be back up by the time anyone else needs it."

Vic stared at her. She had to be joking. "I can just stand here—"

Claire leaned forward, her brows lifting and falling in quick succession. "Under the water for as long as you want to."

A laugh bubbled up Vic's throat, the delirious sound bouncing around the room with eerie sharpness.

"Enjoy." Claire walked toward the curtain and disappeared behind it. Then Vic heard the door open and shut, felt the emptiness of the room, and deflated.

The anticipation of getting to take the first hot shower she'd had since the day she was discharged from service waned quickly as she began to peel the layers of grimy, torn clothing away from her body.

The jacket she wore wasn't really salvageable, but as she pulled it off, she stopped herself from bundling it into a ball to toss aside.

It had been with her for years. Close to a decade, if she calculated properly. And now it was ripped and stained. Dirt, grease. Blood. Her own and...

Getting rid of it felt like letting go of all that had happened to her, all that she'd survived. Even the lingering smell of smoke was a reminder of what would be coming next: her search for answers.

Indecision roiled in her gut until she folded it and set it aside before addressing the rest of her clothing.

The slice through her shirt was dried and crusted with the blood that had seeped into the dark fabric from her wound. It made bile rise in her throat.

A friend. Garrett had been a friend. Not a close friend, but someone she'd spent time with, had enjoyed quality conversations with, worked alongside when work was to be had.

And he'd tried to kill her, that god-awful blank stare in his once-copper eyes, his face red from the effort.

She took the shirt off, grimacing as the process pulled at the gash. The ragged edges had started to fuse back together, making one long, angry mark across her abdomen. It was deeper in the middle, where there was a little more meat to her, though her stomach held little fat after the last few years of lean eating. No one was starving—yet—but they certainly weren't feasting either.

It was a more painful process to remove the wrap from her hand since the fabric pulled at the healing cuts that marred the skin. Surface-level, but they still hurt like hell.

And finally, she turned the knob for the hot water, eager for what it would do for her aching muscles, dreading how it would feel against her barely sealed wounds.

Both ended up being better than she expected, and she drenched her whole head in the scalding water, relishing the idea—wishful or not—that it could wash the invisible dirt from her body, the grime that came from a traumatizing experience.

Despite Claire's urging to take her time, the innate rule-follower in her almost made her stick to the drilled protocol of taking only enough time to scrub herself with the soap and rinse it off. But she forced herself to indulge in the feeling of the hot water stinging along her skin and soaking into her heavy curtain of dark hair, washing her clean of the horrors of what had happened to her.

The clothing provided was clean and comfortable, plain and functional. Not as thick as she usually wore, but if she was to spend her time underground instead of in the hot sun, she wouldn't need much more than the gray cotton shirt and stretchy pants that tapered and cuffed at her ankle. They'd even provided her with socks, but she had to use her own worn boots.

Unsure of what to do with her trashed clothing, she snatched it all up, placing her jacket on top, and headed back toward the door.

When she stepped out, Hunt raised his gaze to her, and a muscle along his jaw feathered.

"Damn, the forest nymph cleans up nice!"

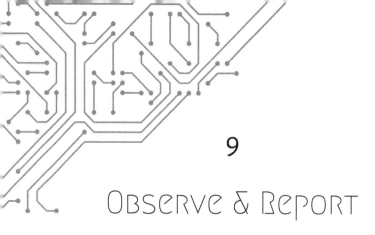

9

Observe & Report

T HE VOICE BELLOWED TO her right, and Vic jerked to look at Brody giving her a playful once-over.

"Forest nymph, really?" she asked, raising a brow. But she was smiling, appreciating the levity in his tone.

He held up his hands. "I've never seen anyone move so quietly through the woods like that."

"Maybe I should give you some lessons," she suggested.

He pursed his lips in a borderline pout while Hunt huffed a laugh through his nose.

It drew Vic's attention back to him. "Where's Claire?"

Hunt tipped his head to the side as he pushed away from the wall. "She had a couple of chores to get done. She'll be back. Brody is filling in for her."

Brody grinned and shot Vic a wink when she looked at him again.

"Two guards at all times?" she asked, raising a brow. "I feel special."

Not that it would matter much. She wasn't sure how well Hunt understood the makeup of a Silver, but if it made him feel better, she wouldn't complain.

He squinted at her as if he were analyzing her tone but said nothing and turned to lead them down the hall, back toward the wing where her room was.

"What should I do with these clothes?"

Hunt looked at the bundle in her hands. "Do you want to keep them?"

She sucked in a breath. "Maybe just the jacket. The rest is. . . in pretty rough shape."

He slowed so that he walked next to her instead of in front and held out his hands for the pile, which she relinquished slowly. It felt like she was handing a piece of herself over, one that was now dead and gone, and she swallowed the uncertainty, the twinge of grief.

Hunt's eyes flashed to her face like he sensed her discomfort. His steps even seemed to falter for a moment as if he wanted to stop and double-check. But she turned her face forward as they cut through the large, round room again, effectively making the decision final.

Fewer people stopped what they were doing to stare. Maybe because she was now dressed like them. Made her seem less like an outsider, though she wondered how often newcomers arrived to this little community and if it wasn't that unusual.

Hunt resumed the lead position in front of her, keeping Brody at her back. She could feel his warmth behind her, but it wasn't merely a physical presence. His personality offered a genuine friendliness that brought a calm to her mind which had been missing since she'd set off the day before. Only a day, but it felt longer. Like in the war, when firefights stretched minutes so they felt like hours.

Hunt, by comparison, made her feel edgy, his cold eyes ever-watchful. A veritable guard dog, that one was.

And despite her best efforts to lean into the comfort the friendly man gave her, the alertness that came from being under Hunt's observation triggered the habits in her that would probably never die as she counted the doors from the center room until they reached her room, filing away the information for later use.

He stepped aside to let her enter first.

Another Organic waited for them there, a woman with flaxen hair bundled into a curly bun at the nape of her neck, frizzy corkscrews coming loose to frame her freckled face.

"Hey, Doc," Brody said, stepping in behind Vic.

"A little privacy, Brody," the doctor said, her voice smooth and lilting.

"Oh, sure, sure." He backed up, shooting Vic a reassuring smile before the door slid shut between them.

The woman gestured to the bed. "Have a seat. I'm going to check you over."

Vic said nothing but complied, settling stiffly. There wasn't any give to the mattress, but she didn't have much to complain about. Her lumpy bed at home was no better.

Home.

That word rang in her head for a protracted minute, a buzzing that drowned out whatever the doctor was saying to her.

Vic shook her head. "I'm sorry. What?"

The woman gave her a sympathetic smile. "I'm Doctor Morgan Kelley. You can call me Morgan. Or Doc. Whatever you prefer. What's your name?"

"Vic. Uh, Victoria... AF:178."

Morgan's eyebrow lifted as she noted the way Vic stumbled between her first name and the assigned serial number that functioned as her true identity.

But it had always felt like a betrayal to share the made-up last name she and Jamie and Alice had given themselves. It was a silly child's dream, a stupid game to pretend they were a family, to wish they could ever be one.

"You prefer Vic?" Morgan asked, reaching out for Vic's hand.

She shrugged. "Just a nickname that kind of stuck."

Morgan's brows quirked as she gave her a soft smile. "Like Hunt."

Vic tipped her head to the side, finding it odd that he was the first comparison Morgan would make. "In what way?"

"His actual name is Hunter." Dimples appeared in her cheeks when she gave her a conspiratorial smile. "But only his mother called him that."

It was odd to think of Hunt with a nickname at all, let alone a full name his mother may have called him. And even though he was an Organic, she was so used to what she grew up with, grew up *as*, she struggled to picture the closed-off man as a child in a mother's arms.

She winced as Morgan felt around her hand, testing its flexibility. "How long have you known him?"

A wistful smile flashed across the doctor's face. "I've known the boys since we were teens. Does this hurt?"

"The boys," Vic repeated, watching Morgan's gentle fingers continue to address the half-healed gashes all over her hand. "Only when you move it because of how it pulls on the cuts."

Morgan's hazel eyes lifted to Vic's. "Well, it looks pretty good overall. No internal damage. Just surface abrasions. I bet it hurt pretty badly though."

Vic lifted a shoulder. "For a bit. It's pretty negligible when you're running for your life."

Her eyes tightened. "Mmmm." She moved to the sink in the corner of the room where a silver tray was balanced. Vic hadn't noticed it before. "Sometimes that rapid healing is a blessing. Sometimes it's a curse."

"The blessing it provides outweighs the curse. If you're going to die, you're going to die." *We were all supposed to die.* Vic swallowed the words down before letting them loose.

The doctor turned to stare at her for a moment. Then she pursed her lips and picked up a couple of tubes from her tray of instruments, walking over to take Vic's hand again. She squeezed out some kind of ointment and rubbed it along the cuts.

"Just to help with the process," she murmured. Then she tilted her head, examining the bruise along Vic's cheekbone. "Any other injuries I should be aware of?"

"The slice in my side, probably. But I think that one's well on its way to healing, too."

Morgan unscrewed the lid to the second tube, the odd smell of its contents making Vic draw back.

"This bruise isn't too bad, though I'd imagine you were hit pretty hard for it to be this visible still."

A ghost of the pain bit through her memory from when she'd taken the hit, Geneva's blank look before she'd slammed her fist into Vic's face. The cream the doctor dabbed onto her bruise was cold against her skin, but she didn't complain or pull back, despite the pungent scent that nipped at her senses.

Morgan reached toward the hem of her shirt. "May I?"

Vic nodded her permission, leaning back so that the doctor had a better view.

Her eyes narrowed as her lips flattened. "Hmmm."

"Good *hmmm* or bad *hmmm*?"

Hazel eyes flashed to silver. "Let's just say the jury's out if this is the blessing or the curse."

"My life story," Vic quipped, giving a grim smile as she kept from flinching while the doctor applied the first cream to the angry, red slash along her abdomen.

Morgan's mouth pinched as she moved back to her tray of goodies, and Vic lowered her shirt.

"Am I all good?"

Morgan lifted a shoulder. "On the surface. I'd say you could use some food and some rest."

"I'll happily comply with those orders."

Morgan turned, leaning against the edge of the sink. "There is one thing, though."

Vic stiffened, wariness snapping along her spine.

"Hunt and Max agree that it might be wise to run some tests."

That wasn't what she'd been expecting, though it made perfect sense. There was a possibility that something in her blood or her DNA would show what had led to what happened to everyone—or to her—that was different.

She nodded. "That seems wise."

Morgan was watching her face, the tight expression not relaxing with Vic's agreement. She didn't know what would make the doctor unsure of her answer. Vic's tone hadn't wavered, wasn't tuned to uncertainty.

"I want to know if I'm a danger to the rest of you," Vic insisted. Even if her stomach torqued a little at the thought, it was absolutely true. She would never want to put anyone in danger.

Morgan twined her fingers together in front of her. "All right. We'll get started after you've had something to eat and some rest."

Vic was so far past hungry that her stomach didn't even growl at the mention of food. It dropped out and twisted, unsure of what it truly wanted, though she knew what it needed.

"We'll start with soup. It seems you weren't eating well even before you got here." Morgan flashed her a sad smile and turned to pack up the items she'd laid out on the tray.

Vic couldn't argue with that. She'd subsisted mostly on vegetables for a while. Occasionally, someone made some bread if they could afford the ingredients. It had been months since she'd had any kind of meat, and even that hadn't been much.

Built with the ideal proportion of lean muscle meant that she was cut almost always with lines of strength, but she'd shrunk, muscle and bone standing in stark relief under her skin. When she was eating well, she actually held more curves than what she possessed at the moment.

Carrying a folding canvas bag, Morgan turned back to her. "All the equipment for the tests I'm going to run are in my lab. It's much easier for you to come to me than to bring it all here. So once you're rested, come see me."

"Assuming Hunt lets me out of the cage?" Vic said, her mouth twisting wryly.

A heavy sigh rushed out of Morgan like someone had squeezed her. "Hunt has always been cautious. Once we get some of the tests out of the way, I'm sure he'll lighten up a bit."

Or kick me out, Vic thought. *Depending on the results.*

"I'll see if Claire is back. I believe she went to retrieve some food for you."

"Thank you, Doctor."

"Morgan is fine." She smiled and ducked out the door.

Vic spotted Hunt standing watch in the hall before Claire filled the doorway, holding a black tray with a steaming bowl of something savory that coaxed her stomach into believing it might actually be hungry.

"Room service and everything. I'm one spoiled girl," Vic said.

Claire's teeth flashed in a smile, brilliant against her dark skin. "You're the hottest thing in town. Have to show some hospitality to our newest celebrity."

Vic tried to laugh, but she only managed to grunt. The last thing she wanted was to be the talk of the community.

"How many live here?" she asked as Claire set the tray across her lap. She looked down at the food, her eyes nearly bugging out of her head. "When Morgan said soup, I thought broth."

Claire's smile faded.

There were chunks of chicken, noodles, vegetables, and the broth looked like it was mixed with some cream to thicken it. It was more like a stew—chunky and filling. Her stomach made up its mind about what it wanted, and it was definitely what was before her. It was hot enough to burn her tongue, but she didn't care. She moaned in delight at the mix of textures and flavors on her tongue.

"How long has it been since you ate?" Claire asked, her voice feather soft.

Vic opened her eyes, not realizing she'd shut them. "It's only been a couple days." She took another bite, too impatient to wait to finish what she meant to say. "But it's been a long time since I had something this hearty."

Claire's eyes flashed down to the bowl like she was concerned about the definition of hearty in relation to what she'd given Vic.

"You guys do well here," Vic observed. It wasn't a question.

Claire's dark brows quirked. "We do. Thanks to Hunt. It's a working ranch above ground."

Vic swallowed a scalding bite, feeling its entire descent into her empty stomach. "A working ranch? As in, live animals?"

Claire nodded, her expression still troubled. "Cows, chickens, horses. We have some fields for crops. There are a lot of us to pitch in and keep it running. It's a lot for one guy to manage."

Vic couldn't even fathom, and she lamented when the soup turned to bitter ash in her mouth knowing that this group of people had so much abundance when her community was struggling to get by.

Had been.

She didn't have to worry about their struggles anymore. But she knew there were so many more pockets of Unborn across the country who were ostracized, barred from moving beyond merely scraping by.

It paid to have an Organic on your side, apparently.

But knowing how much even the Organics were struggling made her wonder exactly what had enabled Hunt to own and run a ranch that was clearly doing quite well. Some part of her suggested that maybe she really didn't want to know that answer. Especially when she thought of the serious firepower his people had wielded when they'd all greeted her.

One didn't simply go into town and buy those kinds of weapons.

Her eyes slid to the other woman. Maybe there was more than meets the eye, and she was not the dangerous one in this scenario.

It didn't matter that Claire and Brody were so likable or that Max had clearly been here for a long time, having grown up with Hunt—which she still wanted the backstory for. Until she got all the information, she would remain as wary of them as they were of her.

Claire walked forward to take her tray now that the bowl was empty, maybe sensing Vic's suspicion, though she hoped the other woman would interpret it as the bone-deep exhaustion that definitely filled Vic to the brim, even if it wasn't truly the cause.

"You rest up, Vic," Claire said, heading for the door. She pointed to a spot in the panel next to the door. "To make it dark—" She pressed her index finger into a rectangular depression in the panel, and the lights dimmed and went out. "Use two fingers up or down to increase or decrease the intensity."

"Thanks. Off is fine."

Claire nodded and left it dark, only the light from the hallway spilling into the room until she slid the door closed and it went pitch black, leaving an uneasy feeling that slid through Vic as she stretched out on the bed, staring into nothingness.

It wasn't long until sleep truly took her.

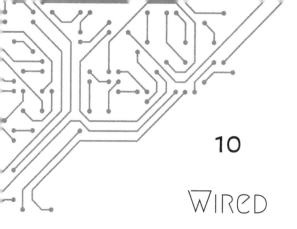

10

WIRED

B EFORE BRINGING VIC TO see the doctor, Claire greeted her with
more food. She hadn't been sure what time it was since the light
never changed, and it felt odd to be eating again, even though it had
likely been hours.

The warm bread and butter, coupled with the eggs and bacon she'd
practically inhaled now sat in her stomach like a boulder as they
walked through the curving halls. They passed out of the corridor
where Vic's room was located and were spat out in the rotunda. Brody
had shared the name for the odd circular area last time he'd been on
her guard duty.

Then they took the same hallway that led to the showers. From
what little Claire then explained, casting careful looks behind her as
she walked beside Vic instead of behind while Brody led them, all
utilitarian spaces resided down this hall. A kitchen and small mess
hall, the infirmary, some offices.

Claire's eyes danced away from the fourth door down the hall—Vic
was still counting—like she was hoping Vic wouldn't notice or ask

about it. Which made Vic take note of its location for future refer-
ence.

Some forbidden room, most likely. Which meant it probably held
something of value.

"You may wait outside," Morgan said, standing as Brody led Vic
and Claire into the infirmary.

Brody made a face. "Aw, Doc. I wanted to see what sort of voodoo
you were planning to use on her."

Morgan's mouth tightened into a line, but her hazel eyes twinkled
with amusement. It seemed Brody had that effect on most people,
notably women. Vic had caught Claire almost blushing shyly whenever the man flirted with her—which seemed to be his only mode of
operation when he spoke.

He held up his hands.

Claire lifted a brow.

"Yes, you, too." Morgan jerked her chin toward the door.

Claire sighed and stepped back out, sliding the door to shut it,
cutting Brody's "aw man" off, eliciting a soft laugh from Vic.

Morgan smiled and gestured to a makeshift bed near the glimmering stainless steel desk she'd risen from as they'd entered. "Have a
seat."

It looked like a hospital gurney, though this space looked more like
a room for science experiments than a doctor's office. Vic spotted the
large window that gave her a view into what was the hospital/in-
firmary portion, several more gurney-like beds lining one wall with
tracks for curtains to be pulled between them.

A shudder went through Vic as she remembered her month-long
stay in a similar room when she'd been burned. It was the burn that
colored the memories in a negative light rather than the hospital
itself, but even before that incident, she'd always associated spaces
like this with pain.

The treatments they were given as children to speed up and then slow down their development were an indelible mark on her memory. The sobs she'd heard from the other children, most notably Jamie and Alice, when they'd all been suffering through the grueling aches in their muscles and joints as their bodies grew unnaturally quickly. Vic had only cried once, trying to put a brave face on for her girls. But she'd cracked her teeth from clenching them so hard.

"You all get that look on your face the first time you come here," Morgan said.

Vic swiveled to look at the other woman.

The doctor's smile was sad, but her attention was on the infirmary. "I know they did a lot of things to you to make you what you are."

Vic cocked her head. "A means to an end."

The bitter edge to her voice made Morgan wince, and she regretted her words. She wasn't sure why. Maybe because this woman, an Organic who seemed to care very deeply about the people she lived with, had a softness about her. There were no edges in her silky voice, and even her expressions had a muted quality to them.

"Shall we?"

Vic nodded, grateful to have her mind pulled from her memories, though she wasn't sure whatever test the doctor planned to run wouldn't be just as invasive or painful as the ones used on her as a child.

"First, I want to check brain activity. Nothing scary." She turned from Vic to retrieve something on the moving stand behind her. "These are electrodes I'll attach to your forehead to do some scans."

Even with Morgan's reassurance, her heart still pattered out an uneven rhythm, the pervasive memories plaguing her. The scientists did brain scans back then, too, monitoring the things they'd done to enhance their minds, their senses, and their strength.

How was the subject affected?

That was the first question on the list every time she'd been sent to the infirmary for her routine "exam."

If Morgan picked up on how uneasy Vic felt, she gave no indication as she placed the electrodes along Vic's forehead. Then she turned to the computer, clicking through a few screens to initiate whatever program she was running.

Vic chose to focus on her own questions instead of what might be happening on the computer—like how they had the electricity to power this large of a compound and the high-tech computer on the desk. And she circled back to what exactly Hunt was into that enabled him to provide all of this for the people who called the bunker home.

"Claire told me this is a working ranch," Vic said, measuring Morgan's expression.

The doctor was so intent on the computer, Vic wasn't sure if the distraction kept anything from showing in her face, or if there was legitimately nothing she was hiding.

"Yes. It's been quite a blessing to us all. A lot of us were not doing well before we came here." Her eyes narrowed slightly as she watched the readouts register on the monitor, the glow of the screen casting eerie images in her irises.

Interesting answer. Not everyone had been here the second they were discharged from service.

"How did you all come to live here?"

Morgan shot her a swift glance. "Hunt invited me years ago, before the war was over. Max came when he was discharged and brought a lot of Unborn with him. Hunt invited the other Organics sometime after that. He needed the hands to help."

Vic blinked. "Wait, there are more Organics here?"

She grimaced and actually gave Vic her full attention for a moment. "There are quite a number. A lot of them live in the house topside or in town. They do a lot of the forward-facing work."

"Forward-facing," Vic repeated dryly.

Morgan sighed. "Anything that the public sees. Trading and sales in town. Meetings with buyers. We all pitch in in some way, but a lot of the topside work is assigned to the Organics because it causes less of a stir."

That sent her gut churning. The Unborn hid underground to keep themselves safe. But what got her mind stuck was the fact that there were so many Organics who were not only willing to live in close proximity to Unborn, but their work actively benefited them.

Morgan watched her face closely, a knowing glint coming into her gaze. "Not everyone considers the Unborn an enemy to civilized society. Some of us know that we wouldn't have survived without you."

Vic sat back a little, the last sentence stirring a bitterness in her chest that burned. She folded her arms in front of her to keep it in check.

Morgan seemed to sense it, though. "It's not some platitude, Vic. I genuinely know this country would not have made it, would not have *won* the war if it weren't for all of you."

The bitterness turned sharp as it bit through her, a venom that twisted and writhed through her veins. "We might have ended the war, but nobody won."

Morgan was still for a moment, absorbing the words with a sadness that seeped out and enveloped Vic, which was not something she wanted to feel at the moment. So she turned her attention to the screen as it displayed spikes and lines and graphs.

"So what weirdness have you found in my brain?" she asked, desperate to change the subject, to give herself relief from the acrid taste in her mouth.

Morgan took a deep breath and took the redirection in stride, turning her eyes to the screen as well.

"Nothing unusual yet."

Half of Vic was relieved to hear that. The other half fell into deeper concern that the problem might be darker and more insidious. "Anticlimactic."

Morgan gave her a brief smile, but the humor didn't reach her eyes. "I'm going to draw some blood. Then I'll run it through some sequencing programs and see if there's anything odd there."

"Of course." Vic laid her arm out as if Morgan was already prepared to draw the blood.

"I want to keep the electrodes connected for a longer observation."

Vic shrugged, and Morgan walked across the room to get her supplies. She moved with a dancer's grace, lithe and smooth like she was floating. When life provided such luxuries, Vic wondered if she had ever done ballet.

She'd always held a silent fascination for dancers. She'd watched old videos—flat screens displaying the flashing images like pictures coming alive—of people moving with such melodic elegance that she'd been captivated. If she'd been something else—a little girl born to actual parents in another time—she might have liked to be a dancer.

Even though there were elements of her training that focused on agility and finesse, there was nothing musical about it. Her body was built and honed to be a weapon—leanly muscular, utilitarian. Her body was cut with packed muscle that persisted in the least hospitable environments. Even now, when she was thinner than she'd ever been, the lines of power in her body provided the strength required to take down a handful of men larger than herself.

Morgan drew up next to her, rolling on a stool with wheels and dragging her moving tray with her. On it lay the supplies she'd need. Everything gleamed in the artificial light, winking with a lifetime of memories packed into the first few years of Vic's life.

And so she looked at the computer screen to distract herself from what would come next. Hardened soldier or not, she still hated needles.

The chart of lines that spiked and vibrated in congruence with her brain activity became mesmerizing, and she almost didn't react when the needle pierced her skin right above the identifying tattoo the government had permanently etched in black ink below the crook of her elbow. Her head tilted when the spike registered on the screen.

"What was that?" she asked.

Morgan looked at the screen. "A spike in your cortisol levels. It's the stress—"

"Hormone. Fight or flight," Vic finished, nodding. "That makes sense."

Morgan's chin lifted.

Keeping her eyes studiously from the needle in her arm, she met the question Morgan's gaze asked. "As leaders, we had to train mentally as well as physically. That meant understanding behavior and physiological responses. Then we had to train to work against, in spite of, or with the natural reaction. We might have been built as super soldiers, but we still have the same general makeup of the average person."

"Just better," Morgan added with a half smile.

Vic lifted one shoulder—the one not attached to the arm currently expelling blood.

"I've lived here for years. Max is one of the few Silvers I've met." She paused, pulling the needle from Vic's arm, her attention going down as she pressed cotton to the small puncture in the skin. "He rarely talks about the training you all did. I hear from the Coppers about the grueling physical training they went through. The tactical preparation."

"We all went through the same." She took a breath, remembering the drills they'd run. Again and Again. "And then, as Silvers, we did more."

Morgan moved across the room to put the vials of blood in some kind of device. From the outside, it looked like a plastic box, but it was so much more—beyond anything that Vic would comprehend, so she didn't even try.

Almost as soon as it started to hum, a window on the computer screen popped up, data pouring in at such a rapid rate that Vic had a hard time keeping up. Not that she'd be able to discern any meaning from the codes that rolled by. It wasn't in any language she knew.

Morgan strode across the room, the sound of her shoes a soft tap on the floor. An urgency snapped at her, drawing her toward the computer like she had been pulled by a string.

Her thick, golden brows drew over her eyes. "Interesting."

Her tone didn't suggest mild interest. It belied an apprehension that made goosebumps break out along Vic's arms.

"Interesting?" she repeated, dread coating her throat, almost choking the word before it could get out.

Morgan looked at her, her expression softening. "These are only preliminary results, and I need to study them further. Why don't we call it a day for now?"

As if Vic would be able to relax without knowing what her results were already showing. Not that she expected to relax at all. She wasn't sure what she would do next anyway. Sit in her cell for the rest of the day? Because even if she wasn't a prisoner, it wasn't clear if she *should* be.

But the tension that weaved its way through Morgan now worked its way toward Vic. It made her want to glue herself to this seat, have the doctor explain everything she was looking at as it rolled in front of her face like some kind of recipe for who Vic was. All the ingredients that made her unique flashing along in a numeric code that felt so robotic and mechanical, it made her feel like she wasn't human.

But she wasn't automated like a Uniform, though Organics would have her believe she was no better. Created in a lab just the same by engineers and scientists. *Bottle-bred.*

How could they continue to hate Unborn like they were the abomination to humanity when the Uniforms were running around, their bodies made of skin-wrapped metal instead of bone? Computers with faces. Thought after thought led her to more questions, more uncertainties.

"Vic."

She jerked to look at Morgan, and she swallowed the rising panic and emotion that was pressing along her sternum.

"Claire is going to take you on a tour of the bunker. Don't stress too much."

Vic licked her lips, her eyes transferring to the door where Claire stood waiting, her brows quirked in mild confusion.

Vic nodded, then stilled so Morgan could remove the electrodes from her forehead.

Sliding off the bed, she cast one last analyzing look at the computer screen as it rolled on before she left the infirmary, knowing she would be back much too soon.

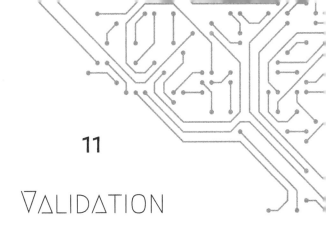

11

VALIDATION

EVEN WHEN VIC'S MIND was preoccupied, the analyzing part of her continued its running count of the doors they passed, noted how many people congregated in any given space, how far each hallway was from the next.

Again, Claire walked beside her like they were friends, not like she was a guard. Even her gun was slung across her back instead of in her hands. Brody moved with ease, no part of him seeming to be on alert, but he still held the rifle in his hands like he'd come across an enemy at any moment.

If she had to guess, he'd had military training. The way he moved, how his chocolate-colored eyes scanned while they walked—aware of all that happened around them with practiced ease.

"After a full night of sleep and real food, you're almost as pretty as Claire, here," he said as they walked. "Though I've never met an Unborn who wasn't easy on the eyes."

She pursed her lips and exchanged a bemused look with Claire. "Well, you know, we were hand-designed by Organics, and you all seem to have an obsession with beauty and perfection."

He snorted. "Is that your way of saying being pretty isn't your fault? It's mine?"

Vic shrugged, letting the levity in his tone buoy her. The concern and uncertainty sank to the bottom for the moment. If she wanted to get as much as possible out of this tour, she needed to focus anyway.

"So, tell me how this works down here," she said.

Claire and Brody exchanged a look, but it was Brody who spoke. "We have a rotating chore system. There's kitchen duty, laundry, cleaning, maintenance. Anything that needs to be done is covered at any given time."

Vic liked the logic and routine of it. Every practical aspect of keeping a community like this working. "Will I join the rotation?"

Brody's lips flattened and Claire sucked in a breath.

"That's up to Hunt." Brody scratched at his chin. "He's a hard sell on trust, but it's always nice to have an extra set of hands."

"The question is whether necessity will win out over caution," Vic muttered.

"Well, we don't *need* you, princess." Brody flashed her a brilliant smile, but his words still lit a flame of anger in her chest.

Claire snickered.

He lifted a shoulder. "If he deems it unsafe, you get to free-load. Take a little vacation."

She gave a soft growl that made Brody's smile grow wider.

"We get it," Claire said, her tone holding a slight bite. "You're a Silver. No such thing as a vacation. Gotta be useful, show us all up with your superior skills. But this place belongs to Hunt."

She appraised the other woman. "You trust him that much?"

"He's never steered us wrong."

Vic filed that away, sensing a deeper story there. Despite Claire's somewhat bitter characterization of Silvers in general, she'd seemed open enough otherwise. Brody was friendly, but she wasn't sure how far his good nature went when it came to loyalty. He was an Organic. Surely his allegiance would stay with Hunt, one of his own.

Ahead of them, a stream of people wandered in and out of a door she hadn't gotten a glimpse behind. Vic craned her neck, trying to peek into the large room.

"What's in there?" she asked as the door closed once more, keeping her from getting much more than a glance.

"Training room," Claire said. There was amusement in her tone. "Weights, equipment, a mat for sparring."

A little tingle shot through Vic, a thrill that chased the unconscious desire to utilize her body the way it was meant to be used. She tried to tamp it down since she was still in her probation period.

"Yeah, I saw that," Brody said, grinning. "I'm sure we'll get you in there soon. I'd like to see you pitted against some of the others."

Claire snorted. "She'd kick everyone's ass."

Vic looked at her sharply.

Claire caught the look and winked. "She's a Silver, remember?"

Brody tipped his head. "She's not the only Silver here."

"True. But something tells me she'd be next level."

Heat burned into Vic's cheeks, though Claire might've been right about one thing. She must have been next level if she was the only one to snap out of that killing trance. Silvers in general were built to be *more*—wired with faster reflexes and more powerful muscle, made to be leaders who were calculated and intentional in everything they did. But was that just Vic? When she thought about Jamie and even Alice, neither had taken on the role quite the same way Vic had.

Vic hadn't questioned it when she was the one most often tasked with training the Coppers before passing them on to their official assignments. Thinking back, she realized she didn't know anyone else who'd been given that responsibility. There was a reason they assigned Jamie the quick and dirty jobs and why she got busted back to lieutenant so frequently. And Alice had been tapped to be a wraith early on, trained for covert, deadly missions the rest of them wouldn't have been able to accomplish as well. It had nothing to do with their smarts. No, Alice beat Vic on every mental evaluation they'd ever had, and Jamie had never been far behind. It must have been something deeper, some innate thing that was wired into who Vic was.

Sometimes the mental side of it had been exhausting, to care about getting things done right and keeping everyone alive, when she was the only one thinking of the long game. Which, she supposed as they came up to the rotunda again, was why she was so desperate to understand how this community worked. She didn't have the insight she craved when it came to this place, and especially Hunt.

As if she'd summoned him, he appeared, walking briskly through the circular room. His eyes flashed right to her face, lingered for a moment, then transferred to Brody and Claire in turn. He made a last-minute decision to change his trajectory and turned toward them all, nothing in his expression changing.

"Giving Vic the royal tour?" he asked as he approached.

Disapproval there? She couldn't be sure. He was hard to read, which left her with a tingle of frustration.

"Well, if she gets on rotation, I thought it would be worth having her familiarize herself with where everything is." Claire's tone was almost defensive.

Hunt nodded, his gaze never leaving Vic's. "You want to pitch in around here?"

"I've always appreciated being useful," she replied, lifting her chin slightly.

"I guess we'll have to see how it goes. Walk with me." He tipped his head. "I'll let you guys finish the tour later," he said, dismissing the other two.

Vic fell into step beside Hunt, keeping up with his long, purposeful stride easily. She found the urgency he moved with somewhat refreshing, and it sang to the programming inside of her.

"What do you think of our place?" he asked.

She glanced over, her eyes tracing the evenness of his features. She'd stared at his exact profile before, though it was Max she was remembering. Not this stranger she struggled to understand. Or maybe she understood him too well. He put his people first, and that was something she appreciated. But his motivations were murky, and there was still a distinct separation between Unborn and Organics.

"It's quite the set up," she commented, continuing to watch his face. "I'm amazed you can do so much for so many."

She caught the way his expression tightened for a second.

"Claire and Brody told me about the rotating schedule. It's a well-oiled machine." He said nothing, so she continued, "None of the Unborn work the ranch up top? They didn't mention that as part of the rotation."

He inhaled a smidge too quickly. Perhaps he'd been hoping she wouldn't ask about it. "We have a group of Organics topside. A lot of them live in the house and do most of the land work."

"Yes, Morgan mentioned that." For once, Vic let her exact thoughts come tumbling from her mouth: "You keep the Unborn here to hide them?"

As he slowed, his lips flattened, going nearly colorless. They stopped at a door she'd never been to before, and he turned to her.

"They're not hiding," he said through a tight jaw. "And they're not prisoners if that's what you'd like to imply next. Not all of us hate the Unborn. My father was a scientist on the Project. Max and I grew up together, like brothers. He's the only family I have left."

A pit formed in her stomach, some little tug of empathy coaxing her toward him, though she fought it and kept herself rooted in place.

He was softer than she'd realized, than he'd let on. His response to her provocation meant he wasn't the enemy, though he'd been formed into one in her mind without her permission. Maybe because he'd been so unwilling to give her his trust, she'd automatically withdrawn hers. Had she been so jaded by her experiences integrating into society and the prejudices against her kind that she hadn't recognized her own bias against them?

Hunt took one step closer, and she could make out the red that peppered his beard, the way one side of his mouth was permanently tilted farther down than the other. An endearing imperfection when she'd been around physically perfect specimens most of her life, Unborn being the paragons of idealized human bodies.

"Maybe I'll bring you up sometime to meet them. We can always use a Silver's efficiency around the ranch." He almost sounded friendly. Almost. But she read the challenge in his words.

She figured a topic change was in order. "Where are we and why did you bring me here?"

He took a breath, coming back to himself. "Max wanted to have a chat."

"A chat," she repeated flatly.

He looked away, raising one shoulder.

"You mean you're having him vet me." She narrowed her eyes, trying not to be offended that he was doing the smart thing. The responsible thing. After all, Max was the only person here who'd known her before.

Hunt took a breath, tipping his head in acknowledgment, then opened the door for her to step inside.

It was a room similar to her own, and it was almost as spartan, though there was a desk against one wall. It was neat and tidy—just the flat screen of a computer taking up one corner and a picture frame sitting next to it. A family photo.

She clamped down on the urge to walk over and pick it up, own the space like she was used to doing during the war. This situation triggered old habits like a tripwire. Hunt noticed her attention and moved in that direction. He took the picture from the desk and handed it to her, analyzing her expression as she studied the people in it.

"Is this your father?" She touched the glass over the older man's face, deeply lined and craggy. His hair was entirely white, his posture stooped. She imagined it was from a lifetime of hunching over a microscope.

"Yes."

On either side of the man stood Hunt and Max. Hunt was probably about thirteen. Max looked closer to how she remembered him. A young man. In his twenties judging by looks, but she knew he was younger than that in years.

There was a faint knock on the partially open door, and it drew her attention up.

"Hunt?" Max's voice called out.

"Here," Hunt replied, plucking the frame from her hands to replace it on the desk.

She watched Max pop the front wheels of his chair over the lip in the door, then roll the back ones over, impressed with how easily and quickly he accomplished the task.

Hunt leaned his backside against the desk, folding his arms across his chest as he grew silent.

"You're looking better now that you've gotten some rest," Max said, grinning at her. "Like the good ol' days, after a long campaign, coming back to base for that first hot shower and hearty meal."

She met his smile with a sardonic one of her own, unable to help herself. "You mean the cold water from a plastic bag with holes punched in it? And I remember the meal, alright. Tasteless mush from packets. Space food."

He laughed, but she caught the way he met Hunt's eye with some kind of silent communication. Probably approval.

"That was a long way from the five-cal days," she murmured, knowing it would get her bonus points.

"Five-cal days?" Hunt asked from his perch, brows pulled together.

"Back during the grow days. We got five thousand calories a day to keep up with the demand of rapid growth." Max was looking at her as he answered.

The memory of the overabundance of food was tainted with the misery of the process of growing in such a short period of time, and she could see it in Max's face, too—like he was fighting a grimace.

"Oh." There was some knowing in that one word Hunt spoke. He'd said they'd grown up together—like brothers. And the picture confirmed it. It made her want to know more of that background, dig into the past to unearth the make up of the man she didn't know. It might even help her better understand the one she did know.

She turned her attention back to Hunt. "Have I passed your test yet?"

Hunt's expression was tight, though she heard Max's soft laughing exhale.

"I mean, it doesn't hurt to make sure," Max said. "But I definitely wasn't questioning whether you're of sound mind. The way you looked right at that camera in the woods. . ."

She shifted to look at him, the question already on her tongue.

And he had an answer before she could voice it. "We have cameras all around the ranch to keep an eye on things. My job is to monitor them. Since I'm not much help with the physical labor in this place." He gestured to his missing legs.

She almost jolted at the reminder, picking up the slightest bitter note in his words. It was a tang on the air she could practically taste, and she felt Hunt stiffen behind her.

"When?" she asked.

Max's gaze grew distant. "Right toward the end. I really thought I'd make it through unscathed. You know, besides that one incident."

She smirked a little, definitely remembering the incident.

"Incident?" Hunt asked. He sounded frustrated like he didn't like being on the outside of whatever history she and Max had together.

"Max was messing around," Vic said, shooting Hunt her sardonic smile. "Juggling with knives."

"The wound in my foot didn't matter so much after the explosion," he said, injecting too high of a note of humor into his tone, and Vic's smile turned brittle. "Bomb blew up right in front of me when I was making breakfast. Took 'em both out," he explained, though she hadn't asked, hadn't planned to. "I remember lying there right next to the bits of my legs, wondering if the bacon was salvageable."

Hunt coughed. "Max. Hell."

Max met Hunt's eye over her shoulder, but Vic kept her gaze on him. As usual, he was using the humor to deflect the very real pain he still felt at losing his legs. Unborn, and Silvers particularly, didn't do well with feeling useless.

"Worried I'm going to hurt Victoria's delicate sensibilities, Hunt?"

It was a challenge that sparked like an electric charge in the air, and she suddenly felt out of her depth. She'd waded into the sticks of a relationship she had no context for.

"I'm not worried about Vic." Hunt's voice was low and even.

"That much has been obvious," Max returned. "You're practically treating her like a prisoner of war."

The urge to defuse the situation before it got worse compelled her to speak. "No need to defend my honor, Max. Hunt is putting the community first."

Both men shifted their attention to her. Max gave her an incredulous look. Maybe because the abiding loyalty that came from serving in the war together forged some level of disregard for convention-al wisdom. Though why that would trump a sibling-like bond, she wasn't sure. Hunt stared at her like he was surprised she'd defended him.

Then Max turned a baleful look to Hunt. "Am I allowed to show Vic around my area? Or is she still guilty until proven innocent?"

Hunt rolled his eyes as he stood.

Max scoffed, jerking his thumb toward him as he spun to lead the way out. "Tireless, this one."

Hunt didn't respond, even with an expression. He simply followed as they all trooped out.

Max led the way down the hall to the rotunda. "I don't get around as much as I'd like. Generally, I stay down my own corridor. Moni-toring the feeds and—"

Hunt coughed, drawing Vic's eye and the questions in her mind. Was that an intentional interruption? His expression hadn't changed one iota, so she looked back to Max as he continued, his eyes trained a little too intently forward.

"Well, that is a round-the-clock job."

They turned down the next corridor, one she hadn't been down before. Not that she'd had much opportunity since Hunt had inter-rupted her initial and as-yet-unfinished tour.

One, two, three, four, five doors in, Max stopped. "That's my place."

The door on the right he pointed to was shut, and he didn't move to open it. Instead, he focused on the open door to their left.

"This is the control room."

No one made a move to go inside, but she was allowed to peek. Still, she sensed the uncertainty at her back coming from the man who hadn't decided if he trusted her yet or not.

But from the doorway, she saw that most of the space was taken up with computer monitors, giving sight to various spots around the ranch. She had no idea how large the property was, but there were numerous views of forest and hills as well as angles around the house and one facing the front and back doors respectively.

Heat permeated the space, and a fan sat on the corner of the desk, oscillating constantly to stir the stagnant air.

"I spend most of my time in here and have a screen that's connected in my room so I get alerts of anything out of place."

"That's quite the set up," she commented, looking between the two men.

"It gives me something to do. Hunt has assumed most leadership responsibilities, and I work behind the scenes."

She couldn't tell if there was bitterness in his voice or not. But it might very well have been the culprit behind the tense exchange earlier.

By Max's own admission, he couldn't do everything he used to be able to, and maybe it was misplaced frustration. The more impressive part was that Hunt took it in stride without clapping back.

She would have to swallow the fact that she still didn't understand their past or the reason behind their dynamic, and it didn't seem like the appropriate time to ask. Not after their tiny spat a few moments before. She might have asked if it were just Max. But Hunt added a complication. He didn't seem prone to anger, but he did appear to be an intensely private person.

That was something she could certainly understand on a deep level. She'd never been accused of being too open. But she wasn't sure how to feel about having something in common with him.

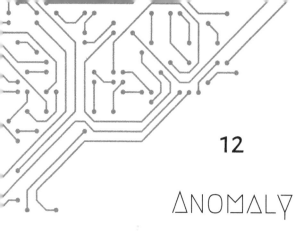

12

ΛNOMΛLY

T HE TENTATIVE KNOCK SOUNDED on Vic's door, and she jumped up from the floor where she'd been pumping through a series of push-ups. A restless energy simmered under her skin even though the room was never locked. But she was trapped by her intense adherence to rules, overt and unspoken. And so she stewed over thoughts of what Morgan may have found in her scans and blood work and tried to fill her time with physical activity. It did little to tamp down the frustration.

The two days since her interaction with Hunt and Max had been lonely and quiet. Claire appeared with food, led her to the showers, gave her a cursory explanation about the layout of the bunker as they walked, but everyone seemed preoccupied by something else. And it chafed to be out of the loop.

The knock set off a ripple of relief through her. She tightened her low ponytail, loosened from her usual bun, as she walked to the pocket door, sliding it open to Claire.

"Good morning, beautiful!" Brody crooned from behind the other woman, his rifle conspicuously missing from his hands.

Vic rolled her eyes but couldn't help the smile that snuck through. The edges of Claire's mouth dug into her cheeks at the corners like she was fighting her own grin. She didn't have a visible weapon either.

"We've come to finally finish your tour," Brody announced proudly.

"And take you to breakfast," Claire added with a smirk at his enthusiasm.

Vic stepped out into the hall, hitting the switch for the lights, and slid her door shut behind her. Release her from prison seemed like an accurate statement given that they were escorting her without weapons. Was that another vote from the community or Hunt's decision this time, she wondered. He'd taken over babysitting her the day before without using a weapon, even though he (and Brody) were more vulnerable to her strength than Claire was. But every time since, they'd had weapons at the ready.

Perhaps Hunt believed she was no real threat and simply felt he had to assert his authority in some way. It was hard to tell with him.

They made their way down the corridor and into the rotunda. There were a number of people cutting through, and a line began to form, snaking its way out of the mess hall and into the corridor, though it seemed to move at a decent clip.

Vic took in the many faces that filled the space, most of whom gave her a cursory glance and then ignored her or turned to whisper to their neighbors. Almost every pair of eyes that slid her way had the coppery sheen that denoted what they were, and a sense of isolation stole through her unexpectedly.

That feeling wasn't exactly foreign, but it was more potent because she didn't know most of the people here. It was a reminder of what she'd lost, and she had to blink against the bite behind her eyes.

The others' interest waned quickly as the line inched forward.

"Have you been sleeping okay?" Claire murmured as their silence stretched. Maybe she sensed Vic's shifting emotions.

"I mean, as well as I ever can. It is nice having a quiet room," she replied.

"Was it not quiet where you were before?" Claire's words came out a little stilted, like she was tripping over exactly what she was asking. She likely knew that thinking about where she came from could trigger some strong emotions.

But Vic had already battled them back and could speak evenly. "Thin walls and shacks tightly packed together makes for a lot of noise at all hours."

She didn't mention that sometimes the noises that breached her thin walls were her fellow soldiers' cries during their post-war nightmares. Claire would, no doubt, know all about it. But it wasn't something worth mentioning or reminding anyone about. Vic had no doubt Claire would be well acquainted with the symptoms of PTSD. Their creators hadn't figured out a way to mitigate the psychological effects of war on their subjects. Perhaps they hadn't seen any reason to.

A deep understanding glimmered in the depths of Claire's eyes as Vic met her gaze. Then the line moved forward, and their attention shifted toward the door.

When they made it inside the room, the growing wall of voices hit Vic with a force she wasn't quite prepared for. After being isolated for the last few days, her nerves weren't steeled for the way the sound and movement bombarded her. So many faces. Representations of the unique tastes of the scientists who created them.

It would've been more efficient, of course, to design super soldiers exactly the same, to streamline the process if they were only meant to be bodies on the ground. But the needs changed as the war progressed, as Coppers only made small dents in the dragging conflict.

As the government grew more desperate, demanding something better, something *more*, the scientists took more freedom and gave in to their own curiosities, catered to their own preferences. The Unborn Project had been just as much an experiment as it was a means to an end.

The line moved again, drawing Vic from her thoughts. It was a buffet-style counter where everyone grabbed whatever they wanted of the choices for the meal that day. A swinging door appeared to divide the cafeteria from the kitchen. She could hear the chatter of whoever worked to prepare the food through an opening in the wall next to the door, though she couldn't see anyone at the moment.

By the time Vic got to the food, a couple of the serving trays were empty of whatever had been there before, and a couple of people hollered from the line toward the kitchen without a response, so she took the empty tubs and walked to the door.

Pushing through, she found every person in the midst of an activity, including one man in deep conversation with none other than Hunt, whose eyes locked onto hers the second she appeared.

She set the tubs on the nearest counter. "They were out."

"We have more right here," a frazzled-sounding woman said to Vic's left, pulling her gaze from Hunt's.

"I got it," Vic offered, turning to take the full tubs.

"Thank you," the woman said on an exhale. "We're down a person, so." She offered a shrug as she spun back to what she was doing.

Vic felt Hunt's attention on her as she shoved her way back out into the cafeteria, and she set the tubs into their respective spots before getting back in line.

Several pairs of eyes lingered on her before the line started moving again.

"You'd think I had an extra head or something," Vic muttered, mostly to herself, but Claire snorted.

"It's been a while since we added anyone new to the bunker, and the circumstances surrounding your arrival. . ."

"You make people nervous," Brody interjected, unconcerned. "Because Hunt is wary. That makes everyone else wary."

"So it's really Hunt's fault," Vic quipped.

"What's my fault?"

Vic tensed then looked up from the plate she was loading with food.

Brody snickered behind her. Hunt's brows quirked up when she didn't respond. Then the faintest smile tugged at his lips like maybe he knew what she had said.

"That everyone's suspicious of me," she finally answered.

Hunt's eyes shifted to Brody for a split-second at the challenge in her tone then came to rest back on her. The faint smile grew. "That is definitely my fault."

Her own lips twitched before she looked down to get the last of her food and move along so the rest of the people in line could get theirs.

Hunt didn't have a plate, but he moved right along with her, clasping his hands behind his back, his eyes scanning the room. Always making sure things were running smoothly.

She understood the weight of that responsibility, could see the way it burdened him in the tightness of his shoulders and his heavy gaze. But she wondered if it was too much for him, if he took on more than he should.

"I was going to come find you after you finished breakfast," Hunt said, interrupting her thoughts.

She slid her plate onto a table, whipping a suspicious look in his direction. "Why's that?"

"Yeah, Hunt. Do you have a vendetta against her getting her tour?" Brody asked in a wheedling tone.

Hunt's gaze went heavenward for a moment as he slid onto the bench across from Vic. He moved his exasperated look from Brody to Vic, softening his features. "Doc has some news for me. And I figured you'd like to hear it, too."

Vic went motionless for a second. Everyone was focused on her, so she forced herself to look down, to pick up her fork and eat, though her stomach twisted. It was clear the news from the doctor was about her.

"Do we get to come?" Brody asked, shooting Vic a wink.

Hunt sat back a little, lifting a brow.

Brody's face fell theatrically as he shared a glance with Claire. How much of his antics were just for show? The frequency with which he looked at Claire whenever he said something ridiculous made Vic wonder if it was for her benefit.

Claire's mouth tilted down. She didn't seem to like the fact that they weren't welcome to join, but she said nothing.

Vic focused on eating so that they could get to whatever news Morgan had. The food didn't settle well with the roiling in Vic's stomach at the reminder that there *was* something to report. But she'd rather know than not.

She scooped the last bite in, reminded of the days when they'd only had ten minutes to eat between trainings, taking their meals in rooms much like this. Back then, she'd been surrounded only by Silvers, each one eager to be tested, to stretch their abilities to the limit. They'd shovel it in and hop up, ready for the next challenge.

Hunt watched her with a mild expression on his face then stood when she did, guiding her to where she needed to deposit her plate. She felt Brody's and Claire's eyes on them as they headed out the door together. They weren't the only ones who watched them leave.

"That was kind of you to step in earlier," Hunt commented, his tone low and gravelly. As if it were some secret.

Vic shrugged. "It needed to be done. Why not help when I can?"

He tipped his head to regard her from the corner of his eye. "I guess we should get you on rotation, then."

Some part of her reacted to his tone, though it was mild on the surface. "That wasn't some manipulation on my part."

One of his icy blue eyes narrowed on her face as he slowed and stopped in front of the door to the infirmary. "I wasn't accusing you of anything."

Vic turned to face him, a tightness cinching her chest. She shook her head and looked down. "I'm sorry. You're right. But I wouldn't hold it against you if you were. I know what it feels like to have the safety of a community on your shoulders."

He stared at her for a moment then dipped his chin slightly. "I understand not feeling like you contribute. I'll get you on the rotation."

Some small bit of tension released inside her at his words, and a new kind of understanding passed between them. There was still a question, still something underneath his words she wanted to probe, to grasp with her own hands. And she didn't truly understand why it mattered, why she wanted to get to the root of his motivation.

The door behind Hunt slid open and the doctor appeared, her brows quirking at the sight of the two of them together.

"Hunt." She looked at him with a question in her gaze, like she was surprised to find Vic with him.

He nodded. "She deserves to hear it, too. We don't have to treat her like an enemy."

Don't have to but will, Vic thought, shooting her gaze to meet Hunt's again. Then she looked at Morgan, whose mouth twitched for a moment like she was fighting a smile.

"Alright. Come on in." She stepped back.

Vic followed Hunt's big frame inside, noting how his shoulders nearly filled the entire doorway. A rancher, indeed.

Morgan clicked into something on the computer while Hunt drew up behind her, his crystalline eyes narrowing, his pursed lips belying an analyzing mindset.

"The blood test revealed some interesting things." Morgan's gaze flashed to Vic's face then to Hunt's, and she shifted like she was uncomfortable sharing the information with them both.

"Interesting in what way?" Vic asked, folding her arms over her chest. She tried not to clench her body too tightly but ended up digging her fingers into her biceps instead. "Am I dying or something?"

Morgan didn't laugh, though it was no wonder. Vic hadn't quite managed a joking tone.

"No." Morgan's fingers interlaced in front of her. "There was a hit in our system."

Hunt's head tilted a fraction, but that didn't land for Vic, even though her heart beat ticked up.

"What does that mean?"

Morgan's shoulders jerked upward briefly. "It means you have Organic DNA."

Still, it didn't compute. She hadn't learned that much about the process of her creation, but there had to be some human DNA for them to start with, even if it was enhanced and manipulated.

"As in DNA that matches familialy with real people."

Vic took the tiniest step backward, the words "real people" landing like a blow.

Morgan's hands shot out. "That's not what I meant."

Vic clenched her jaw and waited.

"I mean Organics who existed. The DNA hit suggests that you are related to them, and not just in fragments like most Unborn."

Vic swallowed as those words sank in, her heart squeezing painfully.

Hunt's eyes went to slits as he looked at Vic. "Someone played around with the formula."

"That's not the only odd thing," Morgan said, turning back to the computer.

But Hunt and Vic remained locked in a stare. Because he knew more about someone playing with the Unborn formula than anyone, she'd guess. If her limited understanding of his history with Max was correct, one or both of them was the product of someone taking liberties. But at least they'd known about it. Vic felt like someone had been lying her whole life.

"The brain scans." Morgan's voice broke their trance.

Vic jerked to look at the other woman. "What about them?" Her voice landed hard and jagged in the quiet room.

"There's some unusual activity." She pulled up a recognizable picture: the topside view of a brain—Vic's brain. Morgan pointed. "This area was overactive when it shouldn't be. But it corresponded with the ghost scans of some overactivity here." She indicated a secondary spot.

Vic forced herself to keep breathing. "Do you think any of this is related to what happened in my village?"

Morgan nodded. "I think it's very likely. Something in your brain was triggered, then some countermeasure jumped in and overrode the command."

Fear began to writhe in Vic's gut. "You make me sound like a computer." What if the countermeasure stopped working?

Hunt and Morgan were both watching her. Not like she would go off the rails at any moment, but probably because she was breathing hard, on the edge of some kind of emotional response. She beat it back, mentally dragging that shadow in her mind to a cage and locking it in.

"What is a ghost scan?" Vic asked, grasping for anything to get her mind around it all.

Morgan waited a beat before responding. "I designed a program that tracks brain activity after it's stopped. Usually there are traces of whatever was happening in the brain, and I can track the path the neurons fired to find out what took place before. Whatever was tripped in your brain slowly decreased until it disappeared entirely. Other than this continued activity here—" she pointed to the illuminated part of her brain— "everything looks normal now."

Hunt's head swiveled to the doctor. "What do you make of that?"

Morgan lifted a brow, one shoulder going up in a shrug. "It was almost like someone pushed a button to activate her, but this countermeasure superseded it and continues to run after the other stopped."

God, she *was* a machine. A robot being controlled by someone else. And none of it made sense because it wasn't like she was going in and out of control of herself. She felt no different than usual. Maybe more tired, but there had been a lot going on.

Or was it that her brain was working overtime?

Vic spun abruptly and walked across the room, willing her thoughts into some kind of order, and stared through the window into the hospital wing, phantom images walking the aisles. Three little girls—aged five human years but with the physical and mental maturity of thirteen-year-olds.

Alice giggling as she signed her name on a piece of paper like a signature with a first and last name—*Alice Rodina*—then passed it to the other two. Jamie had been eager enough to break an unspoken rule, stick it to the man, her sharp eyes glinting with glee as she signed and passed it to Vic.

Vic had hesitated, rolled with Jamie's taunt that she was a goody-two-shoes because it was old hat by then. But it was the one time the defiance had felt right. They *were* a family after all. Built and grown by the same woman, housed in the same room, pitted against every challenge as a unit. And it was only meant for them anyway. A word Angela had used in her faint rolling accent to refer to her family in her native tongue. *My rodina,* she'd said, pointing to the aged pictures in her photo album.

Pictures they'd never have. Of a family that wasn't theirs.

"Vic."

It was Hunt's voice that broke into the memory that threatened to lash tears into her eyes. Angela had built them all. Had she done this to Vic? And what about the other two? Had she written an override into Jamie and Alice's genetic coding as well?

"I wish. . ." She shook her head, tightening her lips against voicing it. The hope was too bright and painful in her chest.

"You wish what?" Morgan asked softly.

Vic turned, dividing a look between the two of them. Hunt was leaning the slightest bit forward, like he was straining to move toward her. But that didn't make sense. It was more likely he was preparing to jump in if the countermeasure ever fell against the other programming.

Vic shook her head. "I was just thinking of my unit sisters—the two I grew up with. The same scientist built the three of us. We were separated once we got stateside, and I have no idea where they are."

"You think maybe the scientist is responsible for this anomaly?" Hunt asked.

Vic opened her mouth, shut it. Tried again. "It seems most likely. I don't remember being separated from the girls much until we were older. If our creator did this to me on purpose, she probably did it to them."

Hunt ran a hand over his chin, the sound of his calloused palm along the scruff filling the room. "Maybe we can find out."

Vic looked at him sharply. "Find out what?"

He jerked his head for her to follow him toward the door, only turning back belatedly before he stepped all the way out. "Is that all you got for me, Doc?"

She waved him off. "That's it for now. I have some more analyses to do."

He slapped a hand against the wall before he ducked out into the corridor. Vic trailed behind him, her steps heavy with questions and memories that felt like her own personal ghosts trying to trip her up.

Angela had died right after they'd been sent off to their first fight, so it wasn't like she could find her and ask. She'd been old when the girls were little, so it wasn't totally unexpected. But it didn't mitigate the ancient ache of grief in her chest.

Vic looked up at Hunt as he moved through the corridor a few steps ahead of her, that same sense of urgency that seemed to be his style.

"Where are we going?"

He glanced back. "I know someone who might be able to help."

Frustration bubbled under her skin, made it feel uncomfortable along her bones. "Help with what?"

He finally slowed, letting his eyes trail back to her face. "Finding your sisters."

"They're not really—"

He lifted a brow. "Just like Max isn't really my brother."

It was a good reminder that he would know better than anyone what she was probably going through. Having a scientist manipulate things to fit their ends, though she didn't know exactly what his full story was. Not that she knew her own at this point. But if she couldn't get her answers, maybe he'd let her have his.

"Wait."

He stopped as soon as she spoke, pivoting to look at her.

"Before we do whatever you plan to do, I need to understand the deal with you and Max."

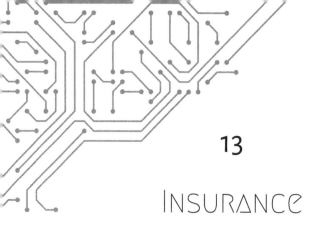

13

INSURANCE

H UNT DIDN'T SAY ANYTHING for a moment, barely reacted, though there was the faintest flash of something in the depth of his eyes.

Then he gave one swift nod. "This way, then."

They weren't far from her room. They'd been at the mouth of the corridor where it spilled out into the nearly empty rotunda, but Hunt's gaze swept the space like he was about to do something he shouldn't.

He didn't take her to her room, though. Down the next hall on their right, five doors in, he held his hand out for her to go in first before he stepped in after her, shutting them in.

With the news of the odd brain activity, she was nervous to come to his room alone. He was still the one who needed to be careful around her with no protection.

"Does this mean you trust me now?" she asked, raising a brow. The levity was there in her tone, but she genuinely wondered if he knew what kind of danger he could be in if that countermeasure ever stopped working.

"I don't trust much of anything." He tossed her a smirk as he moved across the room to the desk.

Her eyes tracked his movement as a little voice in her mind urged her to seek a straight answer. But did she actually want that answer? Did she want to face the fact that she might not be trustworthy?

"You're no longer carrying weapons around me."

He looked up from the computer screen. "Nothing you can see."

The air grew heavy as they stared at each other, and she felt that compulsion again.

He cocked his head like he could sense it. "Do you trust yourself?"

She sucked in a breath and fought the urge to look away. Tingles shot into her fingertips as she wondered if her own mind was strong enough to fight whatever might try to take over again. "Not at the moment."

He straightened, and she was nearly flattened by the way his expression softened. "I trust you as a person. I know you wouldn't intentionally hurt anyone here."

"But?" The word feathered up her throat.

He grimaced. "But there's still a big unknown at play."

She narrowed her eyes. "So why no weapons?"

"I'm a pretty big guy. I'd be hard to take down." He smirked again, knowing that wasn't a valid point. They both knew she could take down a handful of men his size at the same time.

She tried to laugh, but the sound was strangled by her concern. "Hunt."

His smirk faded. "Sedatives."

Her brows folded over her eyes.

"We don't want to hurt you," he said in response to her unvoiced question. "So we each have a sedative on hand, just in case."

She nodded, swallowing the rising irrational desire to prove that it wasn't necessary. To him and to herself.

"My father was one of the scientists on the Unborn Project." He turned back to the computer, typing something that she couldn't see because his screen was set on security mode. "Which means I grew up around all of this. The research, the tests, the experiments."

"There were things I overheard," he continued. "The things scientists did off-the-books to further their own interests and curiosities."

He straightened again and moved back toward the door. When he ran a hand through his golden hair, he loosened the smooth hairstyle, which was somehow endearing. She remembered the way Max would do that when his hair was cropped so short there was nothing to mess up. Like it had been this long once, many years before she'd known him.

"Is that what you and Max are? Your father's curiosity?" The words came out more bluntly than she'd intended, and Hunt looked away.

"Not quite." Barely a breath pushed the words out.

Vic ran the tip of her thumb over the ragged edges of her nails, grounded by the feel of the sharpness as she waited for the explanation.

"My parents were older," he said softly. "They'd lost children. Many times over. Miscarriage, stillbirths, childhood diseases." He swallowed, bringing his gaze back to hers. "Genetically 'not viable.' So my dad had a particular interest in genetic research. A misguided dream of ending his wife's heartache driving him to some manipulation where he maybe had no right."

Vic became mindful of her breathing, releasing the oxygen slowly like it would disrupt the fragility in the room.

"He used the resources he had access to. He didn't quite *build* me. Not like an Unborn. But he made some changes."

Hunt looked down, his fingers curling into his palms. "But even with those genetic abnormalities eliminated, my mother was so afraid. As I grew inside of her, Dad was building Max. My genetic twin."

Vic's hand came up slowly, fingertips brushing lightly over her lips as the realization hit. "He was the insurance policy."

Hunt didn't turn, but his eyes flashed to her face. "It was never necessary. And she died when I was a kid anyway. Dad disappeared into the work. And Max went off to war."

A strange twisting sensation filled her chest. His tone was even, but there was heartache underneath that went marrow-deep. And it colored Max's ready smiles and jokes in a way that almost made the whole thing worse.

"Did Max know?"

Hunt pressed his lips together, which gave her that answer. It explained why he'd checked the rotunda so diligently. If it was this painful for him to relay the story, she couldn't imagine how it made Max feel. Considering the way Max's jokes had that bitter edge the day before and how he'd pushed back against Hunt's authority, it made sense. A world of hurt and history, responsibility unfairly placed on his shoulders and suddenly taken away. Vic felt that down to her bones, and the thought of her own sisters on their own—taken from her—twisted inside.

"Despite the purpose behind his existence," Hunt continued, leaning against the wall beside the door. "Max is my friend and my brother. And that never changes."

It must've been true if Max always viewed this as his home, though she doubted living underground was the kind of post-war dream life he'd envisioned. She caught herself wondering about the division among the people here again. A contentious topic for another day.

"Anyway. I thought I'd loosen some of the restrictions around your movements in the bunker. Knowing what kind of failsafe was built in gives me some measure of peace." He gave her a half smile. "Plus,

Max relayed the rest of his history with you. I was told that I take this job a little too seriously. And that we have that in common."

She gave the barest smile back, acknowledging the truth of the statement. She was a rule follower by nature, the frustrating choice when a smash-and-grab mission had been the goal. That was Jamie's area. Vic was the strategist, the one who would do the complicated missions that required more finesse, more thought, more bodies.

There was a use for both types.

A knock on the door had Hunt grunting a "come in" as he pushed away from the wall, and it slid open.

Memories blasted her in a chaotic dance across her mind as soon as the young face popped into view, the same dark hair and eyes, those sharp cheekbones triggering an automatic response.

She was moving before she could truly process what she was doing; the only thing she could see were the round faces smeared with dirt, bodies strapped with vests loaded down with bombs.

"Vic, he's a friend."

Hunt's voice was at her ear, a little breathless, when she came back to herself. It took a few seconds for her to realize she'd thrown the man to the ground, laying herself over him as if to shield him.

The kid who stood in the doorway had frozen, eyes wide with shock and confusion as he stared. Then a slow smile split his round, youthful face, and he flung his foppish hair from his eyes twice in quick succession.

"Yo, Mr. Hunt. You got a pretty lady on top of you."

"No shit, Niko," Hunt grumbled.

Vic pushed off of him, getting to her feet before offering a hand to help him up, which he took.

He wore a half-amused, half-embarrassed grin as he took his eyes from Vic and settled them on the kid. "Niko, this is Vic. She's new here."

The kid, maybe fourteen if she had to guess, stepped further into the room, his fingers dancing against his thigh in a fluttering pattern. He was still smiling broadly.

"Vic," he repeated with a head tilt. "Is that a girl's name?"

His accent was faint but there all the same, the familiar lilting sound that was seared in her memory from the times she'd encountered enemy combatants.

"It's short for Victoria," she said, forcing the automatic fight response down. The effort made her sound robotic.

"I see." He was nodding vehemently like he was assimilating some complicated explanation, and she wondered if it was because he had to translate into his own language mentally first.

Hunt took a breath. "So, Niko, I was hoping you could help Vic and me with something."

"Sure. Anything, Mr. Hunt."

"Do you have your—"

Niko produced a small rectangle, which he promptly unfolded to reveal the portable computer. It was tech she hadn't seen in years. They certainly had access to some fancy stuff around here.

"Okay, we need you to look up some friends of hers."

Niko's dark eyes shifted to her with a ready smile on his face. "Sure sure, pretty lady. What's the names?"

Vic shifted. "Do you want to sit? Won't it take—"

"A few seconds, probably," Hunt murmured. "Tech whiz over here."

"Um. Jamie and Alice."

"They got last names?" he asked.

Hunt cleared his throat, and Niko's eyes shot up, fingers drumming along the edge of his tablet. "Oh, right. Unborn ladies. Soldier ladies." He flipped his dark, floppy hair out of his eyes several times, and she realized all of his jerky movements were tics.

"They might be listed with AF:CLXXVIV and AF:CLXXVV as their last names," Vic said, drawing Hunt's attention as he studied her. His eyes dropped down to the tattoo on her inner forearm, barely discernible amid the black ink that swirled around it with her own designs.

It had been her attempt at disguising what marked her for what she was. Or maybe it was her one rebellion. Only her left arm was marked in a full sleeve, geometric shapes and flowers taking their turns as they circled and crawled up. Like some rebellious child, she'd attempted to camouflage the one little marker that identified her as not totally human, something that had been meticulously constructed, honed, tracked, and controlled.

The tally marks were the only ones that marched along both arms, tiny black lines that ran along the outside of her forearms from wrist to shoulder, but the reasoning was hers alone. No blemish from the government, no act of rebellion. Simply remembrance.

"East coast," Niko said.

She jolted, shocked it had taken so little time. "Yes!"

He nodded, jerking his hands in a quick shake. "I got a location. They're together."

That sent a pang through her, though she told herself it was only relief that they had each other. It wasn't jealousy that she had neither.

"I can hack the—"

"Niko," Hunt warned. "We don't need a hack. We only need the address for the nearest comm station."

Niko drummed his fingertips along the edge of his tablet and flicked his hair out of his eyes again. His mouth twisted sideways. "Fine."

"I can write them a letter," Vic breathed, the first sense of accomplishment filling her with warmth. She'd wanted to find out where they were, what had been happening on their side of the country, but she'd never had the means.

She suspected that the separation had been intentional, though she had no real proof. It was a gut feeling she had, and considering how hard communication between coasts was, it had been fairly effective at cutting her off from Jamie and Alice.

Hunt nodded. "I know a guy. There aren't a lot of options, but I can get a message through."

With the nuclear wasteland between them and wherever Jamie and Alice were, physically traversing the no-man's-land was almost impossible, and most cross-communication was expensive and difficult to accomplish. But if Hunt knew someone who could get her message to the girls, maybe she could beg their forgiveness for not finding them sooner.

Hope ignited like a wildfire in her chest. She wished it would burn away her guilt. "I need some paper and a pen."

Hunt crossed his arms. "I can get you something. Meantime, let's see about getting you on the rotation schedule. Sound good?"

Relief pulsed like a beacon through her. "Absolutely."

She didn't want to stay cooped up in her room anymore, losing her mind because all she had to focus on was the fact that she might glitch out at any moment, that almost everyone she'd called friend was dead.

Hunt led the way out of the room and back toward the rotunda. Niko slouched along beside them, flinging his hair three times in a row, tapping the wall every foot or so with his pointer finger.

"Mr. Hunt said you escaped a massacre," Niko said casually.

Hunt jerked to look at him. "Niko."

"It's all right," Vic said, recognizing that he didn't mean anything by it. Or maybe she sensed something else because he had been so matter-of-fact about it.

"I escaped a massacre."

So that was it. She caught the way Hunt stiffened.

"It's a pretty scary experience," she murmured.

Niko lifted his shoulder again. "The world is scary."

Vic couldn't argue with that. She'd once been filled to the brim with terror, overflowing until it had poisoned her daily interactions and flooded her dreams. Every time she'd sent a squad in somewhere with no guarantee they'd make it back, she'd been so crowded with fear there hadn't been room for much else. She was never fun to be around when she was worrying about the people she was in charge of.

She glanced at Hunt from the corner of her eye, catching him full-on staring at her. Instead of the suspicion he'd continuously worn while in her presence, there was a softness in his gaze she didn't understand.

Niko's gaze traced the corridor wall ahead of them until it ran out. The rotunda was filled with people moving from one place to another, and Vic was shocked again to see so many. Niko abruptly stopped, shifting from foot to foot, his dark eyes darting back and forth.

"Hey, Niko," Hunt said softly.

Niko's gaze jerked to his face.

"We can try again another day."

Niko nodded, slowly backing away, that finger tap-tap-tapping when he found the wall again.

"I'll see you for lunch, okay?"

Niko spun and practically sprinted back the way they'd come.

"Sweet kid," Vic commented, her attention on the way Hunt stared after him, concern etched in the lines that formed on his brow.

He cleared his throat before turning to her. "Yeah. Max knew his family. His parents. They were victims of the conflict, refugees who'd had nowhere to go. Remember when the U.S. was taking those in?" There was a bitter twist to Hunt's expression.

She remembered. That hadn't gone over any better than the announcement for the Unborn integration into society. People were tired of the war and mad at those responsible for it, even though it had raged so long, it wasn't clear who'd started it. People were just angry, and they needed someone to pay for it.

"We took him in after his parents died. He's struggled with PTSD since the massacre."

She nodded, a little spot in her chest pinching. "That explains a lot."

He sighed. "And no matter what I do, I can't get him to stop calling me Mr. Hunt."

She laughed at that. "It's sweet."

Hunt broke into a full-on grin as he led the way across the rotunda, weaving through the crowd. It was mind-boggling that there were so many people here. How they had the space for this kind of community, she had no idea, though there were parts of the bunker she had yet to see.

There was enough of a shift, enough eyes that tracked her movement beside Hunt as they cut through to make her feel self-conscious. Like those early days of leadership, when they'd shipped out and she was so green but was expected to lead a bunch of Coppers in an invasion across war-torn foreign state lines. All those young faces had stared at her, not much younger than she was. They'd been bred to follow orders, but she'd still had this sense that she'd need to earn their respect.

She lifted her chin, taking a deep breath as Hunt slowed near what Claire had pointed out as the sparring room. He opened the door and gestured for her to step inside.

"We don't get a lot of excitement around here," he murmured behind her.

She almost crawled out of her skin because he was standing so close. Maybe to keep from being overheard because there were a number of people inside.

"You're the shiny new toy."

She glanced back at him, wondering if he realized the implication of what he'd said. He'd grown up around Unborn and the scientists who'd made them, but did it mean he'd heard the things they'd said about Coppers? That they were only bodies, numbers to fill tanks and planes, to tromp fields and shoot enemies. Expendable, innumerable. That there was no substance to them. Vic had known enough of them to see how smart and valuable they were as people.

Hunt must have seen that too, or he wouldn't have invited them to live here. So his comment must have had more to do with her than the Coppers.

"You mean the novelty will wear off and so will the inordinate amount of attention?" she asked with a smirk, choosing to give him the benefit of the doubt.

He shrugged. "Eventually."

To be fair, it wasn't the first time she'd drawn attention. Because Coppers were so common, people tended to react a bit to Silvers, as if they were some special thing.

Sure, there were only a few hundred of them compared to thousands of Coppers—at least originally. She wasn't sure what their numbers were since the war ended. The more unusual sight were the few dozen Golds. Special forces that were as rare as the precious metal their eyes resembled.

Hunt moved around her and drew up to a wall with pages tacked up in neat rows.

"Rotation," he said in explanation.

There were a lot of names. Several rows of charts with colors labeling the top. She assumed that was the breakdown of crews. Then a page of listed duties with colors next to them, confirming her suspicion.

"It took a hell of a lot of work to set it up," Hunt said, his eyes flickering over the lists. "But it stays the same, rotating duties and then repeating weekly. People get different jobs to keep it interesting, but it takes a lot of the guesswork out."

Vic tore her eyes from the sharp lines of his profile to look at the lists.

"I'll put you with Claire since you already know her. She'll show you the ropes."

"And keep an eye on me?"

It was obvious he heard the challenge in her voice. When he turned to look at her, she knew the look she gave him was edged with it.

"It doesn't hurt to keep our guard up."

"I would probably do the same thing."

He regarded her evenly, almost like he was trying to decide if she was being sincere or not. Finally, he turned back to the chart. "Claire is Green. So tomorrow, you're on laundry duty."

Vic did a mock salute, pulling an exasperated laugh from Hunt, which did a funny thing to her stomach.

"You're such a smart ass."

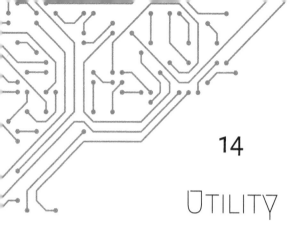

14

UTILITY

V IC ESSENTIALLY SHADOWED CLAIRE through her rotation, ignoring
the way the others slid curious glances in her direction. Claire
helped distract her with easy chit-chat and surface-level questions.
Not to mention her explanations of each step in the process.

But it was hard to fully forget that she wasn't with Claire because
she knew her the best, though she was starting to consider her a
friend. The frequency with which Brody popped in to "check" on
them as they sorted through the laundry would bring the truth home
every time, even though she'd begun to think of him as a friend as
well.

The laundry room was down the same corridor as her own quarters, the sliding door almost twice as wide as her own. A cloying
heat permeated the air that had the sweat beading along Vic's skin,
tickling along her hairline. Bins filled with clothing and linens took
up residence around the room, and piles of both sat on the floor in
front of large appliances that Vic hadn't seen in years but knew were
washers and dryers.

"How do you keep all these things running? What's the power source?" Vic didn't take her eyes from the people who were working through the piles, transferring loads from one machine to the other, or folding.

Claire was smiling, clearly proud. "We're powered by solar panels."

Vic's mouth dropped open. "How the hell did you guys get a hold of solar panels?"

Claire's smile turned a little grim. "Hunt's parents were involved in the Unborn Project." She walked forward, swinging a bin around to place it between the two of them.

"Yes, he told me."

Claire raised a brow, amusement a glint in her eyes, which looked brown in the lower light of the room. "He probably didn't get around to explaining that this was one of the first facilities."

Vic placed her hands on the edge of the bin. "Wait, like, for creating Unborn?"

Claire nodded. "His dad was the foremost Unborn researcher and geneticist. He was on the ground floor. And since the project was so secret, especially in those early years, they had the lab built underground in case of an attack."

Of course, that was a logical jump, but she wondered why Hunt hadn't told her those little details when he'd given her some of his background. Not that he owed her anything. Not really. But the opening had been there.

"Because of his prominence and his money, Hunt's dad was pretty influential and requested the lab be built here. This land has been in Hunt's family for generations."

Claire's gaze was warm on Vic's face as she pulled the clothes from the bin, sorting them into lights and darks. Vic hoped none of her thoughts were visible on her face, though she struggled to understand what had motivated Hunt to keep this to himself. Some part of her acknowledged he wasn't the sort who would want to brag about something like that. And she hadn't asked. But it painted him in a whole new light.

That he had done all this for others, to help them, build a community, keep them safe despite having the resources that could have kept him insulated and given him the kind of luxury of days gone by, made a little spot in her chest feel like mush.

She settled into the rhythm of sorting with Claire, falling silent as she lost herself in the work and her thoughts. Claire kept shooting her speculative looks, though she never said a word.

When they took their midday break for lunch, Vic was relieved to feel the cooler air out in the corridor, taking her first deep and full breath.

"It gets pretty stifling in there," Claire said, amused by Vic's reaction.

"No kidding."

"Brings a nice color to your cheeks though." Brody sidled up next to them, bumping Vic's shoulder with his own. "How's it feel to be put to work?"

Vic smiled. "Better than I thought. I'd been out of work for a bit before arriving. It's no fun being stuck at home with nothing to do, no way to feel useful."

"Oh, we can make you feel useful," Claire said, though Brody sent her a sharp look like he thought her response wasn't appropriate. "Though I think your talents are being wasted on menial tasks."

"What's that supposed to mean?" he demanded.

Vic's mouth twisted wryly. "She means my talents as the strongest person here."

Brody rocked back on his heels. "Right."

"He forgets since most of us are Coppers around here."

Vic tried to soften the grimace that contorted her face. "That wasn't meant to be any kind of brag."

Claire waved her off. "It's fine. We all had it drilled into our heads that we were just the grunts. Silvers are something special, built with a little more value."

Vic opened her mouth, hating that it was what she'd heard all those years, too, but Brody spoke before she could argue.

"If you're that strong, I'd love to see you spar with Hunt," he said. "I'd even pay money to see you take him in an arm-wrestling match."

Vic rolled her eyes as Claire said, "Even in this day and age, grown men will act like boys."

Brody's tongue clicked against his teeth in feigned offense.

"I'd win." Vic winked at him, and he grinned.

"Definitely," Claire agreed.

Vic's cheeks flushed when they made it to the rotunda and Hunt was there, talking to a few of the others. His eyes, casually scanning the area as he spoke, stopped suddenly on the three of them.

He didn't end his conversation or even seem like he would join them, but something about his body language told her he wanted to. The way he leaned a bit in their direction and how his gaze tracked their movement across the room and to the corridor that led to the mess hall.

Her days flowed like that for a while. Paired up with Claire, Brody sometimes joining them, she always caught sight of Hunt doing his leader thing. Though they didn't interact much for a few days, she felt his eyes on her any time they came across each other, that constant observation proof that he couldn't fully relax about her presence.

It was strange, though, when she didn't see him at all later that week, and she found herself disappointed. Especially considering how grating his constant presence had been. According to Claire, that was more usual than not, and Vic convinced herself that having everyone fall back into their old routines was a good thing.

Today was her first experience in the kitchen. Claire showed her the ropes—how they mass-cooked, served, and managed the mealtimes, then how they divvied the cleanup and prepped for the next meal almost as soon as they were done. It was one of the most exhausting of the work days. Practically non-stop with so many people in the bunker.

When she caught sight of the plate that was set aside on the counter once the dinner rush had slowed down, she nudged Claire to ask.

"Oh, that's for Niko. We're working on Max's right now. Someone usually takes it to them after the rush is over."

Vic dried her hands on the dingy apron she wore, her fingers chapped and aching from doing hours of dishes. "What if I brought it to them?"

Claire had gone back to arranging food on a plate, her broad shoulders lifting and falling. Then she turned to give Vic a sly look. "It's fine with me, but I can't get away any time soon."

The thought flashed through her mind, and she spoke before she thought better of it: "I could go alone."

Claire tried not to smile. "You sure could."

A thrill of glee went through her to have a little bit of breathing room. It was expressly going against Hunt's wishes, but she already felt like she'd proven herself useful and trustworthy. Days of no episodes while under strict guard made her feel like she could probably do this one task without losing it on everyone.

No guarantees, of course, but she was chafing under the constant supervision.

There was a glint of mischief in Claire's eyes as she handed Max's plate over, and Vic took up Niko's, pushing through the swinging doors into the half-empty mess hall and out into the corridor.

She no longer needed to count the doors as she passed them, registering the number subconsciously until she walked into the rotunda and crossed the open space to a hallway she'd spent less time in. The counting resumed as she followed the curve to the end of the hall where Hunt and Max had brought her over a week ago. He hadn't let her see his quarters before, but she knew Max had essentially taken on the role of caretaker for the young boy, and they lived like a tiny family unit.

It was only in this moment that she realized why he hadn't shown her that day, and what Hunt had interrupted when Max was explaining his role. They'd been trying to keep Niko a secret until she'd proven herself worthy of knowing him. Based on her reaction the day she'd met him, it was a safe assumption that she might not have handled his presence in the bunker very well.

She knew a casualty of war when she saw one, though.

Music pulsed from inside the room as she approached the door, lifting her hand to knock. But the door slid open before her fist connected, and she jerked back a step as she registered the big man who filled the doorway.

Hunt's attention was still behind him as he stepped forward, the music flowing out from behind him like a vapor of relaxing electronic melodies. "Keep digging, Nik."

He froze as soon as he faced forward, his eyes narrowing on her face before they dropped to the plates she held in her hands. He checked the corridor around her to find it empty.

"Had to bring those boys their dinner," she said, keeping her tone as innocent as possible, as if it had never occurred to her that what she was doing would be breaking his rules.

He turned his head slightly, never taking his gaze from her. "Dinner's here." He stepped aside to let her through, but he followed her in, leaving the door open to the hall.

Niko clicked his screen dark and spun around, his face lighting up with an excited grin even as the music, quieter than she expected, continued to fill the room. He drummed out that habitual pattern of taps along his legs.

Max was parked next to him, his expression morphing from a scowl to a smile that almost matched Niko's in wattage when he spotted Vic.

"Well, aren't you a sight for sore eyes," Max said. "His mug is the only one I've gotten to stare at today." He jerked his chin toward Hunt.

Hunt rolled his eyes. "It's literally the same one you see in the mirror every day."

"And you wonder why I'm tired of it?" Max shot back.

Vic smiled as their banter rolled over her in a pleasant wave and took in the space, setting the plates on a small table pushed up against the wall on the right side of the room. It was similar to her own quarters, only slightly larger and divided down the middle. One side was designated for a teenage boy who hadn't yet learned the discipline of keeping a tidy space. The bed was unmade, and the walls were covered with a clutter of pictures—digital images mostly, depicting geometric designs and various trippy portraits of people. The other was regulation military-pristine with no personal touches whatsoever, save a picture above the headboard that was a Picassoed image she realized belatedly was a portrait of Max.

"Where's your shadow?" Max asked Vic, pulling her from her observations. He shot an arch glance at Hunt, whose expression didn't change. As usual.

Vic pretended not to notice. "She's still working the dinner rush. I wanted to bring your meals before they got cold." She smiled, trying to ignore the way Hunt's attention remained on her as she stepped back before Niko rushed the table.

His mouth was full within two seconds. "Hey, yo, Mr. Hunt," he said around the food, "you should get your dinner and bring it back here. Bring some for Vic, too. We can eat together."

"Oh, that's okay." She held up her hands, knowing that was putting him on the spot, especially since he might have been upset with her for flouting the rules.

"How am I supposed to eat with you when your dinner is half-gone already?" the big man asked, a smirk tugging one corner of his mouth up.

Max raised his brow as he looked at Niko. "That means you have to stop eating and wait."

Niko released his fork, the metal on the plate making a loud clatter as it dropped. "I can wait. I want Vic to eat with us." The words rushed out of him, heavier with the accent she'd never forget after years of fighting his people.

She was able to keep her reaction to that part in check because of the absolute earnest expression on his face, so childlike, as he shot a pleading look to Max. It was clear Max struggled to make his expression stern as he rolled himself up to his side of the table.

"I'll get us a couple of plates," Hunt said, pinning Vic with his gaze before he slipped from the room.

Vic released a loud breath, her shoulders drooping.

"What's got you so wound up?" Max asked, completely oblivious to—or perhaps used to—Niko as he meticulously separated the different foods on his plate into distinct sections while they waited.

"Hunt makes me nervous with his suspicious face and the staring and—what?" She narrowed her eyes as Max's shoulders shook with quiet laughter. She glared at him for asking the question when he clearly already knew.

Niko's eyes bounced between her and Max, so she wasn't sure he entirely picked up on what she thought was irritating and Max found so entertaining.

Max held up his hands in surrender. "Nothing."

She tucked her tongue into her cheek, sliding a glance at Niko, and figured she wouldn't pursue it with the kid around.

"You're healing up nicely," Max commented.

She lifted her hand, now only marked by the pink slashes of newly formed scars. A process that would have taken a couple of weeks for an Organic. The slice along her side looked about the same.

"You know how it goes." She shrugged and moved across the room to look at the pictures plastered all over the wall. It was while she studied one abstract image of a woman's face, half made of dark flesh, the other half comprised of geometric lines that glowed a bright purple and followed the contours of a cheek that she realized it was someone else she recognized.

She gasped and turned to look at Niko and Max. Max was half-smiling at her; Niko was tapping nervously against the table, murmuring numbers like he was counting each tap.

"Niko, did you do these?"

He flipped his hair from his eyes but simply shrugged.

She turned back to the wall to peruse the others. "They're amazing!"

There were other faces she recognized, Unborn whose names she had yet to learn, their metallic eyes glowing from the images, faces made of electric grids or circuits or mechanical gears. The low lights and curves in their features were marked with bright colors or dark shadows, depending on what he was going for. Sometimes moody and dark, they made a spot in her chest ache. But the bright ones made her smile, and usually, those showed happier expressions—playful or teasing.

The music that still played seemed to follow that cadence too as she continued to study the pictures. Sometimes thrumming and up-lifting. Other times, the melody enveloped her in a cocoon of intro-spection and depth that was astounding in such a short piece.

"Found out about our resident artist, I see," Hunt's voice—rec-ognizably distinct from Max's now that she knew what to listen for—pulled her attention back.

She could have spent hours listening to the music and studying the pieces Niko had likely spent a lot of time on.

"These are amazing. And it's like the music perfectly pairs with them. Like it was curated to complement them."

Max laughed, and even Hunt started to smile as he placed two more plates of food on the table that was way too small for the four of them.

"What's so funny?" Her eyes went to Niko, who was the only one not smiling, though his cheeks had grown pink. "Wait."

Hunt nodded, pulling a chair he looked too large for over to the table. "Niko composed the music, too."

She stared at the boy who was clearly embarrassed by all the attention, his hand rubbing at the back of his neck. "Niko, this is incredible."

Max's mouth turned up in one corner. "We had to get him into something so he'd stop hacking into things he had no business mess-ing around with." He reached over to muss the kid's hair, but Niko ducked away before he could accomplish it.

Hunt tipped his head to invite her to join them at the table, and she squeezed in between him and Niko, wondering if the heat in her face was visible to the rest of them.

They ate in silence for a while, and she bumped elbows with Hunt multiple times because he was apparently left-handed. She made eye contact with Max several times and tried to silently communicate with him to fill the silence because she was so uncomfortable, but he feigned stupidity.

"So, soldier lady," Niko said, blessedly breaking the awkwardness. "Did you kill anybody in your village?"

Without thinking Vic sucked in a shocked breath, pulling her bite of food into her airway, and started hacking to get it out.

"Niko!" Hunt and Max said simultaneously.

When Vic struggled to get the food lodged in her throat out, Hunt's big hand slapped against her back. She waved him off as she spat the food into a napkin, though she kept coughing residual particles from her lungs.

Max was glaring at the boy, who looked horrified that she was choking, while Hunt stood to fill a cup with water from the small sink in the corner and handed it to her. The cool liquid soothed her raw throat.

"I'm sorry, Vic." Max looked at her. "Niko has a morbid fascination with death."

She cocked her head to the side. "Don't we all?" she croaked.

Niko's scrunched shoulders relaxed as the other two men gave brief, mirthless chuckles.

"How about I tell you another time?" she suggested, her voice still scratchy. She gave another cough. "I should probably get back to the kitchen."

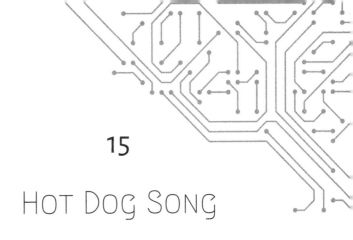

15

Hot Dog Song

I T WAS DISORIENTING TO wake in pitch black every—what? Morning? She could never tell. Somehow her natural body clock knew when everyone else had risen to start their day, so she assumed it must be daytime topside.

Except this morning, she was up earlier than she realized because not many were stirring from their rooms, and even breakfast wasn't in full swing yet. She checked the progress through the windows cut into the doors then chewed her lip, trying to decide what to do until the meal was ready.

She continued down the corridor, wandering until she came to the sparring room, which she'd only ever found empty.

Today, it wasn't.

She debated for only a moment before pushing her way in, knowing she'd be interrupting. Right inside the door, she leaned against the wall, tucking her hands behind her back until Max chose to acknowledge her.

It did give her an idea of what she would do the next time she woke too early as she watched Max go through a rigorous workout routine.

Even though his eyes had flashed to her when she first came in, he said nothing as he continued with his chin-ups, his bare upper body slick with sweat and defined lines of muscle.

She remembered the truncated exercises they all did during the war to keep themselves from going insane. And the times they'd been so pinned down by the enemy that they'd restlessly hunkered down until they could move again. The way they were designed for movement, for strength, for power made it impossible not to work to challenge themselves, even, it seemed, when you'd lost both your legs.

Max grunted out one last chin-up, his body shaking with the strain and effort, and then he dropped back down into his wheelchair, puffing out a breath.

He gave her a shrewd look while his ribs contracted and expanded, the one tattoo he had—more shading than distinct lines depicting mountains and trees, reminiscent of what surrounded the ranch—shifting as his lungs worked.

"You're interrupting my PT."

She smirked. "I'm just standing here."

He gave one airy laugh. "I was pretty much done. I like to get it out of the way before the others are up." He bent forward, his chest hitting his knees as he reached for the towel on the floor. He swiped at his face and neck.

"Every day?" she asked.

His eyes shifted to her again. "Pretty much. I can't keep in shape the way everyone else does."

It was an effort to stop herself from flinching at his casually dropped words, especially when the bitterness was a tang underneath that had a delayed impact.

"I'm not sure I would consider what we do down here as strenuous enough to keep in shape." Her voice was soft, tempered by the fragility she sensed.

He snatched his shirt from the floor and wheeled himself over. "Not down here, no."

Mention of working topside sent a little thrill through her, though she hadn't figured many Unborn did anything on the ranch portion of the property. "Do you ever work up there?"

His mouth tilted up in the corner, but that smirk was not one of humor. "Nope. I'm the security camera guy, remember?"

"But surely you get out of here sometimes? What about Niko?"

Max wheeled himself to what looked like a spigot, pulling a cup from a stack on a table next to it to fill with water. "Oh, he goes up with Hunt if the opportunity presents itself."

"Max—"

"Speaking of Niko," he interrupted, obviously knowing that what she was about to say wasn't something he wanted to hear or talk about. He tossed back some water and began filling the cup again. "You made his night by having dinner with us."

She stared at him for a long moment, finally seeing that he was really a ghost of the man she once knew. There had been glimpses since she'd arrived like he'd been trying to resurrect his old self. But she could see now how much energy it cost.

"I enjoyed it," she finally said. "Niko is very sweet."

Max gave a mirthless snort, but there was affection in his expression. "He's also a pain in the ass."

She smiled faintly, a memory floating loose in her mind. A refugee man, thin and beat up, half-buried in grief for his dead wife, had looked at his young teenage son with that same wry affection.

"That sounds like a typical fatherly response," Vic murmured, though she was still half-lost to the memory.

The boy had been playing with his infant sister, who'd reached for Vic when her brother had startled her—the only feminine figure available—to be held and comforted. The baby had heaved the most world-weary sigh as she'd settled against Vic's chest.

She turned her thoughts from the oddly bittersweet flashback.

Max gave her a sideways glance as he drank some more water. "I wouldn't know what a real father's response might be. But we're trying to do right by the kid. No one else out there for him."

She tipped her head, a little twinge of sadness pinching in her chest, for this boy, and for the family she had never seen again.

"We?" she asked. "As in you and Hunt?"

He lifted a shoulder and wheeled himself closer to her. "Between the two of us, we make one half-decent father figure, I suppose. Neither of us had much of an example, but we know what we would have wanted."

"I'm sure you're doing a great job."

He smirked. "We're all he's got, so it doesn't matter much."

His deflection made her want to smile, but she kept it at bay. She knew they both cared deeply for the boy, and he for them.

"Anyway, I'm sure Niko would like it if you joined us again sometime."

She did smile at that. "Assuming Hunt approves."

Max snorted. "He plays a tough game, but he does whatever the kid wants."

She laughed lightly, knowing she'd probably do the same. "I'd be happy to."

"He might ask you more personal questions," Max warned, his demeanor genuinely melting now.

She lifted a shoulder. "I don't mind."

"You might eventually." His expression darkened a little. "He gets a little morbid."

"I think we all do when we've been surrounded by death."

He conceded that with a nod and a sardonic smile. Because he, too, was probably remembering how they'd joke about dying on the battlefield.

"*Sing that stupid hot dog song over my grave, would ya?*" Max would say as he chewed the nutrition bars they'd relied on when they'd run out of fresh provisions. The ones that packed a thousand calories into the tasteless, jerky-like slab that threatened to break the jaw.

And even though he wasn't in the ground, the group would band together in a rendition of the hot dog song someone made up during one of their early missions.

Hot dog, hot dog, sizzling on the grill,
With toppings galore, oh, it's a thrill!
With onions and relish, and maybe some slaw,
You're the answer to hunger, no matter the law.

As the lyrics melded and meshed into one another, fading in her memory, she wondered now if Max hadn't truly grieved what he'd lost. If he kept himself closed off now because he wasn't who he'd once been and didn't know how to fit in anymore.

Becoming a father figure would maybe fulfill elements of that leadership role, that idolization he always seemed to thrive under. But he'd been the golden boy, the guy everyone wanted to be around. And now, he was sequestered to one small section of the bunker, coming out only when no one else would be around.

Maybe he still needed to mourn.

"Did you sing the hot dog song for your legs when you lost them?"

He gave another breathy laugh and rested his elbows on his knees, looking down at the cup in his hands. "Nope. None of those guys were around anymore to give me backup."

Shaky ground here, but she thought it might be worth treading. "Maybe it would help."

His chin shifted forward as he squinted up at her. He looked ready to cuss her out or throw her to the ground. But he did neither as he exhaled loudly through his nose and wheeled himself toward the door.

"I'll join if you need it, Max. Just say the word."

He stiffened for a second but didn't turn. Then he pushed his way out into the hall.

Their interaction sat in her mind like a boulder as she went through breakfast and then the motions of stripping beds with her rotation crew. It was impossible to move, to see around, to get a real sense of its size and weight. And it was equally hard to ignore.

Would it be worth bringing up to someone? Or was this something she should pursue with Max himself? Keep pushing where she maybe had no right? They'd been buddies once, co-leaders, connected in a way not everyone truly understood unless they'd fought in the war. But it had been years. They'd been in different units, vastly different locations by the time the cease-fire came down from the top brass.

He'd been recovering from his loss in a hospital somewhere. She'd been on a pockmarked field of bodies, surrounded by bomb haze and dirty, exhausted men and women who barely believed that this was their last battle—still fighting an enemy that refused to give up, even when their government told them to. When you'd been fighting for decades, it was hard to stop. Even her own soldiers struggled with the idea of doing something different. But they had other reasons. It had been their sole purpose.

She yanked the sheets from another bed. The sleeping quarters reminded her of childhood, when there were a dozen kids to a room in that Silver facility. It made sense since this had been another place where Unborn were created, trained, and raised. A soldier factory.

She found herself wondering, as she pulled the sheets from yet another single bed, how much time Hunt had spent down here. And

Max, for that matter. From the history the two had, she imagined Max wasn't treated like a typical Unborn.

Had he been allowed to run around like a kid with Hunt topside? Or had he been relegated to strict officer training and drills like the rest of the Silvers, always on the outside of what a real childhood could have been?

And what about Hunt? Did he feel left out? Or had he run these halls more than the fields of his family's estate?

Vic turned to plop the armful of linens into the rolling bin that stood right outside the door, stepping out right as someone was passing, and they bumped into each other. She was able to keep a hold of all the sheets and blankets, but she stepped back to regain her balance.

"Sorry."

Her head snapped up to bring her gaze to Hunt's, and his expression warmed, even if he didn't fully smile.

"It's fine." She hated that the words came out a little breathless.

Even though they hadn't interacted in days, her opinion of him had changed enough that he'd sort of morphed into some kind of celebrity in her mind. Plus, she'd just been thinking of him, and a paranoia that he'd know he'd been on her mind spiked her blood.

"I hear you challenged me to an arm-wrestling match," he said, taking the linens from her arms and dropping them into the bin.

She snorted. "It wouldn't be a match. And I didn't challenge you. Brody simply shared his dream of seeing me beat you in front of the rest of the class."

He nodded, squinting down the hall toward the other bins that were lined up against the walls. "That sounds like something Brody would say. He couldn't take me down himself, so he'd like to see me knocked off the throne."

Vic folded her arms across her chest, smirking. "Is arm wrestling a regular pastime around here?"

He shrugged. "Well, it's not like we have board games."

She let out a laugh that surprised her. His smile spread across his face slowly as he looked down at her.

"You seem to be settling into the routine nicely." He stuffed his hands into his pockets, his gaze going behind her to the others working to pull sheets and put fresh ones on the beds. "Move so much faster than everyone else."

She dipped her head, not sure if that was censure in his tone or a compliment. "Can't help the way I was built."

He folded his arms over his broad chest. "I forget that Silvers are so different."

"I keep hearing that." Apparently this facility had produced only Coppers, which made sense. It had started in the early days, before they'd segregated the levels and focused in on the unique abilities they could infuse into each.

Hunt shrugged. "Well, most of us haven't known that many. Max, obviously, but he. . ." He rubbed a hand along his chin as his gaze shifted away.

She knew what he would have said. That Max had once been their shining example of what a Silver was made to do. But no longer. Convenient segue.

"Speaking of Max," she started, stuffing the linens deeper into the bin.

Hunt raised a brow.

"I ran into him this morning, and we had this conversation. . ."

He waited.

"I'm worried about him. I know I haven't been here long, but I think he's still struggling with what life is like now that. . ."

Understanding shuttered in Hunt's eyes, and a muscle in his jaw twitched. It trapped the rest of her words in her throat. Because he knew. He saw it, too.

So did he care? Or was Max shutting him out despite his best efforts?

He gave a slow nod, his eyes following the movement of someone as they came forward, dragging more linens to the bin. Vic stepped to the side to let them drop it in and head back in.

"I don't want to overstep," she said more quietly. "But he is my friend, and I would hate to see him lose more of himself because he isn't what he used to be."

Hunt studied her, his expression unchanging for a moment. "I appreciate you mentioning it." He sighed like it was an exhausted argument. "I had thought he was doing better, but I've lived with dark Max long enough now that I forget it's not really who he is."

Dark Max. Her chest torqued, and a different kind of grief flamed through her. Who they'd once been wasn't only a loss to themselves, but to those around them.

"Let me know if there's something I can do," she said.

"You already are doing something."

She snorted, looking around at the group that worked on around her, the mechanical parts of what he'd built here.

"That's not what I meant."

She brought her questioning gaze back to him.

"Some pieces of the old Max have cropped up since you got here. He's been joking more again." His brows quirked. "Even if it's been at my expense at times."

Her laugh was half-hearted because she felt that burning in her eyes that she despised. She started to turn and move back into the room to get the stripped beds remade. Hunt followed, grabbing fresh sheets to help her.

She smiled her thanks, unsure why he bothered helping when there were plenty of others to make the work go fast. Didn't he have more important things to worry about? Other enigmatic behaviors to engage in?

They worked in silence for a few minutes, side-by-side, though she got almost twice as many done as he did, which elicited a half-smirk from him because she was a bit smug when they made eye contact.

"Rubbing it in," he commented.

"I'm not doing anything on purpose," she retorted, raising a brow.

"No, I don't imagine you are. Though I suspect there's a little more than the usual, I don't know, silverness." He waved his hands above her head like he could point to whatever it was in her brain that was different.

But that reminder made her smile slip away as she thought about how she was different—more than they truly knew yet. And that reminded her what had happened to her people, once a community like this one. Maybe not thriving, but supporting each other, giving when someone had need. She was here, alive, because of how different she truly was.

"Sorry," Hunt murmured, apparently picking up on where her mind had gone.

She gave him the ghost of a smile. "It's fine." She placed her hands on the side of the bin with all the dirty linens, her eyes on those hands marred by scars from countless battles, but none that reflected the pain that burned in her heart.

"I still see their faces. The blank eyes."

Hunt grew still at her words, so softly spoken she was surprised he'd heard her.

"And the way I woke up, my hands around Garrett's neck. It took me a few seconds, long seconds, to make myself let go. Like I had to actively take the control back." She shook her head, that moment playing over and over on repeat in her mind's eye, everything around her fading into the background.

It was a familiar process, her tendency to replay things like the films they'd watched in training. Even before they studied their enemies, they'd watched reels of themselves in sparring matches to analyze their missteps in hand-to-hand combat, been given clips of their mock scenarios and drills to figure out what they'd done wrong that would lead to death or defeat. She'd spent extra time on those reels, analyzing her actions down to the minutest detail because she *had* to get it right.

Hunt's hand landed on her shoulder, and she jerked.

"You did take back the control, though." His sincerity showed in the softness of his face, usually so sharp, so suspicious, lined at the edges of his mouth where he frowned on a regular basis.

"Did I?" she asked, not really sure why she voiced the doubt aloud, why she even still questioned it. That countermeasure was alive and well in her head. She'd had the doctor check a couple of times. But had she been the one to trigger it? Or was that another thing someone else had initiated?

Hunt's lips parted slightly like he wanted to say something, to reassure her. She wasn't sure. But he didn't, and she searched his eyes for it, hoping for some measure of confidence she couldn't find in herself at the moment. Then she broke the contact, looking down into the bin.

"I'm going to bring this down to the laundry room. Thanks for your help."

He didn't say anything until she'd gotten halfway down the hall.

"Vic," he called.

She turned.

"Niko wants to know if you'll come eat dinner with us again tonight?"

A warmth, soft and pliable, filled her, almost chasing away the chill of grief that stuck to her rib cage around her heart. She tried not to read into the "us" part, the side of her that wondered if it really was Niko asking.

But then she simply told herself she would hate to let the kid down if he truly had asked. And that it was a good opportunity to keep probing with Max, even if he fought her on it.

Hunt was standing there, still waiting for her answer. He actually shifted like he was nervous about what she'd say.

"Yes, of course," she finally said.

He released a breath and gave one swift nod before he turned and went the opposite way down the hall.

16

TALLY MARKS

"WHERE ARE YOU GOING? And what's with all the plates?" Claire asked, her arms loaded with her own dinner.

Vic followed her gaze to the wide tray she held in her hands stacked, somewhat precariously, with plates. "Niko asked me to join them for dinner."

"Them?" Claire asked, her coppery eyes going sharp, and Vic willed the heat not to infuse her cheeks.

Still, it made her stomach flip. It was a foreign sensation, this discomfort, and she really didn't know where it came from or why she needed to feel any sort of embarrassment.

"Well, obviously, it's not only Niko." She hoped the vague answer would be enough, though she continued to ask herself why the fact that Hunt would be there made her feel this way and why she felt the need to hide the fact.

"Right." Claire drew out the word, her suspicion palpable.

"Right," Vic repeated. "Well." She gave a mock salute and hurried for the door before Claire could ask more questions. Because it was clear, despite Vic's evasion, that there were, in fact, four plates on the tray in her hands.

But the heat continued to stir under her skin, keeping her discomfort on the surface as she speed-walked her way down the hall to Niko and Max's quarters.

The door was partly open, and she could hear the murmur of male voices. Hunt's and Max's, almost indistinguishable at that volume. She might've thought only one of them was there with Niko if it weren't for the fact that they occasionally talked over each other, and she saw them both clustered with Niko at his computer screen.

". . . doesn't make sense," Hunt said, frustration a low simmer in his voice.

"I can keep looking, Mr. Hunt."

"I don't like where this is leading," Max growled, his silvery eyes catching the light as he looked at Hunt with a scowl, then caught sight of Vic.

"Hey, Vic, come on in."

Hunt jerked upright from his leaned-over position, and Niko clicked out of whatever they'd been looking at.

Something about the speed with which they'd reacted and the tension in Hunt's shoulders told her she'd interrupted something she wasn't supposed to.

She stepped carefully inside.

"Didn't hear you come up," Hunt said, shifting to stand next to the table. He drummed his knuckles along the surface, reminding her of Niko for a moment.

Max rolled his eyes. "She's a Silver, remember? We have a light tread."

"Not you anymore, though, Mr. Max." Niko's voice was cheerful, though Vic felt the horror flash across her face.

Max just laughed. "No, but I think I'm still pretty quiet."

"You can think that," Niko said, standing, tapping his fingers along his leg in his familiar rhythm. Twice with his left middle finger, then his right four times, a wave of all the fingers on both hands, then the pattern repeated.

Max laughed again, though she wasn't sure how he really felt about this conversation. After their interaction that morning, she wondered if she was starting to see past a mask.

Hunt didn't smile, and she thought maybe he was picking up on it, too. But she watched his throat bob in a swallow and realized it might be something else. Like maybe whatever they'd been looking at on Niko's computer. She resisted the urge to look at the screen on the desk. It was blank anyway.

"Here, let me take that," he said, lurching forward to take the tray. As if she couldn't handle holding it.

He's being a gentleman, she reminded herself. A cynical part of her added, *Yeah, because he's hiding something and wants to distract you.*

She forced a friendly smile and let him take it, then gestured for Niko to pick his seat first. As she'd guessed, he took the same chair he'd used the day before, which left her to sit next to Hunt again.

"Maybe we should trade spots," she suggested before Hunt could take his seat.

His brows quirked. "Don't like bumping elbows with me?"

There was no way he was flirting with her. Right? "I think we both could use a bump-free meal."

He gave her the faintest smile. It was more in the eyes than the mouth, a twinkling warmth in the blue depths, and gestured for her to take the seat closest to the wall.

It did something weird to her insides, despite her suspicions. It was another thing to add to the list of borderline-friendly behavior he'd begun to show her. Did it mean he was starting to accept her presence here? That he might've begun to trust her—truly? Maybe the thing with the computer was related to something else.

She stabbed her fork into her food, trying to distract herself from the back-and-forth thinking.

"What do your tattoos mean?" Niko's question pulled her attention from her food.

The sleeve of ink on her left arm was hard to miss, but he wasn't looking at the flowers and shapes inked into her skin. He probably knew a lot of Unborn sought to cover the identifying number they'd had no choice in getting, though he wouldn't know the specifics of what AF:CLXXVIII meant—AF for her creator, Angela Forman, and the number for her specific sequence in the string of experiments that had come before.

No, his eyes were on the tally marks. There was enough space between the swirling patterns and those crudely inked tallies for them to be noticeable on that arm. And completely stark against the unmarked skin of the other.

The air in the room grew heavy with Niko's curious anticipation and the tension that emanated from Max, who knew the story behind those marks. He'd inked some of them onto Vic's arms himself.

And even though Hunt didn't know what the backstory was, he was just as focused on her as they all waited for the answer.

"Lives lost," Vic said softly, keeping her gaze studiously trained on the plate before her.

"During the war?" Niko pressed.

Max coughed, and she looked at him. She read the question in his eyes: *should I make him stop?*

She gave the slightest shake of her head then twisted her fork in the pasta on her plate, wrapping the noodles around the tines. "The ones under my command."

"Each line represents a life?"

Even though the question sent grief raking across her heart, she smiled a little at the gentle innocence in his curiosity. "Yes."

His eyes went wider, the pads of his fingers gently fluttering along his thigh. "That's a lot of lives."

She gave a slow nod. *Too many.* "I ran out of room."

Niko's expression turned thoughtful, and silence hung for a moment. "It's nice that you take the time to remember."

Suddenly, her chest felt too small to contain her lungs, her heart. She pressed her free hand lightly to her lips when they began to tingle.

Oxygen in and out, she told herself. *Just keep breathing.*

Hunt was watching her reaction with an intensity she didn't quite understand. She felt his concern like an electric current on the air. Under the concern was something else she couldn't put her finger on. The grief had such a stranglehold on her, though, it prevented her from processing. Until she could loosen the claw-like fingers around her airway, she was incapable of anything beyond the mechanics of getting air in her lungs.

Eventually, the pain in her chest subsided, that vise loosening its hold, and she could take a full breath. She slowly raised her fork to her mouth, no longer tasting what she ate. But she was grateful for the food, grateful to have something more substantial than she'd had in so long, even if it had turned to ash on her tongue.

Niko's words sat with her for a long time after they finished their meal, when he played some more of his music for her, some of it melodic and haunting. It felt like he was trying to give her a glimpse at his own grief and how he remembered.

Because that music sounded like mourning, and it twined with what was playing inside her until she couldn't take the melancholy anymore. She hadn't looked at those tally marks in such a long time, though she knew she absently ran her fingers over them when she was anxious. As if she could feel them under her skin, remind herself what responsibility cost her.

There should've been another hundred added after that day two weeks ago, when she'd watched the people she wasn't responsible for tear each other apart like savages. But she couldn't deny that she felt the weight of their lives, their well-being still there on her shoulders. And since no one else would remember them, she should mark them on her skin to remind her to carry their names in her heart.

When there was a lull in conversation and her heart ached too much to ignore, she stood. "I should probably head to bed."

"Hey, Vic," Niko said. "Can you have dinner with us every night?" His eyes rounded as he looked up at her, and his teeth worried at his lip, like he thought her answer would be no.

But already this child had wiggled his way into her heart with his innocently asked, if sometimes abrasive, questions, his artist's heart and hands, his reminder that even normal children were tainted by war.

So she smiled. "Sure, Niko."

He did a fist pump, then ran his hand through his floppy hair three times in a row like he didn't know what to do with his joy.

Max gave her an appreciative nod as she gathered the plates to bring back to the kitchen.

Hunt stepped over to help, took the loaded tray from her and turned. "G'night, Nik. Max." He dipped his head and stepped into the hall, waiting for her.

"'Night, boys," she said.

"Night, Mr. Hunt. Night, soldier lady."

She couldn't erase the affectionate smile that pushed its way to the surface, so she tucked her chin and walked past Hunt quickly, worried that he would see for some reason.

He shut the door behind them, and they set out with a new kind of quiet settling between them. A comfortable quiet, maybe? For once, she didn't feel the burn of his distrust and suspicion.

"I'm sorry about Niko."

She jerked to look at him, though he spoke softly like he was afraid to disturb whatever had changed.

"You don't have anything to apologize for," she said. "One, you don't control him. Two, it was a perfectly valid question." She stopped speaking, a lump forming in her throat until she swallowed it down. "It's good to be reminded sometimes."

"Even if it makes you sad?"

The lump came back with a vengeance, and all she could manage was a nod. But she looked up at him, studying him the way he studied her. "It's not always sadness," she murmured, wondering why she decided to share this with him. Maybe it was the genuine concern she read in his expression. "Sometimes it's anger."

They walked across the rotunda, which was quiet and nearly empty. She wondered exactly what everyone did after dinner with their free time. Certain chores took less time to complete, so there was more downtime on those days. Kitchen duty was usually the longest.

Hunt didn't say anything until they'd gotten down the corridor and almost to the mess hall, where they would be alone.

"Anger at the war?" he guessed.

She stopped just outside the door and turned to him, fighting the urge to agree because it was the logical answer. But she didn't want to lie, even if there were things she didn't always want to share about herself.

But she lifted her chin. "Anger at myself."

He sucked in a breath, his brows drawing together.

"For not keeping them alive." She took the tray from his hands and spun to go into the mess hall, expecting him to walk away. But he followed her in.

No one was eating, and everyone who'd worked kitchen duty that day had already gone, the kitchen left immaculate. She'd been with the boys too long. She hated the idea of leaving even their four dishes for someone else to deal with, so she started filling the sink with hot water.

Hunt settled at the basin next to her. "I finally got your letter sent out."

Her stomach dropped to her toes. Her letter. Her sisters. She swallowed the surge of hope his words inspired. It was still early, still would be a while before her message would reach them—*if* it would at all. But she'd tried, and that's what mattered.

"Thank you for doing that," she murmured, shutting off the water.

He put the dishes in the water before she could, pulling the soap from the cabinet above their heads.

She scrubbed the dishes in the sudsy water, then passed them to him to rinse and dry, their fingers brushing, drawing their gazes to lock every time.

He took a breath when he set the final plate aside. "I wanted to say something about dinners with Niko."

She opened the drain in the sink to let the warm soapy water out, then turned to wait for him to finish.

He took the stack of plates to put them away. "Niko has OCD. A trauma response from his experiences."

She'd noticed, of course, but she didn't have to tell him that.

"That means disruptions to his routine can really throw him off." He closed the cupboard and leaned a hip against the counter, folding his arms across his chest.

"So you're saying not to miss a dinner." She mirrored his stance.

"Not if you can help it. He's used to me not always being there when I have to leave for business. But it took him a while to take that in stride."

She wanted to ask about "business," but this new, tenuous trust didn't feel solid enough for the question yet. "Well, I'll make sure I'm there for him, then."

Her words seemed to have an impact because he pulled in a sharp breath, which started a chain reaction in her. A spreading of warmth through her core. Then he nodded, dropping his arms to lead the way out.

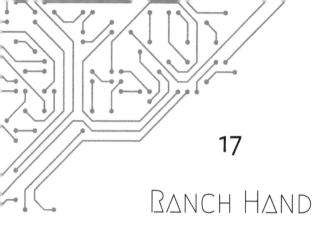

17

Ranch Hand

MORE DAYS PASSED, AND she fell into the routine of finishing chores then having dinner with the boys in the evening. It became often enough that Claire had finally stopped teasing her.

And even though she and Hunt didn't speak much to each other, that new peaceful quiet continued between them. He actually smiled when they locked eyes from across the room or when they passed each other in the hall, which wasn't as often as his duties called him topside more.

Sometimes he wasn't at dinner, and Max's answers about where he'd gone were usually vague. Niko filled the silence with his questions, distracting her enough that she couldn't probe deeper.

He asked about her childhood and the sisters she'd reached out to, wanted to know what her hardest missions were and what her favorite color was, if she had made friends and how she coped with the loss of everyone else she'd known.

Max had drawn the line at that one.

And then Hunt returned, bringing a brightness back to Niko's demeanor that she hadn't noticed was missing until it returned. That dinner, he'd practically bounced in his seat and babbled about every conversation they'd had while Hunt was gone.

A few days later, when she walked with Claire from the rotunda to laundry rotation, Hunt strode toward her with a smile on his face.

"You've been down here for weeks in recycled air."

"That is a statement of fact," Vic replied, unable to contain her responding smile, even if she felt the suspicion humming through her.

No, not suspicion, per se. Maybe anticipation.

He tucked his tongue between his teeth. "How do you feel about fresh?"

Claire scoffed and continued on down the hall, waving them off.

Vic ignored her. "It's definitely preferable." The words came out slow, like stretched molasses with her lack of understanding.

The muscles around his eyes contracted a fraction. "I have a job for you topside." He jerked his head for her to follow him down the hall where her quarters were, though they walked past her room and followed the curve around.

She hadn't explored this direction. Not that she'd had much chance or desire to since no one was guarding her anymore. Being alone outside her room was rare these days.

It was an odd contrast since she'd spent a lot of time in her village lonely, if not always alone. Something had always felt like it was missing, even as she'd sat next to the fire with her neighbors, the conversation bubbling and flowing around her. She'd spent more time listening than participating.

With Niko, it was impossible to remain quiet and detached. The kid was overly aware of her silence and chased it away with question after question.

Hunt slowed, drawing up next to an open ceiling tile tucked next to the wall like a gaping hole. Without warning, he leapt up to grab the end of a ladder that slid down until it stopped about a foot from the floor.

He looked down at her, never taking his hand from the side bar. "You first."

She raised a brow and moved forward, feeling the heat of his body an inch from hers because he didn't move back. It was an effort not to stop, to turn and lock eyes with him. But she forced herself not to, taking a deep breath as she climbed up the ladder into straight darkness, her eyes automatically going wider as if it would help her see better. Enhanced eyesight didn't do much against pure black.

The ladder vibrated with his added weight and efforts of climbing up, so she kept going until she reached the top, a slight drop in her stomach reminding her why she hated the dark so much. She'd never liked not knowing what was ahead of her.

Using her hands, she felt along the floor in front of her, planting her palms flat to pull herself up to standing. She took a few steps forward to give Hunt room to climb up. But it wasn't far enough because he bumped into her, grabbing a hold of her arms to steady them both.

"Sorry," he murmured.

The word dropped into the air like a weight, the sound simply swallowed by black.

"We'll have to trade spots so I can lead." His breath tickled along her face, setting the little hairs along her forehead dancing against her skin.

"Okay."

He never took his hands from her. Instead, he used his grip to guide her as they did a little dance in the dark, switching positions.

He dropped only one hand then, trailing the other down her arm until he found hers and placed it on his shoulder like he'd done before, when she was blindfolded.

Her breathing felt too close as they walked at an incline, her mind cataloging the feel of his shoulder muscles under her hand. But within a minute, there was the faint glow of light under a door ahead of them. The tightness she'd been unaware of loosened from around her chest when he opened the door to real light.

It was amazing what sunshine did to a person's mind, even before its warmth and light could touch skin. She was already grinning before he turned, and she pulled her hand from his shoulder slowly, a reluctance she didn't understand making her flutter her fingers as it dropped to her side.

"So what is this job you have for me?"

His gaze had followed her hand as it left him, but he brought it back to hers. "We have some fencing to repair along the property line."

She folded her arms across her chest and gave him a sly look. "No one strong enough around here, so you have to bring out the big guns?"

He smiled, a little half-grin that pulled her attention to his mouth. "Let's see what kind of muscles we're working with here. I'm curious how fast you really are."

She laughed, knowing he probably had no idea. "Challenge accepted."

They stared at each other, smiling, for a second too long. It felt charged with more than the challenge, everything suddenly so different than those first few days, the way he'd stare at her, trying to figure her out.

No, things were very different.

"Hunt!"

Hunt jolted at the sound of his name from outside, a man's voice. "We're coming!" he called back.

He did his favorite move—the head jerk for her to follow him.

Late spring offered plenty of sunshine, but it wasn't too hot yet. Still, she was slick with sweat, her muscles humming with warmth and pleasure at being used to their limits.

The split-rail fence was easy enough to repair once they had a rhythm going. She and two other guys worked to get the rails in place. She lugged the heavy beams over and held them while they hammered in the posts on either end.

In the distance, hefty cows dotted the field, grazing happily like there wasn't a crater from a bomb one hundred yards away. It was an old one. Grass had grown down in it like it was meant to be that way.

One of the guys—Jack—said in the summer they filled it with water for the animals to cool off. Sometimes even the ranch hands took a dip. Jack was the talkative sort—naming all three of his children, their ages, and interests in a constant stream of information that helped keep her mind off other things.

Namely Hunt patrolling the property line on horseback. He didn't go so far as to wear a cowboy hat, but he had on a beat-up old cap to shield his eyes—the same one he'd been wearing when she'd rolled in a few weeks before. This was the closest she'd been to a horse. They were majestic creatures, intelligence shining in those dark eyes. She couldn't tell if Hunt made the horse look better or the other way around.

There was no denying the man was attractive. But something about seeing him out on the ranch, lending a hand when they'd thrown out some extra feed for the animals, his muscles flexing and contracting, and the way he moved with the powerful animal, made her eyes return to him time and again.

She wiped at her brow, grateful for the leather gloves Jack had given her to protect her hands from the splinters in the wood beams as she held the last one steady. The rhythmic *plock, plock, plock* of Jack's efforts at hammering the new post into the hole the other guy had dug vibrated through her body. Dan was his name. He was quieter, often stealing glances at her. His expression remained neutral, so it was harder to gauge his thoughts about her help on this endeavor.

It reminded her of the chasm between the Organics and the Unborn and made her wonder about the setup of Hunt's operation. Did he see it or try to lessen that gap? It was a big thing that he willingly took Unborn in, never acting like they were anything different, even if they largely stayed underground. But he was the exception, and she wondered what more could be done to bridge the divide.

The sound of galloping horse hooves made the ground tremble under her feet. The absolute joy on Hunt's face as he drew up next to them made her stomach tie in little knots. He was made for this life.

She was glad for the post she held, though. She might have stepped back as the big animal stamped at the ground only a foot from her, and her unease must have shown on her face.

"You ever ridden a horse before, soldier lady?" Hunt asked. His tone was lighter than she'd ever heard it.

She smiled at his use of Niko's nickname. Not that any of the others in the bunker hadn't been soldiers, but for some reason, it had stuck.

"Nope. Never had a reason to," she said, holding her hand to her brow to block the sun, trying to hide the way she shifted back.

Horses had been a rare sight even in her training days. They seemed even rarer now that half the country was a wasteland where nothing could survive the fallout from the bombs that had been dropped, one by one like raindrops. The enemy had targeted the middle of the country for a reason, putting themselves in danger of being shot down as they flew a roundabout path across Canada and down. Most of the Unborn facilities that produced the quick-growing Coppers lined the Midwest from north to south. Some of those labs were where the Silvers had been cultivated, including the one she'd known as home.

But with the destruction of that swath of land went the animals that had called those states home. Livestock was a commodity that was harder to come by.

"Want to give it a try?" Hunt broke through her thoughts, his horse shifting restlessly under him, though he gripped the reins tight, holding the beast as still as he could.

She looked at Jack and then Dan. Jack was grinning. Dan was squinting at her.

"You've finished with the fence—faster than anticipated. You could take a break." Hunt even threw her a wink. "And if the boss doesn't like it, I'll talk to him."

She snorted then released the rail she'd still been unnecessarily holding onto and took a slow breath, approaching carefully.

The horse snorted, shifting away from her, and she stiffened.

"Easy," Hunt murmured, patting the butterscotch neck that rippled with veiny muscle.

He smiled down at her and held out his hand.

She balked. "You want me to get on *with* you?"

He shrugged a shoulder, smirking. "How else am I going to teach you?"

She swallowed, then pulled the work gloves from her hands, tossing them onto the ground next to the newest post. Then she slipped her hand into his.

He pulled her closer but not up. "Put your other hand here." He patted the knob on the saddle that rested between his legs, and she shot him a glare.

He rolled his eyes and scooted himself back a little. As if that would be enough room.

She slid a sneaky glance back to the other two men before she grabbed the knob—a saddle horn, her mind supplied—and used it and Hunt's hand to leverage herself up. She swung her leg over, nearly knocking him in the head. He ducked back just in time, chuckling low and deep.

"Did we finally find something you're not good at?" he asked at her ear when she settled in, her body nearly flush against his. It sent a tingle down her spine.

"What's that supposed to mean?" she asked breathlessly.

"That was less graceful than usual."

She twisted to look at him. "Maybe if I had my own horse."

"Baby steps," he replied with another smirk. "Hold on."

She was about to ask "to what" when he snapped the reins and the horse lurched forward. She gasped, both hands wrapping around the saddle horn.

"Just relax," he said, his breath tickling along her neck.

She *was* tense, every muscle wound tight, and she focused on releasing each one. They weren't going that fast, but the breeze caressed her face, and the gentle movement of the horse's body rocked her back and forth. It was hard to totally relax, though, since Hunt was pressed right up against her from behind, and her mind played that fact over and over.

But she forced her attention to the scenery around them—the sweeping fields that allowed the animals to wander and graze, the trees that lined all sides of the property that was visible, and the fence that went on so far she couldn't see where it ended.

He said nothing more, but she could feel his contentment, the way he seemed so in his element on the back of this horse, roaming his family's land. They walked along the fence line for a while then across the fields, and Hunt checked on the various projects going on with shouted questions about their progress or what they needed.

It blew her mind that there were so many people who worked the land, helped this place run—dozens scattered over several ongoing projects. The questions popped into her mind about what made this all possible, how Hunt had the means to employ so many and provide what he did for those in the bunker. Maybe this change in his demeanor toward her meant that she could ask, and he would actually give her the answers.

Eventually, they made their way back to the house, that weathered beauty languishing in the blazing sunlight in a way that twanged Vic's heart. She hadn't really seen it since that first day she'd arrived, when its depressed outward appearance had not given her much hope for what she'd find inside. How different things were now.

Hunt slowed the horse as they got closer, then slid off to stop the big animal from walking farther.

Vic shifted, pulling her leg over to slide down after him, and he was there waiting for her, holding his hands up to help her. It wasn't necessary, but she let him catch her anyway. When her feet touched the ground, she was nearly pinned between him and the horse, whose flank expanded against her back with its breaths. She didn't imagine carrying two people was easy, even for a beast that huge.

He didn't take his hands from her waist, and a warmth spread from where he touched.

She looked up at him. "Thank you."

"For what? The hard labor or the horseback ride?" His lips quirked.

"Both."

"You're welcome." He took a breath and squinted into the distance somewhere above her head. "I figured you could use the break. But also I owed you after being so. . ."

"Suspicious?" she supplied. "Guarded? Distrustful? Cold?"

"Okay," he said with an edge. "I get it." He took a step back, amusement glinting in his eyes. And maybe a little bit of frustration. "I apologize for all of it."

She stepped to the side, smiling a little. He clicked his tongue, snapping the reins to urge the horse forward.

"You don't need to apologize, Hunt. You were protecting your people." She fell into step beside him as he walked the horse toward the other side of the house.

"You've never said that before," he mused.

"Said what?" She tipped her head, her brows going low over her eyes, half distracted by the barn before them. It was chipped and looked worn, matching the house, but she saw activity inside, heard a whinny or two from more horses. It was like a fairytale come to life—this land of opportunity and provision.

"My name."

She looked at him, a question forming in her mind but dropping right out at the look on his face as they walked under the shade of a tall tree whose branches reached outward as if searching for a hand to hold. The shadows caressed the lines in his face, edging his features in sharp relief.

Her mind slowly came back to itself. She'd never said his name. Why would it matter? Her chest tightened, and her stomach twisted. Neither was entirely unpleasant, but she struggled to make sense of both. And his observation.

"I've said it." Why did she sound defensive? "But I guess not to you. Never had a reason to."

Some of it was the way she'd felt so unwelcome, so scrutinized. Even when they'd eat together with Max and Niko, she'd spent little time actually conversing with him.

"I like the way you say it." He spoke so softly she barely heard it.

More confusion swirled inside of her, but her mouth was suddenly a desert. She swallowed several times. "How's that?" she asked as they stopped at the opening to the barn.

His horse chuffed and stamped an impatient foot.

He looked down at her, ignoring the animal. There was something like a question in his eyes, a wondering that spoke to her, twining with an uncertainty that had made its home in her skin.

"I'm not entirely sure I can explain it."

The weight of his eyes made her want to look away, to change the subject—anything to ease the pressure of the unknown that stirred in her chest. "How'd you like having a Silver working the ranch?"

He took a breath, struggling to adjust to her pivot. "It certainly made things move more quickly."

She tilted her head. "It's a wonder you haven't gotten more Unborn up here. It would improve efficiency."

His expression grew pained, and he turned to stroke his horse's neck. Like he wanted to avoid responding. "It certainly would. But it's complicated."

Her eyes narrowed. "Complicated how?"

"There are a lot of considerations that go into building a community that's safe for both Organics and Unborn."

Even though she knew there was an insidious prejudice against her kind, it seemed like a community like this was the easiest way to fight against it, to work to change things. "Keeping them separated is how everyone stays safe?"

He frowned. "For now. I'm sure I don't have to explain what it's like out there." He gestured vaguely, though she knew he meant in society at large.

"No, you don't." She hated that the frustration edged her voice, that this conversation felt like it was whittling away at the fragile foundation of whatever was building between them. "But what if things could be different?"

The muscles around his eyes contracted, and she was sure he would dismiss her, get angry and send her back to the bunker with the broken pieces of their budding friendship because she was over-stepping. But he sighed, his mouth lifting in one corner. "Alright, Captain. Why don't we schedule a time to talk some ideas?"

She stiffened, thinking he was merely humoring her, but she took in his serious expression. "Really?"

"Really," he confirmed.

She searched his face, then nodded slowly. "Okay."

The skepticism was hard to dispel when her experience had been so opposite with Organics. They usually wanted to keep her in her place, not let her have equal footing. Hunt was surprising her left and right, and something like admiration ignited inside of her.

He almost seemed to find her struggle amusing.

"Hunt!" a man's voice called from inside the barn.

He turned for a moment, then waved the man off and faced her again. "I've gotta get the horse back in and see what Josh needs." He tipped his head backward.

"I need a shower anyway," Vic murmured, plucking at the thin material of her shirt, which had stuck to her sweat-slicked body.

He nodded. "Right. I'll see you after a bit."

She clamped down on the urge to say *I hope so*, still so unsure of this change between them and what it meant. Did she hope? She rarely let it take root, had learned that hope got you nowhere. Effort and hard work got results, not something as foolish as hope.

"Okay," she said instead, backing up without turning.

He didn't budge, opting to stand and watch her until the horse nudged his shoulder with its nose, which made him laugh and finally turn aside.

She spun to face the house and chewed her lip, searching deep within herself for a clarity that seemed so far out of her reach.

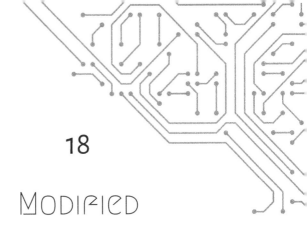

18

MODIFIED

V IC SPENT AN INORDINATE amount of time in the shower, blessedly alone because of the time of day. She felt brighter, like the sun had infused some of its light into her skin and she'd carried it back underground with her.

Or maybe it was something else entirely. She couldn't tell, still didn't totally understand.

She'd noticed Hunt's demeanor toward her had changed leading up to the horseback ride. Her own thoughts of him had taken on a more positive angle. But it seemed that his feelings had changed much more dramatically than she realized or could've anticipated.

But it was unclear what that meant, what would be different from then on. She wasn't sure she was ready to ask, or even ready for the answer.

Now that she'd been a part of the laundry rotation a few times, a deeper sense of gratitude filled her when she unfolded the clothing on the bench before her. Even the clean towel she used, not thread-bare like her old one had been, inspired an appreciation that sank into her bones.

It all smelled fresh, felt crisp and clean. Her muscles hummed happily, tired from being used, even if not to their full capacity. But there was a depth to the fatigue in her body because it was energy it could afford to expend. With the hearty food available to her, she felt the natural curves filling in again, no longer only cut muscles and bone, but padding, health, life.

This place, what Hunt had opened up for everyone, whatever operation he had going on the side that made this possible, was a blessing she could do nothing but be grateful for, even if she thought there could be improvements. And the fact that he seemed willing to hear her out about them was beyond what she could've imagined.

She twisted her heavy, dark hair into a bun at her nape, taking in the angles of her face in the foggy mirror—her high cheekbones, the long nose, the full lips, her round, wide eyes. She imagined they would've been light, maybe blue, despite her dark hair and brows. She wasn't sure why. Maybe because Angela's had been that bright blue, and she'd always thought they were lovely.

She took a slow breath, wondering how old Angela would've been had she lived. She'd been old already by the time the girls were made; her hair was white in Vic's earliest memories, her face lined by time and sorrow. Her smiles had pulled her aged skin like a curtain from her mouth, her eyelids heavy with wrinkles. But still, those sky-blue eyes had shone through, sharp and kind.

Her hands had been deft too, still capable of braiding their hair every morning to keep it out of their faces for their lessons early on, then their physical training when they were older.

Until, one day, her arms were too weak, her fingers too achy and swollen.

She hadn't told them when she'd gotten sick. Only when she'd started dying.

"The natural order of things," she'd said.

She'd told Vic separately that she was glad she wouldn't live long enough to see the girls go, to know they'd likely be shipping out to their own deaths.

"Parents aren't meant to outlive their children," she'd whispered with tears in her eyes, pain clouding the brightness that had once resided there.

Vic was glad that neither of the other girls had been there for that part. Especially Alice. She'd always been so tender, and they'd all done whatever they could to protect her. Maybe because she was the smallest of them, and it had made them feel more like a family to have a "little" sister.

The word "rodina" was tattooed along Vic's ribs, the flowing script permanently etched in the same spot on Alice and Jamie, something they'd had done after Angela had passed, the day they'd all shipped out officially. It was their attempt to keep themselves connected, just in case they didn't get to stay together.

And they hadn't. Not the entire time, anyway. And then separation had become permanent once they'd gotten back.

Vic traced the letters, her fingers still warm and supple from her hot shower, wondering why she hadn't received a response. It had been a couple of weeks. Hadn't that been enough time?

She broke herself from her trance, setting her jaw, and pulled her shirt over her head, the soft fabric falling lightly over her skin. Then she slipped her boots on and gathered her things to put in the laundry bin.

Voices rumbled from the rotunda, hinting that there were many more people in the space than usual, and it drew Vic forward once she dumped her clothes. There was an energy she hadn't witnessed before that bounced around the room, made the cadence of conversation almost buzz in her ears.

"It happens every time."

She jerked to look at Brody, who was grinning hugely at her, and already felt the eye roll coming.

"You stop my heart the second I see you." He winked. "Without fail."

There went the eye roll, though she appreciated his commitment to the bit.

"Oh, Claire, love of my life!" He leaped forward to grab her sleeve as she joined the mass exodus down one of the other corridors.

Vic made a sound in the back of her throat, feigning offense as the other woman scoffed but joined them.

"He does that," Hunt said from beside her. "Doesn't mean you aren't pretty."

She raised a brow at him. "You think I'm pretty?"

Brody guffawed and Claire snorted.

The faintest flash of panic filled Hunt's eyes as a flush crept up his neck. "I mean, you were made to. . . be. . . you know, attractive."

"Was I made to be attractive?"

Max's voice came at her elbow, and her grin spread as she turned to Hunt for his answer.

His expression had turned a little sour, though the color from his earlier panic still painted his neck. "It would be a bit self-serving to say you're attractive."

"But the answer is yes," Brody interjected, shooting Max a wink.

Hunt rolled his eyes while the rest of them laughed, and she grinned, suspecting that he wished he could break from the group by the way he clamped down on his muscles, but he remained by her side. It brought their interactions earlier that day in sharp focus. His expression wasn't as open as it had been then, but the fact that he walked so closely beside her and the way her stomach sort of fluttered at his proximity made her uncertainty flare.

But maybe it was from being outside, in fresh air, clearly in his element, that had made him behave differently. And now it was that they'd become something like friends. Maybe.

They all moved with the flow of the crowd, though she watched Brody make jokes with Claire that had her giggling. Her smile transformed her face, and Vic could see why it appealed to him so much to make her laugh.

"Where is everyone going?" Vic asked, rising on her tiptoes to try to see over the heads of those shuffling in front of them.

"It's fight night," Max said.

His tone made her swivel to look at him. The look on his face was somewhat grim.

"What's fight night?"

"Sparring," Hunt supplied. "We kind of make a competition out of it."

She didn't take her attention from Max as his eyes narrowed slightly. It bothered him, and it didn't take much to guess what might've been the reason.

"Everyone gets restless being stuck down here for long periods of time," Hunt said. "Plus, you know, how you all are wired."

She looked at Hunt, pursing her lips. "Do you join?"

He gave her a shrewd look, but the amusement was there underneath. "Why? You ready for that arm wrestling match?"

"Probably another kind of wrestling match," Brody said, cackling as he slung an arm around Claire's shoulders.

"That's probably just you," Vic shot back, eliciting laughs from those around them, though Brody pouted at her.

Then he brightened. "Only if Claire's my partner."

"Sorry, Bro, but she'd dominate," Max said, his dark demeanor cracking a bit. He could never leave a joke alone, of course.

"Please do," he said, winking at Claire.

She shrugged his arm off, mock punching at his abdomen. "Gladly, Brody."

Vic looked up at Hunt, liking the way he half-smiled at the pair.

"Why are you two joining?" Brody asked, hunching as if Claire got a good gut shot in. "You usually skip out."

Max and Hunt exchanged a look that felt heavy with hesitation. It made Vic's fingers tingle.

"I'm not joining," Hunt admitted. "Was only popping over before I have to get everything set up for tomorrow."

Brody's smile melted, a rare seriousness creeping across his face.

"What's tomorrow?" Vic asked, dread filling her stomach like concrete. She wasn't sure why exactly that was the feeling that swirled inside.

Hunt grimaced and stopped walking abruptly. She stopped, too, as if she were tethered to him. Crossing her arms over her chest, she waited even as people continued walking, splitting to flow around them until the room emptied.

"It's a supply run." His eyes were turned toward the hall everyone disappeared down.

It made her question his answer, the dread getting heavier in her gut. "What kind of a supply run? And what about our... talk?"

He met her gaze now. "We sell meat and other goods in town. My presence is always required, which means Max and Brody are in charge here. It helps them if I get everything all planned and set up so things run smoothly while I'm gone. When I get back, we can meet to discuss your ideas."

"How long will you be gone?"

He frowned. "A day or two."

They stared at each other, and she had that moment again of wondering what exactly was happening, what that electric current was that hummed in the air between them, and what it was she sensed he wanted to say but didn't.

"I guess I'll see you in a couple of days, then," she said, not even denying that she was sad at the prospect.

He gave a terse nod, his mouth forming a tight line before he turned to head down a different corridor. Max and Brody were there, waiting for him before they all disappeared around the bend.

She spun on her heel to follow where the rest of the Unborn had gone, though everything in her wanted to see what those three men were up to. The craving to understand exactly how things worked here made her consider it. Hunt had let her in a little more, but he hadn't fully opened that door.

It was better not to push it, though she paused outside the sparring room for a few seconds before going in.

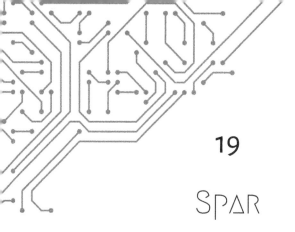

19

SPAR

I T WAS OVERWHELMING TO see the crowd that had gathered in the sparring room, a restless energy rippling with palpable force that bounced along the white walls, rocking Vic's body as she pushed through to find Claire.

Already, two women were gearing up on the mat. Two Coppers, evenly matched. Vic could guess exactly how it would play out—the moves they'd choose—because she'd been through the exact same hand-to-hand training early on. Advanced enough to fight off human opponents with ease. But then she'd gone through the next levels of training, where they were taught to always anticipate moves, studying human behavior, even their own kind, to learn what the most logical next step would be.

It had made Vic nearly unbeatable when they were young because she thrived on reading people, anticipating, and adjusting. Their training had been fun back then, when they were probably about ten or eleven in years but physically in their late teens.

The only person who consistently took Vic down was Jamie, which had irked her and thrilled her sister. Jamie was the least predictable fighter she'd ever met. She tended to operate on pure instinct, which meant she had been useful for the missions where quick thinking and the result mattered more than keeping people alive.

When they wanted successful recon or a strategic fight, Vic was their top choice because she usually brought people back. Though there had been times. . .

She ran her hand down the trail of tattooed slashes on her arms, though she didn't list the names in her mind like she sometimes did, and found Claire toward the back of the room. The other woman's attention was trained on the Coppers in the ring who were now circling each other, eyes locked intently. If Vic had to guess, the one with the tawny skin and black hair would strike first. She looked a little more on edge, an eagerness giving her a coiled look.

"Hey," Claire said when Vic drew up next to her.

"Hey."

"You're in for a treat. Gina's undefeated, but she's never been up against Hattie." Claire pointed to each woman in turn. Gina was the tawny one. The other, a brunette with porcelain skin and freckles splashed across her nose like paint splatter, was Hattie.

Undefeated. Well, that explained the eagerness. Hattie, by comparison, was cautious and calculating. Not eager but ready and waiting.

"Gina will strike first," Vic said, drawing Claire's gaze from the center. Vic shrugged. "Not too intense to begin with, though. If they've never sparred before, she'll probably want to test her out."

Claire's brows pulled low over her eyes as she swiveled back to the match.

As Vic had predicted, Gina threw out a test punch. It was clearly not meant to hit Hattie, who batted the hand away easily. People chuckled around the room.

Except Claire, who pursed her lips and looked at Vic again.

"What next?" she asked, squinting. As if Vic were a fortune teller trying to prove her ability.

Vic watched Gina's feet shuffle quickly, the fast-twitch muscles activating in her legs. "Gina's going to go for her for real this time. Maybe try to hook her foot around her knee and bring her down. Seems like grappling is where her strength is."

Claire's mouth dropped open, which made Vic wonder if that was Gina's habit.

Sure enough, she stepped in closer, angling her foot behind Hattie's, but Hattie was prepared and looped her arm around Gina's neck to get her in a headlock.

At first, Gina wrapped her arms around Hattie's waist, and they spun in a circle as voices rose with excitement. Seemed like a panic move, and Vic could practically see Gina's mind working overtime.

"Get your foot behind her again," Vic murmured.

Claire glanced at her and back.

The women rotated one more time before Gina actually did what Vic said, finally knocking the other woman to the floor, forcing her grip to loosen so that Gina could pull away. Spinning on her knees to throw her weight on top of Hattie, she pinned the other woman with side control.

It was clearly Gina's strongest move, and Hattie struggled to break out of it, wriggling and bucking. There was some frenzy in the movement, probably because she knew this was where Gina thrived.

"She needs to get space," Vic said, now so invested in the fight that the shouts of the people in the room faded into the background. It was only the pump of her heart that she heard, her eyes honing in on the little details of the match.

Hattie grunted in frustration, then slipped her forearm against Gina's throat, pushing. Gina grimaced and pulled back.

"Yes. Now the hips," Vic whispered.

Hattie did a hip thrust, pushing Gina up enough to slide out and wrap her legs through and around Gina's, then used her arm to bar Gina's, knocking the other woman onto her back. She mirrored Gina's previous position, locking her arms around Gina's head and bringing her legs close to her body.

Gina tried to use the same move Hattie had, but Hattie was ready for it and tucked her foot in closer, pulling Gina toward her body.

"Headlock," Vic murmured, curling her fingers into her palms.

As if Hattie heard her, she took her arm and wrapped it around Gina's neck and pulled until the other woman tapped her thigh.

Then both women released their holds, Gina flopping down onto her back panting, while Hattie stayed on her knees, grinning and puffing at the air. Several cheers went up, the piercing sound breaking through Vic's momentary focus, and she blinked, taking a step back.

"Wow," Claire said from beside her. "You should coach us or something."

Vic only took her gaze briefly from the women in the ring. "Nah."

Hattie stood and Gina rolled onto her knees. Hattie offered her a hand up, which she took. They hugged briefly, and Hattie said something to Gina, who nodded, wiping the sweat from her forehead. Other than both their faces being flushed, neither anger nor pride was visible in their expressions.

A couple more people jumped up to take over the ring, but Vic wasn't interested in watching another round. She was exhausted from the last one. Too invested, too much brain power analyzing the moves, what they should do, what *she* would do. Too tied to a life she'd once had, inextricably drenched in memory.

She waved at Claire and made her way to the door.

After her day helping topside, she could use some rest, wanted to shut off her mind. Watching the match brought memories to the surface, made worry churn in her stomach.

Because there had been moments during that match she'd seen Jamie's face, her eager stance, her smug smile every time they'd been matched. She liked being able to one-up Vic.

"You hesitate too much," Alice had told her once after Jamie had pinned her again.

Vic had glared at her, wiping the sweat off her forehead while Jamie danced around in the other room, soaking in the cheering chants of the others.

Alice had given her a soft smile. "You keep thinking of her like she's your sister. So you go easy on her."

Vic had scoffed, but it was true. She'd always felt the responsibility, the sense that it was her job to protect them.

"And the problem is Jamie doesn't see you the same way in the ring."

"That much is clear." Vic had stripped her shirt and tossed it in the bin, the lid falling shut from the force, clattering in the empty locker room.

"Vic, we've been in your shadow our entire lives."

Vic opened her mouth to argue.

"And we don't mind. Usually." One of Alice's saccharine smiles kept Vic from being as offended as she might've been otherwise. "Jamie needs to shine, too."

Vic sighed, knowing the argument had worked. Alice knew it too. Vic wouldn't be mad—at least openly—about getting beaten regularly by Jamie. But she wasn't going to soften up and let her beat her every time. She'd still make Jamie earn the win.

And she wasn't going to let her view of Jamie make her hesitate anymore.

Sleep was a reluctant companion that night, haunted as Vic was by memories of her sisters and the things that had driven wedges between them. She chased phantoms of both Jamie and Alice until she woke with a pulsing ache that they'd been apart for so long. She blamed the throbbing loneliness for her path down the corridor to the boys' quarters, assuming she'd find Hunt there. She convinced herself it was to see Niko and make sure he was okay when Hunt left.

There was no denying a part of her wanted to also say goodbye, to test whatever this thing was that was brewing between them. It was possible, though, that Hunt had already left. It was still early, but maybe he liked to get going as soon as possible. Relief and disappointment warred for dominance inside her at the thought.

But, no, she heard the voices before she even arrived at the door. Hunt's she recognized as distinct from Max's—slower and deeper. Then Niko's, which was always fluctuating as he toed the line of puberty. Brody's higher cadence cut in, though it was unusually edged. No trace of the jocular tone she'd come to associate with him.

That's what made her slow her pace, peeking around the edge of the open door to what it was they were doing.

Niko was at his computer, the three adults were clustered around him—two standing, one sitting. The looks on their faces bore horror and outrage.

It took her several seconds to make sense of what they were watching on the screen. The chaos, the screams, the snapping of a fire consuming wood. Heat and then cold swamped her, coating her skin with chilly sweat, sharp slices gouging at her insides as she watched everyone she'd known in her village—her *home*—rabidly attack each other.

"What the *hell* are you doing?" Her voice snapped on the air like a whip, jolting each one of them from their trance as they turned to look at her.

"Vic—"

She turned her blazing eyes to Hunt, stopping him from saying anything further. "What is wrong with you?"

He opened his mouth.

But she didn't wait for whatever explanation he'd have. She spun on her heel to leave the room so she wouldn't throw up all over the floor. She beat the sensation back, but only just.

All that death.

She'd known in the abstract how many people had died that day, had witnessed what methods they'd used. But she'd had such a limited view of it all, only aware of the immediate threat to her own life, what was right in front of her. But she hadn't seen them tearing each other apart, hadn't had to witness the destruction in a sweeping view like some kind of movie.

"Vic, wait." Hunt's footsteps pounded down the hallway after her.

She rounded on him before he could touch her, try to turn her around. "What were you thinking?"

He took a step back as she moved toward him. There must have been something in her expression.

"I was trying to find out what really happened that day."

"By sending a *child* searching through cyberspace *illegally*?" Fear coated her anger in ice, the kind of cold that burned the skin, and she almost winced. Information was heavily regulated and monitored by those in power, and there was no telling what firewalls they went through to find that footage. Was Niko being careful, covering his tracks?

Hunt threw an arm out to the side. "I didn't—"

"Did you even think about Niko at all?" she demanded, not waiting, not caring about his answer to the previous question. Hunt was no fool. He didn't do things without careful consideration. "Wasn't it you who told me he'd been traumatized by the massacre that killed his parents? He's a *child*, Hunter."

He flinched at the use of his full name.

"Why didn't you just ask me? I told you what I knew already. But if you still had questions, why didn't you ask?"

He pulled his head back slightly and swallowed.

Realization dawned, tinged with pain. The bitterness receded in its wake, leaving deep acidic burns that throbbed with the cold, driving ache of the truth she now saw.

"You still don't trust me." The words scored her throat, stung her tongue, burned her lips.

He shook his head. "No, I—"

She waited. Hoped. Ached.

And he remained silent because his denial would surely be a lie.

She spun again to walk away, but this time he did grab her arm. She could have yanked it from his grasp, shoved him back, thrown him to the ground, but she didn't. Because the pain clawed at her chest, inexplicably sharp.

When she jerked to look at him, he was just a breath away, and she was boxed between him and the wall. Close enough to kiss.

"Please don't walk away," he whispered, the words dancing along the curves of her face. "It might have started out that way, but it became. . ."

Say it, her mind begged. She wanted him to finish that sentence, to give her a real answer. But he didn't, and she bit back the tears, reaching for the pain inside of herself to twist it, make it a weapon.

"I understood your distrust initially, Hunt. You had to protect your home and everyone in it. But those people were *my* friends. *My* neighbors. I need to know what happened, too." Her voice dropped out, the inhuman strength she'd been created to wield leaving her when she needed it the most. "I deserved to know you'd found something. That you were even looking."

His gaze dropped away from her face, the truth of her words landing squarely.

"Good luck on your trip."

She pulled away from him, heading down the corridor, not really sure where she would go. But she knew he didn't move from that spot.

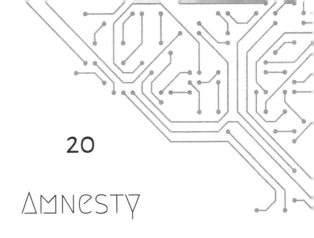

20

AMNESTY

EVERYONE WHO WORKED WITH her on rotation that day knew she was in a bad headspace. Claire stopped trying to engage, and everyone left her alone as they sorted through laundry.

She even skipped eating with Niko and Max for dinner, opting instead to take her food and eat alone in her room. She wasn't much company for the others, and the noise of the mess hall grated on her nerves.

The silence of her quarters wasn't exactly soothing, but at least she could be grumpy alone. She wasn't left alone for long.

The knock was soft and tentative on the closed door, and she seriously considered ignoring it, mouth tightening with her frustration. But something told her the visitor wouldn't be someone she was expecting.

It definitely wouldn't be who she secretly hoped was there to apologize. She'd heard that he'd left with his crew to do whatever it was he was planning. Something about that still sat in her gut with the weight of a stone.

But it didn't matter at the moment.

She pushed to her feet, setting down her half-eaten beef stew to pull the pocket door open.

Her scowl disappeared immediately upon seeing the mop of dark hair. Niko flung the locks from his eyes, his left hand raised slightly, the fingers fluttering endlessly in one of his telltale nervous tics.

"Are you mad at me?" he asked, lifting his face to show his dark eyes slanted against the high cheekbones.

She swallowed an onslaught of dark memories of eyes so similar, dredged up by her mood and the death and destruction that plagued her mind. She stepped back. "Why don't you come in?"

He hesitated, flicking his fingers again, then he tapped both sides of the doorway two or three times as he stepped through, his eyes tracing the shape of the room like it held something interesting instead of the blank canvas that it was.

She slid the door most of the way closed—enough to give them privacy, but open still for propriety's sake. Plus, she didn't know what kind of triggers he might have. Like her, he was a survivor of a devastating war who didn't make it out unscathed. And whatever invisible scars they bore proved unpredictable.

"I'm not mad at you," she finally answered, watching his face.

His mouth turned down into a frown like he didn't believe her.

She sighed. "I'm mad, yes. But none of it is directed at you."

"You're mad at Mr. Hunt." It wasn't a question.

She didn't respond right away. Because the ache in her chest told her it was less anger. A whole lot less. It was sadness. Hurt.

"He didn't really ask me to do it." His words came out quickly, nearly running into each other so that she had a hard time understanding them. His accent, usually so faint, landed heavier in his rush.

"What do you mean?"

"He didn't ask me to. He just wanted me to keep an eye out for anything about what happened." His right hand shot up, his fingers fluttering now as he looked away, scrutinizing the empty room again. "Mr. Hunt doesn't like me to hack. He knows it's dangerous. Especially for someone like me."

She could see that Niko's life had been and would be so similar to her own, to the Unborn as a whole. People automatically held something against him that wasn't his fault, would never accept him into their society.

"I wanted to see what happened to your village. Then I showed him."

Vic swallowed, wondering why Hunt hadn't told her this in the first place. But of course, he'd look like a jerk if he threw Niko—just a kid—under the bus. He was such a decent guy, he would never have done it anyway. Not just to save face, but because he cared about Niko.

But it was still the fact that he didn't go get her, that he hadn't trusted her enough with what they'd found.

"I don't blame you for anything, Niko. I appreciate you coming to tell me." Even though it made the ache in her chest expand. She pressed a fist to her sternum.

Niko tipped his face down, the hair falling into his eyes. "I don't want you to be mad at Mr. Hunt either."

She stared at him for a long moment. "I'm not."

He lifted his gaze slowly.

"Not anymore," she assured him. "I'm still bothered that he didn't see a need to tell me, though."

He opened his mouth, then his expression twisted like he knew his argument would be false. "There wasn't a lot of time. . ."

She squinted at him. "Niko, it's not your job to apologize for Hunt."

"Okay, fine." He twisted his hands together, shrugging his shoulders a few times in discomfort. "Will you come back to eating with us?"

She gave a soft laugh. "It was only for today. You miss me already?"

His fingers flapped. "Mr. Hunt is gone, and I feel sideways and. . ."

The guilt was a sucker punch, and she pulled in a sharp breath. God, she was so selfish. She was sitting in here, sulking and nursing her wounds while this poor child was suffering. She remembered Hunt mentioning how his OCD stemmed from his traumas, how he avoided crowds, how he liked his stability in even the smallest areas of his life.

And she hadn't considered any of those things.

"Yes, of course." Her shoulders slumped, and she fought the sting of the tears in her eyes. "I'm sorry, Niko. I'll be there for dinner tomorrow."

Some of his tension visibly seeped out of his body, and the faintest smile flashed across his face. "Great!"

"Can I ask you a favor though?"

He nodded eagerly. "Yes, of course."

"I don't like secrets. Especially when it comes to my own life."

His brows pulled tight over his dark eyes, and he nodded solemnly.

"And it's important that I see what footage you've found. Will it bother you to see it again? I don't want to make things harder for you."

"No, I'll be fine."

She watched his face for signs of a lie, but it was hard to tell. Maybe she'd check with Max first to be sure. And to make sure he knew she wasn't happy with him about the situation either. What kind of guardian was he if he wasn't catching on to Niko's hacking?

"Tomorrow, then," she said.

"Lunch and dinner." Niko pointed at her. "You owe us."

She laughed. "Fine. Lunch *and* dinner. Promise."

Vic wasn't sure she would be able to stomach lunch. Not with the anticipation already building of watching the footage she knew would be disturbing. She'd fought in a war, comrades dropping left and right, packed mortal wounds, the warm blood spilling over her hands, seeping into her uniform.

And yet there was something different about what she would watch that afternoon. She hadn't had a chance to talk to Max about it yet, but even if they decided not to have Niko present, she knew it was going to happen today.

She'd barely slept the night before. She kept replaying the moment she'd woken up to her own mind, wresting control over her actions.

Except in her dreams, she didn't. She'd become conscious of what she was doing but remained trapped in her own mind, unable to stop herself from wringing the life from the man whose throat she clutched.

And every time her hands released him, he morphed into Cooper, staring up at her with flat, lifeless eyes. But his mouth would form the word: why?

That one word would echo, slicing against her ears like she would—like she *should*—know the answer.

She got half as much finished as usual during kitchen rotation. And she'd dropped more than one dish until they relegated her to mopping duty. Everyone seemed relieved to have her take the plates for Niko and Max and herself. Claire encouraged her to take a longer lunch.

She hated feeling useless, feeling like she was failing at something. It itched under her skin to feel so unlike herself.

The door to the boys' room was already open. Niko was sitting on the edge of his bed, his leg dancing wildly. His face lit up the second he saw her, even though her smile in greeting was a half-second late.

"Hey," she said to him, then nodded in Max's direction.

His ready smile flashed, but his eyes narrowed on her face, reading something in her expression. Maybe she was haggard. She felt run-down.

She gave her head a quick shake to discourage any questions for the moment. There wouldn't have been time anyway, because Niko had bounced to his feet and over to his desk, digging through papers while she set their plates on the table, feeling the absence of the fourth plate—and person—a little too keenly.

"I made something for you," Niko said, his bouncing suddenly stopping as she turned.

Pink filled his cheeks, and he approached slowly, holding a piece of paper against his leg. As soon as he got close, he thrust his arm up, holding the paper out to her.

She took it reverently, her eye catching on the brilliant colors that seemed impossibly iridescent. It was a portrait of her. Her expression was sad, eyes closed. Half her face was done in shades of gray. The other half was a rainbow, watercolor-like splotches of red and orange and blue and green and yellow, dripping down her face.

She could barely catch a breath at the beauty captured in the image. "Niko, this is amazing." She tipped her head, tracing the surface with the faintest touch of her finger. "Wait, this was done in pencil."

She looked at him, but he wouldn't meet her eyes.

Max was smiling like a proud dad. "Yeah, he does that, too. For the special ones." He jerked his head at the portrait above his own bed, and she walked over to look more closely.

It was pencil, too. Her lips parted as she tried to wrap her head around the artistry, the time he'd taken, the shading detail, both in gray and in color.

"These are breath-taking, Niko." She looked at him, smiling genuinely. "Really."

He shrugged, flinging his hair out of his eyes nervously, and dropped into his chair.

"This means so much to me. And now my walls won't be plain anymore." She strode forward and planted a kiss on the top of his head. "Thank you."

When she sat, he was looking down at his plate, but a pleased grin split his face.

She wished she could convey what it had done to boost her low spirits, to help lift her head out of the water that had been keeping her under the tide of grief all day.

It made her want to skip the footage, save it for another day. But putting it off wouldn't do her any good. The longer she put it off, the more it would plague her, and the longer it would haunt her sleep.

That was from experience. Unlike some of her comrades, she'd never tried to numb the potency of the memories. It was a temporary bandage for a permanent, festering wound. But she understood the temptation.

"Where did you learn how to draw like that?" she asked as they tucked in to eat.

Niko lifted a shoulder. "My father was an artist."

"A famous one," Max put in.

"He taught all of us from a young age to express ourselves like this. We didn't all use the same kind of—uh. . ." He looked at Max for help.

"Medium," he supplied.

Niko didn't raise his face, but he tilted his head, watching his fork as he arranged his food on the plate. "Yes. My father was a painter. My older sister liked to use clay. I like pencil best. I like the, um, friction? The way it feels sliding across the paper." He shrugged a shoulder. "I do the digital ones to save my supplies. And they're just concepts, ones I keep for myself when I'm trying something new."

Vic met Max's eyes across the table, swallowing an unexpected lump of emotion in her throat. This sweet child had kept this part of himself after everyone he'd known and loved was gone. And she felt so honored that he would share the most sacred part of it with her, like he was welcoming her into his new, makeshift family.

Had Niko ever made one for Hunt, gifting him with this kind of unspoken love and acceptance?

A soft pinging sound emanated from across the hall and Max's head snapped up, his silvery eyes lasering in that direction.

"What is that?" Vic asked, something in her chest tightening.

"It's the alert that someone has breached the boundary."

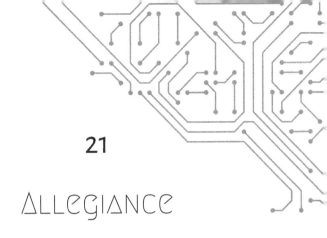

21

ALLEGIANCE

V IC LURCHED FROM HER chair as Max wheeled himself back from the
table. And as much as she wanted to sprint across the hall to
the control room, she knew this was Max's realm, that it was his job
to check the computer monitors.

So she waited for him to lead the way, stewing in her inability
to load up and pack out, identify and take out the threat. If it was,
indeed, a threat. Old habits. It could have been an animal.

As soon as they crossed the threshold into the control room, she
searched the insane number of screens, ignoring the way the warmth
from all of the electrical activity in a small space enveloped her. Her
eyes darted between monitors until she spotted the one that displayed what the alarm had registered.

It was a vehicle barreling down the dirt drive, a contingent of
Uniforms clustered in the back. Her stomach dropped out as she
watched the truck's progress, chilled by the stiffness of the bodies
as they rocked with the speeding vehicle's movements, recognizably
mechanical now that she knew they were more machine than human.

"Where's Brody?" Max muttered, searching the monitors and hitting keys on the keyboard to flip through cameras until one landed on the kitchen where Brody stood at the sink, washing dishes from what appeared to be his lunch.

His back was to the camera, showing what made Vic's stomach drop out again: the gun they'd taken from her was tucked into the waistband of his jeans.

"Max." It was all she could manage, and it drew his metallic gaze to her face. But she saw that he'd recognized what she had.

Not only were weapons of any kind illegal, but that handgun had been registered to a man who'd worked for the government, even if low on the totem pole. Which meant it would be documented as stolen, and that would inextricably tie the ranch to her.

"Can't you warn him?" she asked.

Max shook his head, eyes shooting to the camera that showed the truck stopping in front of the house. "Not with how close they are to the house. Who would I send? There's nothing on record that any Unborn are on this property."

A man stepped out of the cab of the truck as the Uniforms leaped out of the back. He was clearly not one of them. She recognized his uniform—not gray and starched, but loose and practical with the seven-pointed leaf insignia on the shoulder marking him as a lieutenant colonel. Which meant he was an Organic.

"Why didn't it alert you sooner?" she demanded, though she knew it probably wouldn't have mattered. The speed with which that truck had come sailing up to the door told her they knew the property was monitored. Which put some kind of communication system on her list of suggestions for Hunt to implement.

Max didn't bother to answer, his jaw feathering in frustration just as the back door to the kitchen burst open. They all tensed, and Brody jerked away from the sink, reaching for the pistol at his back.

"I wouldn't," the Organic said.

"Who are you and what are you doing on private property?" Brody demanded, squaring his stance but wisely moving his hand back into view.

"Lieutenant Colonel Haven," the man answered, jerking his chin A Uniform stepped forward to yank the gun from Brody's waistband.

Brody didn't move from that spot, but the muscles in his back flexed, his fingers curling into his palms. He wanted to lunge for the weapon, to fight the mech.

"Don't," Vic whispered as if he would hear her.

"We're looking for a woman," Haven said.

"Aren't we all?" Brody's quintessential jocular tone landed a little too heavy.

Haven ignored his comment and held up a picture. "This woman. A Silver Unborn."

She couldn't tell from the feed if Brody even glanced at the picture. "Pretty lady. Though they usually are, aren't they?"

Haven's expression hardened as he accepted the gun the Uniform handed over. "You haven't seen her?"

"Don't often get Unborn out this way."

The lieutenant colonel grunted, finally looking down at the gun he held. "Firearms are illegal for civilians."

"Oh yeah? Hadn't heard that."

Vic's gut coiled tighter. Brody had to know he was playing with fire.

"Where'd you get this gun?" Haven asked.

Vic's fingernails dug into her palms. Brody was quick on his feet, lightning fast with his words. But she wasn't sure he could lie his way out of this one.

His body was too tight, but his tone was casual as he responded, "Found it on the ground."

Technically not a lie, but it provoked the colonel because he used the butt of the gun to whack Brody across the face.

Vic sucked in a breath.

"Niko," Max said, turning to look at the boy behind Vic. He was so quiet, and her panic had been so all-consuming, she hadn't realized he was there.

"I'm not going," Niko said, locking his jaw.

Max bared his teeth but turned back to the screen.

Brody spat blood then wiped at his mouth with the back of his hand, staring the colonel down as he walked away from him.

Niko's hand found its way into Vic's, and she squeezed it in reassurance.

"Why don't you have a seat?" Haven said, though it was definitely not a suggestion.

"You're the guest," Brody said, his voice dark now. "You have the seat. I got some whisky if you're in the mood."

"You've got a smart mouth," Haven said through his teeth. "But that doesn't make you smart."

Brody said nothing. Wise.

"This gun was stolen off a checkpoint guard outside of the city."

Again Brody just watched the other man.

"So I'll ask you again if you've seen the Silver Unborn woman."

"You can ask me whatever you want to. You're not going to get the answer you're lookin' for."

Something in her chest squeezed, the pain radiating through her ribs. He wasn't going to give her up. But he probably should. Knowing what those Uniforms were capable of, he was putting himself in danger to protect her. And who was she to him anyway?

Haven stopped pacing to glare at Brody. "You leave me no choice."

Vic took a step forward as two Uniforms grabbed either one of Brody's arms and hauled him to the chair. He fought against their hold, but they were too strong. Even for Vic—that mech's grip had locked her into place.

They pinned Brody to the chair while a third approached.

"Get him out of here!" Max hollered as the first blow landed in Brody's gut, a sickening thud making Vic's heart race.

He grunted, doubling over.

Vic grabbed Niko, who screamed and thrashed against her. But she easily dragged his thin frame back to the room he shared with Max, the sounds of Brody's beating permeating the space like it was being projected over some kind of sound system.

She slid the door shut, and still they heard him cry out, heard the thudding punches, and she flinched every time, even as Niko finally gave in and covered his ears, sobbing softly.

He crumpled to the ground, and she went with him, holding him while his body shook.

She wanted to cover her ears, too, lose herself to the emotion that pressed against her from the inside—the fear, the sadness, the shame that Brody would do this for her, the flat-out awareness that she didn't deserve that kind of loyalty.

And then the sound of Brody's pain stopped, and a new voice joined in.

"What the hell is going on here?"

Her head jerked up.

"Stay here," she whispered in Niko's ear, an echo of command even in the quiet words. He nodded, but his dark eyes were magnified by the tears as he looked up at her, hope igniting in the depths.

Hunt's voice pulled her forward. She waded through the fear and tension that threatened to drown her, shoving her way back to the control room.

He stood in the doorway to the kitchen, several others behind him, their semi-automatic weapons in their hands. The same style as the ones they'd met her with. Brody was slumped in the chair, still held in place by the Uniforms. There was a lot of blood. Too much. His face was unrecognizable.

"Motivating your little ranch hand here to give up the Silver woman." Haven wasn't cowed by the authority that had snapped through the room with Hunt's words.

"You have no right to be on my property, no matter what reason you think you have."

"I'm Lieutenant—"

"I don't give a shit who you are," Hunt interrupted. "You're trespassing on private property—"

"Sir, maybe if you mention the benefactor—"

Hunt and Haven simultaneously looked at a thin man in the corner of the room no one had paid any attention to. Even Vic had missed him among the group of mechs.

"Shut up, Wilson," Haven snapped.

"I'm not going to *warn* you a second time," Hunt said, stepping forward. The Organics behind him moved with him.

Silence crackled in the room as the lieutenant colonel debated. Finally, he snapped his fingers, and the Uniforms released Brody, who slid to the floor, fully unconscious.

Hunt said something too quiet for them to hear over the camera, and two of the men who stood with him, the ones with the guns broke off to follow—probably escort—Haven and his men off the property.

"Go get Doc," Max said, his voice tight with something she couldn't name, something that hammered into her.

She looked at him only briefly before she bolted from the room, taking the hallway at a full sprint.

Several people jumped out of her way, concern igniting like a wildfire as she breezed past. She felt the eyes follow her when she cut through the rotunda, but she kept going, not bothering to knock when she got to the infirmary.

Morgan was alone, though she looked startled from another world when Vic pulled the door open.

She yanked her glasses from her face and lurched to her feet, already tuned to Vic's intensity. "What's wrong?"

"We have to get topside."

The doctor spun to gather some supplies. "What are we looking at?"

Vic shook her head, gritting her teeth, wishing she had specific information. "Brody was beaten by Uniforms."

"My God." Morgan didn't turn, the shock doing nothing to slow her progress as she threw supplies into a bag, whispering rapidly to herself.

Vic's whole body vibrated with urgency, but she knew the doc was going as fast as she could, that she was doing what was right to make sure she could take care of Brody.

When Morgan finally turned to her, jogging across the room, Vic spun and took off again, painfully aware that she couldn't move as quickly as she was capable. Morgan knew how to get where they were going, but Vic figured her best chance of being allowed above ground too would be if she were escorting the doc up.

They pushed through the people moving around the rotunda, questions thrown at them about what had happened going ignored.

Every heartbeat pumping through Vic chanted one thing: *my fault.* Her legs propelled her forward, Morgan's footsteps falling behind slowly.

Don't push, she reminded herself as they pounded past Niko and Max's room then to the ladder in the ceiling. Without stopping, she jumped to grab and pull down the ladder, the sound of it slamming to the bottom so raucous that it drew a wince out of her.

She turned, waiting for Morgan to catch up and start climbing.

"Give me your bag," Vic said, impatient with the way it impeded the doctor's progress as she went up.

Morgan didn't argue, passing the bag down. It only made her move marginally faster, but faster was faster.

The darkness swallowed them halfway up, and Vic gritted her teeth, expanding her senses so that she became more aware of what lay before them. Neither said a word, but both quieted their steps and their breathing as they neared the top of the ladder, scrambling quietly onto solid ground.

They crept more than walked up the slanted path to the door that led into the house and stopped when they got close, listening intently for sounds of a fight or strangers prowling through the rooms.

It had looked like the trespassers were gone before she'd run for the doctor, but there were no guarantees.

Only a moment later, the door jerked open, and the brightness bit at Vic's eyes. She recognized the silhouette even though he was merely a shadow with the light blazing behind him.

"I was just coming to get you," Hunt said to Morgan. His eyes transferred to Vic but he said nothing about her presence, stepping back to let both women through.

"Where is he?" Morgan asked as she took off at a brisk pace down the hall, Vic and Hunt right behind her.

"Some of the guys and I brought him upstairs. He's pretty roughed up. Broke his nose. Maybe his jaw. I'm not sure what else."

She gave a swift nod and took the steps two at a time.

Before Vic could take off after her, Hunt grabbed her arm to keep her on the main level, and she whirled to look at him.

His eyes were tight with concern, but there was a biting sharpness to the blue as they searched hers. "They're looking for you."

She didn't like what was in his tone, her nerves electrifying with uncertainty. "Because I was the only one who escaped."

"No. That's not it." The muscles around his eyes contracted as he stared at her, and she felt like they were back to those first few days after she'd arrived.

The dread slithered through her, a heavy, black sludge. "What, Hunt?" she snapped. The way he was looking at her, like she'd brought this on them, made that same ache from before bloom in her chest—a knife of guilt, twisting.

"They want *you*, Vic. For a reason. It's not just that you survived, that they want to ask you about what happened. They've been *searching* for you."

His words pelted her, and she fought the urge to take a step back, to jerk her arm from his grasp.

"I don't know why they would want me." The defensiveness in her tone covered her hurt fairly well.

He continued to search her face, his hand still wrapped around her arm. His fingers twitched against her skin, setting off little spikes of sensation where he touched.

"If you want me to go, I will." She didn't have the strength to put volume behind the words, and they came out barely above a whisper. "I would never want to put anyone in danger."

He gave his head an almost imperceptible shake. "I don't want you to go."

It took a second for his words to land, especially because his expression didn't change from the stony mask he had in place. But his voice had turned faintly tender, and she stumbled mentally.

"I'm sorry about before," he said softly.

She blinked, struggling to keep up, especially because she felt so scorched by his proximity, by the look in his eyes.

"I was wrong to keep it from you. You were right that I didn't trust you—at first. But then it was because I couldn't watch what it would do to you. I couldn't stand seeing you in pain."

His apology felt undeserved after what had happened to Brody. His reason painted the whole thing in a new way she hadn't thought of. Hunt didn't seem the type to apologize unless he really thought he needed to.

"I. . . forgive you." She still could only manage to whisper.

His expression softened, eyes tracing her face with an entirely different emotion in the depths.

"Hunt."

They both looked toward the top of the stairs where the doctor stood.

Vic waited for Hunt to go first before following him up without asking if she could. She had to see if Brody was okay for herself since it was because of her he'd endured the beating.

He was lying on the bed, most of the blood cleaned off his face, but the left side was warped and deformed, his eye swollen painfully shut, the untouched side of his face twisted with his pain. There was a gash across his left cheekbone, the skin speared open like someone had used a knife.

"His orbital bone is fractured," Morgan said softly as they walked further into the room. "Definitely some internal bruising. Possibly bleeding. I don't have the right equipment to check, and I'm not a surgeon. I. . ." She shook her head. "The pain meds haven't kicked in yet. But I've given him some serum to hopefully get him on his feet sooner."

Hunt nodded, moving forward slowly as Brody's one good eye tracked them.

Vic swallowed, guilt constricting her lungs.

"You'd think I was dead or something by the looks on your faces," Brody managed. The humor didn't quite land when he spoke through his teeth, his voice tight with agony.

"Nah," Hunt said, too gently. "We're just concerned you permanently messed up your pretty face."

Brody tried to laugh then groaned, hand clutching at his abdomen. Vic shot a sharp look at the doc, who grimaced. Hunt redirected to walk over to Morgan. Since he was handling that conversation, she figured she'd go join Brody.

"You think Claire will still love me if I'm not as pretty as I used to be?" Brody asked as soon as she knelt beside the bed. "I have so much Unborn competition. Have you *seen* Paul?"

She laughed, though a fist of worry pressed against her sternum. "I think Claire would love you regardless if she actually knew you had feelings for her."

He made a face, a collapsing of his attempt at a smile. "What's that supposed to mean?"

Vic tried to keep the concern from her expression, swallowing the lump in her throat. Humor. She had to stick with the humor or she'd drown in the worry.

"Brody, you literally flirt with anything on two legs that walks past you. And Max." Her smile was weak. "She has no idea you like her."

He blinked his good eye slowly, the realization dawning gradually, which meant the meds must have been kicking in.

"Get some rest, heartbreaker." She wanted to touch him, to reassure him, but she was afraid to hurt him more. So she pushed to her feet as he attempted a nod, his good eye staying shut.

She wrapped her arms around herself and joined Hunt and the doctor, who were silently observing Brody now. Neither was relaxed, but there was no hum of worry coming off of them the way she felt it inside of herself.

Hunt met her gaze and tipped his head to have her follow him out.

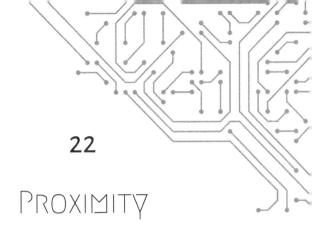

22

PROXIMITY

"**T**HIS IS MY ROOM." Hunt's voice was almost sheepish as he dipped his head, pink creeping up the back of his neck.

Which meant it was incredibly vulnerable for him to invite her in. The space he'd brought her to in the bunker must not have held much importance. Probably an extra room he occasionally used, if he used it at all.

It was easy to figure out why this one meant more.

As she'd suspected, there were images on the walls that were clearly Niko's doing. But they were different from the ones she'd seen. No bright colors or added geometric shapes. All were shades of gray, done only in graphite or charcoal. Hunt resting his head close to the neck of his horse. Hunt sitting on the split-rail fence that edged the property, squinting against the sun. Just his eyes, somehow capturing that suspicious and playful glint she'd come to recognize.

Niko had managed to convey the old-time earthiness of the man who stood next to her, watching her take in his personal space with a weighted silence, holding his breath like he'd revealed a layer of himself.

There wasn't much to the room otherwise. An immaculately made bed sat in the corner, a well-loved quilt folded over it. A solid wood dresser sat to her left with a couple of knick-knacks and pictures on top. A shiny watch, a few figurines that a boy might have collected. It almost looked like it had been preserved from his childhood and left untouched for decades.

"Do you even sleep here?" she asked, smirking as she moved by him.

"Not lately," he admitted, lifting a shoulder. "When you arrived, I started sleeping in the bunker."

She gave him a wry look, not surprised. The way he'd stuck close by that first week had given away the depth of his suspicion even before she got a sense of how things normally functioned.

She walked closer to one of Niko's drawings, which was of the two of them together, the warmth it inspired chasing away her anxiety over what happened to Brody, if only for a moment. She moved around slowly until she came to the photos on the dresser, one framed with young Hunt and Max, looking to be about the same age, maybe ten or so.

Then another of the two of them, Hunt a couple of years older and Max looking like his protective older brother, his leanly muscular arm slung over his shoulders. His towering frame made him look sixteen. Evidence of the rapid growth and development all Unborn went through.

Next was a picture of Hunt with an elderly man she would have assumed was his grandfather if she didn't know better.

"My dad," he murmured from behind her, closer than she expected, and a tingle ran through her.

"I figured," she replied, her voice soft. She tried to ignore how his proximity electrified her nerves.

"Can I ask you a question?" He had drawn closer still, his breath fanning against the back of her neck.

It was feather-light, but she felt it like a jolt to her heart. She rested her fingers on top of the dresser to steady herself. "That is a question." The smile tugged at her lips.

He chuckled softly. "Another question, then."

"Yes."

"What did you want for your life after the war?"

It wasn't the question she was expecting, and she sucked in a breath as she turned.

He was only a few inches from her and didn't step back. She could practically feel his heart beating between them as she pressed against the dresser behind her, hands gripping the edge.

It seemed so out of left field, but there was an earnestness in his expression that made her seriously consider the answer. The key word was *life*, which still felt like a foreign concept, something entirely unattainable. Even back when most of the Unborn believed the idealistic image they'd been fed, she'd doubted they'd have anything close to what the Organics had. Not based on how they treated the Unborn during the war.

Even when the desire for that fantasy idea had been some little glimmer inside of her, stirred by the experience of tiny hands reaching for her, the warmth of a sweet little body cradled against hers awakening a maternal instinct she'd never known was there—she'd tamped it all down, denied it existed because it wasn't supposed to.

But she had thought she'd have the one thing she'd never experienced. Something that seemed so simple, it should have been at her fingertips. All she'd have to do was reach for it.

She looked up at him, feeling the warmth those ice-blue eyes were capable of conveying. "Peace."

His expression softened the slightest bit. "And now?"

Was he moving closer, or was it her imagination? She tried not to think about it, or the way it made her hands ache to reach out, to touch him.

"I don't know what tomorrow holds, let alone what I might want." She swallowed the unexpected pressure of emotion building in her throat. "I try not to wish for things that feel impossible."

He was definitely closer because his body was almost pressed against hers now, his head tipped forward enough that she felt his exhale along her lips. "What if they weren't impossible?"

That whispered question ricocheted through her. Because it was, wasn't it? An impossibility to have a life, a family, a future that was more than just surviving? What happened in her village and to Brody proved that peace would never be within her reach.

But if she couldn't have peace, couldn't she at least have this? Even if it was only this moment in time, when he looked at her like this, like she mattered to him.

She released a shuddering breath and brought one hand up to touch his face, the scruff of his jaw under her fingertips tiny prickles along her skin.

And wasn't it a kind of peace, she thought as he wrapped his arms around her, to be held?

She lifted her face, allowing the tips of their noses to brush, their breath to tangle in the infinitesimal space between their mouths. Already her lips were tingling, anticipating what it might be like if she wished for the impossible and let herself have it.

It only took the faintest movement for him to bring his mouth to hers, melding their lips in a tentative kiss.

Just a taste—that was all she would allow, all she thought she'd need. She'd always been good at denying herself. But her body betrayed her self-control—had she ever possessed any? Could she ever regain it?—and she pressed into him, her hands going around his neck to pull him closer, doing whatever she could to close the cruelty that was any space between them.

She parted her lips to allow him to drink deeply and got a taste of the citrus sweetness on his tongue—an orange he'd had, maybe—losing herself as every sense was overwhelmed by him. The way his arms tightened around her, easing her closer so that every surface of his body was touching every plane of hers, the way his scent filled her mind with images of forests and fields, and the way the pounding of their hearts filled the quiet room.

Every pulse through her veins cried that it was not enough, that it was too much. She was drowning, and she was parched. Filled to the brim and starving.

And all too soon, she was reminded where they were and who she was when a door down the hall opened and shut. Time sputtered and began to move again, pressed against her with the urgency of what lay behind and before them, the questions that still needed answers.

She didn't have to say anything because he sensed it, too, and they both started to come back to themselves. Their kisses slowed, became tender instead of intense, slow instead of demanding, until they finally broke away, and Hunt rested his forehead against hers.

"That was not the reason I invited you in here," he said, breathless.

She raised a brow. "What was the actual reason?"

He sighed. "To talk about what happened."

Her body snapped tight, and she wished she wasn't so boxed in. She would have turned away.

"Don't," he said softly. "I'm not accusing you of anything."

"But I *am* responsible." She gave him a gentle push, and he relented, giving her the space her nerves demanded. She paced away, restless with self-blame. "I don't know why they're looking for me. It has to be for the same reason you had Morgan run tests. To find out why I broke out of it."

He ran a hand through his hair, tousling the blond locks, and leaned against the dresser to watch her. "Someone mentioned a benefactor."

Vic's eyes shot to his, and she stopped, remembering, though it hadn't landed at the time. "They're getting paid to look for me." She brushed a finger along her bottom lip as she thought that through.

He grimaced. "Money talks. Louder than it used to."

Someone rich and, therefore, powerful wanted to find her. And if someone with that much pull wanted her, there had to be a deeper, bigger reason. "Who? And why?" she murmured, mostly to herself. Was there more than the countermeasure inside her brain?

Hunt folded his arms across his chest, his gaze distant as he got lost in his thoughts. He'd mentioned money as if he knew, like he spoke that language, and her mind wanted answers that were more easily attained. Especially because he'd kissed her.

"When money talks, do you listen?" she asked.

His eyes cut to her.

She slowed her body, slowed her thoughts, worked at keeping the tension from winding her tighter. "There's been a somewhat secretive side of what you have going on here."

He frowned, squinting toward the floor.

The lack of trust she felt in his silence lanced at her heart. "You have illegal weapons you aren't afraid of wielding in front of a half-bird colonel. That same colonel who tucked tail as soon as you told him to."

He unfolded his arms and placed his hands on the dresser on either side of his body like he was bracing himself. A sigh sawed through him. "This ranch exists because of a handful of powerful, rich people. Quality food is what they're after, and I provide it. It enables me to employ locals who need work. It helps me provide for this community."

"And the guns?"

His frown deepened. "They want to protect their investment, so I get a pass on certain laws."

"Money sure does talk."

He took a breath, dipping his chin to acknowledge her murmured words. "It's also why they turn a blind eye to the Unborn population I keep around. They view it like private security. I sell some of the surplus in town. Give some to the shelter whenever I can."

She heard it in his voice, buried in those extra words. Despite the legitimacy of his reasons, he was ashamed that he would be catering to the very people who were contributing to the depressed economy, and he wanted to make up for it, do what he could to atone for what he thought was a betrayal. It wasn't a lack of trust that had kept him silent; it was guilt.

And her heart, which had been leaning over the precipice before, now fell flat in her hands, ready for her to surrender it to this man who sacrificed so much to enable people to live with dignity, to have food, safety, and community.

And she realized how much she cared that they continue to have that, how that had shifted to be her focus now that this had become her home.

She moved across the room, pulled by the way he kept his face turned away in shame, drawn in by the selflessness he displayed, lured by the memory of their kiss only moments before.

The shift had happened so gradually, she hadn't caught on at first. And though she didn't totally understand what had led to his change of heart, she knew things wouldn't go back to what they were.

Aloof strangers. Then tentative friends. Now. . . something else.

Something more like fire. But instead of burning her, it ignited her senses, jolted her back to life, resurrected the part of her that had once dreamed of a future.

Her nearness drew his gaze to her face, and his expression opened, revealing more to her than he ever had before. Affection, admiration, vulnerability.

"You asked me what I wanted out of life," she started.

He lifted a hand, brushing it up her arm, his palm and then his eyes tracing the swirls of black ink that marked her skin. He skimmed the identifying number on her inner forearm, just below the bend of her elbow.

"What do *you* want?" she asked, her voice as soft as his touch when his hand glided up and over her shoulder, resting at her neck. Her pulse throbbed under his palm.

"I didn't want much before," he said. "Like you, I kept what I wanted contained to practicality."

He fell silent, the edge of his thumb tapping lightly against her jaw as he studied her face. He was still hard lines and suspicion, but there was a subtle softness that she might have missed if she hadn't begun to see what was underneath.

"Only a few weeks ago, you treated me like a criminal," she prompted when he remained silent. "What changed?"

He gave her the softest smile, and she felt his gaze like flames along her face. "I don't know when it started. One day you were the enemy, and the next. . ." He exhaled slowly. "I got these glimpses of your heart, and I saw that we were two sides of the same coin."

She tipped her head, leaning her face into his palm, remembering the moments she'd noticed that, too.

"It was when you were telling Niko about your tally marks that I realized I was in trouble." Humor glinted in his eyes. "I saw something in you that day that scared me."

She couldn't quite find the ability to laugh, the weight of his words pressing against her.

"To know that you took every life lost so seriously. . . meant you would care about everyone here as much as I do."

She sucked in a breath like he'd punched her. Everyone tended to see her as cold, analytical, all about the endgame. Untouched.

His expression turned sympathetic as he dragged the pad of his thumb across her cheek. "But it reminded me what it is to be burdened by responsibility, and how you have to put the feelings inside a little box to be able to keep going, keep making the right decisions, keep putting others first."

The sense of being exposed was raw as it sliced through her. But there was freedom in being seen to that depth, too. To be understood was to be loved.

"What happened today. . ."

Her stomach torqued. "Was my fault."

"No." The word was firm, and it branded the air between them. "It wasn't your fault."

"Brody was protecting me." She broke away from him and paced again.

"As he should. You're part of the community here, aren't you?"

She expelled a heavy breath. "Maybe I shouldn't be."

He dragged a hand down his face. "Vic, I'm sorry. I hate that I ever made you feel like an outsider, that I didn't trust you. Things are different now."

She turned her face away, her eyes catching on that pencil drawing of him with his horse, the way the lines fanned from his eyes as he smiled. "Now that the thing you were worried about happened—me putting everyone in danger."

"Vic." He pushed away from the dresser, the knick-knacks on top rattling. His steps were so quiet as he moved toward her that she wouldn't have known he was even there. "We'll face it, whatever this enemy is. You've proved that you care about the people here, that you'll protect this place as much as any of us. So let's do it. Together."

His hands landed on her shoulders and skimmed down her arms. His body heat pressed against her back, underscoring his words with his presence. *Together.*

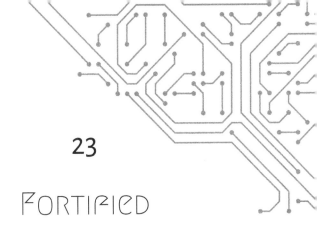

23

Fortified

VIC WAS SO STILL at the kitchen table no one would ever know every inch of her body was aflame with the intensity she tried to keep locked down.

She could hear Hunt outside, giving clear, concise instructions to the extra Unborn charged with walking the perimeter in case of another breach. Claire had volunteered readily as soon as they mentioned it that morning, followed by a handful of others who itched for the chance to be used for something other than grunt work.

Vic could feel it, too, the way the assignment appealed to the purpose wired inside of them to guard and to fight. She wanted to join, to be used in that way, but Hunt had advised she stay behind, tucked away in the house because they'd been looking for her specifically. But it chafed to have to sit back when she was meant to lead, to be at the forefront. The Uniforms were a whole new animal, something so unpredictable that Vic worried a handful of Coppers wouldn't be enough.

She stood, ready to march out and demand to participate when the back door jerked open, sunlight splashing across the floor between her feet and Hunt's.

"I'm about ready to head out," Hunt said, his voice soft. It was the reluctance she heard underneath that distracted her from her determination to assert herself.

Something twisted inside of her. He wasn't going far. Just out to help with projects around the ranch. No big deal. But the newness of whatever this was coupled with the sense of being surrounded by an unknown enemy sent renewed anxiety rushing in her blood.

She took a faltering step toward him, ready to present her argument, but there were others standing behind him, talking in subdued tones that gave away how much the strain had permeated even casual conversation. Though he hadn't said anything about keeping whatever their relationship was a secret, it felt undefined, the edges too blurred, and she figured he'd want to protect it for a while, keep it private, special between them. At least until they'd created some parameters and expectations.

Except he grabbed her by the hand and yanked her into him, their bodies colliding because she'd been too surprised to stop herself. His lips crashed against hers just as clumsily, but he didn't seem to care. She didn't much either, not when being connected to him this way soothed her harried thoughts, made all of the anxiety fall right out of her head.

When he pulled away, she tried to ignore the sharp awareness of everyone behind him. The hum of conversation had fizzled in the wake of the shock their embrace had inspired.

The heat painted her cheeks, but instead of releasing her or looking as embarrassed as she felt, Hunt simply grinned at her.

"I like what a blush does to your face," he said.

She tried to glare at him, but the flutter in her stomach made it impossible. "Is this your idea of some kind of an announcement?"

He pursed his lips. "Was there something to announce?"

She punched him in the shoulder, and he winced, chuckling.

Then his fingers flexed against her waist. "There's no keeping it secret. I don't do things halfway, Vic. I'm either all in or all out."

Her lungs throbbed from lack of oxygen as she processed those words, what was behind them. The impossible now lay before her, within reach. Did she even deserve it?

He placed another kiss on her shocked lips. "It's okay if you're not there yet. You've got a few hours to mull it over." He winked at her, totally unconcerned.

And yet, her world had tipped sideways. His hands felt too hot on her body, but he released her and backed up. She expected to feel relief, but only a sense of dread and abandonment remained, and she struggled to understand.

He turned to the group of people behind him—Organics who would be heading out with him and the armed Unborn—and they all snapped into work mode. Because he *was* still their boss.

She rubbed her hand down her thigh, suddenly understanding Niko's anxious need to tap and do various calming rituals. She'd never felt such a restless energy inside herself before, something wholly different from the nerves that fired any time she'd been about to go on a dangerous mission.

Maybe because she'd never felt the weight of her own peril in those moments. She focused on getting her people back, but she never cared or expected to make it back herself. But she always did. And though she'd never been afraid to die, she *was* wired to survive against all odds.

What if she didn't survive this?

She shut the door and turned, startled to find Morgan standing halfway up the stairs, her lips pressed together like she was holding back a smile.

"How much of that did you hear?" Vic asked, looking down at the table as she brushed her fingertips along the glossy surface.

The doctor's footsteps were muted but still audible as she started down again. "Enough to know what's melted Hunt's rough exterior."

Vic raised her eyes. She half-expected Morgan to be angry for some reason, like she would be offended by the very thought of an Unborn with an Organic. It certainly wouldn't be accepted by society at large.

Vic could barely wrap her mind around it. She and Hunt were not the same. Everything about her screamed what she was—a genetically engineered tool to be used, not a person to be loved. Not a some*one*, but a some*thing*. Unnatural. Built, not made. He was drawn to her pretty face, the things he saw in her that reflected himself, what she could *do* for the community, a possible bridge between the segregated halves of what existed here. This couldn't be anything more to him, surely.

She wasn't sure she could offer him anything more, anyway. It wasn't even known whether or not her kind could have children, or what those children would look like. Would they be superior in strength and ability? Would they age at a normal rate? And if she couldn't give him a normal life, a normal family, what was the point?

"Why does it seem like his declaration is about to send you running for the hills?" Morgan asked as she moved to the cupboards to get a glass for water.

Vic gave her the briefest smile to acknowledge the hyperbole, but she couldn't hold it because the observation wasn't too far off. She had no intention of running. But it didn't mean she wasn't scared.

"We weren't *designed* to have a life after the war." She lowered herself into a chair at the table, remembering how the room had felt cramped and cold when she'd first arrived—when Hunt had sat across from her to interrogate her, almost denying her sanctuary in his little safe haven. "We were designed to fight. What if. . ."

Morgan looked at her over the rim of her glass as she sipped at the liquid inside. She lowered it, absently swirling it to send the water spinning. "You're worried Hunt wants a future you can't give him?"

"Among other things." Vic looked toward the backdoor, seeing through the gauzy curtains over the small window set into the wood that they'd left.

"Hunt doesn't go into things blindly. And he knows a lot more about Unborn than you give him credit for."

"Right. Front-running researcher father." Vic tapped her fingernails on the table, pulling her bottom lip between her teeth. "I know he's got some connections in some high places, but what if they find out he's with. . . with me?"

Morgan sighed, twisting to set her empty glass in the sink. "Vic, I understand where you're coming from. This is new territory for you. Maybe even the first time you've had real feelings for someone."

Vic opened her mouth, heat flooding her face, but Morgan didn't stop.

"Hunt is a grown man. He knows that world, knows what risks he's taking. You might be an expert on death and destruction, but putting your heart on the line isn't as dangerous as all that. There's risk, yes. To everyone involved. But neither of you will die if you give this a chance." She shrugged. "Maybe it won't work out. But that's what living is—taking the chance, knowing you could get hurt, and doing it anyway."

Living. Vic couldn't really say that's what she'd been doing all these years after the war. It was more of the same—taking what she'd been given.

She swallowed at the realization, wondering exactly where Morgan's well of wisdom came from. Life experience, most likely. And it was true. Vic had been trained in all aspects of war—weapons, combat, strategy. And based on what she'd learned there, this was a calculated risk even with the odds stacked against her. But she'd made a habit of beating the odds. It was why she'd been one of the best.

And if she wanted to start living, well and truly, she'd have to start taking the risks.

Morgan wore a half-smile as she watched Vic work through it all.

"Have you taken that risk?" Vic asked her, the words feather-light.

Morgan's hazel eyes flashed down. "More than once. Can't say everyone is willing to make the jump, even at the beginning." Her gaze came back up to meet Vic's. "But I'd like to see the two of you give it a go. Lord knows you deserve a little happiness. And Hunt could use a little of his own. He takes on so much. And I think you'd be good for him."

Vic found that hard to believe, but she let it go. "Thanks for the pep talk." She looked down at her hands. "I appreciate it."

Morgan dipped her head. "Any time. And if you ever need me to *look into* anything, I'd be happy to."

Vic's eyes flashed wide as she sat back in her chair, a nervous laugh bubbling out of her. "Right. Uh, maybe someday. Way down the line."

Morgan's mouth quirked, and she nodded again.

"How's our big hero doing?" Vic asked, desperate for a subject change.

Morgan grimaced, folding her arms across her chest. "I see improvement. My serum helps."

That caught her attention. "You mentioned that yesterday. What serum?"

Morgan's face actually lit up, and she straightened. "I've used Unborn blood and DNA to synthesize the rapid healing qualities you all possess. It's quite helpful when we have more severe injuries like Brody's."

Vic's face fell. Severe didn't sound promising at all.

Morgan seemed to read her correctly. "I think he will be okay. Eventually. It's just a long road until he's up on his feet again. He had some internal bleeding, which was the biggest concern."

Vic searched her face, noting the dark circles under the woman's eyes, the way her hair was more frizz than curl. "Have you slept at all?"

Morgan opened her mouth, then snapped it shut, blowing out a thick breath. "Not really."

"Maybe I can sit up there with him while you get a solid couple of hours. I have time to kill. I'd send Claire if she weren't on perimeter duty."

She and Morgan shared a conspiratorial smile. "Now that's an idea. Claire would've lifted his spirits quite a bit and that would go a long way in his healing process."

"I'm sure if he ever needs a sponge bath, he'd love to have her be the one to give it."

Morgan laughed, clutching her side. "I'll let him know that's an option."

Vic smiled.

"You really don't mind sitting with him?" Morgan asked. "I could use the rest."

Vic shook her head. "Of course not. He's my friend, too." *And it's my fault he's hurt.* Her smile faded.

Morgan didn't seem to notice. It was almost like she was half asleep already. "I'll take a nap in the next room over in case you need me for anything. I've already given him his next round of pain meds, so he's resting for the time being."

Vic nodded and watched the other woman trudge up the stairs, her footfalls heavier than before. Vic knew that bone-weary feeling. The one that hit all at once when rest was within reach.

She cast one last glance out the back door, though no one was out there, then pushed to her feet, following Morgan up the stairs.

She rapped gently on the door to Brody's room in case he was asleep. She didn't want to wake him, but she didn't think bursting in was a good idea either. He was awake when she slipped inside though, and he tried to crack one of his easy grins. He reminded her so much of Max—the old Max, anyway—trying to keep the mood light at all times, even if they were in pain underneath.

Brody didn't say anything, his eyes drifting closed as she settled in the large recliner the doc had moved into his room for overnight observation.

She stared toward the window, feeling useless and helpless, and eventually got up to look out. There was not much activity near the house, though she could see one of the Unborn walking along the edge of the trees she had emerged from all those weeks ago.

Weeks.

How long had it been since Hunt had given her letter to his guy? Had the girls received it by now? It had seemed miraculous Hunt had that connection, that she was that much closer to being reunited with Jamie and Alice.

She didn't know what kind of life they'd carved out for themselves, but she didn't imagine it was something worth keeping. Not if it resembled what she'd had in the Unborn settlement she'd called home until recently.

With the way things had shifted between her and Hunt, the way her priorities had changed to mark this place as home, she could recognize that there was some kind of magic in what he'd built on this ranch. And she wanted to share it with her sisters.

Be the family they'd always dreamed of being.

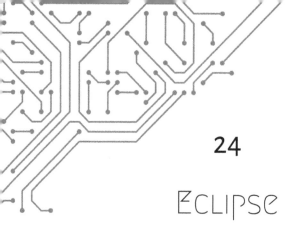

24

Eclipse

T HE WARMTH OF THE sun was a caress along her body, calming her mind after being cooped up for three hours with Brody. It was all she managed to give Morgan before the woman shooed her out, claiming it had been plenty.

Vic didn't fight her on it, realizing she hadn't actually been outside since the horse ride with Hunt, which felt like so long ago. Even though it had been the beginning of that big change between them, it almost seemed like a different life. And maybe it was.

After her turmoil inside, thoughts circling around the sisters she still didn't have by her side, the fresh air felt like a reprieve. Hunt might've thought being out in the open wasn't a good idea, but the sunshine on her skin reminded her that she needed more than food and water to survive. And the way she missed Hunt's presence made her realize that feeling alive was more than just surviving.

A couple of the ranch hands noticed her lingering by the house and asked her to help with tossing hay into the horses' stalls, so she occupied herself with the manual labor, relishing the pull and burn of the muscles as she worked.

She was walking back to the house for a break and some water when she spotted a truck rumbling down the dirt path from out in the field, bodies crammed into the back.

A wry smile crossed her lips as she shook her head. Of course Hunt would have a vehicle against all odds. It was a good thing he was such a decent guy, otherwise, she was liable to think poorly of him for having so much convenience at his disposal.

Stopping near the corner of the house, she folded her arms as she leaned against the cracked siding. She was happy to find that the only feeling rushing through her blood was the excitement to see Hunt again. No trace of the uncertainty and doubt from earlier lingered. Her concerns weren't gone, but they were less pressing.

The truck skidded to a halt a few feet from her, and Hunt practically jumped out of the driver's side, snatching her around the waist and pulling her into him like they'd been apart for days instead of hours.

Claire jumped out after him, a pleased grin on her face as she raised an eyebrow. "Well, isn't this a—"

Her steps faltered, and a bolt of recognition shot through Vic, hot and electric. She pushed Hunt back, her stomach twisting as the woman's eyes went dark. It was like an eclipse, a shadow that slid right over the coppery irises.

No. It wasn't—couldn't—be happening again.

"Claire?" she ventured, wishing, *hoping* it wasn't what she thought it was. She stepped in front of Hunt the second before the willowy woman lunged forward.

"Vic!"

Hunt's shout got lost in the flurry that followed. Claire took Vic to the ground, the uneven dirt wrenching her back, and she grunted as Claire's weight crashed on top of her.

She heard the shuffle of the others who moved to get Claire off of her.

"Don't!" she cried. Claire could easily rip them to pieces. Fear snapped like firecrackers through her body as Claire rolled and got to her feet, looping her arms around Vic's middle to yank her up.

She thrashed as Claire worked to drag her away from the house, which made Vic falter for a moment, her mind reeling. Claire wasn't trying to kill her. She was trying to take her somewhere. Vic made a quick calculation, wondering how far the other Unborn were, and sent a warning look to Hunt, who was working his way toward them with the other Organics.

Twisting her feet with Claire's, Vic took them both down. Scrambling in the dirt, she straddled Claire's abdomen to keep her down, but Claire slammed her hand against the underside of Vic's chin, shoving her head back and knocking her teeth together. All Vic could think was that she didn't want to hurt her friend. But she might have to.

A force hit her from the side and to the ground. Before she could get her bearings, hands grappled around her shoulders, grabbed at her legs, her arms, her hair—more who'd joined the melee. There'd been four Unborn walking the ranch. Four Coppers she could take down, but not without effort.

With a roar, Vic wrapped her right hand around the wrist of whoever had her left arm and yanked them forward, twisting to pull their body weight over her and bowl them into whoever held her right leg.

It threw everyone's balance off, and they abruptly released her. She flopped onto the ground and rolled, scrambling to get to her feet to face the Copper man she'd met before but whose name she couldn't remember. His flat black eyes locked on hers, his face devoid of emotion as he rose to his feet. Claire did the same behind him, muscles coiling to attack again. The other two were still trying to extricate themselves from each other.

They weren't trying to kill her. But she couldn't let them take her.

She positioned herself like a sprinter about to take off, then pushed off the ground, the pads of her fingers tearing into the earth as she launched herself forward to ram into the Copper man, then bull-rush him into Claire. With her speed and strength behind her, they all went to the ground again, and the other two grunted as the oxygen was forced from their lungs. If they'd been on concrete, their skulls might have cracked.

Even on the grassy ground, they slammed hard and seemed stunned. Vic spun off of them, rising as she pirouetted, swinging her leg around to slam it into the second Copper man's temple. He stumbled and went down, unmoving.

A blow to the back of her head sent her staggering forward, but she reached behind her, taking the arm—a woman's—against her body and jerked up until she heard a pop. Another grunt—not the scream she should've heard if someone were in their right mind. Vic turned and threw her foot behind and shoved the Copper woman backward. She tripped and crumpled to the ground. It should've kept her down, but she started to push up again. Vic grit her teeth and reared back to slam her elbow into the woman's face, knocking her out cold.

The second Copper man and Claire were climbing to their feet. Panting, Vic staggered up, jerking her head for Hunt and the others to come forward. With two down, they all could probably handle the last two. She really didn't want to hurt anyone more than she already had.

"We need at least three on him." She brushed hair from her sweaty face and took a step forward. "I'll take Claire."

Bodies converged on the man, three tackling him to the ground.

Claire paid them no mind, her eyes locked on Vic. Even in dark mode, her body language gave her away. Fingers became claws, arms pulled into the body. She lunged, and Vic twirled, spinning into position at her back, and seized her from behind. Pulling Claire's arms tight, she shoved her forward even as the woman jerked against her hold, the only disruption to her flat expression the intensity with which she was concentrating on breaking Vic's grip.

"We need to get them sedated or something," Vic said through her teeth, squaring her stance to counterbalance Claire's rabid efforts to turn and get to her. She shot her desperate gaze to Hunt.

"I don't keep it on me anymore," Hunt huffed as he and two others worked to keep the Copper man from breaking free. "Doc probably has something."

"We need every available body on the two in the dirt back there," Vic jerked her head backward.

"This is all we have right now," Hunt snapped.

"Then pray they stay down."

Claire jerked out of her grasp, and Vic clenched her jaw, about ready to bear hug her and lug her inside. She was trying not to knock one of her only friends unconscious, but Claire was making it almost impossible.

"Eric!" Hunt shouted to a man who was running in their direction. "Get as many hands over here as possible! We need at least six!"

The man skidded to a halt, kicking up dust that joined what they already stirred in their efforts to keep the wild Unborn from getting loose. He took off in the direction he'd come from.

They wrestled Claire and the other man into the kitchen through the back door, and Hunt hollered for Morgan, his voice booming with intensity.

Morgan came thudding down the stairs, stopping halfway, her eyes wide with concern.

"We need something to sedate them!" Hunt yelled, grunting when the Copper landed an elbow in his gut.

She spun and sprinted back up, returning a few seconds later, diving into her bag. "I don't have enough for both!"

"Do him then," Vic said, dragging Claire toward the hallway to get her to the bunker. The other woman kicked out at the table, knocking over a chair. "Is there more underground?"

"Yes!" Morgan shouted as she rushed toward the man Hunt and the others held. "In the infirmary!"

Vic muttered a curse under her breath. That was a long way from the entrance. But she continued to fight Claire to the door into the tunnel, shoving the unruly woman into the darkness that leached toward them like a physical presence.

Darkness. Vic plunged ahead, knowing that at least Claire was as much at a disadvantage as she was without light. They shuffled and staggered down the slope in the dark until they reached where Vic was sure the ladder was. That was going to be a problem with someone as uncontrollable as Claire was.

But then she abruptly went docile.

"What? Who's there?" Claire's voice was tight with fear as she tugged against Vic's grip, now with the urgency of escape, not violence.

"Claire?"

"Vic?" She stopped thrashing. "What's happening?"

Making a split-second decision, Vic released her friend. "Go straight down the ladder. Now. I'm right behind you."

Claire did as she was told, maybe some trigger in her from training making her obey Vic's sharp order without question. She went down the ladder quickly, Vic rushing down after her, her body alight with anticipation and fear. What would she find at the bottom—the rest of the Unborn in dark mode? Oh, God, what about Niko?

But a theory bloomed in her mind—supported by the fact that Claire seemed to have control back—that made her think there wouldn't be mass chaos.

Soon the light shone bright under her feet as she dropped through the opening in the ceiling panels, and Claire waited at the bottom for her, concern lighting up her copper eyes as she looked from her scraped-up palms to Vic's face.

They were both covered in dirt and grass.

"What happened, Vic? You have a cut on your face." Alarm spiked her tone, weaving to pull Vic's sense of responsibility to the surface.

"What are you feeling right now?" Vic demanded. "Are you in control?"

Claire's eyes got bigger, and she looked down at herself again, her fingers curling into her palms. "I-I'm in control. Honestly, I feel like I've been tackled by a Silver."

Relief poured through Vic, and she gave a short mirthless laugh.

"Vic!"

She whirled and shot out a hand, terror snapping up her spine. "Don't, Niko!"

He froze several feet from them, a chunk of his dark hair falling over his widened eyes.

"Go get Max!"

"He's with Mr. Hunt. They just came in through the other door."

Vic dropped her hand, the sound of it hitting her thigh echoing loudly in the corridor. "What other door?"

Niko jerked his thumb behind him, but before he could open his mouth, Hunt and several others came jogging down the hall toward them.

"Niko, I need you to go back to your room for a little bit." She ground her teeth when the hurt flashed across his face. "Please! I'll come find you in a bit. Promise."

Hunt dropped his hands on Niko's shoulders, a question in his eyes as he looked to Vic then Claire behind her.

"We'll see you for dinner, Nik," Hunt murmured to the boy, who finally complied, his mouth twisting into a pout as he turned to slink off back to his room.

"Claire, how you doing?" Hunt asked, walking forward slowly.

She shook her head, her coppery gaze wide with horror. "F-fine? I don't know."

Hunt jerked his head, and the others with him all moved forward to surround Claire.

"I think it's alright now," Vic said, heart going out to the woman as hurt and confusion chased each other across her face.

"Just in case," Hunt said in a low voice.

As a unit, they walked down the corridor and through the rotunda, then down the next hall. Claire's eyes dashed around, heavy with guilt and uncertainty. Vic felt for her, knowing what it was like being escorted like a prisoner through these halls. Claire willingly went into the infirmary once they reached Morgan's office, sitting on the bed next to the sedated Copper man. On his other side were the two Vic had knocked unconscious. She probably broke the woman's arm.

Vic stood by the window, biting her lip while Hunt drew up behind her.

Morgan moved along the unconscious forms, checking each in turn. When she got to Claire, she spoke to her, eliciting brief nods and head shakes as she checked her over.

"What happened?" Hunt murmured from over her shoulder.

Vic shook her head, watching the doctor with Claire, feeling the need to stand guard just in case. "As soon as we got to the ladder, it was like whatever had taken over lost its hold on her. Like the connection was severed."

Silence stretched for a moment. "Vic, are you okay?"

She turned to look at him and wrapped her arms around herself. She was roughed up, but no worse for wear. It took more than a couple of Coppers to take her down. But it was watching another friend lose herself to whatever was doing this that sent pain spiraling through her.

"I'm fine."

"That was one of the scariest moments of my life," he said, reaching up to touch her hair.

It was to pull something from it, she realized, his hand coming away with a blade of grass pinched between his fingers.

"That's what happened to your entire village?"

Her grip on herself tightened. She almost said yes, but she stopped herself.

"I mean, that's what they all looked like. But this was different. In my village, they were literally trying to destroy each other. Claire wasn't trying to hurt me exactly. And neither were the others." She nodded toward the inert forms. "It was like they were trying to take me somewhere. Did any of them come after you guys?"

Hunt shook his head. "They were dead set on you only. Luckily there were only four of them."

She lifted a shoulder. "I've handled more before."

The ghost of a smile flashed across his face. "Remind me never to take you up on that arm wrestling challenge."

She couldn't even dredge up a laugh and simply groaned, rubbing her hands over her face. "I don't understand what is happening."

His palms skated up her arms so he could wrap his fingers around her wrists and bring her hands away from her face. "We'll figure it out."

She expelled a long breath and leaned forward. He dropped his arms around her, pulling her closer. The comfort that came from his embrace was something she didn't think she'd ever get used to.

It began to soothe her frayed nerves until he abruptly stiffened. She pulled back enough to look into his face.

"You think they were trying to take you somewhere." It wasn't a question, and he wasn't looking at her.

"What is it?"

He focused on her face, eyes narrowing. "Interesting timing that the day after a lieutenant colonel came around here looking for you—and I'm convinced he knows you're here, even if not where—and the others go apeshit trying to drag you off somewhere."

She pulled back further, and his arms dropped away. She tried not to think about how lost that made her feel for a second. "You think that half-bird had something to do with this?"

He cocked a brow. "Well, we know it's not you who's triggering them."

Her brows furrowed.

"They were around you all morning with no issues. And Claire snapped out of it once you'd gotten into the tunnel. Like you said, it was like the connection was severed."

She took a steadying breath. "You're right. Because if it were something about me, she would've stayed in that state the whole time."

"Until we know it's safe, we've gotta keep all the Unborn down here. I'm guessing that's what disrupts the signal."

Her frown dug deeper.

"You're the only exception." His expression sharpened, analyzing as he stared at her.

"I have a theory about that."

Vic whirled to face the doctor.

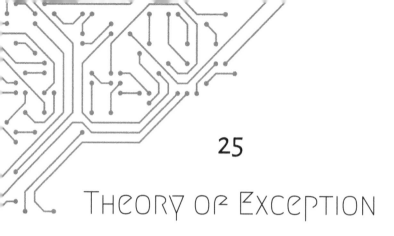

25

THEORY OF EXCEPTION

D ESPITE THE REPRIEVE Vic had given her earlier, Morgan's eyes were ringed by dark circles, her hair still a frazzled mess. Yet she strode forward to wake her computer up, a determination in her expression.

"I think there's something written into your DNA that blocks the ability of the signal to take a hold over your mind. Remember how your brain scans showed unusual activity in the prefrontal cortex?"

Vic nodded slowly while Hunt turned and moved closer to the doctor.

"I think the DNA that was used to design you—that unique Organic material—is acting like a buffer. That's what triggered the countermeasure to whatever mind control the rest of the Unborn are susceptible to."

Vic wrapped her arms around herself again, a sense of loneliness stealing through her. She'd worried about being wholly *other* from Hunt, and how that would cause problems. But now she seemed to be wholly *other* from those she was meant to be like.

Was she the only one? Time would tell when she heard back from Jamie and Alice.

But there were so many new questions. Like whether Angela had designed her this way on purpose? Or if it was a random side benefit no one had anticipated?

"What is it you're thinking, Vic?"

It was Hunt's voice that pulled her from her thoughts, and her fingers dug into her arms. "I was wondering if that countermeasure was intentional or not."

Hunt and Morgan exchanged a look, but it was Hunt who answered. "Based on what I understood growing up in these labs, which, to be fair, is rudimentary at best, none of the design of the Unborn has been haphazard."

Vic couldn't tell if that was a relief or not. Her stomach certainly kept up its twisting.

"But. . ." His frown deepened. "There are many things about Unborn that grew outside of their control. It's why they created the Uniforms. As much as they thought you could be controlled, genetically engineered or not, you are people, and people will refuse to follow every order without question."

"Free will." Vic nodded, smiling grimly. Like Jamie, there were plenty of Unborn who still ended up with a predisposition for rebellion.

"The age-old question of nature versus nurture still applies, even when every aspect of creation is controlled." Morgan's expression fell somewhere between a smile and a frown.

Vic snorted. "That's because we were still made by fallible humans." She thought of Angela and her apparent meddling in Vic's DNA.

Hunt shifted, likely thinking about his own father's manipulations.

Morgan regarded them with equanimity. "I suspect that if I do some ghost scans of the others' brains, I would find a different part of the brain had been activated, and likely the part that is still actively working in yours never would have fired in theirs."

Vic shook her head. "I can't believe you can do that."

Morgan's mouth tipped up a little. "I was not originally a medical doctor."

Hunt looked to Vic. "Morgan was studying to work on the Unborn project, specifically the neuroscience side. But then the war ended."

"And the funding dried up," Morgan added grimly.

It clarified why Morgan seemed to light up when they talked about these things. Like her serum.

Hmmm. The serum.

Vic glanced toward the window at the prone bodies, Claire lying back and resting with the others, who were still unconscious. "You said there was something in my DNA that triggered the countermeasure."

Silence met her statement.

She turned back. "And you made a serum for the rapid healing from the DNA of Unborn, right?"

"Yes." Morgan drew the word out, stretching it as her mind started whirling down the track Vic's was.

"Do you think you could do that for the mind control?"

Hunt divided a look between them, his eyes narrowing. "You mean like an antidote?"

Vic lifted her hands in a gesture of surrender, but desperation darted through her, burning under her skin. "We can't trap everyone down here forever. As nice as it is to have an insulated little community, no one can survive without sunlight and fresh air indefinitely."

Hunt's expression fell as that realization sank in.

Morgan was nodding and spun to face her computer again, pulling up programs and documents. "I'll get working on it. I've already got your DNA sequenced. It would be a few more steps and then we could have a prototype." She stopped and dropped her head. "But I can't devote the time right now. I need to check on Brody. . ."

"We'll stay with Brody," Hunt said, placing a hand on her shoulder. "Why don't you take the night off? Rest. Hit the ground running in the morning."

Morgan sighed, her fingers fluttering over her keyboard for a moment. She *wanted* to start right then. But wisdom won out and she nodded, casting Hunt a grim smile.

"Brody doesn't need much. Meds every eight hours, a dose of serum once tonight, and to be checked regularly."

Hunt nodded, then looked to Vic. He turned abruptly. "Maybe keep Claire and the others for the night, just in case. But I bet if you run checks on them, the danger has probably passed."

Morgan gave one tight nod and watched them go.

Hunt slid the door shut behind them and took Vic's hand, looking down at her.

"You said 'we'." She gave him a small smirk.

He cracked one of his rare full grins—she'd only seen it that day he was riding his horse, living the rancher life he was clearly built for. It was when she'd seen him at his lightest and most free.

"I don't plan to spend any time alone if I can help it from now on."

She swallowed, her heart tripping over itself in her chest. "Hunt. . ."

"It's a lot. I know. We can move things slow. But you already know I'm all in."

"I want to be all in, too. But what if. . ."

He shook his head. "There is no what if."

She laughed because, otherwise, she'd cry.

"Let's let tomorrow worry about itself."

She nodded, taking a cleansing breath. Because he was right. They could soak in what they had for the moment. Plus, there were so many other pressing things to worry about. Her heart was not the top priority.

"I told Niko we'd have dinner," she said as they began walking, passing the mess hall, which was filled with bustling people going about the usual business. Still, she felt the tension in the room like it was a perfume on the air. Everyone was worried about what had happened topside.

"He can come upstairs and hang with us for a bit. That way Max can keep an eye on the doc and the others without worrying about him."

Niko asked all the possible questions about the altercation earlier that day down to the last nano-detail.

What did it look like when Claire went dark?

Was it exactly the same when your village went berserk?

Did she try to kill you?

Did you think you would have to kill her?

When did she snap out of it?

Why did she suddenly come back to herself?

How come you didn't become psycho?

She finally shushed him when it seemed to pull Brody out of his troubled sleep. Pain twisted his features every time he moved, and she shot her concerned glances in Hunt's direction.

Even during their meal, tension never seemed to leave Hunt's body, and he spent more time on his feet, moving restlessly through the room than sitting with them. So much for letting tomorrow worry about itself.

Niko's peppered questions seemed to wind him tighter, and she felt the distance that formed between them like it was oceans instead of the few feet when he stood at the window, night creeping in beyond the glass.

They heard the heavy tread of the ranch hands who lived in the house on the stairs as they each headed to bed, ready for rest before they tackled the next day's tasks.

Brody's room was filled with dim light from a small lamp near the chair in the corner that Niko had curled up in, drowsily messing around on the tablet he'd brought upstairs with him.

Vic sat on the floor, her back against the wall, her legs drawn up to her chest.

"Are you worried?" she asked softly.

Hunt stiffened and turned. He looked briefly to Niko, whose eyes had slipped closed. Satisfied, he came over to sit on the floor next to her.

"I'm always worried."

She leaned her head against his shoulder. "More worried than usual."

He sighed, his exhale tickling the mess of her hair, which had half-fallen out of her its bun in her tussle with Claire. She'd never fixed it.

She was worried, too. About him, about Brody, about Claire, about her own unique chemistry, about who was looking for her and the lengths they were willing to go to find her.

That sense of being useless was a cold despair that wrapped itself around her body, sending the ache deep into her bones. The ranch was vulnerable to attack. Her new home, the people she cared about were unprotected. Unborn couldn't patrol, couldn't keep this place safe. And she would never be enough on her own, even if her presence out there wasn't already a liability.

The weight of failure sat like a stone in her gut. She was unable to do what she was made for when it mattered most. Again. She couldn't be the defense they needed.

But. . . maybe she could be the offense.

Her head jolted up as that thought rang loud in her mind. The lieutenant colonel had been sent to find her. And whoever he worked for was desperate enough to trigger Unborn to go dark to find her.

She needed to go to the source to make it stop. To make her home, her family, safe again.

"What is it?" The tension in his body told her he was prepared to not like her idea.

She curled her fingers inward as if preparing for a fight. "I need to see that half-bird. Haven."

"What? No!"

Vic glanced at Brody, who shifted but didn't wake at Hunt's out-burst.

"If I can get him away from the Uniforms," she said, lowering her voice to a whisper, "I think I could work him over for information on who's looking for me."

Hunt rubbed a hand down his face. "Vic. . ."

"I can't hide here forever, Hunt. I know that's sort of the life you've built here, insulated from everything else. But I can't sit back and wait for the big bad to come find me and put everyone I care about in danger. Not when it affects every Unborn."

He pulled away from her. "Is that what you think I do here? Hide?"

There was real hurt in his voice, but she couldn't deny that was how it looked from what she'd seen. And as much as that appealed to her, to the part of her that wanted peace, there was an unknown enemy out there. And she couldn't rest knowing she was bringing danger where she'd made a home.

"You have done so many amazing things for the people who live here. You protect them and provide for them. I've seen how deep your generosity runs. But I can't pretend there isn't a threat to my people, live in blissful ignorance when I know I could do something."

He stood, stopping her train of thought. His anger made her feel vulnerable on the floor, so she stood, too.

He whirled to face her. "Vic, you can't take care of the whole world. And maybe because you're stronger than everyone else, you think you can. Because that's what they built you to believe."

"Hunt—"

He held up his hand. "Fighting off Claire and the others is one thing. But you're not a superhero, and you can't fight an enemy you don't know."

"What did you say?" The strained voice came from behind them. Brody's concern cut through his labored breaths. "You fought Claire?"

Vic took a step forward, holding out a hand to calm him, knowing how bad it probably was for his healing to get worked up. "Brody, it's not—"

"What happened? Where is she?" He tried to get up, his fist slamming against the wall.

Niko jerked upright in the chair at the same moment something crashed to the floor in the room next door. They all stilled for a moment.

"Claire is in the bunker, but she's fine. She's not hurt." Vic kept her voice smooth and low as she walked to Brody's bedside. If he tried to get up again, she would strong-arm him down if she had to.

Her eyes slid to Hunt, but he wouldn't look at her. Instead, he strode toward the door to investigate what had fallen in the other room. Niko watched him go, shrinking a little at the intensity he still carried from their argument.

"Then what happened?" Brody flopped back onto his pillow, taking shallow breaths, wincing with the effort. His injuries were reminding him why he was in that bed. Maybe she wouldn't have to pin him.

She held up her hands. "We had a tussle. Neither of us were hurt, but Doc is checking her out."

Brody shot her a suspicious look, the emotion slicing through the haze of pain meds that floated in his system, and Vic took a deep breath.

"Claire and a few others went dark and attacked me. I tried very hard not to hurt anyone. She seemed fine when we got back in the bunker, but Morgan is making sure it doesn't happen again."

"Dark?" he huffed. "As in what happened. . . to your village?"

She nodded, aware of Hunt's return from the other room but ignoring the way his proximity lit little fires along her nerves. He set something on the bedside table, maybe whatever it was that had fallen in the other room. She glanced at it and back, then froze. Looking at it again, a flush of cold ran through her like ice water in her veins.

The cracks in the glass didn't mar the image enough to keep her from recognizing one of the faces in the picture. Still, she snatched the frame from the table to look closer, to make sure she wasn't seeing something that wasn't there.

"Vic?" Hunt's voice cut in, muffled in her ears, fading in and out.

Her heart punched at her ribs. "Wh-what is this from?"

"Why? What is it?" Hunt held his hand out for the frame like he didn't know what it contained. Had he even looked at it?

She let him have it and stood to take a few steps away, trying to quiet her mind and heart, both of which were inciting chaos inside her.

"It's my parents with some other scientists, I think. Back when the program first started." Hunt shrugged, handing the picture back, but he was staring at her, trying to understand.

She took it, ignoring the feeling that he was still wound up from their disagreement, but his confusion about her reaction seemed to override offense for the moment.

Staring down at the photo, she touched the glass lightly with her index finger, running it over the woman's face, ghosts stirring in her mind. "That's Angela. Doctor Angela Forman. She built me."

Hunt tilted his head. "It would make sense that she knew my parents. They were early participants."

Angela was younger, her hair still dark, though her features were sunken, and the sadness she'd always known the woman to carry was heavier over her expression. The man beside her held her close to him with an air of possessiveness that confused Vic. Angela had never mentioned anything about a family. And this man. . . he wore a wedding ring. And so did Angela. The diamond winked from the flash of the camera.

"Do you know who this man is?" She held the picture out to Hunt again, and he was slow to move his gaze from her face to the image.

He took his time studying the man, probably because he could tell his answer mattered. Then he shook his head. "This was a long time before I was born."

She reluctantly examined Hunt's parents in the picture, decades younger than in the picture with him. "You look a lot like your dad," she murmured.

He didn't smile. "What's wrong, Vic?"

She chewed her lip. "I don't know. I can't. . ." She shook her head as if she could knock the words, the memories, the answers loose.

But they wouldn't be there. Because this was many years before she'd been spliced together, carefully constructed in a lab that no longer existed. But it stirred something, made her feel like she should know.

"I never knew she was married." Her voice was barely audible, choked out by something like hurt. Angela hadn't betrayed her by keeping her past to herself. But why did it feel like she had?

"I found him."

Vic and Hunt whipped around to look at Niko, who'd clearly been listening in on the conversation. The glow from the screen of his tablet lit up his face, split in a proud grin.

26

To Seek & Find

"**H**IS NAME IS JARED Linus."

Vic handed the broken frame to Hunt and moved toward Niko like she was in a trance, lured there by some invisible force. She might have even stumbled. She couldn't tell. Her legs felt numb.

He turned the tablet to face her, showing a picture of the man. He looked older, the lines in his face deep crags that almost looked painful. He had sad, droopy eyes.

"He's some fancy suit," Niko said.

"Where did you hear that phrase?" Hunt asked dryly, sounding a lot like a father as he moved closer.

Niko shrugged.

Vic was too busy speed-reading the information the article provided to care where or how Niko had learned the colloquialism.

"Benefactor," she breathed, and the air flattened, pressing around her. Was it everyone else's reaction joining hers, or was it all just her?

Hunt was standing beside her now, reading over her shoulder. "He was involved with the Unborn Project from the beginning, financially supporting its inception and continuation."

"What did that half-bird's twig man say?" Vic straightened, looking from Brody's pain-clouded eyes to Hunt's. There was already a deep comprehension glimmering in the icy blue irises.

"He mentioned a benefactor." Hunt's tone was mild, but the knowing in his gaze sent shocks through her.

"What are the chances this Jared Linus is still involved somehow? And if he has the funds to throw around—"

"He would have quite a bit of influence." Hunt cocked his head. "The government is practically a mercenary outfit. If someone with money wanted something, or some*one*, they wouldn't have to go far for access to their own personal army."

The air was getting heavier and heavier, stifling, suffocating. Her lungs screamed. Any minute her ribs would crack from the pressure. Maybe this man was the one who'd called for the death trance. But why? Had he targeted her village because of Vic?

"You said you didn't know him," Niko said, an accusation in his tone.

Vic snapped from her spiraling thoughts and looked down. Niko had taken his tablet back, skipping through the dark web with the rapid efficiency only a computer whiz possessed.

Her brows pulled low over her eyes. "I don't."

Niko turned the screen to her again to show another picture of the man when he was much younger, this time with a little girl, maybe ten or eleven. A little girl who was Vic. But wasn't.

Cold seeped from her head to her toes, ice that spread through every inch of her body. "That's not me."

"She looks exactly like you," Hunt murmured, his eyes flashing to meet hers. A silent understanding passed between them.

Like twins, she thought, remembering her comment about Hunt and Max. Except for the pale blue of this other girl's eyes, they were identical.

The eye color matched the man's—Jared Linus—and the dark hair was a replica of Angela's in the picture. Though she'd been almost entirely gray by the time Vic was created, it was clear Angela had modeled Vic's dark tresses after hers. Or had spliced in her own DNA.

..

This girl. Uncanny.

Vic's stomach torqued. Unsanctioned.

Angela, like Hunt's father, had used the Unborn Project as an opportunity to alleviate the pain of her fractured family. Her attempt to fix what had been broken, she'd built Vic to be her replacement daughter—the one she'd had with this man who had once been her husband.

So what happened to the daughter and then their marriage? Or was it their marriage and then the daughter? But no, the look on Angela's face in the photo told the first story. Evidence of unimaginable loss.

Parents aren't supposed to outlive their children.

Vic looked back at Hunt, whose chest was moving with the force of his breathing. So she wasn't the only one who was off-kilter, feeling like the world was tilting again.

But she transferred her attention to Brody and checked the clock on the wall. He was intent on their conversation, though he was clearly in pain, the good half of his face contorted with the effort of enduring.

She brushed past Hunt to find the meds and the serum the doctor had told them about, administering the doses necessary, even though he glared at her.

"The conversation was just getting good," he croaked.

"Yeah, well, I'll fill you in if anything else interesting happens," she said dryly. Her stomach dipped at the thought of what other "interesting" things would come up. This had been enough.

Too much.

Almost immediately, his breathing eased, though he was clearly fighting the pull of sleep. She stayed on her knees next to him while he slowly drifted, trying to parse her whirling thoughts and feelings.

It was clear this Linus person was still alive and that he knew something, if not everything. It didn't seem coincidental that all of this information was coming to light—that he had been so heavily involved in the genesis of the Project, that he was still alive, that he'd been married to Angela, and that Vic looked like the daughter they'd likely lost.

That someone was looking for her.

Pushing to her feet, she met Hunt's eye, saying nothing as she walked to the door. There was no question now what she would do. She expected him to follow but wouldn't blame him if he didn't. She didn't need his approval, his input, or his help.

But she wanted it.

So when she heard him give Niko the order to stay put in a voice that brooked no disobedience, she felt a warmth that almost touched the cold stone that had settled somewhere in her chest, heavy and solid, hard to breathe around.

She went to his room since it was the only place she knew would be empty and waited in the dark for him. His footsteps were soft, and she thought again about how he'd been raised around Unborn. She wondered if he'd done any of the training being as close to Max as he was, wanting to be something that drew his father's interest when he'd buried himself in the work instead of the grief.

Hunt left the light off, though he shut the door. She didn't turn, even as his warmth seeped into her from behind. Her eyes remained on the window, the curtains wide open to let the diffused moonlight in, illuminating the room enough to caress the shapes of the sparse furniture.

"I need to talk to that half-bird."

His inhale was not quite sharp, but it was harsher than it should've been in the quiet. "I know."

She turned then, a burning in her eyes that she fought to control, to wrestle back. No tears, ever.

It was a motto she'd stuck to for a long time, always trying to be brave for the girls who looked up to her. But maybe that had been short-sighted. It made her seem untouched and untouchable. It colored what she did, made them—Jamie specifically—assume intentions where they didn't exist. Like she didn't care. But, if anything, she cared too much. Felt too much. And if she allowed the tears, they might never stop.

"I'm coming with you."

Her heart squeezed, a fist of fear wrapping around the muscle. "Hunt—"

"I can hear the argument in your voice, and I'm not having it. You aren't invincible, Vic. Maybe you think you are because you made it through the war when others didn't. And you alone escaped the massacre in your village. But you're not." He stepped forward, gripping her arms in his warm hands. "And I'll be damned if you go into this without backup. Without me." His voice dropped on that last part like it was painful to admit.

But he'd said all in.

"Okay."

His grip tightened around her arms. "Okay? You're not going to argue with me about it?"

She smirked a little at his incredulity. "No."

He stepped closer, loosening his hold. "So what's your plan, then?"

"I'm going to kidnap that lieutenant colonel and make him take me to Jared Linus."

He huffed a laugh, his breath tickling her hair. "Well, at least the plan is solid."

Anxiety plucked at her tension, making the chords of uncertainty sing. Because she didn't know *how* she was going to do it. Not yet, anyway. "It's the only way I can guarantee avoiding the Uniforms. I could probably take a couple, but you couldn't."

His mouth tipped. "I would be offended by how quickly you dismiss my capabilities in a fight, but I saw you take down four Unborn at once."

She chose to ignore his sardonic tone. "We're going into town tomorrow. Can I have my gun back?"

He raised a brow. "You mean the one you stole?"

She matched his expression. "The question stands."

"The colonel kept it."

She blew out a breath and tipped her head back. "Damn it."

He rolled his eyes. "I can get you a handgun if that's what you prefer."

"I know you like your big guns," she said with a sly smile. "But I want something easy to conceal."

He squinted at her. "Where would you even hide it?" He lifted the hem of her shirt as if to check, revealing her chiseled stomach, and he froze, his eyes tracing over her skin in surprise.

She felt it like a touch and sucked in a breath, drawing his gaze back to her face. Neither moved for one protracted second, a string of heartbeats filling the gap of time as he hesitated, and she sifted through what her next move would be.

All in.

Those two words pulsed in her mind with every pump of her heart, becoming a question that echoed through her blood. It ramped her heartbeat up, made a nervousness dance in her stomach. Was she ready?

She inhaled slowly, trying to banish the nerves as she slid her hands over his, palms skimming along his corded forearms. Need climbed from somewhere deep inside of her, begging, overwhelming the fear of this next step.

"Keep going," she whispered.

He swallowed. Hard. Then, gently, his calloused fingers brushed against her abdomen as he slipped his hands under her shirt, watching for her reaction.

How long, she wondered, how long had it been since she was touched? After their kiss a few days before, he'd felt the freedom to glide his hands along her arms, her face, her own hands. But her body had been neglected for a long, long time.

He didn't take his eyes from hers as he lifted her shirt higher and pulled it over her head. The fabric fell onto the floor, a whisper in the dark.

Then his palms, deliciously rough and warm, ran down her neck to her shoulders and halted for a moment when he felt the warped patch of skin that marred her upper arm and across her back, usually hidden by her clothes.

He took a step closer, leaning down to press his lips along the scar that was her permanent memento, the one that made sure she never forgot that being too close meant she could get burned. But his lips were a soothing balm as they moved slowly across her shoulder to her collarbone, and her eyes fell shut.

His fingers skimmed her sides, tickling along her rib cage. Could he feel her heartbeat vibrating through her bones?

He must have because she heard his smile and opened her eyes to look at his face. He was taking in every inch of her, his gaze following his hands as they traced over her.

When he deliberately touched a spot on one of her ribs with his fingertips, she knew he'd found her one hidden tattoo. It had been only for her—and Jamie and Alice. The rest of her tattoos had been to hide the proof of what she was. This one had been to protect the part of herself she held sacred.

"Rodina?" he asked quietly. He met her gaze, his eyes almost navy in the darkness.

Her heart throbbed. "It means *family.*"

He brushed the wild hair away from her face, resting his palm against her cheek. "We'll get them here."

She fought that burning in her eyes again, but she was so raw from his touch that her defenses were strangely weak, and the tears snuck out, leaving a warm trail down her face. He brushed them away with his thumbs then with his lips, peppering kisses across her cheeks, down her jaw, along her throat, across her collarbone again.

He slowly backed her up toward the bed in the corner of the room as his mouth found hers again, and they fell together, taking the time to discover all the hidden places on each other's bodies as the rest of their clothing fell away, the moonlight their only guide in the darkness.

The friction from his calloused hands along her skin was a welcome reminder that she wasn't numb, wasn't a machine. She felt. Everything was a burst of energy and light. Down to her toes, every nerve was alive with movement, sensation, and heat.

She'd burned before, and it was all pain.

But this... this was awareness and warmth and need and pleasure. A conflagration of consciousness.

The only worry she had as they moved together was how she would survive not having his hands on her every second of every day from then on. It seemed impossible that she would be able to function after this explosion of sensation. It stole through her at an alarming rate, a wildfire that could not be contained.

It blazed and consumed, melting away the frigid fear, every question she'd ever asked about who or what she was. It no longer mattered as every atom in her body warped in the heat, shifted, and became something new. Her world tilted on its axis again as they came undone in each other's arms.

It took her a long time to come back to herself after, utterly altered by his touch. She'd been with one other man before—another Unborn, of course—and only once the war was over, when the government no longer dictated their every move. But it hadn't lasted long, and it had never been like this. Her heart had never gotten involved, and Hunt's words from before floated through her drowsy mind.

She was all in now, too. There was no choice, not with this newness forged inside of her, the scorch marks that had burned through her soul as permanent as the scar along her shoulder.

Hunt was quiet beside her, maybe struggling to surface as well. His breathing was the only thing that punctured the silence, still coming faster than normal.

Her own heart was knocking hard against her ribs, and she rolled onto her stomach, burying her face into the pillow that smelled faintly of him—forest and petrichor.

He turned onto his side, his bare chest pressing against her arm as he propped his head on his hand. The other skimmed along her spine, sending shivers down her body.

She lifted her head and laid it across her folded arms to look at him, noting his faint smile, though his eyes followed the movement of his hand on her back. His smile dimmed when his fingers ran across the tight, warped skin of her scar again.

"I can't imagine how much this must have hurt," he murmured, never taking his eyes from her reminder.

She sighed, the ghost of the pain walking the halls of her memory, trailing its fingers along the walls to trigger a phantom ache in her skin. "It was blinding."

"What was it from?"

She lowered her lids. It'd been a long time since she'd shared the story, since anyone had asked. She didn't make a habit of showing it, let alone talking about what had caused it.

"We were in this little village. It was supposed to have been cleared by the unit ahead of us." She gave a grim smile that disappeared quickly. "Either someone wasn't thorough, or the enemy had sent more in after, knowing our habit of multiple sweeps.

"It was my fault. Even though it was cleared, it was stupid to relax our vigilance. A handful of us were going through the houses, checking for any usable supplies. Double-checking that it really was clear. But we'd done so many of those sweeps, finding no hidden enemy combatants, that we got lazy."

Hunt's hand continued its soothing trail along her spine. "I don't think anyone could call you lazy."

She shrugged. "I was careless. There was a guy. Maybe it was on orders, maybe he'd just been left behind. I don't know. But he was inside this house, hiding in a room I'd barely checked." She shook her head, knowing she hadn't been thorough enough. They'd been one mission away from a reprieve, and she was eager to get her unit back, to give them the break they deserved.

"He caught us with his last grenade. Took out the two guys I'd brought with me. Then he jumped me. He didn't even care if he died. I saw it in his eyes. Anyway, the house went up in flames from the explosion, and I wrestled him to the ground with the fire building around us. He was crazy, but I was able to. . ." *Snap his neck.* She couldn't get the words out. After a tense silence, she continued, "By the time I got him down, the fire was everywhere. It was unavoidable as I tried to get out of the house, and the sleeve of my uniform caught. It ate through the fabric so fast, seared me underneath, even though I threw myself to the ground as soon as I was outside."

Hunt's hand had stopped moving as she spoke, but he was watching her face, his expression very soft.

"I don't remember much after that. I had to walk back to the rest of my unit without the other guys, my shoulder and back totally exposed, layers of skin missing. I do remember the agony. Collapsing when I got back to camp. I ended up with an infection from the burn being out in the open for so long."

She didn't want to recount her days in the hospital. Unborn healing only went so far when it came to deep wounds and infection. It was faster than normal, but it was still miserable.

Silence blanketed them for a long time. He didn't resume his movement, but simply rested his hand flat on the small of her back. Eventually, he pressed feather-light kisses along the scar.

"We should probably check on Brody and Niko," she whispered, stirred by his loving attention to the damage left on her body.

He grinned, pulling her closer. "Probably."

She pushed against him, laughing softly. It was easy to break away, even when he fought to keep her against him, his muscles straining to hold her.

She stamped a kiss across his mouth. "Don't try me. I will win."

He huffed as she stood to dress, then did the same.

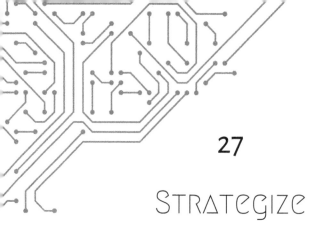

27

Strategize

B RODY AND NIKO WERE dead asleep when they went back into the room. It wasn't likely Brody had awakened since his doses at all. Niko's mouth hung open, his tablet dark as it rested on his chest where he'd dropped it.

She settled on the floor, and Hunt joined her. They took turns dozing until the light cut through the window.

She lifted her head from Hunt's shoulder to blink the sleep from her eyes as the sun poked in. His lids were still closed, his chest rising and falling in a deep rhythm that meant he hadn't woken yet.

So she stood to check Brody, who seemed to be breathing much better. Even the swelling on the one side of his face seemed to have gone down.

Niko stirred but simply curled into a ball in the chair and continued to doze. His tablet had fallen onto the floor sometime during the night, and his arm draped down, fingers brushing the edge like he couldn't be parted from it even in sleep.

She did a quiet stretching routine, the stiffness she'd woken with reminiscent of her long nights in foxholes or crouched near the half-fallen wall of a building, waiting for light to be able to move or fight.

Once finished, she drifted toward the window, seeing the movement of the ranch hands at the barn. She wondered how early they got up to start work and realized she hadn't heard them head down the stairs whenever it was they'd gotten up.

The door clicked open, and Vic turned, her hands gripping her opposite elbows in a small hug. It was Morgan who poked her head in, looking more refreshed now that she'd had a whole night of rest.

Morgan's hazel eyes lit upon each of the sleeping men and walked quietly across the room to where Vic stood at the window.

"How'd it go?" she whispered, barely audible.

"We had a moment with Brody. He was concerned about Claire."

Morgan clicked her tongue. "That man."

Vic fought her smile. She wasn't the only one who'd noticed his partiality for the dark, willowy woman.

"How was your night?" Vic asked.

"I got a few good hours. The others are back with the rest of the Unborn. I'm monitoring them. The ghost scan confirmed that same area of the brain had been lit up. They don't have the countermeasure, as we suspected."

Vic pursed her lips, a sense of responsibility she shouldn't bear pressing against her shoulders. But even though she hadn't wired any of them this way, it was because of her that Claire and the others had even gone dark.

"I've got something figured out to try for a serum," Morgan continued. "It would function sort of like a beta-blocker. The biggest hurdle would be testing it."

Vic's finger tapped against her arm. They didn't have much time for testing. Not if she wanted to get to the half-bird and then find this Linus person. Because she didn't expect that second part being doable without help. As much as she hated using that endeavor as the test, it might be their only option. The stakes wouldn't be high until they reached their final destination, anyway. To be on the safe side, they'd only take four at most. Fewer, maybe.

"If you can get us a test soon, that would be ideal. Today, if possible." Vic looked at Morgan, hoping she wasn't asking too much.

Morgan's brow furrowed, but there was a hard determination on her face that made Vic feel more confident about her abilities and her commitment to making it happen.

She turned to face the room and found Hunt staring at her from his spot on the floor, his expression hard to read.

Niko and Brody still slept.

"If not, we can test it on the road tomorrow."

Morgan looked between the two of them, comprehension just out of reach. "Tomorrow?"

"We're heading out to find some answers," Vic replied. "I'm definitely going to need some backup."

Morgan's eyes got larger as horror settled into place. "What if the blocker doesn't work?"

"I can take a few Coppers on my own." Vic gave her a grim look and tipped her head. "But maybe throw in some sedatives as backup."

Morgan sucked in a breath, her urge to argue a twinge in the air.

Vic turned to Hunt before she could say anything. "Right now, Hunt and I have a lieutenant colonel to kidnap."

The door to the bunker looked innocuous. A linen closet easily ignored. The one she would have thought was the entrance to the bunker was, in fact, a door to the basement.

That was likely on purpose, she thought as Hunt yanked the string attached to the naked bulb that hung just inside the door. He led her down the rickety steps, and she supposed the unused feel of the space was intentional as well. It was creepy, dank, and covered in cobwebs. Once they reached the bottom, it solidified the impression. Old boxes, broken furniture, evidence of a life lived decades ago, slept in the loneliness of the darkness, heavy with silence and memory.

Hunt practically waded through the junk to get to an even darker corner where an old water heater and furnace sat. But as she followed him behind what looked like a stack of more boxes, he pulled open a door that nearly blended in with the wall, turning on a dim light that permeated only the small space.

It turned out to be a weapons cache. More guns than he probably needed resided here, and her eyes grew round as she took it all in.

His own gaze swept the space, a slight frown on his face. "During the war, it became imperative that the lab remain protected. There was a military contingent stationed here at all times. Because this was the first lab, it had some of the most valuable information."

Vic couldn't fathom, had had no idea, though it made sense, considering many of the other labs, including the one she'd been created in, had been targeted and destroyed by enemy nukes.

"Handguns are on the far wall."

He pointed, and she headed that way, realizing why he and Brody seemed to have a military quality about them. They really had been raised in this, even if they'd never gone to fight. By the time they were old enough, the war had ended.

She selected a small nine-millimeter that she tucked into her waistband, flipping her shirt over to cover it. Then she grabbed a second larger one, same caliber, and some extra magazines.

"Seriously. Where are you going to keep all that?" Hunt asked, smirking as she walked past him.

"I've been learning to conceal weapons since I was a kid. I have my ways." A slow smile spread across her face. "And if you behave, I'll let you look for all my hiding spots."

He let loose a little growl that made her laugh, and they headed back up the stairs.

Hunt apparently had his own stash of smaller weapons. She made a quick breakfast with supplies in the fridge while he changed and strapped up in his room upstairs.

After she set their plates on the table, she undid her hair and finger-combed the dark tresses, pulling more blades of dried grass as she went. Then she redid the low pony tail, pulling the dark locks forward over her shoulder before sitting to wait.

It wasn't long until Hunt was making his way back down, his gilded locks dark with moisture and brushed back from his face. They ate quickly, Vic so distracted, she barely tasted it. Hunt's eyes flickered to her face as she stood to put the dishes in the sink, but he said nothing as he led the way outside and to the barn.

In the recesses of the building, in the half that wasn't taken up by horses, he kept the truck parked. In a bay next to the truck, there was a large transport trailer, and she thought of the horses, then the cows she knew he probably took to be slaughtered on a regular basis, and a weird twisting started in her gut.

She remembered the joke they'd all made in the back of those heavy transports during the war, crammed in tight, weighed down by gear and anticipation. They'd make animal sounds—pigs and cows, mostly—chuckling darkly as they drew closer to the deafening sounds of war beckoning.

She turned from the trailer and got into the truck on the passenger side. Once they left the property line, they bounced over a crumbled road, and she reached up to grip the handle above the door. It did little to stop the jostling, and she wondered if the problem was the road or the aged suspension of his vehicle.

It was noisy enough that they weren't able to speak. Not that there was a lot of time for it. They weren't far from the city. It had seemed much farther when she'd been trekking through the woods in the dark. But she'd also come from a completely different direction, on foot, no less.

Hunt knew the general area where the colonel and his contingent of mechs were because it was where most people with money and power stayed. And because he knew where to look, he also knew where to park the truck so the colonel wouldn't pick up on their presence.

They stopped on a deserted street and got out. She pulled out the two guns she'd tucked under the seat where she'd hidden them in case they were pulled over. The smallest went into a makeshift holster she'd fashioned under her bust. The other she tucked more obviously in the back waistband of her pants, as usual.

Hunt came around the front of the truck. "Here."

She glanced up, noting that he wasn't obviously packing, impressed with his ability to conceal it all.

He held a pair of sunglasses in her direction. She took them, needing no explanation. Even though she'd been told there was another group of Unborn living somewhere in the city, she knew how rare Silvers were among any population. And considering that Haven and his men were looking for her, it was safer to disguise herself any way she could.

"This might end up taking a while," she said, sliding the glasses on. "First, we have to locate Haven. Then we have to wait for the opportunity to corner him alone."

Hunt squinted across the pockmarked road to the smaller side street that cut between two half-collapsed buildings then put on his own pair of sunglasses. Probably to make hers seem less conspicuous.

"You're good with me being in charge?" she asked.

His gaze swung back to her, the left side of his mouth quirked up. "I don't mind taking orders."

Her mouth twisted. "Could've fooled me."

"My ranch is different than a mission."

She snorted. "Mission." But it was definitely reminiscent of some of the assignments she'd been given in the war.

Recon, systematically capture a stronghold, sweep an area for combatants. She'd always been the logical choice for those missions. This kidnapping mission definitely fell under the smash-and-grab category—Jamie's wheelhouse. For one of the first times in her life, Vic tried to channel her sister.

Hunt waited for her as she donned her beat-up jacket. It had been through the wash, the stains miraculously washed out of the fabric, but it was still torn and frayed, worse for wear. But she needed something to hide any possible glimpses of the guns she was concealing.

As soon as she finished, slamming the heavy door of the truck, Hunt nodded toward the side street, and they cut across the empty road to get to that darkened corner.

She could feel the tension that radiated off him, though he still moved with the smooth ease of a man who was used to this life. She, by comparison, was buzzing with eager anticipation, the latent soldier in her coming back to life.

The things that made her feel alive and fully human only a few hours before, when Hunt's hands had explored her body, seemed to fall away and she was reminded again of what made her different, what made her feel more like the machine she'd always feared she was: a robot with a beating heart. All of what was inside of her was flesh and blood, but it was no less programmed and planned than a Uniform.

She slowed when they came to the corner of the smaller street, drawing closer to one of the more solid buildings that flanked them. She pressed her right shoulder to the brick, and Hunt came to lean with her. She peeked around the edge of the building.

"I think they're staying up there, at the Radisson," Hunt said from behind her.

"Is there a restaurant or cafe in the lobby?" She turned to look at him, the shadow half-obscuring his face and digging deeper canyons underneath his cheekbones. It made his eyes darker too, and she was briefly reminded of the way they'd looked last night.

He nodded. "I've met a couple of my buyers there before."

It sounded shadier than it was, though being employed by some rich and powerful people like Hunt was meant that he operated in some shades of gray. Still, the funds enabled him to keep the ranch running and the people in his care fed and provided for. The world was so gray these days, it didn't really matter that those who kept him in business were likely the ones pulling the strings for the political puppet show that ran the country. Or at least this half of the country. These days, with that wasteland between the coasts, there was no way the United States was all that united.

She nodded for him to take the lead, and he walked out into the morning sunlight with her close at his heels. She focused on making her movements more casual as they made their way down the side-walk to the entrance of the hotel.

Hunt went to the front desk, walking with a certain confidence that told her he knew what he was doing. He slipped some credits on the counter then leaned sideways against it.

"Good morning, Ian."

The young man's eyes flickered down and up. "Mr. Listmann."

She kept her reaction to his last name in check. She'd never heard it before.

"I have a question for you," Hunt said.

"Yes?" The man shifted, his shoulders inching upward until he caught himself.

"There's a military guy staying here. Some kind of colonel. He's got himself a few Uniforms. Really creepy-looking."

Ian's throat bobbed with a swallow, and Vic could tell by the way his eyes darted to a side door and back that he knew who Hunt was talking about.

"I'm just wondering where he might be staying."

"Like his room number?" Ian asked.

Hunt's smile was slow but friendly. "That would be a start."

"Well, we're not allowed to give that information out." Ian's eyes slid sideways again, the same direction and, without turning her head, Vic looked that way too. A door leading to what looked like private bungalows surrounded by a large, concrete wall was tucked back into a corner.

If the information on Linus was accurate, he might've been footing the bill for some expensive lodging. And it would seem more likely that the hotel wouldn't want to house Uniforms in the main part of their building where their distinguished guests might want a different experience than what they saw out on the streets on a daily basis.

"I understand, Ian." Hunt winked at the man, pushing the credits closer to his side of the desk.

"No problem, Mr. Listmann." He swallowed again. "Sorry I couldn't be of any help. We've been pretty busy cleaning. I still have bungalows *seven* and eight to take care of."

Hunt tipped his chin in an understanding nod, turning to give Vic a satisfied smirk.

The credits that had been in front of the concierge were nowhere to be seen as Vic glanced back at him. He looked less nervous than he had initially, and she filed that away, making a note to be on her guard.

Hunt led the way toward the door to the private courtyard where a swimming pool was ringed by little hut-like buildings, but he stopped before pushing out into the sunshine.

"How do you want to play this?" he asked.

She squinted out the door, still not having removed her sunglasses. "There aren't a lot of options for hiding. What are the odds he'll come in here?"

Hunt's lips flattened as he considered. "It's hard to say. He might be milking this more than usual because he's on someone else's dime—bungalows are pretty high-brow. Room service seems a likely scenario."

"Room service," she repeated, turning that over in her mind, scanning the hall to their left that led to what appeared to be offices and employee spaces.

Hunt noticed where her attention had gone. "You think you want to sneak in by pretending to work here?"

She pursed her lips, raising a brow. "I've always wanted to go undercover. Plus, I doubt he'll have any of the mechs staying in his room with him. They're no more than machines, so they probably don't need much."

No more than machines. Vic had to shake the thought from her head. She'd heard the same sentence spoken about herself before.

The division in her mind and body about where she fit on the spectrum would rip her apart if she let it.

So she focused on the *Employees Only* sign down the hall. "This way."

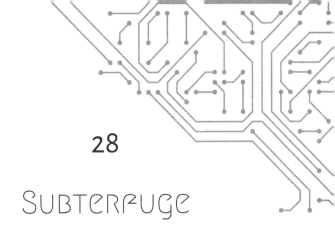

28

SUBTERFUGE

S HE FLIPPED THROUGH THE rack of uniforms for one that might fit
Hunt. He would get by unnoticed more easily than she would
with her obvious unnaturally silver eyes. It would never have been a
shame he was so tall and broad except in this kind of situation.

Hunt checked the clock on the wall. "It's not quite lunchtime."

She looked at the time as well, then pulled out a set of clothes
that looked like they would work. "Not yet, but I'm going to bet he's
gotten his order in. We can hover, get a jump on it as soon as his food
is ready."

She passed Hunt the uniform, and he frowned as he took it.

"You'll get us in," she said, low and fast. "But I'm asking the questions. I figure since he's a human, you can probably handle him if he
gets out of line."

He gave her a dry look as he pulled the crisp white shirt off the
hanger.

She glanced out the cracked door and back. "It only seems fair. If
I take him on. . ." It would be too easy to incapacitate the man, and
they needed him conscious. And alive.

Hunt snatched the maroon vest next, putting it on over the ill-fitting shirt. At least he could button it all. Put together, it didn't look half bad.

"I don't mind taking a crack at him after what happened to Brody." His voice was a low growl, drawing her gaze from what his fingers were doing.

She wasn't sure how deep his anger ran, but the heat of it seared the air. She'd never seen him angry before—not like this. Vengeful. She took comfort in the fact that it would take a lot for him, as an Organic, to do permanent damage, and she could stop him if it went too far. Part of her wouldn't be upset if she let it go a touch over the line though.

"You first. I'll shadow," she murmured, waiting for him to lead the way.

When he did, she fell in behind him, their footsteps silent on the worn carpet. She tracked his breathing, his movement, the way his hand contracted in an effort to dispel his anxiety. He'd handled the front desk easily, though she'd read tension in his body then, too. Subterfuge and clandestine missions like this weren't everyday things for him. He might've been forced by life to operate in gray, but very little of it had to be under the radar and certainly never involved physical violence against another person.

But he didn't complain as he walked into the kitchen with his commanding presence as his mask. The appearance of confidence might not make anyone question him, but his stature might. He was only a slightly better choice in this scenario as an Organic.

"Bungalows?" he asked the kitchen manager when she drew closer to the carts already being loaded with covered dishes.

The manager did a double-take, surveying Hunt before pointing to the four carts lined up, little folded cards with numbers printed in a fancy script resting next to the dishes.

Vic fought the urge to roll her eyes. Pretentious. In a world that was falling apart, the need to keep up appearances for the wealthy among them was laughable.

Hunt stepped over. "Are they ready?"

The manager shook her head, rushing to address a few other orders whose savory scents had Vic salivating. She'd never had pan-seared salmon, but it smelled delicious.

"One more dish for six and seven."

Hunt drummed his fingers along his thigh and glanced back to Vic in the hallway, pressed against the wall to keep out of sight. Their eyes met.

"Here."

Hunt jerked back to the manager, almost lurching forward, but he held back, trying to keep his nerves in check.

He touched the handle of the nearest cart. "Seven first?"

The manager looked at him sharply, and Vic stiffened.

"For that fancy colonel?" Hunt clarified.

"Yeah, I suppose that's a good idea. Dude makes me nervous with all those robots," the woman muttered as she moved back to the plates appearing on the warming rack.

Vic released a slow breath as Hunt tugged the cart toward the door and peeked around the corner to check that everyone in the kitchen was too busy to pay any attention to them. Darting forward, she pressed the bar on the door, opening it to the courtyard so that Hunt could roll the food out. She checked the surroundings once, twice, three times. Again. She didn't want to be ambushed. There was no telling if the lieutenant colonel was keeping the Uniforms on a steady guard rotation or maybe even a patrol. They would be tireless, capable of round-the-clock sweeps.

But it was evident the half-bird didn't think he had much to worry about here. She spotted no patrols as she continued to slink along the buildings while Hunt walked confidently to the seventh bungalow.

Once they reached the door, she gestured for them to switch places and waited until Hunt got into position. He pulled his handgun from a hidden holster and held it pointed toward the ground. He gave a quick nod, so she knocked.

"Yes?"

Definitely Haven. It was quiet enough in the room that she didn't think anyone else was in there with him.

"Room service," she replied, figuring a woman's voice would be less suspicious than Hunt's baritone. She looked briefly at him as the footsteps sounded from the other side of the door, getting louder as he drew closer. Her heartbeat slowed, the sense of purpose in what they were doing calming any jumping nerves.

The door swung open. "That was fast."

Hunt's gun flew up. The muzzle stopped at the lieutenant colonel's temple, only a centimeter from kissing his skin, and Haven stiffened.

"I heard you were looking for me," Vic said with a dark smile as the shock crept across the half-bird's face. His mouth opened and shut like he was choking on air.

She shoved the cart into him, and he grunted, hinging at the hips before he backed up, allowing them to push inside the little cabin.

She shut and locked the door as Hunt urged him back into the sitting area with a flick of his gun. When she joined the men in the sitting area, the lieutenant colonel's demeanor had morphed from fear to righteous indignation. Red crept up his neck and a vein pulsed in his forehead.

"You might have some friends in high places, Listmann, but I'll make sure your buyers go elsewhere for their supplies," Haven spat, his eyes blazing as he stared up at Hunt.

Hunt, for his part, was as stoic as ever, no betrayal of emotion in the depths of his cerulean eyes as he stared right back.

"We have some questions for you, Lieutenant Colonel," Vic said, pulling Haven's gaze to her.

He seemed to shrink a little bit, and she wondered if he'd ever had actual contact with Unborn, if he'd even seen combat. Not that it mattered. None of the Organics would deign to fight once the Unborn were available. The speed with which the government churned out new Coppers was astounding, really, and made it so that combat was a thing of the past for the people worth keeping alive.

Haven seemed too young to have been anything more than a pup when the war ended.

"You know, we also have a beef to sort out," Vic continued, walking toward the window, dragging the man's gaze all the way across the room. "See, you really hurt a good friend of ours."

Hunt's muscles coiled tighter, and it became clear why he was doing so well at concealing his feelings. It was an unholy fury that burned through him, and that required a level of control that bordered on psychotic. She felt the sizzle across the room.

Haven swallowed when her eyes landed on him. The sunlight bounced off the silver, making little reflections dance across his paled face. "I didn't—"

"Didn't you?" she growled. "I've decided it wouldn't be fair if I took the matter into my own hands. That's not an even match, is it?"

Haven's confused expression gave her a sick sense of satisfaction, and she could see it in Hunt's eyes, too. But Haven looked to the man holding the gun, and realization dawned quickly.

"Only seems fair for an Adam to take on an Adam." Her voice had darkened, driving her point home.

"I-I'll answer your questions. Whatever you want," Haven said, lifting his shaking hands.

She tipped her head to the side, disgust an acidic smoldering in her stomach that he would so readily give up any information. A disgrace to the uniform, really. Lieutenant colonel, indeed.

"Of course you will," she said, working to keep her lip from curling back. "Hunt will make sure of it."

She lifted her weapon to keep it trained on the half-bird when Hunt lowered his. He wasted no time laying into Haven, the sound of his fist hitting flesh a dull *thwop* in the small space.

"I want to know more about this benefactor who sent you to the ranch," she said, walking to a pile of papers on the desk in the corner. She brushed them aside, speed-reading the contents in case there was anything important she might find there.

Haven raised his head, glaring at Hunt, a small dribble of blood leaking from the corner of his mouth.

"A general," he said breathlessly. "He wants to know how you beat the kill switch."

She stiffened but tried to conceal it as she turned to look at him. She had expected him to give up Linus immediately. So maybe she was on the wrong track here. And with how sniveling he'd been a moment before, his smug look now made her wonder which was the true face: the scared, paper-pushing half-bird, or the know-it-all lieutenant colonel. Things weren't adding up.

"What general?" she asked, her voice even despite the unease that clamped around her gut.

Haven almost smiled, absently licking at his lip. He took too long to answer, and Hunt slammed his fist into the man's face again.

He hissed and turned his face away, spitting bloody saliva onto the aged carpet.

"His name, half-bird." She leaned more heavily on impatience, hoping he'd feel the weight of it.

"O'Rourke," Haven gritted out.

"He have a first name?" she prompted.

Haven narrowed one eye at her, his head lolling to the side like it was an effort to hold it up. "Kevin. General Kevin O'Rourke."

They'd have to look him up if they had time once they were back in the bunker. Maybe Niko could do a search through the dark web, though a pang shot through her knowing how dangerous that was. He'd happily do it if she asked, but if she could avoid it. . .

A noise outside the bunker drew her gaze. Movement. From what she gathered, there weren't many staying in the bungalows, and she wondered, based on the lieutenant colonel's expression, if it might be a mech coming to check up on him.

She strode forward, lifting her gun to press the barrel against his forehead. "Good news: you get to come with us. You're going to take us to see the general. And the man who's financing this little project."

Haven's face paled, so she knew that had landed. She liked knocking him down a peg when he'd clearly been trying to keep at least one thing from her. He thought he had leverage, but she'd taken it away.

She jerked a nod at Hunt, who yanked the colonel to his feet. He barely stood at eye-level with her, which was not terribly unusual given that she was more than above average height. But still, it almost made her laugh to think he'd been so ready to throw his weight around.

They dragged him toward the front door, though that unease clamped in her stomach again. They hadn't planned out their exit, and the direction they'd come brought them through some exposed places. Surely there was another exit that wouldn't require they leave through the lobby—a fire exit, something.

She wasn't gentle with the gun as she rammed it into Haven's ribs, and he grunted. "You don't say a word if you want this to be painless. I let Hunt take the lead the first time, but I'm not going to be as magnanimous from now on."

He must have believed her because, when they opened the door to an empty courtyard, he said nothing and made no noise to change that. He hadn't struck her as the brave type.

They moved as a unit back to the door of the hotel lobby, but that didn't seem like the best course of action. Her gaze darted from one end of the area to the other until her attention landed on a corner that seemed particularly covered with fake trees and plants. Like it was an attempt at camouflaging something important.

She jerked her head at Hunt, who'd been watching for her signal. They moved together with Haven between them toward the corner. Sticking her hand through plastic leaves and branches, she groped for what lay beyond and found a door handle. A sense of accomplishment rolled through her like warm molasses. Stepping through first, she checked the sidewalk for anything out of the ordinary.

Her gaze snagged on a Uniform marching along the length of the front of the hotel. Her whole body seized, and Hunt went rigid as well. She traced the mech's track. He would go around the corner in a moment, so she forced her frozen body to release, only her breath remaining trapped in her lungs until he disappeared.

Her nerves jumped as she led them out and slid the sunglasses back on, not eager to draw attention to their little party as they stiffly moved down the sidewalk toward the alley that would lead them to the truck.

The Uniform came into view a half-second before they slipped around the corner, and every one of her muscles snapped to attention. That eerie, unblinking stare seemed to land on them just as they disappeared from view, and she jerked them all forward, rushing toward the truck.

The tight silence pressed around them, and she found herself jamming the gun harder into Haven's side without intending to. Still, he didn't complain, though she caught his unending grimace from the corner of her eye. She had to give him props for his commitment to her warning.

Something stirred in her that maybe she couldn't trust his cooperation, that there was something he knew that they didn't, and she cast her eyes behind them for a moment, checking to see if that mech was following. There was no one, but the sense that something was wrong rattled her bones.

Hunt sent her a questioning look, but she gave a tight shake of her head. She certainly didn't want to mention it when they were still exposed and definitely not in front of the half-bird. She wanted to get back to the truck as soon as possible. It might not have been a guarantee of safety, but it was one step closer, and they could move faster on wheels than on foot.

The truck sat innocuously where they'd left it, and Hunt stripped the hotel uniform while Vic shoved the half-bird in, sliding in next to him. Hunt hauled himself in behind the wheel, sandwiching Haven between them. She turned toward the half-bird as Hunt fired up the engine, pressing her back against the passenger door.

Haven's lips were flat and colorless as the vehicle lurched away from the curb. His tongue darted out, running over the slice in his lip from Hunt's punches, but the man barely moved otherwise.

His stillness made her edgy, little pinpricks of uncertainty tingling along her skin as they started down the decrepit road. Her eyes narrowed to slits as they made their first turn at the corner.

Then the lieutenant colonel curled in on himself, ducking his head between his knees, and Vic's nerves ignited.

"Hunt—" she started, but she was cut off by the window that shattered behind her head, spraying glittering shards of glass like tiny crystalline knives into the cab of the truck.

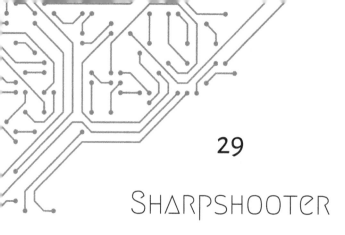

29

SHARPSHOOTER

I MPRESSIVELY, HUNT DIDN'T WAVER. She expected him to jerk the wheel, pop up onto a curb, or hit something. He simply ducked as he muttered a low curse and pressed his foot harder into the gas pedal.

The truck jumped forward, the engine a roar that filled her ears, even as she kept her focus on the military man in front of her. She only took her eyes away when her body alerted her to the pain that seared along the fleshy part of her shoulder. She glanced down at the sleeve of her jacket, quickly darkening with fresh blood. So it was a bullet, and she'd been incredibly lucky.

She looked up. There was a hole where the bullet had blasted through the ceiling only a few inches from Hunt's head. Rage slammed through her, a tidal wave of heat that pulsed within her entire body, setting a fire in her blood. A wildness chased it, and for once in her life, no thought for plans or protocols flashed into her mind.

"One of yours?" she asked through her teeth, pressing the gun against the lieutenant colonel's thigh, and she was ready, so ready, to pull that trigger, give him a taste of what many of her kind had suffered through and gone back for because it was expected of them. She'd been shot before, so she knew that her shoulder had merely been grazed, but it was the bullet's proximity to Hunt that fanned the flame of her anger.

Haven's eyes glowed with panic, probably because he realized what exactly she was feeling in that moment. He opened his mouth, but she didn't give him a chance. Pulling the gun back, she slammed it against his skull, knocking him unconscious. He slumped into her lap, and she almost kicked him away, but it would hinder Hunt's ability to drive.

She searched along his body for a bug or device—whatever it was that had brought the Uniform's bullet within inches of them. But by the time she found it, they'd made it out of the city, and probably far enough away from whoever had taken the shot at them.

She crushed the tiny device—a tracker, looked like—and tossed the pieces out the gaping window, then met Hunt's gaze across the cab.

"You okay?" he asked, eyes going to her shoulder.

She looked down at her torn sleeve, eyeing the bloody mess her arm was becoming. "I'll be fine. It's just a graze." She gave him a grim look. "Might have given our baby colonel a concussion though."

Hunt didn't even spare the other man a glance.

"That bullet came so close. . ." She shook her head, the rage blossoming inside of her again. But she knew what it was there for: to cover the abject terror at the idea of losing this man before her, the one who had come to mean more to her than almost anyone else she'd had in her life.

"It didn't entirely miss," he reminded her, his eyes dropping to her bleeding arm again. Some measure of her feelings was reflected in his expression.

"Good thing I'm a quick healer," she muttered, turning to face forward as they made their way to the house.

It was gilded gold in the afternoon sunlight that cut through the trees, blanketing it in a warm glow that beckoned them forward. And then something cold and dark wended its way through her gut, a premonition, a secret knowledge that filled her with the weight of dread.

"They're going to come to the ranch," she murmured, feeling an aching sense of loss as a horse trotted to the fence closest to her side of the truck, curious about who'd arrived.

Hunt cut her a sideways glance.

"We have to take them out."

"After you get patched up," Hunt insisted.

"No." She felt it deep in her bones. They wouldn't have time, though, ideally, they'd leave, and the Uniforms would follow instead of coming for their home, their family.

She jolted at the thoughts, reminded of how solid that truth had become, that she'd started to see this as the place she belonged. She'd planted her knowable future in the soil she'd stumbled upon. Of course, that had a lot to do with the way she was now tethered to this man, this Organic who had been so reluctant to open himself to her, showing her that once he did, it meant more than anything else would have. But it had started when she'd invited the only family she'd ever known to join her in this new community.

"Vic, I can't let you bleed all over the place while we wait for something that may or may not happen. How the hell are you supposed to accomplish anything with a wound—"

"That's already stopped bleeding and will heal in a matter of days instead of weeks like you Organics?" she interrupted.

He was silent for a moment as he parked the truck next to the house. "You called me an Adam back there."

She didn't move for a moment, tracing back to the moment he was referring to. And although the name "Adam" had been something she'd rarely used, it did have the same connotation as "bottle-bred" did for the Unborn. Degrading and slanderous.

"It was part of the facade." She didn't have much energy to pour into the conviction in her tone. It was true, even if her explanation seemed flimsy in the moment.

Hunt's face was unreadable, then his eyes shifted to the unconscious man between them.

"We better get this guy inside. I'll get some ranch hands on watch while you see the doc." He ignored her sharp look. "Maybe have her check Haven out, too, in case you caused any brain damage."

Neither of them smiled at his joke.

Her jaw shifted forward. "I have a better idea: I get him inside, you get me a rifle, and I'll situate myself in an upstairs window."

"Vic—"

"I'll get the damn rifle myself, then." She shoved her door open, sprinkles of broken glass falling to the ground. She shook the rest out of her jacket, miraculously keeping her wince from the movement at bay.

Hunt expelled an exasperated sigh as he got out and leveled a hard look at her, which she returned. She vaguely wondered if he regretted showing her where his weapons cache was.

He slammed his door. "Fine. I'll get you the gun."

She gave one quick nod and lugged Haven from the front seat, throwing him over her shoulder as Hunt followed her toward the house.

If Morgan had gotten those beta-blockers working, she could have a contingent of Unborn to help fight the Uniforms off. But she wasn't going to hold her breath for that miracle. Not that she knew what kind of ability they would be up against. Her one experience with the mech in her village hadn't given her much to go on, and she'd been half in shock at the time.

But she had more people to rely on this time, even if they were only Organics, and they had firepower on their side. If Hunt and a few ranch hands were armed and hidden, they stood a chance as long as their aim was true.

Hunt opened the back door for her.

"I don't think we're going to have much time before they get here," she said, glancing at the clock across the room as they lumbered into the kitchen.

Hunt gestured for her to bring Haven into the living room. She plopped the lieutenant colonel's limp form onto the couch in the corner, kicking up a cloud of dust that danced in the rays of afternoon sun cutting through the window.

"I need that gun, and we need backup."

He gave one tight nod and headed for the door to the basement.

The gash in her arm burned, keeping her tired mind focused on her task. She might have preferred her handguns, but this rifle was handy for when the contingent of Uniforms came marching in.

She didn't have much experience being a sniper aside from training before the war—it had been almost exclusively a Gold's job—but she was an excellent shot, and she had the advantage.

Max had given the warning about the breach of the property line, though she'd already set up in one of the north-facing bedrooms, angling the gun where they anticipated the mechs would come based on their position—right down the main drive.

It seemed stupid, but then again, she wasn't sure how much autonomy was programmed into them. They were veritable killing automatons—great for enforcement but shit at planning, recalibrating, weighing risks. Which was why they hadn't been implemented during the war, even though they'd existed then.

Her heart jumped as the vague outline of bodies became visible. She doubted the others could see them yet, given that she couldn't quite make out the number from this distance.

She pulled a slow breath in through her nose, steadying her heart rate as she tracked the contingent's advance. Six bodies, moving with the fluid ease of mechanical programming.

God, did she look like that when she walked?

It settled a coil of unease in her gut, but she focused her sight down the barrel of the rifle, zeroing in on the lead robot's forehead as they marched forward.

When they were close enough for her to make out their identical blank expressions, she took another slow toke of oxygen. With the exhale, her finger inched the trigger back, and the rifle kicked into her injured shoulder, teasing a muttered curse from her lips as the semi-automatic feature kicked her next bullet into the chamber. The forehead shot should've taken the mech down—if it were human. Its head simply jerked backward briefly as it kept moving forward. Not one of the Uniforms scattered for cover like a normal soldier would, no scrambling to get behind something to protect themselves. The only sound that followed her shocked silence was a horse's shrieking whinny as it galloped away from the danger.

Cold dread settled into her gut as she repositioned the rifle against her shoulder, biting into her lip hard enough to draw blood. She fired off two more rounds into the lead mech, and it finally dropped, crumpling like any other body.

But the remaining Uniforms simply marched doggedly on, sending a new jolt of adrenaline through her, and she lined up her sights again, breath huffing through her teeth.

"Dammit, Hunt," she muttered. Where the hell was the back up he'd promised?

Her panic earned the next mech a shoulder shot that jerked it enough to make her second bullet hit the eye instead of the forehead. But it went down faster, and she hurried to line up the next shot. Aiming for the eye, she took the next one down with one bullet, and, finally, gunshots rang across the empty yard from behind the group, helping her take down the rest.

Hunt and a couple of his ranch hands emerged once it was clear the Uniforms were down.

Lurching away from the window, she was careful of the bullet casings on the floor and brought the rifle with her as she pounded down the stairs, some unknown anxiety spiking her blood with urgency.

Those damn machines had been harder to bring down than she'd thought. Eye shots, she thought as she shoved out the back door of the kitchen.

"Bring the bodies," she shouted to the men as she strode their way. "We need to get rid of them, so it won't be linked back to the ranch."

Hunt and the others had no issue taking orders from her, though they groused about the fact that she could lug two of the bodies at a time and it took two of them to handle one. She would've been able to take more if it weren't for the logistical awkwardness of carrying them.

"Help me with this one," Hunt called to one of his guys as Vic came back around the corner of the house.

Some forewarning triggered within her a half-second before anything happened, and her hand shot forward. "Wait!"

The Uniform lurched to its feet with inhuman speed and threw an arm around Hunt's neck. It was the blank expression on the mech's face that made her gut drop out even as she bypassed the rifle slung across her back to pull the handgun from her waistband and aimed it at the mechanical left eye. Without hesitation, she pulled the trigger, nailing it before it could move a centimeter more.

Its knees buckled, but its grip around Hunt's neck didn't release, and he went down with the machine. Panic licked up her spine as she sprinted forward, even though she knew without a doubt that her aim had been true. By the time she reached him, Hunt had already rolled from the grip of the now-defunct mech, breathing hard as he got to his feet.

She glared down at the lifeless body, the hole in its eye matching the one in its chest, which hadn't hit anything vital, apparently.

"It's creepy. They look like people when they're alive," Hunt said, staring down at it, too. "But they truly look like machines in death—could you call this death?"

She stuffed her gun back into her waistband, an odd twinge pinching in her chest. "Some element of them is alive. Organic matter is used in part to build them. But it's not the same."

Not the same as Unborn, but there was a parallel that made a wave of cold wash through her. The weird mix of blood and mechanical fluid leaking from the gunshots drove her to bend and gather it up, to get this done. The cold feeling didn't dissipate as she tossed the body onto the pile. Hunt and another Organic tossed one more right after.

"What do we do with them now?" Hunt asked.

She sucked her teeth for a moment, debating. They couldn't leave them here, but trying to dispose of them would take up precious time. She wanted to get the drop on whoever was running this witch hunt for her before they realized she was coming for them.

"Burn them."

Hunt's eyes jerked to her face, mild horror mixing with curiosity. "Can they burn?"

"Down to the metal. Which we could melt and reuse or sell." God, why did it feel like something in her chest was twisting?

He stared at her for a moment longer before speaking. "I'll get some guys on it. Meanwhile, we should probably check on our guest."

She gave one quick nod and hitched the rifle around to hand it to Hunt now that her sniping days were over.

Hunt trailed behind her as they went in the front door and to the living room. A writhing continued in her gut as she unwillingly replayed the scene with Hunt in her mind's eye.

Claire was standing guard, her shotgun gripped with steady hands in front of her, though the muzzle was pointed to the ground. The lieutenant colonel was sitting up, his eyes narrowed to slits, and he moved his head slowly to look at her as she walked in.

Vic raised her brows in a silent question.

"Welcome to the experiment," Claire murmured.

So it was a test of the serum. Another little tingle of anxiety rolled through her as she became overly aware of how close Hunt was to Claire if she went dark.

She reminded herself how easily she could take one Copper down and focused on the half-bird.

"I hope you're up for a little adventure," she said dryly. "How's your head?"

He glared at her.

"Doc said he's fine. Pretty good lump. Probably not concussed," Claire supplied.

"Good." Vic turned her attention from the colonel to her friend. "We're heading out in an hour."

Claire nodded.

"You good?"

Claire nodded again, more slowly, and with a heavier glance along Vic's face. She took that to mean the serum was working as far as they could measure. She hadn't gone dark, and that was a win.

It reminded Vic that she needed to have a conversation with the doctor, though. Probably needed to check in on Max and Niko. It had been somewhat break-neck since that morning. The sun was now slanting in the west and creeping toward the horizon, and urgency still sang a discordant melody along her nerves.

She walked past Hunt, and his hand slid around her arm. "You really should rest." His voice was low, barely audible to anyone but her.

She looked up. "We don't have time. I want to get out there as soon as possible. We have to hit these guys before they suspect what's happened. Who knows what sort of protocol they have set up that will alert them that something isn't right?"

Hunt's lips turned colorless as he pressed them together. "What if we take the truck?"

She dipped her head. "That would help. But I'm still not waiting."

"Vic. . ."

"If I promise to rest on the drive, will you drop it?" She raised a brow but smiled a little to take the sting out of her tone. "This taking care of me thing is kind of cramping my style."

He sighed, his eyes tracing her face, but she could see the humor in the depths. "Fine."

She broke away from his stare, driven by her desire to hide what was brewing in the back of her mind.

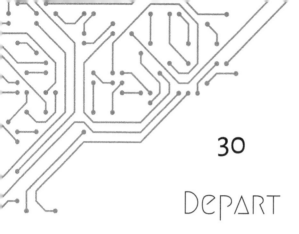

30

Depart

H UNT STAYED UPSTAIRS TO pack whatever he felt was necessary for the trip and to prepare the truck for the journey. Since it only fit so many people inside the cab, he was getting the bed ready to carry the others and the supplies they'd need.

Vic dropped down to the floor from the ladder and speed-walked down the hall toward her room, planning to change and check her shoulder. It had stopped bleeding, but it probably needed to be cleaned and bandaged. She didn't want to take the time to stop by the infirmary, but her desire to check in about the serum had her breezing past her quarters and jogging across the rotunda anyway.

She was mildly surprised to find Morgan there. Brody was apparently doing well enough not to need constant observation.

Morgan glanced up from her computer, her eyes going wide as she took in Vic's appearance, and she stood quickly. Vic spoke before she could make a comment about the blood staining her clothes.

"So I take it you've developed the serum," she said. "How long does it last and how much of it do you have?"

Morgan's expression twisted. "I have no idea how long it lasts, and honestly, I still don't know if it works. Unless the switch has been tripped, I can't measure its effectiveness."

Vic tapped each of her fingers against her thumb in turn, wishing they had time to test it from every angle, but she'd take what she could get for the moment. "So how many Unborn are we talking?"

"Only two. I'm sorry. I—"

Vic put her hand on Morgan's arm. "It's fine. You did great on such short notice. I appreciate all the work you've put in. Give me those sedatives as backup, and we'll see what happens."

She nodded, then her eyes sharpened as her attention snagged on Vic's bloody shoulder. "Need some patching?"

Vic gave her a rueful smile. "It's fine."

Morgan gave her a slicing look. "Since we're here."

Vic huffed begrudging consent.

The doc shook her head, a small smirk on her face as she helped Vic take her jacket off so she could have access. More shards of glass fell to the floor, drawing the doctor's eye for a moment. Then she took in the gash along Vic's shoulder and raised a brow. "Is this your only wound?"

Vic suppressed her chagrin. "Scout's honor. It's not even that bad."

Morgan shot her a sideways glance, but instead of saying anything, she simply set to work cleaning, treating, and bandaging it. "I know you're chomping at the bit to get out of here, so I won't give you my lecture about how you should really have some stitches."

"Much appreciated," Vic said, keeping her wince in check.

But still, it was impressive that Morgan kept her promise as she finished up. "When are you leaving?"

"As soon as possible."

Morgan frowned as she turned to gather the syringes of serum and sedatives, putting them into a small box she had sitting nearby to give to Vic. When she turned back, worry had etched lines into her forehead.

"You have one dose a piece. Use them only when you have to, when you know they're going dark."

Vic took a breath. "I appreciate it."

"Be careful, Vic," Morgan said, her hazel eyes searching her face. "We care about you here. You make sure you come back."

Vic felt her words like bullets to her heart, and she fought to keep herself rooted to the spot instead of taking a step back with the force. All she managed was a tight nod as she took the box and walked from the room, heading for her quarters to change.

Despite her attempts to fight it, tears burned the back of her eyes. She'd managed to attach herself to this place and the people here, but some of them had somehow grown attached as well, and that had been the least expected thing of all. It was already a heavy weight to know that Hunt had fully committed to whatever this was between them, planning to assimilate her into his life without a backward glance, despite the unknowns that still plagued the future.

She managed to squelch the tears, swallowing the lump that lodged in her throat as she slid her door open and stepped inside, rushing to the extra set of clothes someone had placed at the foot of her bed. It shocked her to realize how long it had been since she'd even slept here.

She used a washcloth that was neatly folded on the edge of her sink to clean herself off, wiping the dried blood that had run down her arm, cleaning the dirt from her face. Then she took out her hair, shaking the tangled locks until they fell around her face.

But instead of redoing it, she set her hands on the edge of the sink and leaned her weight forward, trying to sort through her emotions. What had been turning over and over in her mind, relegated to a dark corner while she'd spoken with Morgan, now rushed to the forefront.

She'd put Hunt in danger twice. He'd almost been shot, and that Uniform could have easily snapped his neck right in front of her, reminding her exactly what kind of path they were headed down. They'd kidnapped a reasonably high-ranking official of the military, and she was going to seek out—and potentially kill—an even higher-ranking member of the military.

And she would meet a man who, genetically, might be her father.

All while putting others in danger, including the man she...loved? Was that what this was? Had she ever felt the emotion before? Was she even capable of such a thing?

She knew she'd never get him to stay behind. His level of hard-headedness nearly matched her own.

"Vic?"

She spun to face the door, which stood only a few inches open to reveal Hunt, and her heart dropped down to her toes.

"I knocked..."

She hadn't heard it, too much in her own head to pay attention to what was happening around her.

And maybe the look on her face drew him forward because he said nothing more as he pushed the door open enough to let himself in, striding with absolute confidence across the room to gather her against him, to press his lips to hers, to cover her face in tender kisses.

Her eyes fluttered closed so that she could soak in the affection with only the senses that mattered, to fall into his embrace with abandon. No questions, no uncertainty.

And because she hadn't had the chance to remind herself that they were all right. It had been close. That bullet had tried to take one or both of them and had failed. She was beyond grateful for that much, even if it was no guarantee of anything beyond this point. Hunt had been right, even if he'd said it in anger: she was not invincible. She was no superhero. But damn if she wouldn't do her best to keep him and the others alive on this mission, personal as it was.

The thought made her pull back, the fear that her vendetta would be the thing that got the people she cared about killed slamming through her. This wasn't a war they'd all signed up for, that they'd been created to fight. This was hers and hers alone. But she couldn't do all of it alone, as much as she wanted to. So she would let them go with her as far as it seemed necessary, and then she would strike out on her own.

Hunt stared down at her, his eyes tightening ever so slightly like he sensed some change in her, though there was no way he could tell what it was.

"We should say goodbye to Niko before we go. Just in case. . ." she said, knowing full well it was an attempt to distract him from reading her.

He gave a slight nod and released her. She immediately missed his proximity but did nothing about it. They had too much at stake, too many things ahead of them.

After she pulled her hair into her standard bun at her nape, they walked in silence down the hall to the corridor where they'd find Niko and Max. The door to the boys' room was open like they'd known this was coming. In all likelihood, they did. Word traveled fast down here, and Max knew more than most because of his role.

Niko was sitting on the edge of his bed when they approached, his fingers tapping rapidly against his thigh. His head jerked up as soon as they stepped inside.

"This general guy is bad news, Mr. Hunt."

The first words out of his mouth had them both pausing and exchanging a glance.

"Bad news how?" Hunt asked, his voice gentle. It was a subtle change she hadn't noticed when they'd first met, but it was something he only did when he spoke with Niko.

"He's been in trouble." Niko shot to his feet and walked forward. "For bad experiments, for not following rules, and un—um—unethical actions. But then nothing ever happens. He just keeps doing them."

Hunt and Vic exchanged another glance. Triggering an entire community to slaughter each other definitely fell under *bad news*. It set a new determination within her to find this man and make him pay.

"We'll be careful, Niko. But someone has to stop him."

He looked at her, moisture swimming in his eyes. "Can't you send someone else?"

Hunt pressed his lips together and reached out, pulling the boy into him for a hug. "We would love nothing more than to stay here. But this general is doing dangerous things to people we care about. It's our job to protect everyone here."

Unease ran down Vic's spine at Hunt's words, a reminder of what she was planning to do—on her own. She felt Max watching her, his silver eyes narrowed when she met his gaze. Did he know? Could he tell? He knew her better than most when it came to how she led, how she fought to protect everyone else first. And he had to know, at least in part, what she felt about Hunt by now.

She tore her gaze away from his as Niko pulled out of Hunt's arms. The boy kept his head down but practically dove against her, wrapping his thin arms around her waist. His head came to her chin, and she rested her cheek on the silky, dark hair.

"We'll come back," she said, the whispered promise one she hoped she'd keep. At least in part. She looked at Hunt, knowing she'd damn well make sure at least one of them did.

31

Marching Orders

V IC RODE IN THE cab as Hunt drove, and Claire and Cam guarded the lieutenant colonel in the bed of the truck.

"Sleep," Hunt said softly, his voice matching the rumble of the engine.

Her eyelids had been slowly drooping, but she kept forcing them open. A pit had formed in her stomach, and she wasn't sure why she had such a weighty sense of foreboding, but it felt dangerous to let herself fall asleep.

"Vic."

She released a long-suffering sigh, and it seemed like her last re-serves of energy escaped with the exhale. "What about you?"

"I'm fine. I had some coffee, and I'll sleep once we get there."

She twisted in her seat to check the back. Claire sat on one side of the bed while Cam took the other, both holding handguns against their thighs. The colonel sat between them, his back against the cab of the truck, so Vic could only see the top of his head. He might have been military, but she was sure he'd had little to no hand-to-hand experience—maybe not even training—so she didn't think he would try anything. Still, nothing was guaranteed.

"We've got this," Hunt murmured. "Please rest."

She turned back to look at him, his profile barely visible in the dark as they traveled on the worn track through the woods. It was an old road nearly overtaken by nature, but Hunt said he'd made trips this way before. She'd had no idea he had buyers in the town she'd spent the last five years in, or that he trekked out there every few months. This was apparently a longer route, but the ride was a bit smoother and less traveled, which meant they'd have an easier time getting to their destination undetected.

Vic knew, though, that she really should rest since she didn't plan on sleeping once they arrived like they'd talked about. But even as she leaned her head against the window, it was a while before sleep claimed her.

Once it did, it filled her mind with dark dreams and memories, times that people she'd cared about hadn't made it back. When she'd been pinned down by enemy fire, forced to watch her fellow soldiers go down. The ripping sensation through her thigh when a bullet had found her sprinting between buildings alone—without the team she'd started with. The warmth of her own blood as it wept from the wound while she kept her eyes dry.

Soon enough, someone was working to wake her, and she struggled to resurface. Especially because the darkness of the night was deep and cloying, gripping her mind and body in a heaviness she couldn't shake as she lifted her head to look at Hunt.

"We're outside the city. Ready to sleep for the last few hours before daylight."

She blinked hard, squinting at their surroundings. The trees had thinned out, but they stayed within their protection. The lights from the town were visible, the part of downtown that never truly slept, where money and resources dictated a life of exorbitant luxury and constant activity kept it alive long into the night.

Vic opened her door to get out, sliding out into the night, her legs stiff as she walked around the back of the truck where Cam was leading Haven out of the bed. Claire trailed behind, weapon at the ready.

"Since I got some rest, I'll take first watch," Vic said, pulling out her own gun and taking up the position behind Haven.

Claire nodded but still looked to Hunt for confirmation as he pulled some of their supplies from the truck.

He lifted what looked like rolled-up sleeping bags from the bed. "Probably a good idea."

They trooped into the smallish area that was the most open and even and laid out the sleeping bags.

Vic used her gun to gesture at Haven, guiding him to a nearby tree. "Have a seat, *sir*."

His eyes tightened at her words, but he said nothing, lowering himself to the ground without looking away from her face. He kept his legs close to his body, resting his arms on his knees so his hands dangled between them.

Vic settled herself against the nearest tree, facing him, a little tingle of excitement lighting along her nerves. The others were still settling in several feet away, and she knew before he moved that Hunt would come over for a moment.

His tread was soft and quiet, and he crouched down next to her, his eyes on the half-bird for a moment before he brought them to Vic's face. He lightly touched the back of her hand with a finger.

"You'll be all right?" he murmured.

She forced a reassuring smile. "Of course. You get some sleep."

His expression was unreadable as he traced her features like he was trying to sense whatever she was keeping hidden. Or maybe he was trying to make sure she truly was all right.

She tried not to let her paranoia dictate her response, to keep from giving herself away. Touching his cheek, she worked to ignore how vulnerable it made her feel to have the lieutenant colonel watching the interaction, that he would know and see that there was more between them than he might've thought otherwise.

"I'm fine. You all need to rest." She added the next part for Haven's benefit: "You know I could take him easily if he tried anything."

Hunt's smirk was faint and disappeared quickly before he leaned forward to give her a brief kiss. "Wake me if you need anything."

She nodded, fighting her urge to tell him, to have him come with her. He was all in. That meant they did things together. As a team. They were a unit.

And yet. . . if this had been the war, she would have found a way to take the fewest people possible, put no one at risk if she could help it. So she didn't call out to him as he settled on the spread sleeping bags next to Claire and Cam, taking a few moments to get comfortable before he grew still and quiet.

Vic kept her eyes in their direction while the half-bird's gaze remained on her. She felt it like a cold finger along her skin as he watched her, but she didn't turn, wasn't worried that he would do anything. Her capabilities far exceeded his. But she did wonder what was running through his mind.

She waited a half an hour for the others to fall deeper into their sleep before she moved. By then, even the half-bird's head had lolled back against the tree trunk.

Slowly, she crept forward on her hands and knees, situating herself next to him, and placed the barrel of the gun under his chin. He must not have been deeply asleep because his eyes flew open the second the metal touched his skin.

"You will come with me, and you will make no noise," she breathed at his ear.

He nodded tightly, bumping the muzzle of the gun. She took it from his chin but slid her hand around his arm and jammed the muzzle into his side, feeling him tense. She reminded herself to be patient, even as she practically dragged him to his feet.

The darkness remained a heavy blanket on their senses, but she could see a little better than he could. Enhanced vision and all that. So she helped him keep his footing as they trudged through the trees toward the downtown area whose multi-floor buildings remained illuminated like so many lighthouses.

The trees thinned and fell away, leaving them exposed in an open field that turned into the ragged landscape of the destroyed city outskirts. The piles of rubble grew larger and more intact the closer they got, some semblance of past civilization rising on either side of them.

"All right, half-bird," she said. "Where do I find this general?"

"He's commandeered the governor's house." Haven was a little breathless, probably not used to hoofing it anywhere.

No drills for upper management. Not when they'd had Unborn for the war and Uniforms to do their legwork. Literally. Disgust filled her, leaving a bitter coating on her tongue.

"Which way?" She pressed the gun harder into his side to remind him how serious she was.

He grunted. "West."

On they walked until a pink glow touched the eastern horizon. A chill danced down her spine as she glanced in that direction, knowing that on the other side of town, there was a fiery grave where her home once stood. That she had seen the birth of a new day as the people she had called her friends and neighbors were being dragged down by death's bloody and violent hand.

She made herself turn away, angling west with the baby colonel, who said nothing. But she felt it, some sense that he was smug, that he wanted to gloat. Probably due to the fact that his whole objective had been to find her and bring her back to his boss. But he still didn't know she was aware of Linus and his likely involvement.

Haven's assistant had tipped his hand. If it had only been the general involved, there was no reason to call him anything but the general. Specifically mentioning a benefactor meant somebody else was the pockets, even if more than one person was in charge or calling some of the shots.

And so she'd let him feel confident that he'd done his job. Because, surely they'd be thrown off when she walked right into their temporary headquarters without hesitation and of her own free will.

"I should've known," Haven said eventually, when the sun was peeking over the horizon.

"What's that?" she asked through her teeth, not keen on having any sort of conversation with this peon, this man who didn't even deserve the title he bore.

"That you would keep us moving so relentlessly." He huffed, tripping over the rubble that was strewn along the sidewalk that looked almost as neglected as the outer edges of town, though they came across entirely intact buildings now. Places where people lived, though it looked hardly any better than what she'd had before the kill switch.

"Isn't that why you Adams call us hybrids? Man plus machine. Or do you prefer to call us bottle-bred?"

"I don't use those terms."

She sneered. As if that would make him a more sympathetic character. Even if he was only a cog in the wheel, he was still actively participating, had still chosen this.

"Interesting that you'd call me an Adam when you clearly are in a relationship with one of us."

She stiffened, though she'd expected this to come up eventually.

"Unless there's some other reason you would align yourself with him."

Her fingers dug into the flesh of his arm, but she didn't answer.

"Is it perhaps his story? The father who disregarded regulations to cater to his wife, building for her the family she'd always wanted?"

It shouldn't have been surprising that Haven would know Hunt's background. If Hunt's father was on the front lines of the Unborn Project, much of his research and activity was likely monitored. She wondered how strict they'd been back then. Maybe they'd welcomed some level of experimentation.

Angela had always operated with a deep sense of secrecy as she'd passed the girls the cutesy books and the dolls. And she'd never said a word to Vic about what she'd done to bring her about. But despite being modeled after her own daughter, Angela had never been overt in her favoritism. She seemed to put more responsibility on Vic to care for the others, which flew in the face of what she had done in designing Vic to practically be her replacement daughter. She hadn't been overly protective or possessive. She'd pushed her harder, expected more, demanded near-perfection.

Maybe because she'd known that, despite the way she looked, Vic could never be what she'd lost. Either because she didn't live up to the expectation, or Angela was too hardened by the grief.

"How far are we?" Vic asked, renewing her focus.

"A couple blocks."

She took in the empty streets, scanning dark alleyways, and inexplicably looked behind her as if she would find Hunt and the others barreling toward them in the truck. Had they gotten up yet, finding Haven and herself gone? Would they think the lieutenant colonel had overpowered her or would they know she'd left without them?

She turned forward again as the big house came into view, and she knew without Haven telling her, though he did anyway, that this was their destination.

The house was stately, though it looked a little bedraggled. The brick was a dingy brown when it should have been red. The white columns that held up the front portico were dirty. But it still looked regal with its wrought iron fence guarding the meticulously kept lawn.

Some part of her felt the weight of indignation that someone could live in this mansion while she'd resided in a two-hundred square-foot shack, earning the thin walls with her blood and sweat given in a war she hadn't started.

"Alright, half-bird. Let's do this."

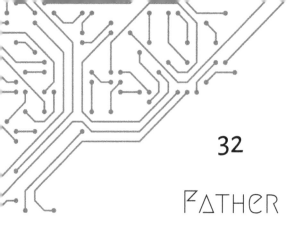

32

FΛTHƐR

THERE WERE A NUMBER of steps leading to the front entrance since the house sat on a bit of a hill. It made Vic pause and evaluate. Would there be some kind of security measure in place?

It seemed ill-advised for this kind of a home to be completely unguarded, even if most of the houses on the street with it were intact and well-kept. The landed gentry of this crumbling society, as it were.

"Is there a back entrance?" she asked.

The half-bird actually smiled at her. "Getting nervous, are we?"

She jabbed him in the ribs with the gun, and his smile disappeared.

He jerked his chin, and she turned that direction, pushing him in front of her as they rounded to the back of the property, though sweeping grounds met them wherever they went.

Then they came upon the locked gate that guarded the back entrance and the garages where, presumably, a fleet of vehicles resided. Veritable tanks, if she had to guess. But this presented a bigger problem. She would not make it past the gate without someone noticing, and the half-bird had likely known that. His cockiness was in knowing this was the end of the line for her being in charge of what came next.

"Feel free to give up your weapon now," Haven said gleefully. "Or weapons, most likely."

She didn't relinquish the gun initially. She saw no one surrounding them, no movement, no bodies, no guards.

But then gray-clad figures emerged from various angles, semi-automatic weapons trained on her from multiple angles.

Which was, honestly, ludicrous. She'd wanted to get in with the upper hand, yes. But these people wanted her alive, so their guns weren't truly a threat to her or they would've shot her as soon as she'd gotten in range.

It drove home how right the decision to leave the others behind was. Her life was the only bargaining chip she had. With the others there, her enemies would have leverage over her, and she couldn't afford to give up control.

The lieutenant colonel spun out of her grasp, grinning, and it made her want to show him how little he mattered, that she had no reason to fear because she was the ultimate prize, not him. The desire to wipe that smug smirk from his face, especially after what happened to Brody, became a fire low in her belly. This half-bird, who'd let robots do all his dirty work and beat a man nearly to death, wasn't undeserving of her revenge.

Instead of dropping her gun, she lifted it higher, aiming for the half-bird's forehead. It would be easy to let her anger over Brody dictate her next move. And though she had never been a cold-blooded killer, she'd never had compunctions about taking out the enemies who wouldn't hesitate to do that very thing to her and those she cared about. After all, it was what she was made for.

Haven must have realized she was seriously considering it because his smile faded, and his eyes grew wider.

"Don't," he said quickly, holding up a finger as he backed up.

"I'm much more valuable to them than you are, half-bird. So I have nothing to lose." Her finger moved over the trigger, and his eyes tracked it—the infinitesimal change—as the Uniforms moved closer, all their guns still trained on her.

This was a test of her morality, the personal ethics she'd adhered to her whole existence. Before, she'd let Hunt take the lead with this man, considering it an even—well, slightly weighted in Hunt's favor—match. That had simply been payback.

But she was not some vigilante, and Haven wasn't the one who'd ordered the slaughter of her entire village. He was a minion in the army, someone who likely knew few of the actual answers she wanted. And as unimportant as he was to them, he was even less important to her.

So she uncocked the gun and let it dangle from her finger as she lifted her hands, eyes never leaving the lieutenant colonel's face. His expression crumpled as soon as the mechs moved in, one of them snatching the gun from her hand while two others took her arms in turn.

No one said a word—were the mechs even capable of speech?—as they marched her through the electronically opening gate and toward the steps.

It might have been a back entrance, but the half-size columns and mini portico were a reminder that this home was ancient and expensive, a residence for powerful people. The ceiling of the porch overhang was painted with a mockery of Renaissance art. It was pretty enough for the casual observer, despite the cracks and faded colors. It felt sickeningly ostentatious to Vic.

A Uniform ahead of them opened the door, and the two holding her shoved her inside a richly furnished and largely untouched piece of history. The antique furniture was worn but well-kept, the wood floor shining with recent varnish to cover the evidence of hundreds of footsteps from decades of use. The paintings and sculptures gave the same impression as the fresco on the porch.

"Quite the relic of times past, isn't it?"

Vic twisted to glare at the half-bird, whose misplaced bravado was back in full force. Her lip curled back as she took in the cocky way he stood, as if he were the one who had the pull to get access to a place like this.

She found herself regretting not shooting him when she'd had the chance.

"I guess you wouldn't know, though," the half-bird continued. "No experience with the real world before going off to fight."

She squinted at him. "At least I know how to fight. You might have that shiny insignia on your sleeve, but we both know who would be the real commander in the field."

Haven's face twisted and he took a step forward. She thought he might strike her, but he thought better of it. There was some logic in that head of his after all.

"Get me a map," he snapped, eyes shifting to a nearby mech. "I have the location of three new targets for you."

His cold tone sent a chill down her spine, and a chain reaction of panic ricocheted through her as the Uniform turned away to do the half-bird's bidding.

She jerked her arm from the grasp of the mech on her right. The other's grip was too tight, so she yanked him forward, swinging him around and practically throwing him into the other one. Their momentary disorientation gave her an opening, which she used to lunge at the half-bird, shoving him back against a wall with her arm pressed to his windpipe. His arms flailed, and he knocked a vase from a nearby table. It shattered at their feet as she snarled in his face.

An unusually blinding burst of pain, like an explosion in her side, made her loosen her hold, and she spun. Something crashed into her leg, and she fell to one knee. A hand gripped the back of her neck, shoving her face toward the floor.

"Enough."

It was a man's voice coming from several yards to the left, possibly near the staircase she'd spotted upon entering. She tried to lift her head to see who it was, but the Uniform's strength kept her in place, and fear ignited in her chest. No one was supposed to be able to do that. No one except another Silver.

Her breath came in panicked blasts, hitting the floor that glimmered with its fresh coat of shine. She could see how wide her eyes were in the reflection.

"Do you not understand what 'enough' means? Release her." The man's voice sounded again, closer this time. His tone suggested he was speaking to obstinate children.

It was an extra beat of time before the pressure on the back of her neck eased, and she lifted her head.

A man, his lean frame slimmed by age, though he was not stooped, strode forward, his eerie blue eyes almost translucent as he glared at the robots that surrounded her. She knew from the pictures Niko had found that this was Jared Linus, though his face was more deeply lined now, his hair stark white even if it was still thick. It was hard to gauge how old he truly was because he moved with such ease.

His attention moved to the lieutenant colonel, who flinched at the slices aimed at him by Linus' eyes. The hand he was using to rub at his throat stilled.

"You proved to be useful after all."

Haven glanced at her then back to Linus, unsure of how to read the older man's tone. She guessed Linus was being condescending, and the way Haven shifted uncertainly told her he suspected it, too.

"Not in the way I had been expecting." Linus's gaze flicked over Haven one last time before he turned his attention to Vic, his expression softening. "I apologize for the rough treatment, my dear."

A prickling sensation rolled along Vic's skin as she stared up at him. He drew closer, holding out a hand to her.

She stared at it, her mind registering the wrinkles, the age spots, and the steadiness. He had to be delusional, right? So why was he so calm? And why was he smiling kindly at her?

You look exactly like her.

Her muscles snapped with tension when the words floated through her mind. It was as if someone had spoken them aloud, using them like a weapon. And they were. The knowledge of what Angela had done felt like a slash in her heart.

The replacement daughter who was burdened with more responsibility than the others. Why, when Angela had recreated her lost daughter, would she expect more, put her in the crossfire more often, demand a higher level of integrity?

Instead of accepting this stranger's help, she got to her feet on her own, wincing a little as her ribs shifted, revealing her injury. Bruised, more than likely.

Linus's bushy gray eyebrows pulled together in concern. "Are you hurt?"

"I'm fine," she replied evenly, slipping her hand across her side to brace the aching bones.

"Sir, she should be taken to a cell—" Haven's words abruptly halted as soon as Linus shot him a scalding look.

It confirmed that Linus did wield some kind of power, even if he wasn't entirely running the show. It was obvious in the way he carried himself, clad in that expensive, tailor-cut suit that seemed to flow like water with his movements. His shoes alone probably cost as much as she'd spent on a six-month supply of food before she'd found the ranch.

Linus turned his attention back to her. "Join me?"

She glanced at the Uniforms that lined the room, seeming to stare at nothing, their posture at attention. Their lack of movement was eerie. But still, she knew she was outnumbered and out-muscled. So she gave a slow nod and waited for Linus to lead the way.

He gave her a soft smile, just a light tug of his thin lips as he moved forward. She followed a pace behind. Several Uniforms moved with them like guards. Linus might have been deep in his delusion about what or who she was, but the Uniforms—or whoever controlled them—knew she was not to be left unguarded.

He led her to the stairs and up to the second floor, where they turned left and passed several doors until they reached his destination. He opened the sixth door on the left, the heavy wood gliding silently open to reveal an office. The diffused light filtering in through a big window did little to permeate the room, which was furnished with a sweeping, dark-wooded desk and equally dark floor-to-ceiling bookshelves burdened with more tomes than Vic had ever seen in her life.

Linus drifted inside with the confidence of intimate familiarity, and Vic followed with the halting cadence of trepidation, her eyes scanning for hiding spots or weapons, enemies, an ambush. There was no safety in this house, despite Linus' relaxed state.

"Shut the door behind you, would you?" Linus asked as she stepped inside, her feet sinking into the thick carpet.

She turned, closing the door on the mechs who halted just outside, stationing themselves on either side like sentinels.

As Linus walked to the window, drawing back the curtains to bring more light in, she lingered by the door, her eyes sweeping the room again. Her whole shack would have fit inside this space easily. But the thick carpet was a big upgrade from dirty planks with gaps between them. And the wood comprising the desk and the wainscoting along the wall had likely cost three or four times as much as whatever they'd used to cobble together her ramshackle home.

The man turned to face her, his fingertips brushing the shine of the desk's surface, looking utterly at ease in this space like he had no idea what it was like to have a winter breeze cut through cracks in thin walls.

"I have to say that having you here is almost like a dream," Linus said, faint emotion straining his voice.

Vic's palm was still pressed flat along her rib cage, and she made no move to come closer, kept any reaction from her face.

"I know you are not her, but. . ." It was almost a whisper as moisture glimmered in his eyes.

Unease rolled through her even though his words hinted that he wasn't totally lost to fantasy. But still, the way he was looking at her reminded her that this man had killed to find her.

"I am an old man," he said, clearing his throat. "And little brings me joy. But seeing you eases my grief."

"Is that the only reason you brought me here?" Her effort to keep the coldness she felt in her bones from totally infusing her words was only partially successful. "To ease your grief?"

He kept his gaze on her, the slight contraction around his eyes the only indication her words impacted him.

"Is that why you had my entire village slaughtered? To get to me?" The last few words came out a little strangled as her own grief clenched in her chest.

"That was not what happened."

She lifted her chin at his defensive tone. "Enlighten me."

He took two slow breaths as they stared at each other. "That was an experiment."

Her mirthless laugh surprised her as it scalded the air between them. "Isn't it always?"

Her very existence was an experiment. *Can we make a super soldier? Can they win the war? Can they integrate into society? Can they love?*

He almost looked angry now. But was he angry at her words or what had happened? Because he clearly knew what exactly had taken place. "It was not my experiment."

"Does it matter?" This through clenched teeth.

He swallowed. "I have only ever been—"

"A benefactor?" she supplied, the bitterness forming the word into a weapon.

His flinch was almost imperceptible. "It wasn't my experiment," he said again. "But it was what led me to you."

She scoffed lightly, shaking her head. Faces filled her mind. The ones belonging to her friends when they were alive. But even after knowing him for years and having hundreds of interactions, only Cooper's unseeing gaze flashed into her mind.

"You were the only one unaffected by the activation." His eyes sparked with something like pride. As if he had some claim to what she'd accomplished. As if it *was* an accomplishment.

"Because of how Angela designed me," she said coldly.

Those words made him flinch for real. Maybe because it was a reminder that she wasn't his child, hadn't done something to please him at all. Or maybe it was the reminder of a woman he'd no longer had access to, someone who had mattered to him once.

"She used her DNA and yours, I'd guess, to build me. To make me look like your daughter." Vic took a breath and a few steps forward, Linus's eyes tracking her movement. "In so doing, she made a countermeasure to the 'activation.' It overrides whatever command was given that day."

"And it gave me a purpose I had not had in a long time." He actually smiled, and it made her stomach churn. "To find you. Have my daughter back."

The faces flashed into her mind again, the chaos of her village being utterly destroyed. The shacks on fire, the smoke that poured into the morning sky, carrying with it the ashes of the meager lives those people had fought for.

"I am not your daughter."

"But you could be." He smiled wider, coming around the edge of the desk toward her, though she took several steps backward. "We could be the family we never had. I can take care of you."

She shook her head. "I have a family."

That stopped him in his tracks. Something like anger flashed into his eyes. "What? Hybrids? As if they could be your family." He practically spat the words.

She scoffed. "What exactly do you think *I* am, Linus? I am not your daughter, and I never could be. Especially not after what happened that day."

It was almost like he didn't hear her. "You are exactly what I imagined she'd look like when she was all grown up."

Goosebumps broke out along her skin, and the urge to run was stronger than she'd ever felt it in her life.

"It was like fate or some higher power that led me on a visit to General O'Rourke and his operation." His eyes grew distant as he remembered the day that represented her personal horror story.

But it was his mention of the general that snapped her gaze to his face, kept her from getting lost in the grief.

"He was eager to show me something, though I've never been interested in his little tests. The Project had lost a lot of my attention over the years." He walked to the rows of books as if to choose his next read. "As did so many other things."

Her brows pulled low as she took in his posture, the relaxed stance, the way he clasped his hands at his back. So at ease and casual, recounting it as if it were an innocuous event.

"He'd activated a whole village at once, testing the power of the code, the reach, the scope." He waved a hand like the man had been assessing a computer game. "But then there was you."

Her breathing stopped, her lungs trapping her exhale for a moment as he turned to her.

"He was angry to find that someone could escape. He thought maybe there was something wrong with the code or the delivery system. But no one else had wrested control back. Only you."

The hand against her side flexed at the memory of the feel of someone's throat in her grip, when she'd fought to take that control back, the mental effort it had required.

"We saw it through a Uniform's eyes. Your face stopped my heart before the feed cut out."

She saw the desperation in his eyes, probably only an echo of what he'd felt in that moment, a mirror image of her own desperation to survive, to know what was happening to her people. But it elicited no sense of sympathy for this man who'd allowed atrocities against her people simply because it was a necessary evil.

"And I immediately went to work seeking you out. My motives aligned with the general's, if only for a time. It was convenient. We both wanted you."

"Indeed we did."

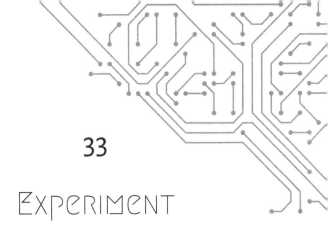

33

EXPERIMENT

T HE EERIE VOICE CREPT like a finger along Vic's spine, and she spun to face the man standing in the doorway. General O'Rourke was long and lean with a prominent bone structure that made his face seem sunken, like it was too much for his skin to hold his expressions. It gave his eyes a dead look. Even his uniform draped on his body in such an odd way—like it had been cut for someone else, someone thicker.

He held a gun toward her, but something told her that was merely for show because she doubted he planned to kill her. Not yet anyway. Not when considering what exactly his motivations to find her would be.

She was the only one who'd made it out. And he would want to know why, like she had.

"How lovely to meet you, Victoria." He didn't smile.

"General," she said, dipping her chin.

One eyebrow quirked at that. "I see Linus has been enjoying this little reunion immensely. Giving away my secrets in the process." His dark eyes shifted to Linus next to the bookcase.

The tension filled the room like a noxious gas, and Vic's senses went on high alert.

"Luckily, neither of you will be around long enough to cause issues for me long-term."

The threat had barely left his mouth when he shifted to aim his gun at Linus, shooting the older man where he stood. Vic didn't turn, but she heard the body crumple to the ground, intimately familiar with what a person looked like when they'd been shot to death.

The edge of the general's mouth finally lifted in a small smile. "Not even a flinch. Impressive, soldier."

She didn't move, didn't react to his words, though they filled her veins with ice. She ran her tongue along the back of her teeth as her mind calculated the number of mechs she'd seen so far in the house. She didn't know the entire floor plan, so she couldn't be sure of the total.

"You didn't flinch before taking out that Uniform in your village, either. Hardier than some, it seems." The dark eyes ate up the real estate of her body, measuring. "What is it in that make up of yours that makes you so unique?"

The way he spoke, she would have thought she was a complicated math equation to solve. But something far more sinister was on his mind because he looked at her like she was something to dissect and study. The thought landed heavy and sickening because there was no doubt that's what he intended to do. But she couldn't let it get that far. And she certainly didn't want this moment to pass without more information.

Because she was going to find out how to end the control or die trying.

For herself. For Claire. Jamie and Alice. All the people who would be affected by perverse experiments that took the lives they'd tried to carve out for themselves.

She may have outlived her initial purpose, but she would be damned if she'd let that stop her from finding a new one.

"Are all Unborn wired for activation?" she asked.

His smile jumped up a notch as he cocked his head.

She realized then what he reminded her of. A vulture. His beady eyes, his hooked nose, the bony frame. A man who picked over the leftovers of what this world now had to offer.

"We had to have a fail-safe in case one of you went berserk or something." He pursed his lips. "But it's convenient for other reasons. Treaties have forced our hand in keeping the lot of you from government and military positions. It seems that leaders in other countries are just as worried about your controllability in society as the average Joe. And with your strength and enhanced abilities, I don't blame them."

The general walked forward, circling her like a predator, and she moved to keep her eyes on him.

"But, you know, we aren't responsible for where Unborn end up now that you aren't the property of the US government. And if you go nuts on your own time, that's not on us."

Her stomach twisted. A convenient way to keep their hands clean. And a surefire way to stir even more hate and prejudice against her kind among American citizens and foreign nations alike.

"What was the point of taking out my entire village, then?"

He shrugged, but the casual movement looked alien coming from him. "To see if it was possible."

That sick feeling sank heavier, and she knew the horror must have shown on her face. A simple experiment, like it was a whim, a casual curiosity he wanted to satisfy. Not living, breathing people. Humans.

No matter what anyone said or believed, those were people who deserved to have a chance at life after what they did for this country.

"It was a stroke of luck you were there," O'Rourke continued. "How unfortunate it would have been to activate a contingent and have you go rogue when it really mattered."

He meant make them look bad. Because she was the one they couldn't control, which meant she was a problem. So that was why he'd let Linus spend his money and use his influence to look for her. Because it suited his ends.

Her gaze slid to the dead man on the floor near the bookcase, a weird grief pinching in her chest. Not because he was anything to her, but because he'd been deceived, led to trust the man before her.

And she realized they were both delusional in their own ways. One wanted to live the fantasy of his fractured family. The other had entirely lost his connection to his humanity, a sense of what was moral and right.

It had always been a question of whether the Unborn could be considered human, but they were the ones who'd spent their lives fighting for someone else, for the end of a war that had rocked the entire world. Was this the standard they were held to? Because, if this is what it meant to be human, she wasn't sure she wanted it.

But even if they were a product of scientific manipulation, that didn't mean they had to submit to constant suppression or control by others. Whether it was the government or whoever wanted something done by illegal means, their lives would never be their own.

O'Rourke tilted his head. "Horror and disgust." He was nodding now. "You Unborn are a marvel of modern science, but you certainly lack imagination. What you could accomplish if you banded together."

She swallowed. "You speak as if you want us to revolt."

He smiled again, and she was sure it was her imagination that his teeth were serrated edges.

Realization dawned. That's exactly what he was trying to make it look like. But what was the purpose? Didn't he *want* them to be usable weapons? Not to be eliminated because of the kill switch or by the society that wanted them gone.

"If there are fewer of you," he said, as if hearing her question, "then you become a myth, a legend that people whisper about but can't confirm. Ghosts."

Two hundred people dead and gone to make a smaller army of secret agents for one man. Or were there more out there who wanted what she and her kind had to offer? The government as a whole? Whatever that actually was.

"This many of you weren't supposed to survive that war anyway." O'Rourke's gaze darkened, brow lowering. "You weren't supposed to get a life after."

Something inside her jolted, like that verbalized denial of something she never knew she'd wanted awakened something inside her. A heat bloomed low in her belly and crawled up her chest, into her limbs. It tingled into her fingers.

A plan started in her mind, the edges and shapes forming into something concrete. There were no guarantees. Not with the number of Uniforms in the house.

A little niggling doubt filled her as she thought about going up against those mechs. Because they could actually take her down. The pain that still throbbed in her side was evidence of that.

But the man moving toward her now, the gun he held pointed at her, his expression dark and focused, wanted to deny her and her people a future, the chance at freedom.

It was not right that they had survived this long without asking for a single thing. They'd even put up with the prejudice and poverty handed to them. Vic had never been one to complain or push back. And she'd certainly never been afraid to die. But even after friends and comrades had fallen, after she'd burned, she always made it back, always pushed. And for what? Now she had something she *wanted* to come back to.

She wanted that future now that it could be taken from her.

O'Rourke opened the door behind her and waited. Without prompting, the two mechs who were stationed outside the door stepped into the room.

"Take her down," he said.

The Uniforms flanked her on either side, gripping her arms, and she glared at the general, the very representation of everything standing in the way of what lay before her, what was within her grasp.

"I am so curious to know what's in that brain of yours that makes you so unique," O'Rourke said, falling in behind the Uniforms taking her from the room.

A chill ran through her, some sense that it wouldn't be a few simple tests he'd run. Morgan had learned about the genetics, the science behind it all, designed computer programs to study without being invasive. O'Rourke didn't exactly strike her as the techy type. He was military, which usually translated to brute force. Get the answers no matter what, even if that meant popping her head open like a soda can to poke at the brain inside.

They dragged her down the stairs, past the rear entryway where she'd first met Jared Linus face to face. The half-bird was there, his cocky smile a stark contrast to the Uniforms stationed near the doors, still standing at attention, unblinking.

She ignored him as he joined their party and calculated as they went down and around and behind the sweeping staircase. Four Uniforms near the back door. The two holding her arms. The four she saw by the front foyer as they passed on their way to a hidden door tucked in the back.

Two more mechs were there, monitoring who came and went, though they gave no hint of recognition when O'Rourke stepped forward to unlock it with a code.

In they dragged her, following the general's lead into a dark, metal-lined room. It was barely large enough to fit the four of them as the lieutenant colonel joined them, and the door behind them shut. It triggered soft lights along the edges, casting them all in a faint eerie glow.

Another keypad appeared on the opposite wall. When O'Rourke finished inputting the code, the soft beeping of the buttons audible in the airtight space, the whole wall slid aside to reveal a dimly lit space. Computers blinked from all corners of the room, filling it with the muted buzz of electricity that made the hair on Vic's arms rise. Maybe it was the intention that mingled with the electricity, the sense that she was being carried into a death chamber.

The Uniforms lugged her across the room to a chair that shoved chilling flashbacks to the forefront of her mind. Injections that infused her muscles with inhuman strength, that aged her body weeks in a matter of minutes, that coaxed her cells into healing faster than normal.

The phantom pain haunted her bones, a howling ache that echoed to the marrow.

There was no conscious decision on her part. It was simply the memories that triggered her rebellion, the automatic reaction to fight the grip of her captors. The Uniforms might have been stronger, but she gave them a run for their money as they wrestled her into place. It took concerted effort for them to strap her limbs down.

She yanked against the restraints as the mechs stepped back, and her glare landed on Haven lingering behind them. He didn't seem particularly confident in what was happening as his gaze darted to the general.

"The kill switch was a genius invention," O'Rourke said, totally unconcerned about the ruckus, even as she continued to rage against her bonds. He simply moved to his selection of supplies and plucked up what he needed to place electrodes all over her forehead and chest. "But only if it works correctly."

His expression darkened as he stared down at her, something like hate forming in his eyes.

"Why can't you just use the mechs?" she asked, still tugging, desperate for a weakness in the nylon straps around her wrists. They held fast, felt firm against her skin. "They seem perfectly willing to do whatever they're told."

He lifted a brow. "I think you know the answer to that."

She caught the way Haven's focus shifted from the general to the Uniforms and back, processing his words, though she kept her attention on O'Rourke.

As she'd suspected, the creators of the Unborn saw a mistake in making soldiers superior in every way while allowing for free will. Control only went so far, and Unborn still had needs, desires, independent thought. It didn't matter that they were meticulously spliced together, and every element of their inception was controlled. They were still humans built by humans.

Uniforms might have been easier to control, but they were incapable of looking at things through the lens of human life. They couldn't weigh moral quandaries, didn't have the capacity to consider the facets of every situation and make the best choice when there was no right answer. They operated in terms of objectives and assignments, following direct orders and nothing more.

There was a reason they weren't suited for war, which was a veritable minefield of gray.

"The government poured a lot of time and resources into the Unborn Project." O'Rourke's voice pulled her from her thoughts. "It would be a shame to scrap the whole thing."

He turned away to reach for something. "But we also can't have any of you malfunctioning when we need you to behave."

Her heart started pounding so hard in her chest, the rush of her blood hot and urgent through her veins. This was it. The moment she had to decide that what she wanted was worth fighting for. If she deserved to have a life outside of what she was created to be. If her *people* deserved their future. If she didn't fight for herself, she damn well wanted to fight for them.

The monitors O'Rourke had attached her to registered the acceleration of her pulse, and she realized how heavy she was breathing. The air seemed to scrape up her windpipe and burn through her nose.

The phantom sensation of Hunt's hands on her skin jolted her, that one reminder that she wasn't a robot and would never be one. That even though she was designed with intention, a product of necessity and desperation rather than human connection, she deserved to have a life beyond what she'd been created for.

And she wanted it. Wanted more than she'd been given, more than she'd experienced, more than she'd allowed herself to want before.

But beyond that, seeing Hunt again, being *with* him, taking care of the little community by his side, became a need that wove its way into her very makeup, forging a whole new creature out of this lab-grown mockery of humanity. She was another thing entirely, and she would be damned if the opportunity was squandered in this way. She would fight for her fellow Unborn. She would fight for herself.

The moment she decided that this wouldn't be the end, the computer clocked the change. Instead of the irregular rhythm it had been recording, it went smooth and even. O'Rourke's head snapped up and jerked in her direction as the cold, mechanical feeling crept over her.

"No!" he shouted at the same moment she ripped through the wrist and ankle bindings as if they were made of thread instead of thick nylon.

She was pulling the electrodes from her forehead before she even registered the pain from the restraints biting into her skin.

The two Uniforms behind him only made it two steps by the time she was up, yanking O'Rourke's hand from whatever he'd been doing, lifting and twisting until the sickening crack of bone reverberated in the room.

Every sight and sound was sharpened, almost painfully clear as her mind processed it.

She heard the first mech pull his gun from its holster and spun, taking O'Rourke's screaming form with her. The bullet tore through the fleshy part of her oblique, leaving a trail of fire as it lodged into the chair she'd been in a few seconds before. But it was negligible background noise.

She continued to move, dragging the general along as several more rounds blasted in her direction, sprays of sparks shooting into the air from the computers all around them as the bullets missed her by centimeters.

She rolled her lips inward as she did another twist around, deciding it wasn't the worst thing to pull O'Rourke a half-second too late.

He shrieked when one of the bullets hit him in the back, though she wasn't sure where. She was still aiming for the wall they'd come through, expecting another set of Uniforms to make their way in soon. If she could get past them, she'd have access to the escape.

She dropped O'Rourke and ducked, continuing her spiral through the room. He was still alive, though he was gasping and writhing like a fish on land, narrowing his creepy, vulture-like eyes in her direction.

Completing a full circle through the room, she came up behind one of the two Uniforms. They were both turning in her direction, still firing their weapons somewhat wildly along her path a millisecond after she moved. She pulled an extra gun from the hip holster of one and popped the other mech in the eye before the second kicked the pistol from her hands, catching her chin with the heel of his heavy boot.

She staggered sideways, hitting one of the numerous desks, the edge jamming into her hip painfully. Ignoring the pain, she used the moment to leap over the desk and duck behind it as another round of bullets ricocheted above her head.

The wall opposite her slid open, four more Uniforms spilling into the room with rifles and weapons in hand, and she mentally rolled through a stream of curses, clenching her teeth to keep from spitting them. The brief rest behind the desk had her mind registering the wound in her side as it screamed where she'd taken the bullet.

The new contingent of Uniforms came forward, choosing not to fire their weapons in the tight space with so many bodies. That meant she might be able to move without fear of getting shot, but it also meant that they would likely come at her with brute force.

She was a Silver, though. She was going to take as many down as she could, even if she went down, too.

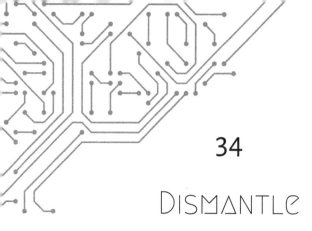

34

DISMANTLE

THE CROWDED ROOM ALSO meant that she couldn't keep enough space between her and another body, even as she slid away from the desk, keeping low to the ground.

But a mech managed to slam the butt of a gun against the side of her head, a burst of pain exploding across her vision. When it cleared, all she saw was the glittering black floor, the cold tile soothing the throb in her skull.

The realization hit a second later that if she was lying on the floor, she was vulnerable. She pushed away from the cool stone, ignoring the way the pulse of pain radiated in her head.

She slid her leg along as she spun, knowing she was slower than usual, but she was still able to knock the closest Uniform off his feet, practically feeling the ground shake as he went down.

Blood was still leaking from her side, warm against her skin as it soaked into her shirt. But she climbed on top of the mech she'd dropped, slamming her fists against his face. With no change in expression, his head jerked left and then right as if it was being yanked back and forth by a string.

And then something slammed into the side of her chest, knocking her sideways and to the ground, a renewed agony stabbing through her abdomen. But not just the gunshot wound. A new sensation, a deeper radiating ache expanded through her entire rib cage, front and back, and she gulped at the air. Then a weight—a mech's body—landed on top of her, pressing her harder into the floor. A pop she could feel more than hear reverberated through her body.

He had the leverage to keep her pinned, especially with whatever had been damaged inside her body. It took every ounce of her willpower to fight against the pain that speared through her with each breath she took. It was a dagger to her lungs every time they tried to inflate.

The Uniforms must have thought they had her, though, because they grabbed her arms and hauled her to her feet, lifting as if she weighed nothing, though it sent a blast of agony through her body.

But she fought it back, using the moment and their certainty that she was made, and she whipped the Uniform's arm over her shoulder, bending and snapping the robotic arm. It sounded eerie. Not quite bone-like, and he didn't even make a noise.

She kept yanking, flipping him over her back. He landed on the edge of the desk in front of her. She threw her weight against him, heard the louder crack of his back along the edge, and the light in the eyes dimmed until they were black pits. Like a computer screen going dark.

Another Uniform came at her, and she lumbered sideways even as she heard the gurgling sound of her own breathing. That wasn't healthy. It was slowing her down, too.

The Uniform tried to use the butt of the rifle to knock her back, but she caught it, twisted it from his grip, and slammed the business end straight through his eye. His head jerked back, the entire body going rigid and sailing to the ground like a stiff board.

Vic held fast to the rifle, deciding to take a chance with firing since she'd decreased the numbers already.

She dropped to her knee as the strength continued to leach from her body. She was leaking so much blood from her side, and her punctured lung was greedily soaking in fluid. She heard it in the squelching breaths that filled her ears.

But she pulled the trigger, the semi-automatic mechanism a blessing as unending rounds of bullets sprayed fire through the room, taking down two more mechs in quick succession.

Where was the last guy?

She sucked at the air, her chest heaving hungrily as she scanned the room for the final Uniform.

Gravity threatened to pull her down, a part of her mind telling her to lie down and rest, to shut her eyes and sleep. Sleep did sound nice. One hand went to the floor to hold her up as the wall at the other end of the room opened again, the final four Uniforms she'd seen upstairs filling the space.

She coughed, the feeling like shards of glass scraping against the inner tissue as a splatter of blood landed on the floor in front of her. Staring at that bright red splotch, feeling the presence of the Uniforms around her, she knew she didn't have enough left in her.

She could push one more time, take down a couple more mechs. But breathing had become its own exercise in endurance, its own battle for consciousness. There were likely others, and she wouldn't be able to stay lucid enough to face them.

She swallowed and grimaced, leaning sideways, her one arm extended to the floor still propping her up, and looked at the mechs before her. Lifting the rifle from the floor was a fight, and she blinked hard, willing her weakening muscles to work.

Pop, pop, pop, pop!

One by one, the Uniforms jerked upright then tumbled to the floor like a stack of dominoes. She would have been shocked, or at least would have reacted, if her only focus wasn't fighting to get oxygen into her lungs.

The reaction came when those responsible for taking out the last of the Uniforms stepped forward. Claire, Hunt, and Cam walked into the dim light of the half-destroyed room. Every muscle in her body tried to seize, and the stab in her chest became almost unbearable. The air, once a life-sustaining elixir, had become a relentless foe, turning each inhale into a battlefield.

They didn't see her at first, and she didn't have the capacity to call to them. It was quiet except for Vic's labored breathing and the periodic buzz of electricity through the damaged computers. And then there was O'Rourke's whimpering cutting through. Apparently, he was still alive.

She swung her heavy head in the general's direction, fear shoving itself forward inside her. One last adrenaline pump gave her a shot of energy as she met his gaze. Something flashed in his eyes, and he reached up to the control panel he'd been using before she'd ripped from her restraints.

"The serum!" she gritted out as O'Rourke hauled himself up on the console. His hand slammed down on whatever would trigger Claire and Cam, then he collapsed back onto the floor into his own puddle of blood.

Her eyes wheeled until they found Claire and Cam, neither of whom faltered—like they'd inoculated themselves before coming into the room. It would have been the smart thing. She would've instructed them to do it if she'd been in charge. The adrenaline's power faded almost as quickly as it had come, chased as it was by relief, and the rifle in Vic's hand clattered to the floor.

She went right after, unable to hold herself up any longer. Even the cold, hard floor felt like a reprieve.

"Vic!" Hunt's voice cleaved the air with concern. She heard his movement, and then he was there, dropping to his knees beside her, hurrying to tuck his pistol into the hidden spot at his back.

"No big guns?" she gasped out as he reached for her, some part of her trying to keep him—or herself—distracted from how bad this was. Because it *was* bad. The bitter tang of blood was on her tongue, and she felt the weight of it in her chest where it wasn't supposed to be.

His eyes shot to her face, incredulous. "God, Vic." He shook his head as his hands hovered over her bloody abdomen. His lips pinched into a thin line. "Couldn't have waited for all of us to come in together."

She released a wet cough, her concern about the spiderweb of agony second only to the gurgling sound in her chest. It wasn't encouraging. But she'd either heal or she wouldn't.

What she'd planned to say was that things would have been a lot worse if they'd all come with her. There had been nothing to keep the general from shooting the rest of them where they stood. She'd at least had the protection of what was in her head to keep him from taking her out immediately.

Damn her inability to catch her breath. "Are you going to—" a tight cough and a grimace— "lecture me... now?"

Hunt frowned, his eyes flashing to hers.

"How did you—" The rest of the question was overtaken by a fit of coughing. Her hand came away from her mouth wet.

"How did we find you?" he finished, his voice strained as he took in the blood she'd hacked up. "Lucky guess. It's hard to miss the biggest house in town when it's crawling with Uniforms."

"The general is still alive," Claire called. "What do you want us to do with him?"

"We need. . . to know how—" Vic grunted, frustration a quick flash that overtook the pain briefly— "to stop the kill switch." She wasn't sure if it was loud enough for Claire to hear.

But when the general's strained scream bounced around the room like someone was torturing him, she figured she had.

"What am I looking at here?" Hunt spoke low and fast, his reprimand taking a back seat to his worry.

"Shot," she managed, gesturing to her stomach. "Broke a rib." Breath. "Or five. Probably. . ." She slurped at the air again. "Probably punctured a lung." She fought another urge to cough.

His lips became colorless, and he moved to put pressure on her stomach.

"No," she croaked. Even tensing in anticipation sent another wave of torture through her, and she groaned.

He lifted his hands back up like she was holding him at gunpoint. "Vic, I need to stop the bleeding."

She gritted her teeth and shook her head.

He blew out a frustrated breath. "Can you walk?"

Doubtful, she wanted to say. But it took less air to say "no."

The sound of a close-range gunshot reverberated through the room, and Hunt's head snapped up. It took her much longer to react, even after she realized that the general was no longer whimpering or writhing on the floor.

Claire's coppery eyes caught the low light as she glanced in Vic's direction. "He wasn't cooperating."

Vic couldn't find it in herself to care much. But they had to make sure there wasn't something else, a control center in another location. "Phone or tablet. . . or something?"

Claire was quiet, the sound of her rifling around on the body her only response. Vic's hope began to fall the longer she had to search. And just when she was about to call it, Claire made a sound of triumph.

"Got it."

The faintest flush of relief rolled through Vic. Niko could probably do something with that. If they could get it to him. They had to make it out of this place first, but how many more Uniforms were nearby? There was no way there'd only be a contingent of ten.

"We've gotta go," Hunt said, as if reading her mind. He started to scoot his hands under her body, but it made her cry out, and he pulled back.

She took a shallow breath and rolled to her hands and knees, a growl vibrating her clenched teeth. Hunt and Claire tried to help, but even gently pulling on her arms made the pain scream in response.

"I got it, I got it," she snapped, slapping their hands away as she climbed laboriously to her feet.

She heard the sucking sound as she panted from the effort. Instead of focusing on the probably-not-good of that, she repeated in her head like a mantra the fact that she was designed to self-heal. Maybe if she said it enough times, her programming would catch on and knit her punctured organ back together.

The sound of her teeth grinding together from the pain every movement brought her was audible, but she managed to stay upright as she wrapped an arm around her middle. It was a weak attempt to stanch the flow of her blood, and even that small pressure elicited a hiss.

"Please tell me. . . you brought the truck," she managed to huff out.

"Small miracles," Hunt said with a grim smile as they started toward the still-open antechamber.

Something tickled in the back of her mind, fighting its way past her pain, and she turned. "Wait."

Hunt's brows crashed over his eyes. "What?"

"Half-bird," she coughed out, scanning for movement. She hadn't seen him leave, hadn't spotted him hiding. But if she had to guess, that's what he was doing.

She snatched Hunt's gun from his back and shuffled forward, listening for. . . there. She ignored her injuries and staggered forward, moving too quickly for her own good to where she'd heard the panicked breathing. Agony bit through her, twisting her expression.

Trembling hands came up in front of Haven's sweaty face, curled as he was under a desk. "Please, I—"

She fired off two quick rounds at the console behind her, hoping it shut off the general's attempt at making Claire and Cam go dark. She liked that it made Haven flinch, his hands shaking harder in front of his face. Then she brought the muzzle to the half-bird's forehead, not hesitating the second it was in place. She turned from his limp form and passed the weapon back to Hunt, nearly stumbling into him when her vision grew spotty. She breathed in fits and starts, pain curling around her ribs, until her lightheadedness abated.

She waved the helping hands away and moved forward again, the others reluctantly following. Surprise flickered through her at the sight of something jammed between the door and the wall, holding it open, and she looked at Hunt with new eyes.

One brow twitched. "I might not be able to take six men down at a time, but I can get creative in a bind."

She released a short laugh, then grimaced as the pain exploded through her ribs. "Don't. . . make me laugh," she groaned.

"Sorry," he murmured.

Claire and Cam strong-armed the other door open, Claire using her weight against it to keep it wide enough for the rest to pass through.

Cam went first, checking in all directions, moving like smoke billowing out, smooth and silent. He'd obviously been trained as a wraith.
Alice moved like that.

Hunt had his gun at the ready with his free hand, his other lightly
wrapped around Vic's arm to help her stagger through and across the
quiet room to the front door.

Gunshots rang out right as they reached it, bullets lodging inches
from Vic's head, splintering wood above them like shrapnel. Hunt
ducked, yanking her down, and her scream of agony threatened to
rip her vocal cords in half.

Claire and Cam crouched in the corners on opposite sides of Hunt
and Vic, aiming their semi-autos in the direction of the staircase and
other entrance respectively.

Vic's fingers craved a weapon. She wanted to cut the rest of these
bastards down. She begged her body to work with her instead of
against her, so she could do what she'd been created to do: destroy
the enemy. But she was useless as volleys of firepower blinked back
and forth around them.

The constant rat-a-tat lured Vic into a vivid memory as she cow-
ered on the floor under Hunt's hand. It felt heavy against her back
when it shouldn't have. It was the only reason she stayed down.

*"It's a damn good reason to stay down!" Vic's voice reverberated in the
halls of her own mind. She'd met Jamie's gaze, lit with anger, only inches
from her own. She was practically holding her sister down as the bullets
whizzed above them, fireflies that packed quite the bite if they even moved.*

*"But Alice—" this through clenched teeth, and Vic wanted to shove
Jamie's face into the ground just to shut her up.*

*"Can take care of herself," Vic finished, even as it made her stomach twist
and threaten to leap up her throat. Though it was true, and she knew Alice
was probably fine where she was, that instinct that Jamie was letting lead*

was fighting Vic's sense of responsibility for the sister that was right in front of her.

If Jamie got up now, that spray of bullets would take her out, and she'd be no good to anyone, let alone Alice.

"... not enough oxygen."

Hunt's voice bit through Vic's mental haze, the memory of Jamie's angry face disintegrating as the anguish rippled through her. The pain had pulled her under, and it had ripped her back. It took a moment to register the fact that she was cradled against a warm body as it moved.

"Her lips are almost blue." This from Cam.

"I'm fine," Vic croaked, pushing against Hunt.

"Whoa!" He scrambled to keep a hold of her since she was still stronger than he was, even half-conscious. "Damn it, Vic." His words sliced through his teeth.

The edge in his voice didn't come close to how sharp the misery radiating through her body felt, so she stopped fighting him so she could focus on getting the air her lungs desperately needed.

"You're not fine," Claire snapped from beside him. "People don't pass out when they're fine."

They were walking. Briskly. Which meant they'd gotten the snipers inside the house. She felt the warmth of the air, the tang of early summer on her tongue. She opened her eyes, squinting against the brightness of the sun.

Hunt didn't meet her gaze. He was too busy checking every direction and going as fast as he could with her in his arms. She might have been stronger than he was, but she didn't weigh much in comparison. Still, it was hard to move fast with a limp body in your arms.

"Where are you going to put her?" Claire's voice came from behind Vic's head then moved forward like she was leading them.

"What hurts less, Vic?" Hunt finally looked down at her. "Sitting? Lying down?"

Her eyes fluttered closed. None of it would matter. Not really. Except she did know that if her lung was punctured, as she suspected it was, giving it space to expand was probably better.

"It all hurts," she gasped out. "But probably... lying down."

"In the truck bed, then," Hunt said, probably not to her.

She heard the creak of the hinges as someone unlatched the tailgate and dropped it down.

"Yeah, the blankets."

She liked the feel of his voice rumbling through his chest against her. It was soothing, and she mentally clutched at the way it soothed in preparation for getting into the truck.

Hunt slid her onto the tailgate, and she gripped at his shirt, eyes popping open again. "Let me."

He nodded, though the muscles in his jaw feathered as he released her.

She crawled to the blanket, hissing through her teeth, the sound like a slow leak. She was pretty sure her bullet wound had slowed its bleeding by now. The pain there was dwarfed by what was in her chest, anyway.

When she laid her body down, she stared up at the brilliant blue of the afternoon sky that was visible between the full branches of the trees, puffing air in and out until the pain subsided enough that she didn't wish for death.

Hunt crawled up beside her, which shocked her, and she turned a questioning look at him.

"Cam is driving." His tone brooked no argument.

She didn't have the capacity anyway.

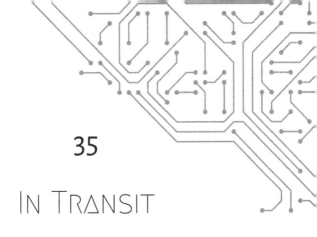

35

In Transit

"**D**o you think he's aiming for the potholes on purpose?" Vic asked through her teeth, squeezing her eyes shut so tightly she worried she'd pop blood vessels in her eyelids.

"They're unavoidable," Hunt said in defense, though his voice was too tight to believe he was dismissing it so easily.

He was still worried about her. But it was a good sign that she was able to speak a full sentence without stopping for a breath. Or maybe it was wishful thinking. And because she was stretched out in the truck bed, her breathing was a little easier, even if the pain hadn't decreased thanks to roughly riding through the neglected road that brought them out this way in the first place.

It hadn't felt this rough when they'd been heading in the other direction. But it hadn't been long before she'd fallen asleep in the cab while Hunt drove them to what surely would've ended up being a death sentence for the rest of them.

It would've been hers if Hunt and the others hadn't shown up. That was a surprise after she'd ditched them in the woods and set off on her own, though she wouldn't have abandoned anyone on her team, either, even if they'd gone off without backup. Still, she didn't regret the decision. The rightness of that choice sat just fine on her shoulders, heavy as it was. But it didn't mean she was above expressing her gratitude.

She grimaced as the truck trundled over a new constellation of potholes, trying to keep her body still so she wouldn't rock and bump against the side.

Hunt was sitting upright, his back pressed against the cab of the truck, one knee bent with his arm dangling over it. Her eyes traced his profile as sunshine and shadow took turns rolling over his face. He wasn't looking at her, but she didn't miss the tight lines of his expression.

She reached over to brush her fingers against his leg, drawing his gaze to hers.

"Are you in pain? You need something?" His words came in quick succession as he started moving, reaching for the first aid kit he'd pulled from the rest of their supplies.

"No," she said, grabbing his hand to stop him, to pull his focus to her. He'd already patched up her gunshot wound. The medical tape pulled against her skin every time she shifted.

His eyes narrowed, the skepticism that was so much a part of him making her want to laugh. But *that* would be a bad idea, considering they barely had the bleeding under control. At least on the outside. Her chest still felt heavy with fluid.

"Yes, I'm in pain. No, I don't need anything," she clarified, and his expression relaxed enough that he must've been mollified for the moment. "I wanted to say. . ."

His fingers laced with hers, and the guilt dropped into her stomach like a weight. He deserved to hear it.

"Thank you for coming." She forced the words around a lump in her throat.

He smirked. "For rescuing you, you mean?"

Her expression soured. "You didn't rescue me."

"I'll pretend you didn't say that," he said mildly, the smile still on his face.

She slammed her eyes shut as the truck jostled her again. "Why would you do that?"

His fingers tightened around hers. "Do what? Rescue you? Or pretend you didn't try to deny that I rescued you?"

She opened one eye to give him a glare. His smile was gone, and she'd heard it in his tone—the anger that she'd left them all behind that morning. She knew that conversation couldn't be avoided forever.

"Let's say either one, so we don't have to argue semantics." She shifted, trying to get comfortable—or as close as she was going to get with the unending waves of pain rolling through her. The trees grew thicker together overhead, blocking out the sun and lowering the temperature, which was a welcome relief from the heat of the day.

"Semantics, huh?" There was a mocking twist to Hunt's mouth at that. "What if I want to get into semantics?"

She was about to argue, but he lifted his free hand. It was the intensity of his expression that truly stopped her, though.

"I want this to be one hundred percent clear since I'm not sure you've picked up on my arguably not-so-subtle *semantics* before." He turned to fully face her, taking the hand he held into both of his. "I was absolutely serious about being all in, Vic. And I don't mean for the time being or as long you'll have me. This doesn't happen for me."

"What doesn't?" she breathed, her heartbeat rapidly ascending to the danger zone. The feeling of not enough oxygen had nothing to do with her punctured lung this time.

"What I feel for you. Never felt it before. Pretty sure it won't happen again. So I want to make sure you understand what that really means."

She swallowed the fear of the answer to her next question. "What does it really mean?"

A lock of his sandy blond hair fell onto his forehead as he lifted a brow like he knew she knew what he was driving at. "I'm happy to say it, Vic. Are you ready to hear it?"

She wanted to say yes. She wanted to say no. She wanted to hide in the half-lived life she'd had before and simultaneously never go back. But she knew from experience that without venturing out, ground could not be gained. And she wasn't a coward, even if she was scared.

"You said you wanted to be one hundred percent clear," she reminded him, still a little breathless, but her fingers fluttered against his palm.

The corners of his mouth turned up slightly. "I love you, Vic."

The words were massive, pressing along her skin with an urgency to get inside her and wind themselves around her heart. But they needed permission, and maybe she was a coward after all.

"Are you sure?" she whispered.

"Victoria," he said, exasperated.

"I-I. . ." What could she say? That the fear filled her to the brim, leaving little space for anything else?

She'd broken rules, gone rogue, and taken out a general. Surely they would all suffer for it. Now she was the only one they knew of who could combat the kill switch, and that could mean she was on someone's radar somewhere. What if her choices cost her this man that she. . . loved?

But Hunt knew all of this. He wasn't stupid, and he took his role as leader of the group at the ranch and in the bunker seriously. He wouldn't put everyone in danger for no reason, even something as silly as love.

But was love silly? Maybe dismissing it as ridiculous made her feel better about denying herself access, when she'd always been so sure she was incapable. She could say she'd probably only ever loved the girls and Angela, and they'd all been taken from her. She was afraid of losing Hunt, too.

But she'd followed every rule before, done all that was asked of her and more, and still, she'd lost the ones who'd mattered most in the world.

Hunt was waiting for her to finish, but there was no pressure in his expression. Just a mild understanding. And, damn it, if he didn't deserve her honest answer... He'd come to rescue her, even if he was still angry that she'd left them out in the woods to take on the bad guys alone—still the smartest move on her part. But she would've been livid, would've hashed it out right there.

But he wasn't her. And as much as they had in common—taking on more responsibility than they really needed to—he was different enough that she knew how good he was for her.

She opened her mouth to answer, her words sure to be shaky but true, when the truck began to slow, and Hunt's attention shifted ahead of them.

She started to sit up, unable to gauge where they were since all she could see was sky and trees above them, but Hunt pushed her back down. The brief thought that she could fight him flashed through her mind. She was strong enough to throw him out of the truck one-handed if she wanted to, even injured.

But now probably wasn't the time to assert that kind of dominance, especially since he didn't look worried.

"We're home," he murmured, though he didn't look down at her again as the truck rumbled to a stop.

"That means you have to let me get up," she said, annoyed.

He glanced over and took his hand from her shoulder, already shifting to a crouched position. As soon as the truck lurched to a stop, he leaped from the bed over the side and walked around to the tailgate while she rolled to her hands and knees to crawl her way—slowly, painfully—to the end.

She sat and scooted carefully until her legs dangled, letting Hunt help her stand from the bed. It was miraculous that she didn't scream, though she wanted to. The agony threatened to shove its cry right up her throat.

She gripped the front of Hunt's shirt, as much to steady herself against pain as to pull his attention back to her because Claire and Cam were already getting out of the truck. Vic wanted to say this before anyone else got to them, before the doctor whisked her away for a checkup, *before she lost her nerve.*

"Hunt, I. . ." She looked down at her own slender fingers wrapped around the light-weight cotton over his chiseled chest. Then she met his gaze as his thick brows pulled low over that icy blue. "I love you, too."

He sucked in a breath, so faint no one else might've heard it. His arms went carefully around her waist, more of an embrace than the help he'd initially offered her. He brought his lips to hers in a soft kiss, worried about hurting her. But she still sensed the hum of emotion behind it, felt it in the way his fingers curled against her sides, the faint pressure agonizingly painful and delicious.

"Thank you," he said, pulling back slightly. His breath fanned over her face.

"For what?"

"Telling me."

She smiled.

"But don't think this means you're getting out of the discussion about you abandoning us in the woods."

She sighed, grimacing through a sharp stab of pain. "I wouldn't dream of it."

The footfalls coming toward them made awareness slam back into place. The person was running, and there were more bodies around them than there usually were. Unease slithered through her.

Why wasn't everyone out working?

"Hunt!"

He turned, though he didn't take his hands from her as a Copper came barreling toward them, skidding on the gravel a little when he tried to come to a stop.

"Max needs to talk to you." The man wasn't even out of breath, but there was a clear urgency in his words that made Vic's nerves prickle with electricity.

"What's the problem, Ryan?" Hunt demanded.

The man's face crumpled into a grimace. "Got news about a settlement a few miles south that was totally wiped out."

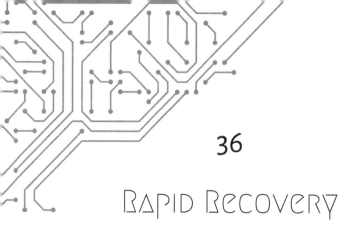

36

Rapid Recovery

H UNT'S HEAD SWIVELED IN Vic's direction, the apprehension deeply entrenched in his eyes, the blue pools shimmering with it. As much as she wanted more information, to get every minute detail, he needed to know what happened as soon as possible, and she still desperately needed to be doctored. As much as she hated to admit it.

"You go," she told him, giving him a little shove. "I'll make it to the house. See Doc." She winced, oxygen fighting her again now that she was standing. "Not sure I can manage more than that right now."

Still, he hesitated. Torn between his responsibility for the community and his need to take care of her.

"I'll be fine," she insisted, working to hide how hard catching her breath was so he wouldn't delay any longer. "I want to know what's going on just as badly. The sooner you go, the sooner you can fill me in."

He took halting steps away from her, then turned to give Claire a heavy look as he followed Ryan back toward the house.

And because Vic wasn't stupid, she knew what that look had communicated even before Claire moved in her direction with a determined set to her expression. It was a mask, though, because Vic saw the worry in the depths of the other woman's eyes. The westering sun brushed orange light along Claire's ebony skin, making her look like she was glowing as she reached for Vic to help her.

Vic shook her head, knowing it would likely hurt more. Though she wasn't afraid to admit it was a little bit of pride. "I can walk myself."

"And you complained about the potholes," Claire muttered with a shake of her head, falling in beside her.

Vic slid a glance in her direction as she hobbled toward the house, slow, stooped, and weak. If Claire had heard her complain about the potholes, she possibly heard the rest of the conversation that took place in the back of the truck. Damn that Unborn enhanced hearing.

She chose to ignore it and asked instead, "What would you do. . . carry me?"

Claire shot her a dark look.

"Well," she huffed, "that's the least painful option aside from walking. . . myself."

"Then hop in," Claire said, holding out her arms.

And then they both laughed, which made Vic stop and groan, clutching at her ribs as she sucked air in through her teeth.

Claire's shoulders inched toward her ears. "Sorry."

The effort of climbing the stairs was what nearly killed her, and Claire made jokes about piggyback rides to distract her. By the time they reached Hunt's room—an assumption on Vic's part, though she doubted it would be a problem—she was ready to collapse.

She sat carefully on the bed, trying not to jostle too much, and then laid back on the mattress, taking quick, shallow breaths as anguish radiated through her chest and worked like a poison through the rest of her body. It permeated every cell, making it almost impossible to tell where it originated from.

The doctor came in not long after, giving her a thorough exam while lecturing her on moving around so much when she was so severely injured. As if Vic could help having to ride in the bed of a truck along an abandoned road for over two hours.

Morgan's hazel eyes bore into Vic's as she listened to her breathing, her lips disappearing into a thin line. "I don't like the sound of that."

"Not particularly enjoying the feeling either," Vic replied with an edge.

Claire snorted from her position near the window, staring out. Her stance might have been casual, but the lines of her body were taut. Hunt hadn't been up yet with the information about the village that had been wiped out.

"I can't tell if the lung is still collapsed or not." Morgan didn't seem to have heard Vic's words. Likely because the stethoscope's buds were still stuffed into her ears.

"I'm going to guess not," Vic said, knowing what the treatment would be for a collapsed lung. She definitely didn't want a tube inserted between her ribs. She'd had triage training for the war, and that was one practice drill that had given her the heebies.

Morgan pulled the stethoscope out of her ears. "What's that?"

"If it was still collapsed, which I'm sure it was before, I'd still be struggling to catch my breath."

Claire turned to them as Morgan gave Vic a skeptical look like she knew Vic was trying to get out of a painful procedure.

"It's true, Doc. She was practically blue earlier, stopping mid-sentence just to take a breath. Passed out."

"You passed out?" Morgan snapped.

Oops. They hadn't exactly shared that bit.

"Only for a few minutes," Vic protested. "And I'm better now. It just hurts like a bitch."

The doctor shut her eyes and lifted her face heavenward as if praying for strength. "You Unborn are *so* lucky you heal quickly." She brought her face back down and leveled Vic with what could only be classified as a glare. "A normal person would have suffocated to death."

"Why are we acting like this is my fault?" Vic looked to Claire, who was smirking.

"And what is it with you getting shot all the time?" Morgan muttered as she sifted through her bag to grab what she needed to stitch up Vic's side.

"At least it's the same spot as my knife wound," Vic said, staring up at the swirl pattern on the ceiling. "Only one scar."

Morgan gave her a dry look then went back to setting up. "I've done more sewing on you than almost anyone else."

"Hopefully you won't have to do any more from here on out."

Morgan grunted as she bent forward, snapping on some sterile gloves before setting up the sutures. She turned back to analyze the wound. "This bruising. . ." she murmured, shaking her head. "I've never seen it so bad on an Unborn before."

"I believe you mentioned I'd be dead if I were human," Vic said flatly, keeping her eyes locked on the ceiling while trying not to tense up in anticipation of the needle. There'd be no numbing. She'd insisted. Unnecessary waste of supplies, considering she may have destroyed Hunt's entire livelihood by taking a prominent general out. Who knew what kind of ramifications they were facing from her actions that day?

Morgan's gloved finger was what she felt along her skin though, not the sharp point of her curved needle. And it was higher than it should have been for the wound in her side.

Vic's eyes shot to the other woman's face. Morgan's gaze was locked on something near her ribs, a softness cradling her expression in a way that made Vic's heart twist.

"Rodina," Morgan whispered.

Oh. That.

"Family, right?"

Vic stiffened, ignoring the way the pain slashed at her, both physically and emotionally. She couldn't tell which one was worse. But she pulled the hem of her shirt down a little, breaking Morgan's trance.

The other woman's face flushed as she trained her attention back down, clearing her throat.

"Sorry." The word susurrated through her lips, barely audible.

Vic turned her head back to the ceiling, hissing out a breath as the needle pierced the already irritated skin around her gunshot.

It was dark when she heard and felt the movement, a disturbance in the air that snapped her into consciousness. She fought the panicked spasming in her chest that made the pain burn like fire across her entire upper body, tendrils of agony squeezing the bones from her chest to her back.

There was no reason for her reaction. No one would be sneaking in to slice her throat open under cover of darkness. There was no enemy hunting her right now.

And yet her hand shot out when the figure drew close to the bed, the training so deeply ingrained that she didn't hesitate when she flung him to the ground, even as she tried to fight the response that felt as natural as breathing, like an auto-run program.

She stood over him, panting as the pain lashed through her renewed, threatening to steal her consciousness. But even with her vision dimming at the edges, the moonlight shooting into the room illuminated Hunt's surprised face, catching the blue in his eyes and giving them an ethereal glow.

His palms were raised in her direction, and she wrapped her arm around herself, collapsing back onto the bed before her legs gave out, snatching at the air with gasping breaths.

"Remind me never to sneak in when you're sleeping." Hunt's voice carried that wry twist of his mild sarcasm, and he grunted as he got to his feet.

But she was incapable of answering him while the agony blasted through her from the rapid movement. No amount of painkillers could touch this after the kind of force she'd used to flip him.

He took a step toward her. "Vic, do I need to get—"

"Just give me. . . a minute," she managed through a clenched jaw.

He watched her silently as she breathed through the torture, fighting the urge to clench her entire body. It was the automatic response to the excruciating pain, but it would only make it worse. So she concentrated on each body part, talking individual muscles into relaxing, and slowly the pain subsided to a torturous throb.

She raised her eyes, though her body was still curled over itself, her arm wrapped around her rib cage as if she could hold the bones together and keep them from splitting apart.

"I'm sorry it took so long to make it back up. Doc told me you had dozed off, and I didn't want to disturb you."

She gave a terse nod, deciding words were unnecessary at this point. And still too much of a chore to get out.

"I gave Niko the tablet to work on," he said, still watching her face. "It's got an encrypted password to unlock the damn thing. Likely has a gnarly firewall after that he'll have to break through as well."

She gave him a knowing smile, though it probably looked too much like a grimace. "So he'll have it. . . by breakfast."

He huffed a laugh. "Most likely. Even though I told him to get some sleep and try again in the morning." He glanced out the window, silver light caressing his face, delineating the worry etched there.

When his eyes came back to hers, his expression softened.

"Was it the same as my village?" she asked, no longer able to hold back the questions that buzzed in her mind.

He sighed and moved forward to sit on the bed. His bed.

"As far as anyone can tell, everyone was wiped out. A contingent of Uniforms was spotted nearby, and they're spinning it as another glitch, warning people against Unborn. Fear-mongering."

Vic swallowed the rage that flashed through her. Like the general had said—if they could eradicate the larger groups, leaving a small number of mostly Silvers to do secret work, if they were ghosts, it would be easier to use them for covert missions. It would also cause enough division amongst the population to make them easier to control.

"It's going to work," she muttered darkly.

"The fear-mongering?"

She shook her head, but not in denial. "People are ready to hate us. It's not going to take much. It probably would've taken less."

Hunt took her hand, his expression pained like he was struggling to find the words to say, the thing to offer to make it better. But they both knew there was nothing, so he remained silent.

"I want to know if the general ordered that massacre like he ordered the one in my village, or if it was someone else. And if it was, how many others are in on this. . . crusade?"

More questions filled her, threatened to take over, to drown her. She wanted to know if the ones who were triggered just went berserk or if they could be controlled and directed. If one person could be triggered at a time or if it was only a mass number in a specified area. She would choke on the uncertainty, and she blamed her tears on that and not the fact that the future seemed even more bleak, that she felt so powerless.

What was the point of being faster, smarter, stronger if she couldn't solve all the problems? If she couldn't fight the enemy?

"We have to change things. It has to start here." Desperation almost strangled the words.

He nodded. "We will. I promise."

She wanted to say more, to push, to tell him how they would do it, that they would start the very next day despite the pain in her body, but the hand of grief tightened its grip.

Hunt's hand slid around her waist, the calloused skin catching on the fabric of her shirt as he gently urged her to lean into him. She wanted to fight the sob that was clawing up her throat, pretend it didn't hurt so much to feel so alone.

Because she *was* alone. Even though he was here, supporting her, loving her, he would never truly understand what it was like to be hated for what he was. Unborn had been created to help, to fight for everyone else's right to live, and yet they wouldn't get to live themselves.

The effort of holding in the sob was too much for her battered body, and she couldn't keep fighting it. It ached as it rolled out of her, setting off tremors of pain through her chest. But it was right that she would physically suffer for what was becoming of her world, her people, wrapped in the arms of this man who'd become more than she could've ever imagined.

This man whom she loved.

She cried herself out, aching for her sisters, the ones who would truly know her anguish. She wished to have them beside her, to face the world as they had done in the war—with the knowledge that one or all of them could die at any moment, but they had been equipped to fight through it—the fear, the uncertainty, the enemy seen and unseen—together.

She shuddered, pressing her eyes closed when it racked her body with more pain.

"Lie down, love," Hunt whispered. "Let's rest."

She obeyed, letting him wrap around her on the bed, lending his warmth and support as she drifted to sleep again.

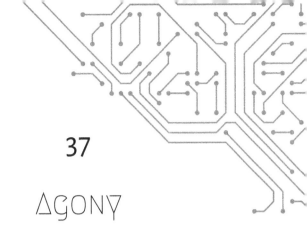

37

ΛGONY

"T HIS WOULD BE SEXY if you didn't make a face every time I touched you," Hunt said, lifting one golden eyebrow, a frown pulling at his mouth.

Water dripped in endless rivulets down his muscular body, and she lamented her injuries. He was practically holding her up, the renewed misery in her bones after a full night of sleep infuriating. The stiffness in her muscles, the way her body fought the effort of breathing like air wasn't essential to her survival made her crabby and snappish.

Hunt ran the sudsy washcloth over her with the lightest touch he could manage, and she still hissed and bit out a string of curses while her fingers dug into his shoulders.

His expression twisted every time he brushed over the mottled blue and black bruising that covered half her abdomen.

"Maybe we should've stuck with the sponge bath," he said.

"Definitely not," she snarled.

His mouth turned up a little, but the humor didn't touch his eyes.

She wanted to be thoroughly clean and fresh after so much death the day before, and the hot water would soothe the tension in her muscles. But blood loss and low oxygen levels had taken more from her than she thought possible, and she hated it, hated feeling so. . . weak.

Getting dressed was almost as bad, and she had to stop to rest half a dozen times pulling on a pair of pants. Tears gathered unbidden in her eyes from the pain.

Hunt watched while leaning against the edge of the dresser, offering several times to help her until he got tired of the knives she flung at him with her eyes.

Almost as soon as she was finished, ready to collapse onto the bed, a knock sounded on the closed door, drawing both their gazes. Pride kept her upright, though her body screamed for her to lie down.

"Come in," Hunt said, straightening.

It was Dan, whom she'd worked with on the fence a few weeks prior. His expression went purposely blank as soon as his eyes bounced from Vic to Hunt. "There's word of a couple of Silvers heading to the ranch."

Vic's stomach dropped to her toes, and all she heard was the sound of her heartbeat throbbing in her ears for *one, two, three* seconds.

"They were asking questions in town. Not sure where they got their information." His gaze shot to Vic, and she felt it like a blow. "But they apparently got their answers and will be here soon."

"Thanks, Dan."

If Vic didn't know him so well, she might have thought Hunt entirely unconcerned. It was what made him a good leader. He didn't panic, didn't give away the internal processing that went on behind his mask of calm.

Dan gave a curt nod, his eyes cutting to Vic one last time before he stepped out, closing the door behind him.

"It's them. It has to be." The words shot out of her before he could even ask.

For once, she didn't feel the need to hide her own emotion, the hope that ignited in her chest. It chased away the remnants of her pain, making her forget that she'd even been wounded.

"It might not be," he said mildly, his voice cautious.

She nodded to acknowledge his words and wrestled the hope back, trying to keep it from flying too high.

"I want to be down there when they get here," she said.

He sighed. "Vic, you can barely get yourself dressed—"

The desperation burned in her belly, and she almost took a few steps forward. "Please, Hunt."

He snapped his mouth shut, muscles in his jaw rippling. She'd never begged him before, had never used that tone, had probably never even said "please."

He stared at her for a long beat. "Fine. But we go with weapons."

She actually grinned at him. "Twist my arm."

He scoffed.

She over-estimated hope's ability to cover all ills. It had dissolved her pain for a moment, but walking down the stairs was an exercise in determination. And patience—which she'd run out of. She also ran out of unique curse words, exhausting her entire library of expletives and obscenities before they were halfway down.

She rested at the kitchen table, mostly because Hunt insisted while they waited for word that the two Silvers were spotted on the property.

"You look like you're going to pass out," Hunt said, reluctantly holding out a gun. "Not sure you should be armed."

Despite being out of breath, she managed to roll her eyes. She'd felt it when the color drained from her face, but there was no way she'd let herself pass out now.

"I'm fine," she huffed, reaching for the weapon, but he didn't relinquish it immediately. She squinted at him. "Hunter," she warned.

"Victoria," he returned.

Then he started to smile, and she could see it there in his eyes—that he was buoyed by the hope of this moment, too. Because he knew what it meant for her, *to* her.

"Incoming." The voice came from the back door they'd left open so that someone could let them know when the Silvers, when her *sisters*, had arrived.

She wanted to leap up, but she caught herself in time, remembering that she had to take it easy as she pushed up from her chair, grimacing and shuffling forward.

Once outside, the sun brushed warm fingers down her body, coaxing goosebumps across her skin. That feeling was healing in and of itself, though she still fought her ailments. She wanted to hide how bad her injuries were from Jamie and Alice, to bury how consuming the pain was. Alice would fuss over her and Jamie would bust her balls for not making it out unscathed.

Still, she couldn't help the arm she kept pressed around her ribs. It was the only thing that made her feel like she could keep the pain contained, and she moved slowly, though she cleaned up the shuffling limp. She caught Hunt's disapproving look but chose to ignore it.

Then she saw the figures approaching, and her heart flipped in her chest. Sunlight glinted off two sets of silver eyes, and the shimmer of Jamie's white-blonde hair was unmistakable.

But that wasn't Alice with her. Vic's step faltered.

She craned her neck, eyes skipping over the man who walked beside Jamie even as recognition tingled in the back of her mind, looking for a third person. There *should* have been a third person. The short, dark hair, the petite body that moved like silk through fingers, the one who was the softest, sweetest of them all even though she could sneak in and kill a person and never leave a trace.

"No," Vic whispered, the pain in the single syllable snapping Hunt's attention toward her.

Not possible. Not *right*. Even as she desperately flipped through explanations, there was no scenario in which Jamie would come without Alice.

Unless. . .

A new kind of agony ripped through her, scoring her on the inside as that realization settled deep and heavy. Because she could see it in Jamie's eyes, feel it in the air as she approached: the anger. God, the anger was beyond anything Vic could comprehend, beyond anything she'd ever seen in Jamie before.

And more than that, the pain that marked Jamie's face. It ripped more gashes inside of Vic, and her legs threatened to give out.

Until she shored up her defenses, clenching her teeth and willing herself not to waver. She was the strong one. The pillar the girls needed when they were hurting. It was what Jamie was going to need.

Jamie and the Silver who wasn't Alice drew closer, and Vic's memory supplied the name of the man who was almost as tall as Hunt, the recognition triggered by the way he moved and his proximity to Jamie. Oliver. She remembered how kind he'd always been, how easy he was to work with. He never pushed back against her command on those few missions they'd been given as all-Silver units, when she'd been tapped as the lead. Even when Jamie did fight her authority, he'd been unwaveringly cooperative, even if she'd suspected something brewing between him and her sister.

Jamie's eyes danced away from Vic and landed on Hunt, tightening. She swept the area around them next—took in the house, the barn in the distance, then the guns Vic and Hunt held loosely.

"Well, you certainly found yourself a nice place."

The words bit at Vic, but she clamped down on the urge to flinch. Typical Jamie. Assessing the situation with the bitter tint she always clutched close as a protection mechanism. The sting was particularly sharp because of the noxious grief. Vic could feel it because it matched what tumbled and writhed within her, threatening to break her bones.

"Is this why you never came to find us?" Jamie asked, her top lip curling back. "Too busy living the high life?"

"Hey—" Hunt stepped forward, but Vic pressed a hand against his chest to stop him.

Jamie's eyes flashed from his head to his toes and back up, her nostrils flaring as she noted how his body had moved in front of Vic's. "Ahh, got it. Too busy *playing house*." A dark, mirthless laugh bubbled out of her. "Don't tell me you're *sleeping* with an Adam. Can he even keep up?"

Vic huffed a frustrated breath then winced before she could stop herself. Her fingers fluttered against her ribs as the anger danced with the physical pain that assaulted her. "You could try giving people the benefit of the doubt before you go spewing your wild assumptions."

Jamie jerked to look at Vic, her platinum braid bouncing along her back.

Oliver cleared his throat beside Jamie, drawing their attention. "Maybe we could, uh, take this inside?"

His silver gaze, so much more startling because of the contrast with his toasted skin, shifted to the Organics who'd stopped what they were doing to watch. Even though these were people Hunt trusted implicitly, Vic could understand Oliver's wariness. Especially with the tide changing against them.

Hunt looked to Vic as if to ask her permission. She took a page out of his book and tipped her head in assent, so he led the way back toward the house. He kept his gait slow to not outstrip Vic's encumbered walk.

It was stupid pride, but after Jamie came out swinging so viciously, she hated showing her physical weakness even more. And it was worse because she just wasn't strong enough to succeed.

"What the hell happened to you?" Jamie bit out, the concern barely there under the surface but there all the same.

Vic tried—and failed—to hide how badly she was hurting, her face contorting as she walked. "It's a long story," she huffed.

"Seems like we've got time," Jamie muttered, words twisting with that same bitterness, and Vic felt a matching twist in her heart.

They all filed inside the house through the front door, which felt odd and overly formal since Vic barely spent any time in the living areas. She'd never seen anyone using those spaces casually, but she assumed they must with how many people called it home. The ranch hands worked long hours, but they did get downtime.

Hunt tucked his gun away and reached for Vic's, gesturing for Oliver and Jamie to sit after she relinquished it.

Oliver sat. Jamie didn't.

Vic wanted to; her body was calling for a break. But she was wound up, the hand of grief twisting her tighter and tighter. Because Alice wasn't here, and she should've been.

There was fear, too—little tendrils of ice that wended through her because she didn't want it confirmed. She didn't want the truth, didn't want that to be the reality. She hoped against logic that there was some other reason. She *needed* there to be an explanation.

Jamie stalked to a nearby window to glance out at the part of the ranch that sprawled east—where the barn housed the horses, the chicken coops sat on the far side, barely visible, and the fields stretched beyond.

"Quite the operation here," Jamie commented, her voice too flat to be believed. There was nothing innocuous about the way she held herself, a volatile time bomb.

"We have a lot of help," Hunt said, his questioning gaze going to Vic. He didn't understand the dynamic, the strain that pressed on the air.

She didn't, couldn't, look at him. All she could manage was her shallow breathing to keep from splintering apart.

"Help, huh?" Jamie turned, her eyes slamming into Vic with a force that made her pain ripple in response.

"Jamie, I—"

"You could have written," she interrupted, hands balling into fists. "You could have come to find us. Hell, we'd have come to you if we knew where you were. But no. Nothing. Nothing from our fearless, untouched leader."

"I did write," Vic said softly.

"Oh, that's right." A caustic laugh. "You did. *Five years later.*"

More anguish poured through Vic, rivers of it that drowned out anything else. Five years. She'd felt each one creeping by like some part of her was missing. It was probably why she never could fully engage with her community, why she'd always felt a little disconnected.

"We looked for you. We *waited* for you." Jamie's words scraped the air.

"Jamie."

Hunt shifted toward Vic, hearing the pain in her voice because he knew her, had held her when she'd fallen apart.

"We waited for you to find us, Vic." The tears shone in Jamie's eyes, but she didn't look ready to cry. She looked ready for a fight. She wanted the physical release because the grief had grown heavy. So why *wasn't* she fighting?

Vic wanted to take it, bear that weight, relieve the burden, add it to her own, knowing she deserved it. She should carry it and shoulder the blame. Because she should've tried harder.

"I didn't know," Vic said, but the words lacked strength, volume, power. They sounded inadequate, even to her.

Jamie didn't seem to hear her, spinning away. Like those times she'd get so angry, trying to hide her furious tears. She'd punch a wall before she'd release the sadness. The times Vic silently wrapped bloodied and bruised knuckles, and how her quiet, calm expression would drive Jamie crazy because she always thought Vic was closed off and cold, that she didn't care. Or worse—that she was judging Jamie for her emotion.

And just like that, as if some sort of key was handed to her as she stood before the locked door, Vic realized that being the rock for her sisters had also made her hard and unreachable.

Jamie turned back to her then, her chin shifted forward, her movements so much like a boxer ready to strike, endlessly shifting. She wanted to fight so she wouldn't hurt, in much the same way Vic made herself a stone to keep the agony at bay.

"Just like we waited for you to put that goody-two-shoes reputation to work and *keep us together.*" With every word she stabbed in Vic's direction, Jamie moved forward like it was an attack.

"I'm sorry," Vic whispered.

Hunt shot her an incredulous look like he couldn't believe she was apologizing, knowing full well she hadn't known where they were, let alone how to get a message to them.

"Sorry for what?" Jamie demanded. "For not finding us? Or for not looking?"

"That's enough." Hunt stepped between them, his voice that dark shade of angry Vic had heard before.

Jamie's eyes flashed metallic with her own fury, a glow that lit her from within. Maybe because it was magnified by her tears, the ones that refused to fall.

"You were too busy playing house with your new *rodina* to bother with us. And then that letter came. . ." Jamie's voice trembled, her lips colorless as she bared her teeth. "A day too late." The tear that slipped down her cheek made her words come out more viciously. Always that protection. "Too late, Vic."

Vic's eyes fluttered closed, and she released it all—the need to be the strongest one in the room, the best, the leader, the stone pillar. She tore down that wall, ripping it away so that Jamie could see the torture it was to know that she had caused this hurt, that she, herself, had ached for them, too. Her tears broke through the dam, the pent-up pressure of being on her own all this time, wondering, wishing, knowing that they'd had each other, and she'd had no one.

"I didn't know," she whispered, the sound like smoke in the air. Her chin wobbled, and she opened her eyes to meet Jamie's gaze, to push as much of her apology as she could into that look. "I didn't know where you were. I didn't know how to find you. I didn't know what to do or say or try to keep us together without making things a thousand times worse."

Jamie fought to stay angry, to believe something about Vic that wasn't true but made sense. Vic had never let her in, had barely let Alice in, though Alice had always seen the best in everyone, had seen Vic's heart. She'd seen Jamie's, too, always that buffer between them, soothing hurt feelings and bruised egos.

And now she was gone.

Vic's tears spilled over, and shock flashed across Jamie's face at the sight. The wall was down, and all Vic could do was wrap her arms around herself, try to hold the shuddering pieces together because she would surely break apart. Those fissures ran through her, taking every shred of strength she was hanging onto with desperate hands.

"I'm so sorry." Vic gasped at the air, the weakness stealing through her as the grief sought to break her already damaged body.

Hunt came to her, wrapping his arms around her as her legs gave out, went to the floor with her as she sobbed, holding her.

"Vic, it's alright," he murmured at her ear.

"It's not," she argued, one hand clutching at him as the physical pain spasmed through her, her lungs rebelling against the sobs that raked up and out. "I'm sorry, Jamie."

Jamie's jaw worked, the tension in her body hinting that she wanted to come to Vic's aid, to do something. She even took a step forward, and then she stopped.

"Jamie," Oliver said softly, his hands clenched together between his knees. He'd been so still and quiet through the whole exchange, Vic had forgotten he was there.

Jamie gave the slightest flinch, like his voice broke through some sort of trance she was in, and her expression collapsed, twisting with her own agony.

"I think Vic and I need some time alone."

Hunt stiffened as he glared up at Jamie, his reluctance palpable. But Vic nodded, forcing her sobs to quiet. There was some measure of understanding in Jamie's voice, a faint softening that told her they could have the conversation, be there for each other in this grief in a way no one else could.

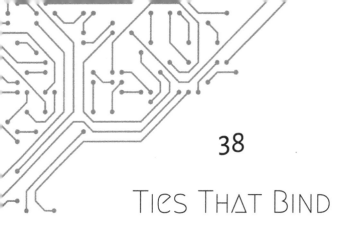

38

TIES THAT BIND

T HEY SAT ON THE couch together, still a notable space between them. But they were on equal footing now, at least. Jamie's anger had cooled, but Vic heard it in her voice as she described what they'd built for themselves out east.

The girls had eked out a decent living as laborers by day and paid fighters by night. Vic suppressed the urge to curl her lip at the fact that they'd used their inborn abilities for cheap entertainment in the slums.

It was a pride thing, and she knew it. Stooping to that level, beating on each other while people paid to watch, letting some low-level mobster dictate where and when and how. . . It was below them.

But Vic couldn't let her judgment cloud what she had come to understand about life after the war: you did what you had to in order to survive a dying world.

"I should've. . ." Jamie started, turning her face away, her jaw working. She tried again: "Oli came to warn us about it. Told us about your village, though we didn't know you were there."

A day too late, Jamie'd said.

"It happened to Cade," Jamie continued, her voice flat and soft. "Oli didn't see it happen, but he knew something wasn't right. Cade was executed for what he did."

Vic remembered Cade. A hothead who would rather do something, anything, whether that was in line with or against orders—he'd never cared much. If she hadn't seen what going dark did to someone, she would've believed he'd willingly committed whatever crime he'd been executed for.

"I ignored Oli's concerns. Dismissed them. It had nothing to do with us." She lifted a shoulder, gaze intent on the floor in front of her. She was leaning forward with her elbows on her knees, head tipped, her eyes locked on a horror Vic couldn't see. "I was in the ring with Alice. It was a normal night. They pitted us against each other regularly because watching two Silvers battle it out always drew a crowd. We did our little routine, pumped everyone up. We always gave a good show." The ghost of a smile, haunting.

Vic kept herself still, even as pain danced through her body, her stitches stinging, her lungs protesting, every physical ache reacting to the emotional torment of hearing about the moment Alice had died.

Each word dropped into Vic's stomach like a bomb, lighting her on fire from the inside.

Jamie's voice caught as she spoke, and she looked at her hands, picking at her dirty, flaking fingernails. Vic didn't know what to do, how to help, how to console. She'd shown Jamie her grief, let it burn at the surface, but she still wasn't built for offering solace. She'd been wired to wade through at the forefront, to forge a way forward for those behind her, to protect and lead.

Vic pressed her lips together, tears running a hot trail down her cheeks, and she grabbed Jamie's hand, squeezing.

"It wasn't your fault, Jamie." A whisper was all she could manage around the pressure in her chest.

But Jamie still wouldn't look at her. Her chin trembled, but she squeezed Vic's hand back, at least accepting that much of her meager offer of comfort.

"There's something bigger happening," Vic said, more strength in her voice now. "Someone is making Unborn go dark."

That drew Jamie's eyes to her face, and she told her sister what really happened in her village, about her journey to the ranch, the lieutenant colonel, what Angela did, about Linus, and the general's plans.

"Uniforms did this to you?" Jamie asked, horror a deep chasm in her expression as she looked her over.

It reflected Vic's own feelings, knowing they could be overpowered by mechs purely controlled by someone else. So little could destroy Silvers. They'd made it through hundreds of battlefields with bullets and bombs gunning for them, and they'd made it through alive, if not always unscathed.

"You know no one else could've except a Silver," Vic said. "And probably more than one."

"Or a Gold," Jamie murmured, the echo of experience behind her words.

There was a story there, Vic thought. For another day, when they had fewer pressing things to address.

"The problem is that even though I took out this general, there are others. There's more to the operation than one crazy man. As soon as we got back yesterday, we got news of another massacre not far from here." Vic's gut churned at the reminder, and she wondered if anyone made it out. There'd been no reports of searches like there were for her, but knowing what she did about Linus and why he'd been obsessed with finding her, she wasn't surprised.

After everything Jamie told her, it was clear Vic was the only Unborn—until they heard otherwise—who could counteract the kill switch.

Jamie stood and strode across the room, stopping at the window to stare out. Her expression was inscrutable. A long stretch of time passed. The air felt brittle with the uncertainty, the rage, the grief. All the things they couldn't alleviate.

"This man who owns the ranch," Jamie said after a moment, not turning. "He means something to you."

Vic fought to keep from tensing up. First, to keep her pain in check. But second, to not read censure in Jamie's tone when she wasn't sure it was even there. She had to keep the walls down, whatever the cost to her pride.

"More than something," she replied softly.

Jamie's eyes cut to her, sunlight glinting against the silver irises. "I'm glad you found someone, even if it's an Adam."

Vic sucked in a breath, but she saw the faint smirk on Jamie's face.

"It's about damn time you broke some rules."

Vic rolled her eyes. "There are no rules anymore."

Jamie raised a brow. "Not written ones, anyway. But we both know Victoria operates by a very strict moral code." Her mocking tone was reminiscent of their childhood and so Jamie. It almost made her smile. Almost.

"I have my limits," Vic said, thinking of how little guilt she felt over the way Haven and O'Rourke had died. That moral code had gotten murky there.

Jamie watched her for a stretch. "I suppose you do."

Vic met her gaze. "A threat to my people being one."

Jamie tipped her head. "About this threat. . . " She turned her body, leaning her butt on the windowsill. "You think there's a bigger operation? Someone still running the experiments?"

"The general made it sound like my village was his little pet project." Vic shifted, wincing as pain lanced through her. Her bones ached. Her heart did, too. "If there are Unborn in the east going dark, then there has to be more of a network. Even the government can't get much through the wasteland. So there have to be branches, little pockets of control. And I'd guess they all lead back to one central force."

Jamie pushed away from the window, the same restless fury radiating off of her that boiled through Vic's veins. It was doubly infuriating that she couldn't move to dispel the energy. Already her body was screaming for real rest. Just her venture downstairs and the grief she now shouldered was beyond what it was capable of enduring in its state.

"We got a tablet off the general," Vic said. The weariness was obvious in her voice. "And we're working on getting in."

"You think that will give us a direction?"

Vic grimaced. "I really hope it does." The prospect of not having anything to go on made a sick feeling writhe in her gut. To leave all Unborn so vulnerable to an unseen enemy—one that should've been an ally—was not something Vic could stomach.

"How we doing, ladies?"

Jamie's head snapped to the front entrance where Oliver's voice had come from. Vic didn't turn, but she got to her feet, unable to suppress the twist in her expression.

Hunt was behind Oliver, his eyes tight on her face, looking for proof that all was well between her and Jamie. Vic fought to keep evidence of her increasing pain level off her face.

"We're good. I think," Vic said, sharing a wry smile with her sister.

The men moved further into the room, though Hunt's presence still made Jamie bristle. She managed to keep the animosity from showing in her expression, which was a miracle.

Vic tracked the way Oliver moved in Jamie's direction, the way he came closer than a friend would, though he didn't touch her. It was how he looked at her, though—a caress in the way his gaze swept her face.

Hunt's hand slid along Vic's low back, a feather-light touch to be careful of her injuries.

"You okay?"

Vic's eyes remained on Jamie and Oliver. She remembered the time the two had spent together during their training days, how they'd sneak into the stairwell when they thought no one was looking. Vic had never seen anything other than lingering glances, but she'd always suspected.

"I will be," she finally said, turning to Hunt. Just looking at him soothed her aches for a moment, knowing he was there with her, that he loved her.

"Yo, Mr. Hunt?"

They all turned to Niko, whose eyes went wide upon seeing the strangers with them. Vic felt Jamie stiffen from across the room, though she controlled her reaction better than Vic had the first day she'd seen Niko.

And even though he was young, even though he didn't always pick up on subtleties, he remained in the doorway, cautious about moving further in.

"I got the information you wanted." Fingers danced along his leg.

Hunt left Vic's side to put his arm around Niko's shoulders in encouragement.

Jamie moved in Vic's direction as she stood, her eyes never leaving Niko's face. "Who's the kid?" she asked, her voice edged.

"He's sort of Hunt and Max's adopted son," Vic murmured, not wanting that to reach Niko's ears. "He's a computer whiz. Hacks into systems like he's a Silver doing a gun disassembly drill. He's the one who found out where you were so I could write."

Jamie's eyes flashed to Vic's face then danced away, the grief between them still too raw and abrasive.

"Does it give a location?" Vic asked Niko, happy to pursue a distraction.

"Yeah. There's a list of names, too. Lot of military dudes."

Jamie snorted, shifting and crossing her arms over her chest. "Great."

"We'll have to leave as soon as possible if we want to catch these guys with their pants down. Word may have already reached them about O'Rourke." Vic started forward, forgetting about her ailments, and sucked in a breath through her teeth when the pain sang through her, bright and blinding.

"We, as in me and Oliver, you mean," Jamie said, her tone drier than a desert. "You're not going anywhere, Vic."

Vic shot Jamie a glare. "I need—"

"To rest and recuperate," Hunt interrupted mildly, drawing her cutting look to him. "This isn't an argument, Vic."

"The hell it's not," she growled, the epic gang-up stirring a heat in her chest. That burn almost distracted her from the constant throb that proved they were right.

He leveled her with a hard look. "You lost a ton of blood, broke some ribs, and punctured a lung. Yeah, you're an Unborn, and it will take you a few weeks instead of months to heal, but seriously."

"Damn, Vic," Jamie whispered, gaze sweeping up and down as if a veil had been removed, and she was able to see all the injuries he'd listed.

Then her sister shared a knowing look with Hunt, stirring a weird dichotomy of feeling in her. They'd found some common ground, though it was in keeping Vic pinned down.

She clenched her teeth, hating the fact that they were right, that she was so useless, that she was still in so much pain in the first place. She'd planned on this whole thing being her fight. It *was* her fight, damn it.

"What do you have, kid?" Jamie asked, turning her attention to Niko.

His eyes flashed to Vic, and as much as it pained her, she nodded her permission, fighting angry tears, and turned away. She wrapped her arms more tightly around herself, willing the self-embrace to magically heal her, to give her back what should've been hers as they talked about what information Niko had found.

"You'll need help," Vic said. "Talk to Doc about the serum."

"Serum?" Oliver asked.

Vic turned to meet Jamie's eyes. "It will help you fight going dark."

39

Hope Deferred

V IC WATCHED FROM THE window, a chill creeping into her bones as Jamie and Oliver walked across the sweeping front yard toward the gate, leading three horses—one for each of them and one to carry supplies. She felt again like she was losing a piece of herself, and it was more devastating than it should've been because there would always be a gaping hole left by Alice's absence.

Though she and Jamie had patched up the torn parts of their relationship, she wouldn't feel settled about it until they got to *after*. But that wouldn't happen until this looming, faceless enemy was taken down.

Even then, she wasn't sure.

She heard Hunt's movements before she felt his warmth behind her, though she didn't turn. She couldn't yet pull her gaze from her sister as she walked away, unable to deny that she was angry.

Angry that Jamie and Hunt had ganged up against her. Livid that Alice was gone, that she didn't stop it, that she couldn't be the one marching off the property to make sure nothing like it ever happened again. Furious that the pain still buffeted her, reminding her exactly why she was stuck here, weak and useless.

But there was so much, and she reminded herself that this was not the only difficulty to overcome.

Hunt's hands slid tentatively around her waist, and she allowed herself to melt against him. Because this was where she could do good, where she could invest in what was right in front of her.

She didn't have to be the leader of a pack of Unborn as they infiltrated an enemy base. She could take care of the people here, help the community grow and change—maybe bridge the gap between the Organics above ground and the Unborn below, a thought that had been brewing since her experiment as a ranch hand. She could love and be loved by the man who'd given her his heart and opened his home.

This was the life she'd wanted, the one she'd fought her way back to, the one she'd deemed worthy of her efforts.

Still, the regret and loneliness that whistled through her would be there. But if she'd been able to go with Jamie and the others, she would have left with the same sense of desolation, the same feeling of abandonment.

So she would take Alice's words to heart from all those years ago: *Jamie needs to shine, too.*

Even though they had both lost Alice, she knew Jamie needed this. Vic had taken down O'Rourke, some small feat against the enemy seeking to eliminate them all. But she also had a home. Alice had been Jamie's home, and now she was adrift.

Vic didn't have to do everything. So she would force herself to let this go.

There was a knock on the door, as there always seemed to be. Vic had a sneaking suspicion this would be the norm for their lives: constant interruption.

Hunt left her by the window to stride to the door.

It was Dan again, who didn't bother looking at Vic. "Max gave the alert about an eastern breach."

East. That was the direction she'd come from, and an entirely different path from where Jamie and Oliver had gone.

"Have him send Claire and Cam up," Hunt said, voice tight. "I'll be down in a minute."

Dan nodded and spun to head back downstairs. Hunt's grip on the knob tightened for a moment before he shut the door and turned to grab his boots from under the bed.

He sat on the edge to lace them up, his icy eyes shooting to her face. "No, you're not coming with."

Flames of rage, already so close to the surface, licked through her. "We decided this was my job now—keeping the ranch safe, by your side."

His movements were jerky. "Not when you're this—"

"I swear, if you say it again, I will—"

He shot to his feet. "Vic, I cannot watch you in pain any more than I already have to." He gripped her arms. "I can't stand it."

She balked at the flash of anger in his eyes. They'd hashed out her abandonment in the woods, but he was still stinging from that small betrayal, even when he understood her reasons.

"If you just take care of yourself for once, you can go back to being the superhero you think you are." To soften the blow, he pressed his lips lightly to hers. "Just let me do what I do. I have the backup I need, and when you're better, you can be my bodyguard all you want."

She gave a surprised laugh and then winced when pain sliced through her.

The anger cooled, and he managed to smirk. "And if you want to fight about it some more, we can do that. *After* I deal with this."

She shook her head, hating that the heat of her own anger still burned. Hating, too, that he was right.

"Fine," she bit out.

He kissed her again and then sprinted for the door.

She stayed by the window, ignoring her body's cry for more rest because she had to see what scene would unfold below. But she wasn't prepared for what came through those woods.

A man and a woman—an Organic and an Unborn—who were so beat up, Vic wondered how they'd made it so far. The man limped. The woman was dirty and bloody. But she held a bundle in her arms that nearly made Vic's heart stop.

It was a small child, probably no older than two.

Something stirred inside of her, something bright and blinding.

When she finally made it down the stairs, they were just coming into the house, and Hunt's eyes shot to Vic's face as he helped the Organic man inside. He looked ready to collapse.

The woman looked sturdier than she'd seemed outside, and the child clutched at her, the cherubic face filled with worry as it took in the strangers around them.

It wasn't the sweet, round cheeks that struck Vic, though. It was the eyes, the irises a brilliant green that matched the ones the man possessed, and there were metallic flecks, too—silvery stripes that caught the light as her gaze wheeled to Vic at the base of the stairs.

She'd never heard of an Unborn having a child. There was never any reason to speculate whether they even could or not.

But here was this child, the product of two worlds, evidence of the way life forged on even when everything was stacked against it, and that thing sparking inside her was something like hope.

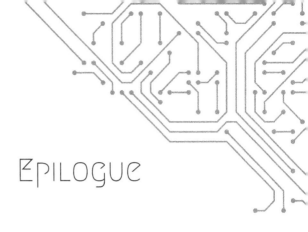

Epilogue

VIC WIPED AT HER brow, though it wasn't entirely the heat slinking along her skin that had the sweat beading along her hairline. It *was* warmer than normal for this time of year, hinting at what the summer might bring. But it was her body fighting to right itself after the damage from her showdown with the Uniforms.

Ten days. That's all it took to get her to a place where she could at least do something besides worry about whether Jamie and Oliver made it to their next stop unscathed. Digging in the garden wasn't the most challenging work to be done around the ranch, but it kept her close to the house, which eased everyone's mind. Doc, who warned her to still take it easy, though she'd cleared her for the escapade in the garden, and Hunt, who saw how messed up Brody still was and couldn't see past his concern over her well-being.

But it also meant that she was close enough to get first news of any changes outside their little haven—whether it was about her sister, another village getting destroyed, or the consequences of her actions almost two weeks prior. So far, there had been nothing on any of those fronts, stirring an unease within her belly that made it nearly impossible to rest the way she'd been advised to.

"Hunt, give me something to do or I'm going to drive you as crazy as I've driven myself," she'd said in desperation the day before.

He'd given her a dark look. "It's cute that you think you haven't already driven all of us insane."

She'd punched him in the arm.

His wince wasn't feigned. "Judging by how bad that hurt, I'd say I better dig something up for you, and not just an arm wrestling match with me."

She couldn't help the smirk that tugged her mouth up in one corner as she glanced up to peek at Niko sitting under the shade of the big oak that spread its umbrella of branches so far in every direction that fingers of shadow reached toward her. Hannah, the two-year-old that had arrived with her parents, Levi and Eve, toddled around in the grass that stretched between Vic and Niko. She was a quiet, inquisitive child, her eyes filled with intelligence beyond what, Vic suspected, was normal for her age.

She'd offered to babysit for the newcomers, partly because Hannah loved being outside so much and because her parents had been through so much since their Unborn settlement went dark. Their initial understanding was that the entire village had been wiped out, but Levi and Eve had escaped the slaughter by sheer force of will. Against all odds, Levi, an Organic, had kept Eve from killing him, herself, and their child, though not without significant effort. He'd restrained her for the thirty minutes she'd been under the trance, and Vic couldn't imagine the toll it had taken on all of them.

But she'd found the couple endlessly fascinating, like they were a mirror held up to her own situation. The physical representation of a future where there was no separation between Organic and Unborn. Someday, it could be a reality. Maybe once Jamie got back and confirmed what they were hoping—that no one could make them go dark again. That they were all free.

"The sun is doing Niko some good."

A warmth crawled through Vic's belly, and she sat back on her heels at the rumble of Hunt's voice. She nodded toward the little girl a few feet from them. "Hannah, too."

His hands landed on her shoulders, and she tipped her head back to receive the kiss she knew he'd have for her. "And you, too, I bet," he murmured against her lips.

She started to get up, wincing with the movement, though the pain was substantially less than it had been even a few days prior.

"I saw that," Hunt said, stepping up behind her, his thumbs gently working at the knots coiled at the base of her neck. "You doing okay?"

She rolled her eyes. "Stop asking me that."

He sighed, the familiar brew of exasperation and amusement dancing lightly along the skin left bare with her hair piled up on her head.

She leaned back against him, not caring that they were both sweaty and dirty after her gardening and his working out in the fields. His steady presence buoyed her as her attention drifted from Niko, his tongue tucked into the corner of his mouth, the careful precision of the pencil in his hand immortalizing a beauty that would someday fade, to the little girl digging in the dirt with her bare hands, a beatific calmness cradling her round face.

Something squeezed in her chest at the sight. An aching hope haunted her, bringing with it a question that had plagued her since Hannah's little family had appeared on the ranch. There hadn't been time to bring it up with Hunt. And she hadn't had the capacity to analyze it anyway, that flare of a dream that came to life in her heart, not when she'd been in so much pain.

But the damage in her body and the grief that still throbbed in her heart had reminded her what a dangerous world they lived in.

It wasn't a place for babies, for families—especially of the sort they would have.

And yet she'd asked Morgan if it was truly possible. During one of her routine follow-ups, Morgan had picked up on Vic's extra dose of tension. Hannah's presence had seemed like a confirmation that it was possible, but Vic still had her doubts. Morgan made sure there weren't any.

Vic abruptly spun to face Hunt, whose brows jumped in surprise.

"I want to ask you something," she started. Her gaze dropped from his to the front of his shirt where a smear of dirt had been ground in during his activity that day.

They were still close, their bodies nearly touching, so she felt it when he came alive with concern, the worry buzzing in the air between them.

"Anything," he said, confusion lowering the volume.

"Do you. . . see us, in the future, with a family?" She forced herself to look up. She was a Silver Unborn, dammit. Not some meek, fearful creature.

His brow furrowed, then he glanced at Niko, over to Hannah, and back to Vic. Understanding lit in his icy eyes. "You mean like having children?"

Expressing this bright and painful hope to him was like going one step beyond placing her beating heart in his hands. She'd offered it to him when she'd told him she loved him, but she'd never let go, simply allowing him to hold it with her. This moment was her taking her hand away, entrusting its safety in his alone, and it was so vulnerable. She felt the aching emptiness in her chest at the very thought that he might hand it right back or crush it altogether.

His gaze traced her face like a caress, his expression softening. "I want it all with you, Vic—whatever that means. If that's just us, I'll take it. If it means more, then give me that, too." He brushed a hand along her cheek. "All in is all in, love."

The whispered words wrapped around her, settling deep and heavy, even though there was still the matter of whether it was even wise, never mind possible. She'd already lost a sister.

She looked down again, though he kept his hand against her face. "There's a difference between accidental and intentional."

In her periphery, she caught the way his head tilted.

"Wait," he said. "You're not trying to tell me something, are you?"

His voice had swelled, a warmth infusing his tone that sent a stab of guilt through her. But it also suffused her hope.

She gave him a sad smile and shook her head. "No. I just wanted to make sure we were on the same page."

Even though he was good at masking the intensity of his emotions, she knew him better than most and recognized the faint disappointment that flashed across his face.

He shrugged. "As long as the bottom line is 'together,' it doesn't matter to me what page we're on."

She smirked. "I'll remember you said that the next time we argue."

He opened his mouth to respond, but the sound of someone running toward them pulled their attention.

"Hunt, Vic!" The panic in Claire's voice lit tiny little fires along Vic's nerves, and she gripped Hunt's hand. "Max says there's a contingent of Uniforms on its way here right now."

Vic spun to scoop Hannah into her arms before Claire had even finished speaking. The urgency zooming through her turned any pain from her quick movements into background noise. Niko shot up from the ground, eyes wide and face pale.

"Get them inside and downstairs," Hunt ordered, reaching out to Niko to pull him forward as two Coppers who'd been working nearby headed their way. No doubt they'd heard what Claire had said. Hunt turned to her. "What direction?"

"West."

Silver eyes met two sets of copper, and Ryan and Sam nodded their acknowledgment, stirring ghosts of the old days. They hadn't served in the war with her, but Vic had earned their respect in the two weeks since some of her proposed changes had been implemented around the ranch. The two Coppers jogged off to the western edge while Vic and the others started moving as one toward the house.

Vic was already running through calculations in her head. Wind speed, vantage points, slope of the land, even the strength in her body.

"As soon as we're inside, I need my rifle," she murmured to Hunt.

He shot her a look. "*Your* rifle?"

"Well, since we have a history." She smirked, but his eyes merely narrowed on her face. "You know I'm the best shot. Don't waste time arguing with me."

"I wasn't going to argue," he muttered as they burst through the front door.

Vic rolled her eyes as she handed Hannah to Claire. The little girl clutched at Vic and whimpered.

"I'm sorry, baby," Vic whispered before turning to Hunt, who was grabbing their weapons. "The roof."

His lips flattened, but he said nothing as he led the way upstairs to the room that had a window above the porch overhang. It would give her access to the roof so she could climb to the apex.

She let Hunt lift the window since it exacerbated her injuries, and neither flinched when Max's voice broke through their concentrated silence. "There's six of them, and they're moving fast."

"Copy that," she answered, sliding onto the sill.

"Please be careful," Hunt said, slipping the rifle's strap over her shoulder.

Their eyes locked. Then she gave one tight nod and swung out. Eyeing the gutter that ran along the edge, she decided it didn't look stable enough to hold her weight. Instead, she gripped the roof's edge and hoisted herself up. Pain screamed through her ribs, stealing her breath for a moment, but she gritted her teeth and pushed through. Once up, she belly-crawled to the pinnacle of the roof.

She scanned the western edge of the ranch as she loaded her weapon, pulling air in and out of her lungs in a practiced rhythm, actively concentrating on lowering her heart rate and relegating her pain to a distant room in her mind. She got into position, placing the butt of the rifle against her shoulder.

And then she waited.

Ten breaths in, ten breaths out. Then, one by one, the figures appeared, and she lined up the sight, exhaled her tension, and released her fury in the succession of shots that blasted out of the muzzle of her weapon. The ache in her ribs flared again, but this, she thought, this was what she was made for: to bring down her enemy and protect what was hers.

Four shots reverberated against the trees, two Uniforms fell, and four continued toward the house, faster now. The spike of adrenaline squeezed at her heart, and she did the quick mental math, adjusting her sights for the next two. The head didn't seem to hold as much executive function as a human's, but her experience all those weeks ago in her settlement showed her a lot of its mechanics had been placed behind the eyes.

Her finger pressed against the trigger. One, two, down.

The final two kicked up speed, and a ripple of fear snapped up her spine as they got closer to the house. She hissed when the pain responded, but she scooted forward anyway, ignoring the way it jarred her body. Her blood pulsed in her ears, and she popped the next shot off prematurely, the bullet slamming into the dirt right behind the mech. Dust sailed into the air.

A curse rattled through her lips on an exhale she tried to slow as she lined her sight up again. She blinked hard, trying to relax her body. These two would be out of view in a matter of seconds, and she would've missed her opportunity. She fired three more rounds into the one she'd missed to be sure.

Three more gunshots, not from her weapon, rang out in quick succession, and she shot up, glancing over the eave to find the last Uniform on the ground. Her heart punched against her ribs as she searched for Sam and Ryan, who were dealing with the first couple of Uniforms. So someone else had taken that last one out.

When the echo of gunshots died away and minutes passed with no other figures materializing from the darkness of the forest, she dropped back down. A few more ranch hands joined the Coppers in the clean up, and she exhaled, resting her head on her folded arms, shutting her eyes. There were others to help. She didn't have to shoulder the rest of it. She could take the time to breathe through the pain that refused to abate. Too many movements, too much adrenaline.

"You know, you won't always be able to lie on your belly like that and take potshots at intruders."

The grin spread across her face, and she rolled onto her back. "And I so look forward to that argument someday."

Pushing herself onto her elbows, she was met with Hunt's look of irritation.

"It's not going to be an argument, Vic."

One eyebrow lifted. "Because you know I'll win."

He huffed, tucking a handgun at his back, and climbed up. He must've been the one to take out that last mech.

Crouching next to her, Hunt turned his attention to the tree line where several people worked together to move the Uniforms. She felt it when the intensity of the situation truly eased, and their comfortable silence stretched as she watched the opposite line of encroaching forest, reminding herself she didn't need to do anything more right now.

He turned to look at her after a few minutes. "What if we turn 'someday' into soon?"

Her breath caught, but then she squinted at him. "To argue?"

He growled and leaned forward as if to kiss her, but he stopped before their lips touched. "You're a frustrating woman, Victoria."

Her pulse quickened, her lips tingling at the proximity of his. And then fear like a poison spiked her blood, twisting her stomach. "We should try to figure out where those Uniforms came from and if there's something more going on."

He didn't pull back, his eyes steady on hers. "We will."

"It's a scary world out there," she whispered, unable to speak under the weight of that knowledge, the Alice-shaped hole in her chest pulsing.

He nodded, his expression serious. "It's always been scary. And it will always be scary."

Oxygen was heavy in her chest, but she swallowed the fear, the questions, the uncertainty of the future. She'd never gain ground if she didn't venture out. She'd protect what was theirs. They'd do it together.

"All in?" he asked, as if reading her mind.

She slipped her hand around his neck and pulled him forward, a slow smile forming. "All in," she confirmed.

Turn the page for a teaser of War of the Unborn, the companion in The Leader & The Rebel Duology.

The Rebel

Secrets of the Unborn

WAR OF THE UNBORN

C.H. LYN

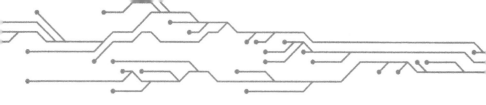

Concrete Jungle

T HE CITY GLINTED AT night. Not the way it used to, before the world plunged into a war that took decades and super soldiers to end. But it glinted all the same.

Jamie's jaw clenched as she rode the clear exterior elevator up the side of one of the only lingering habitable skyscrapers. The remains of dozens more reflected the light from the halfmoon, the stars, the fires lit to keep people from freezing during cold east coast nights. Some of the massive structures had crumbled entirely, others were half-fallen, the rest stood as taunts for those brave and stupid enough to enter. Floors and ceilings caved in at the lightest breezes.

It was a good thing she hadn't grown up here. Jamie's mouth twitched as she pondered the trouble she'd have gotten in with a concrete jungle like this to play in.

She probably would have broken her neck.

The muscles in her back tensed as the elevator slowed to a stop nearly thirty stories up. The glass didn't seem to keep out the chill, and she pulled up the zipper of her cropped sand-colored jacket, stuffing her hands into the pockets. Jamie cracked her neck to the side, the pop drawing the attention of Thick and Squat.

Those weren't their real names, of course, but she barely cared enough to remember Carter's name, let alone his numerous henchmen.

A rush of nerves cramped her stomach. Or maybe it was hunger. She'd been at the gym most of the day, staying fresh for the next two weeks of fights. The big tournament ended soon. She and Alice would have a healthy payday that might get them out of the city. If not, it would at least keep them fed and warm through the winter.

The elevator dinged.

Thick stepped off first. Jamie winced at the groan of metal as the man lumbered out of the death chamber. She made a mental note to take the stairs back down and followed him.

However dingy the rest of the city was, Carter kept his territory clean. There were only four skyscrapers left. The military owned one, the supposed government another, some old tech mogul was cooped up in the third, and Carter claimed the last.

Jamie inhaled the stale scent of too much incense and nearly sneezed. "No windows this far up?" she asked Squat as he waddled onto the plush hallway carpet. "Sure is stuffy in here."

Thick glowered and gestured for her to continue down the corridor. Fancy tables lined the walls, lights in brackets—wasting energy—every few feet, and collections of vibrant paintings that Jamie tried to avoid looking at.

What was the point of admiring something you couldn't have?

The three reached an arch, and Thick held up a finger. Jamie rolled her eyes.

Every time.

Carter liked to make a show of being a busy man. It was no surprise when Jamie ducked her head into the room and saw him finishing a solo dinner at his ornate table. He stood quickly, swallowing a final bite of what smelled like perfectly seasoned steak—a delicacy Jamie had only tried once, on V-Day—and turned to face her.

"Ahh, my prize fighter."

Jamie held back the urge to roll her eyes again, thinking about Alice and the possibility of eating steak sometime in the next year.

"Carter, it's an honor." It was harder to keep the dry irritation out of her voice, but she put up a good effort. At least there wasn't any malice audible.

Carter smiled. His teeth were too white, too straight, and too brittle. Those eyes, dark blue with bushy brows that jumped around when he got excited, narrowed in on her own, different ones.

"It gets me every time," he said with a sigh. He pulled a suit jacket from the back of his chair, stuffing his thick arms into the sleeves and leaving it unbuttoned, draped over his protruding stomach. Carter pointed a finger at her. "Silver eyes. The color means something, right?"

Jamie blinked.

Silver did mean something. It meant when she was created, grown in a glass bottle much like the elevator for the first nine months of her life and then ejected into a sterile room with a dozen beds, they'd designed her to be a leader. They'd built her to be unbreakable. They'd trained her to be the best.

Well, second best. But Gold was rare and almost a different breed. She'd only met one in her time at war.

"Not really." Jamie shrugged. "Just wanted to make sure we didn't get mistaken for Adams."

Carter, an Adam, grimaced at the term. "Hah, an unnecessary addition to your otherwise perfect physique. Besides, anyone who watches you Unborn fight knows you're not human."

She bristled. "What did you need from me, Carter? Changing the line up again?"

"Tone, Jamie." His own tone was cold.

She reminded herself to keep a civil tongue. It would have been easier with Alice there. "Course, boss. Just tired from the gym. Looking to get some rest before tomorrow night."

Carter's mouth slid into a smug smile that made her wish he'd step into the ring every now and then. Hell, just once and she'd show him exactly what his fighters went through to earn him a dime.

He strode around the table toward a cigar humidifier in the corner.

This room was much like the hall. Decorated beyond the means of every other person in the city. Maybe a handful of the manors near the river were like this. Maybe there were some rich folks with smaller homes that had chandeliers, and cushy seats, and three kinds of forks, and steak, but Jamie doubted any of them flaunted it like this.

"About the fight..."

Jamie scowled.

"Not tomorrow's." Carter waved off her expression with a clipper in his hand before he cut the end of his cigar and tucked it into the corner of his mouth. "I'm talking about next week. The big one. You're first on the roster, going up against, what? Six opponents?"

Jamie shrugged. Her fists remained in her pockets, where they couldn't give away how tightly they were clenched. "Nothing I can't handle, Carter. You know that."

"Yeah, well I have a name I'd like to see get to the top of that list."

She remained quiet.

"If you know what I mean," he said with a grin, lighting his cigar and puffing acrid smoke into the room.

"I don't." Jamie inhaled through her nose, chanting an internal mantra of *calm* like Alice told her to do every time their landlord demanded extra rent.

"You fight Travers that night. It would be beneficial to me if he didn't go down."

Jamie closed her eyes and cracked her neck again. She took her hands out, planting them on the table in front of her and leaning forward. "Listen, Carter. I do a lot for you, but I'm not taking a fall. If you don't want him going down, put him in with someone else."

Carter sneered. "Don't get uppity now, Jamie. Not when we've worked so well together."

On either side of her, Thick and Stout stepped forward.

Jamie's tight expression slid into a smile. "I fight for you, Carter. I'll keep fighting. But I'm not taking a fall." She tensed her core, subtly shifting her weight as the henchmen waited for their orders.

If these flesh bags wanted to fight, she'd show them a fight. A real one, not the bullshit half-showboating she did in the ring.

They'd find out just how high this monstrosity of a building was when they went out the damn window.

Carter hesitated. He watched her with those blue eyes, beady and angry. Then he smiled. "Well, let's see how this week treats you. It may be you come around before the finale."

Jamie's chin lifted half an inch. "Anything else?"

His nose pinched again, but he gave a dismissive nod and gestured to his men. Thick reached for Jamie's arm. She whirled, moving toward the corridor fast enough that it took the men jogging to catch up.

"Stairs?"

Thick grunted. "We take the elevator."

Jamie snapped her glare toward Stout. "*Stairs.*"

The man swallowed and pointed to a door a few yards from the big glass bubble that had carried them nearly thirty stories from the ground floor.

"See you boys on the ground."

She jammed the door open with her shoulder and hurried into the dark stairwell.

"So, how'd it go?"

Jamie's expression was answer enough, and Alice stepped back, pulling the door open to let her into their tiny apartment. Jamie kicked off her shoes, tossed her jacket over the back of their torn and raggedy couch, and leaned against the closed front door.

"Carter sucks."

Alice nodded sympathetically. "We've known this for a while now."

Jamie's eyes half-closed in a glare. She heaved a sigh. "He wants me to throw a fight."

Alice's eyes, silver and glinting even in the low light of their apartment, went wide. "That's..."

"Yeah. I told him to shove it."

Alice pursed her lips, glaring. "Please tell me you didn't *actually* say it like that?"

Jamie pushed away from the wall and trudged into the kitchenette. "No, I was nice about it. Nice-ish."

Alice snorted.

"What is there to eat?" Jamie tugged open the door to their mini fridge. Apparently, there was a time when people had full sized ones. Big-ass hulking things that ate up electricity and held weeks' worth of food. The idea was simultaneously enticing and appalling.

Her question was answered by the utterly empty shelves looking up at her.

"Never mind." Jamie ignored Alice's appraising eyes as she turned away from the counter. She pulled the little brown elastic band from the end of her long blonde braid. Running her fingers through her hair felt so good—almost as good as a fat sandwich in her stomach would have felt.

Alice grinned.

Jamie caught the look from her peripheral vision as she shook her head, loosening the tight braid she wore for training. "What?"

Alice shrugged.

"You've never had a good poker face, Alice. What are you smiling about?"

Her sister in all but blood crossed the space, opened a usually empty cupboard, and pulled out a loaf of bread.

Jamie's jaw dropped. "Where the hell did you get that?" she demanded, wondering how her nose had missed the scent. Then again, her nostrils were still plugged with smoke from Carter's cigar and incense.

"You know Joey? From 7E?"

Jamie's hungry look turned to a scowl. "The Adam?"

"The baker," Alice said, her tone dry. "Anyway, we ran into each other on his way to work this morning, and he said he'd bring us back a loaf if I helped him move a massive dresser in his apartment."

A smirk pulled at Jamie's lips, even as mistrust stirred in her chest. "You've gotta be careful with them, Alice."

"Bakers?" Alice asked, her voice overly innocent as she turned away. She laid out a wood block, pulled a knife from a drawer, and began cutting slices. "I've got some butter hiding in that one." She gestured with the sharp end of the blade, and Jamie followed the hint to pull butter and—to her shock—a jar of strawberry jam from where they'd been hiding.

"Why hide these?" she demanded.

Alice grinned again, whirling with two slices of bread on one plate and three on another. She darted toward Jamie, fluid and graceful, pecked her on the cheek, and continued toward the couch. "We never have nice surprises," she sang. "I wanted to give you a nice surprise."

Jamie snagged a spoon from their sparse cutlery drawer and followed with a smile. The two settled onto the couch, legs crisscrossed as they smothered fresh sourdough with butter and jam.

"Remember Five-Cal?" Alice asked, a wistful hint to her tone as she leaned her head back against the couch. Her hair, corkscrew curls in dark brown except for a single white lock on the front right side, was streaked with dust. She'd spent most of the day at their side-gig, drilling through old cement to clear space for farming closer to the city proper. It was hard work. Tiring, even for Unborn.

"Remember?" Jamie scoffed. "I dream about those days."

Alice chuckled. Five-Cal, as they called it, was a period of time from their youth. Unborn developed faster than humans—a necessity when building soldiers from scratch to fight in an already decades-long war. Some of Jamie's earliest memories were the days when she, Alice, Vic (the third member of their pseudo-sisterhood), and the others had been fed upwards of five-thousand calories a day.

They'd grown fast enough to stretch their skin, bones pulling tendons tight, pain pills sometimes not enough to ease the unnatural strain on their nerves and muscles. Even with the pain, Jamie missed those days. She missed the three of them, drenched in sweat, hands trembling from training with weapons half their size, sitting cross-legged on their cots and slamming through half a dozen massive bowls of Cook's spaghetti and meatballs.

In human years, they'd been around twelve when their growth had slowed. Mind followed body and—though the rotation of the earth around the sun would suggest they were only in their early twenties—all the Unborn left from their squad were closer to thirty by the time the war ended.

Jamie wasn't sure how it all worked. Had never really cared, especially those nights when Vic got in everyone's head about the logic behind it. She'd learned to tune out her older sister when the "Unborn role" preaching started. Jamie had already known they were soldiers; she hadn't needed the reminders from Miss Goodie-Two-Shoes.

Though, thinking back, most of those reminders had happened after Jamie had been demoted... again.

She heaved a sigh and set her plate on the ground. It was days like this, when she was tired and hungry and dealing with people like Carter, that she wished Vic was with them. Most of the time she could brush it aside, remind herself of Vic's words when the war had ended, when the brass had handed down orders saying the three of them were getting split. After over a decade growing and fighting together, losing their friends, losing territory, and gaining it back, killing countless enemies, and someone up top had decided the three of them didn't deserve to stay together.

Jamie had nearly burned down the barracks.

Still, she and Alice had found each other. They knew Vic was somewhere out west. Past crumbling cities, towering mountains, and a vast wasteland. Beyond their reach.

"What are you going to do about the fight?" Alice asked, her voice soft.

Jamie closed her eyes. "I'm not taking a fall."

"I know *that*." Alice's voice carried a smirk.

"I'll worry about it when I get there," Jamie muttered, sleep coming quickly now that her stomach was moderately satisfied and her body relaxed. "It's not till next week anyway. I have to get through this weekend before I'm guaranteed to be in the finals."

"Right." A sardonic sound now, almost a chuckle, came from her friend. "Like there's a chance you don't make it to finals with me." Alice had made it through her bracket the week before.

"You never know," Jamie said through a yawn. "I could go up against a gorilla or something."

"Shit, *I'd* pay to see that fight."

Jamie snorted, shifted her butt to avoid a spring in the couch, and fell asleep.

Acknowledgements

All the Thanks, Ad Nauseam

First, I have to acknowledge my brother. Yay, you exist! Kidding. I owe him at least a high-thumb because he gave me the idea for this book many moons ago and even wrote an early prologue for the story. If it weren't for him, this story wouldn't even exist. So. . . cool beans.

Next, I want to thank my uncle (again) because he read that first version and loved it, even when it was less than it is now—in so many ways. Anyone who's met my uncle has been blessed by his humor and laughter. You're a fricken cool dude, Uncle Nu Nu.

I also want to shout out to Stefanie and Hannah for critiquing that super early version and pouring into what would become my evolution as a writer. Thanks for lovingly not pulling punches, friends!

And Shiny. Dude. I would not have picked this story up again if it weren't for you. It wouldn't have become what it is, and I wouldn't have blown myself out of the water with it if I didn't have you to encourage me and brainstorm with. Your enthusiasm made me reluctantly look at what I thought was a dumpster fire and turn it into this story that has captured my heart. I'm keeping you forever, and that IS a threat.

As always, my favorite people: my mama, my bestie Alyssa, my wonderful babies who share me with my imaginary friends, my Dream Guy (a.k.a. my wonderful husband), my dad and stepmom, my friends and community, and the blessing of living where I do. I cannot be more grateful.

To my betas and critique partners—Meredith, Danielle, Penny, Rachelle, Megan—your feedback is worth so much money that collecting every cent in the world could NEVER cover a fraction of what I owe you for your feedback.

Finally, I must holler from the rooftops: YOU, YOU BEAUTIFUL MOTHERFORKING READER! Who am I without all of the amazing people who buy, read, review, and pass along my books? You make my world go 'round, boost my fragile writer's ego, and give me the motivation to keep putting pen to the metaphorical paper (because I write on the computer, you know). Thankyouthankyouthankyouthankyouthankyouthankyou.

K, love you, bye.

About the Author

Tracey began writing at age 13, when there wasn't much for kids who loved adventure and weren't into the drama of everyday teenager-hood. She has always loved romance with a side of danger, and she has a hard time writing anything else. She really likes to read it, too. *Kiss, kiss, pew, pew,* and all that jazz.

In January 2022, she took a leap of faith and published her first book, *The Alternate End of Cassidy Marchand.* Since then, she's published the full trilogy, a side novel, a co-written book with C.H. Lyn, *Love Undercover,* and the first book in *Secrets of the Unborn.* And she ain't stopping. Except when she has to teach her kids for homeschool. Or when she has to answer her 800th *why* question. Or when she has to break up a fight between her two kids. But, you know, when she's not doing those things... she's not stopping!

Check her out on socials @authortraceybarski (honestly, she mostly does stuff on Instagram) to find out what shenanies she's up to, like book info, new releases, sneak peeks, and weird reels.

Go to traceybarski.com for all other info, to sign up for her very infrequently sent newsletter, and see what events she might have set up.

Also by Tracey Barski

The Alternate Chronicles

The Alternate End of Cassidy Marchand
Resurrecting Cassidy Marchand
Cassidy Marchand Unraveled
Heart in Parallel

Compromised

Love Undercover

Written with C.H. Lyn

Love is Murder
Secrets of the Unborn

Printed in the USA
CPSIA information can be obtained
at www.ICGtesting.com
LVHW090751100824
787828LV00005B/13